COLD AS HELL

Also by Kelley Armstrong

Rip Through Time

Disturbing The Dead   The Poisoner's Ring   A Rip Through Time

Haven's Rock
The Boy Who Cried Bear
Murder at Haven's Rock

Rockton

The Deepest of Secrets   Watcher in the Woods
A Stranger in Town   This Fallen Prey
Alone in the Wild   A Darkness Absolute
City of the Lost

Cainsville

Rituals   Deceptions
Betrayals   Visions
Omens

Otherworld

Thirteen   Living with the Dead   Industrial Magic
Spell Bound   Personal Demon   Dime Store Magic
Waking the Witch   No Humans Involved   Stolen
Frostbitten   Broken   Bitten
Haunted

Darkest Powers & Darkness Rising
The Rising   The Reckoning
The Calling   The Awakening
The Gathering   The Summoning

Nadia Stafford
Wild Justice
Made to Be Broken
Exit Strategy

Standalone novels

I'll Be Waiting   Every Step She Takes
Known to the Victim   Wherever She Goes
Hemlock Island   Aftermath
Someone Is Always Watching   Missing
The Life She Had   The Masked Truth

Age of Legends
Forest of Ruin
Empire of Night
Sea of Shadows

The Blackwell Pages (co-written with Melissa Marr)
Thor's Serpents
Odin's Ravens
Loki's Wolves

COLD AS HELL

A Haven's Rock Novel

KELLEY ARMSTRONG

MINOTAUR BOOKS
NEW YORK

First published in the United States by Minotaur Books, an imprint of St. Martin's Publishing Group

COLD AS HELL. Copyright © 2025 by KLA Fricke Inc. All rights reserved. Printed in the United States of America. For information, address St. Martin's Publishing Group, 120 Broadway, New York, NY 10271.

www.minotaurbooks.com

The Library of Congress Cataloging-in-Publication Data is available upon request.

ISBN 978-1-250-35179-1 (hardcover)
ISBN 978-1-250-39165-0 (international edition)
ISBN 978-1-250-35180-7 (ebook)

Our books may be purchased in bulk for promotional, educational, or business use. Please contact your local bookseller or the Macmillan Corporate and Premium Sales Department at 1-800-221-7945, extension 5442, or by email at MacmillanSpecialMarkets@macmillan.com.

First U.S. Edition: 2025
First International Edition: 2025

10 9 8 7 6 5 4 3 2 1

COLD AS HELL

PROLOGUE

As Kendra stumbles onto her residence porch, she tries to recall how much she had to drink. The answer should be easy. Two beers consumed over two hours, which should not make her drunk. The second one had been a black velvet, combining beer and wine—totally Yolanda's fault for ordering a round—but still, that wouldn't even put Kendra over the legal driving limit. Not that driving matters in Haven's Rock, where there are no cars. The point is that two drinks over two hours should not have her tripping over her own feet.

The problem, Kendra decides, is that even two beers is more than she's had since college. Kendra's idea of "going out drinking" means she goes out and has a drink. One. She knows most people would blame this on her growing up Indigenous in the Canadian north. But, really, it's just Kendra. She doesn't mind a beer, but she's just as happy with a soda. Unfortunately, there is no soda in Haven's Rock.

Kendra stands on the porch and blinks. It's past midnight and pitch-dark and freaking cold. Okay, she's being a wimp about the cold. Haven's Rock might be in the Yukon, but she grew up at a higher latitude, and for late March, they've actually been having a warm spell. Tonight, though, a fierce north wind slices right through her sweatshirt.

Sweatshirt? Where's her parka? It might be a "warm spell" but it's still hovering around zero.

Did she leave her parka in the Roc? Why would she do that? Because she's drunk.

Okay, but why is she on the residence porch instead of getting her ass inside where it's warm?

Right. The bathroom situation.

The residence has three toilets, perfectly reasonable for a building designed to house a couple of dozen people. Kendra should know. During town construction, she'd been hired for her unique combination of talents—a social worker with extensive experience plumbing in a northern climate. They needed the plumber part and wanted someone to help with any psychological effects of the isolation. That was also why she'd been offered long-term employment after construction was done. Because a town with an off-grid sanitation system needs an on-site plumber, and a town this unique needs all the mental-health experts they can get.

Why is she thinking about her job right now?

Right. Because she needs to pee and there are no available toilets because residents flushed nonflushable items down *two* of them. The fixes require replacement parts. She'd also ordered *extra* replacement parts for sanitation in a town with people accustomed to being able to flush whatever crap they wanted.

Damn it, she really needs to pee, and the Roc just closed, and she wasn't fast enough getting back to snag a toilet, so now she's left staring into the forest and considering her options.

Dropping her trousers in freezing weather should not be one of those options. Especially in a pitch-black forest. But it won't be the first time she's done it. When you head out on the land to hunt, you don't haul along a chemical toilet.

Still . . .

She should just wait for a stall to be free. How long can it take?

A moment later, Kendra finds herself on the edge of the forest and stops short. How did she get here? She was just on the deck, thinking she should wait it out.

Something's wrong.

She shakes off the internal whisper. She's drunk and not accustomed to being in that state.

You shouldn't be blacking out after two drinks.

She didn't black out. She's just confused, and as long as the forest is right there, she might as well use it.

She takes two steps, and her foot slides in the melting snow. As she's righting herself, she hears a crackle behind her, like a boot breaking through a skin of ice.

Kendra spins, and her foot slides right out from under her, and she collapses into the wet snow and—

She's on her feet again. She goes still and looks around.

Did she imagine falling?

No, there's the skid mark from her boot and the handprint from where she landed. When she clenches her fist, her fingers are wet.

Wait, where are her gloves?

Why is she outside without gloves or a parka, like some newbie to the north, thinking *I'm only walking a hundred feet?*

Is it the booze, making her not feel the cold?

She remembers when she was in college, studying the "starlight tours" in Saskatoon, where police would drive drunk Indigenous men past the town limits and leave them there, often improperly dressed for the weather. Three froze to death.

She shivers and shakes her head sharply. Her brain is zipping all over the place, and she needs to . . .

What did she need to do again?

Her aching bladder reminds her, but when she looks at the forest, something else nudges at the back of her mind.

She heard something. That's why she stumbled.

She peers around.

No one's out here, and even if there were, it'd just be someone heading home from the Roc.

Why isn't she seeing people heading home from the Roc? She'd left at closing, and there'd still been others behind her.

She checks her watch.

Past *twelve-thirty*? How is that possible? The bar closed at midnight.

Her watch must be wrong. Even if it's not, hearing someone out at one isn't a cause for alarm in Haven's Rock. They'd just be heading to or from a lover's bed, the lucky—

Wait. That's why she'd had a second drink. She'd been flying high because one of the new residents, Tish, has been making what seems like a concerted effort to "bump into" Kendra as often as possible. Kendra thought she might catch the right vibes, but also feared that after nearly a year of celibacy, she was seeing what she wanted to see.

Damn it, her brain is like a terrier tonight, chasing everything that runs across its path. Forget this nonsense. By now, there has to be an empty stall in the bathroom.

Kendra takes a step toward the residence, and the next thing she knows, she's flat on her back with no idea how she got there. She pushes to her feet.

Something is definitely wrong. Two drinks do not cause blackouts.

Is she having an allergic reaction?

In college, her first thought would be that someone slipped something into her drink. But this isn't college, and she didn't just walk out of a bar full of strangers. There are seventy people in Haven's Rock. Dose a woman here, and you'll get caught.

Hell, it's not even a remote worksite filled with guys who might think that's a perfectly fine way to get laid, especially if the woman you're eyeing "claims" she's not into men. Kendra had narrowly avoided that once on a remote job, saved by a guy who'd caught the offender tipping something into her drink. It's one reason Kendra had joined Yolanda's construction team—it was seventy-five percent female. Which, to be honest, made her happy in more ways than one.

Kendra smiles . . . and then she remembers what originally prompted that memory and the smile evaporates.

Was she dosed in the Roc?

No, she was just arguing that she couldn't have been.

Stop thinking. Start moving. Get her ass inside and lock her damn door—

Crunch.

Kendra wheels just as something slams into her back, and her first and only thought is *This is it.* Someone hit her from behind, and now, instead of spinning and slugging them, she'll slip and fall. Or she'll just black out. Because someone put something into her drink, and that is not fair.

It's not fucking fair.

At least give her a chance to fight. She isn't very good at it, and she isn't big or strong enough to power through, but at least give her a literal fighting chance.

She doesn't slip, though. Or black out. She even manages to half spin before another blow comes. This one knocks her face-first into the snow. She manages to get one hand down in the slush, ready to push up, when her attacker grabs her feet and yanks so hard that she face-plants in the snow again. She tries to flip over, but she's being dragged.

Someone is dragging her into the forest.

Scream!

She opens her mouth, but time jumps again, and now she's in the forest and there's a hand over her mouth.

Bite! Kick! Scream!

She bites as hard as she can and clamps down on a wool glove. She kicks backward and somehow—*somehow*—her foot actually makes contact. Her attacker grunts, and the grip on her mouth slips, and she screams. She screams with everything she has, and from the town, a voice answers.

She doesn't know what the voice says. It's just a voice, alarmed, and her attacker drops her. They try to grab her again, catching her by the sweatshirt, but she lunges free and runs.

There's a figure up ahead. She can't quite make it out, but someone's running her way, and she waves frantically and then her foot slides and she goes down, and—

Darkness.

CHAPTER ONE

A fist pounds on our chalet door. I lift my head to squint at the clock. 1:16.

A knock in the wee hours of the morning is never good.

Beside me, Dalton makes a noise that could be a curse or could just be a still-half-asleep grunt.

"I'll go see what it is," I say, patting his arm as I rise.

He starts making another sound, one that might be sleepy acceptance. Then he bolts upright.

"No!" he says, as if I've suggested running into a burning building. "You stay. I've got this."

"I'm already out of bed."

"Then get back in it."

In the moonlight I can see Storm, our Newfoundland, look from one of us to the other. Then she sighs.

"Sorry, pup," I say, patting her with my foot. "He's a little weird these days. I have no idea why."

"For the same reason you're petting the dog with your foot instead of bending down to use your hand." Dalton points at the cause of my inability to bend—my eight-month-pregnant belly. Which, yes, is the same reason he's leaping out of bed to answer the door instead of just gratefully staying where it's warm.

"I'm fine," I say. "Even April's long list of 'things Casey can't do' does not include answering doors."

"Yeah, but if it doesn't include 'going down the stairs in the middle of the night,' it should."

I could point out that going down a flight of stairs while sleepy is always dangerous, and no more so when heavily pregnant, but when we started this journey, I knew I was going to have to deal with Dalton's protective streak. Or, more accurately, deal with him using my pregnancy as an excuse to indulge his protective streak.

Also, granted, it's not purely indulgence. Old damage to my uterus means I could have issues. In eight months, I've had two scares, one where I'd been certain I'd miscarry, and one a month ago, where there was some concern I'd gone into early labor. Being seven months along meant it would have been a premature birth. Not a huge problem . . . if I were living down south with access to proper preemie care.

Dalton had been ready to take me to Vancouver so we could spend my last two months in an apartment, preferably one close enough to a hospital that he could carry me there in an emergency. My sister had been on his side . . . because as the local doctor, she's the one who'd need to deal with premature birth, and she's a neurosurgeon, not an obstetrician. Fortunately, my actual obstetrician convinced them both that I was fine where I was. In an emergency, Dalton could fly me to Whitehorse himself and she would come up to the hospital there.

So I understand if he's fussing over me walking down the stairs. It isn't as if we intentionally put ourselves in this position. It was an accidental pregnancy that we decided to continue while knowing the risks. And I decided to continue it while knowing he was going to freak out if anything went wrong, including false alarms.

Another pound on the door below.

"Stay here," Dalton says, pointing at the bed.

When I glower, he says, "Keep her here," to Storm. Then he leaves, and Storm heaves to her feet, walks three paces, and collapses in the doorway.

I turn my glower on her. "Traitor."

She only lets out a slobbery sigh and watches me with all the patience of Nana in *Peter Pan*. Having a Newfoundland means I understand why Barrie chose one for his canine nanny. She's the sweetest and most patient dog imaginable, but also, if she's in that doorway, I am not getting out of this room.

Below, Dalton answers the front door.

"We have a problem," a voice says. "I know you aren't going to want Casey getting up at this hour, but I think she needs to take this one."

I scramble to get ready without even hearing my husband's probably profane response. It isn't that the caller sounds panicked or even stressed. The voice is perfectly calm with just the right hint of apology.

If I didn't know the speaker, I'd think that tone meant a very minor problem, an inconvenience and an annoyance that unfortunately did require my personal touch . . . such as our deputy being unable to access the gun locker because baby brain meant I misplaced the key again.

The speaker, though, is Sebastian.

Sebastian had been our youngest resident in Rockton, and at twenty-two, he's still the youngest adult resident in Haven's Rock. He came to Rockton because he's too infamous to live a normal life down south. At the age of eleven he killed his parents. He had his reasons, but no court would consider them a defense. If he *had* a defense, it's that he was an undiagnosed sociopath who thought this seemed a valid solution to the problem of rich parents who wouldn't let him attend school because it interfered with their social calendar. He served his time and while serving it, he dealt with his diagnosis and continues to deal with it. He's not a serial killer. He has no interest in hurting anyone. He just needed to understand that murder is not a valid problem-solving strategy.

All this means it's really hard to rattle Sebastian. Maybe impossible. He could stumble over a dead body, and unless it's someone he cares about, his response would be purely practical. Go find someone to deal with it.

I dress and tell Storm to move. Her eyes roll up to meet mine, her disapproval clear, but she's technically my dog, and she knows it. She lumbers to her feet and down the stairs.

I expect Dalton to spot her and tell me he can handle this, but before Storm's even down the stairs, he's at the bottom, looking up, his expression grim.

"You do need to handle this," he says.

"What happened?"

Sebastian pops in behind him. "Kendra was attacked. She's fine—unhurt, that is. But it seems . . . Well, it looks as if someone dosed her in the Roc and dragged her into the woods."

"Dragged—"

He lifts his hands. "They didn't do anything to her. She got away in time. But, yeah, that's why I, uh, thought you should come. Because it looks as if they planned to . . ."

He trails off, and genuine emotion flashes over his face. He likes Kendra, and that flash is undiluted anger. He reins it in fast.

"I thought of going after them, but that didn't seem like a good idea. So I helped Kendra instead."

"Thank you. Where is she?"

"At the clinic with your sister."

Sexual assault had always been a serious concern in Rockton. The population had been three-quarters male with no couples allowed, and as law enforcement, we'd been dealing with the potentially explosive situation of women escaping victimization and men who could be victimizers snuck in under a cover story. Explosive and completely unacceptable, but Dalton's only option had been solid policing and the strictest of penalties. Oh, and there was a brothel—women residents were allowed to sell sex. Isabel and I had endless disagreements over that, the feminist politics of consensual sex work versus the fact that it presupposed men needed that outlet or there'd be trouble. Yep, it was complicated.

Haven's Rock has no sex trade. Unless you count Gunnar, but he's free, so there's no "trade" involved. We allow couples, and we have a mixed group of men and women and sexual orientations, so . . . Well, if you want sex and you aren't an asshole about it, you can probably get it, especially if you're a straight woman because . . . Gunnar.

Now, as a cop, I'm the first to say that sexual assault is not always about sex. The type that *is* about sex is the sort that involves coercion and dubious consent, where someone has manipulated a situation to get what they want. Drugging a woman in the Roc could be that sort or it could be the other sort, where it's about control and violence.

Coercion sexual assault is the most likely scenario, whether it's Rockton or Haven's Rock. One would hope that anyone driven to drag a resident into the forest would realize he was going to get caught. We have seventy people in Haven's Rock and a professional police force of three.

But if you've convinced yourself that you just "talked her into it," you don't see a crime. Even if drugs are involved, it's their word against yours, and besides, you didn't give them any drugs and so you thought it was consensual sex. Really.

If Kendra was attacked and possibly dosed, there is no way I'm turning this over to Dalton and Anders, as I have—grudgingly—with most of my late-pregnancy workload. I absolutely trust both of them to treat it with all due gravity and respect, and if I weren't here, they could handle it. But I am here.

The clinic front door is unlocked. That's the only way I know April is inside, because the windows are shuttered, blinds drawn. To avoid giving the town away at night, all of the buildings have been designed to be as close to dark as possible, even if someone has a light on, because in the dead of winter, you can't expect people to be in bed by four when the sun sets.

I still tap on the door as I open it. Inside, it remains dark, meaning my sister unlocked the front door but didn't turn on the waiting-area light. I don't make it to the next door before it's yanked open.

The first time Dalton ever saw April, he knew she was my sister. Of course, siblings often resemble each other. It's genetics. But I grew up hearing how different we looked, and I realize now that what people really meant was that I have distinctive features that favor our Chinese-Filipino mother, and April does not, and by "distinctive features" I really mean just eye shape and skin tone. It only takes that, though, for me to look Asian and her to look white.

Get beyond that, and it's very obvious that we're sisters, with the same straight dark hair, heart-shaped face and cheekbones. But those differences are one of many things that drove a wedge between us growing up, the other main one being April's previously undiagnosed place on the autism spectrum.

April steps out, flipping on the light and closing the door as she glares at me. "What are you doing here?"

I make a show of looking around. "Have I lost clinic-visit privileges? Or sister-visit privileges?"

"Both if it's one in the morning. I thought Eric was handling all this for you." Her glare moves to my shoulder and hardens to annoyance when Dalton isn't there to receive it. The fact that she's glaring at all tells me she's out of sorts. When it comes to irritating April, Dalton gets the free pass that her little sister never does.

"April?" I motion toward the door and for her to make sure her voice is lowered so Kendra can't hear.

Her eyes narrow.

"Considering the nature of the case," I say, "I'm going to be here."

"She was not sexually assaulted. Nor is it clear that was her attacker's intention. If it were, I would have asked you to be here myself."

"Even if the motivation is unclear but she *was* dosed, that could mean other residents have already been dosed and assaulted."

"No one has come to me with such concerns."

"But . . ." I gentle my tone. "If they were dosed, they may not be aware that what happened was nonconsensual. Or they may not come to the doctor unless there was . . . damage."

"Oh." She colors a little. "Yes, of course. I had not considered that."

"May I see your patient, April?"

She nods. Then she pauses, and visibly girds herself before saying, "You were right to come."

I could tease her about finding that so hard to admit, but it *is* hard. Being wrong upsets her. It feels like failure.

April leads me into the examination room, where Kendra sits cross-legged on the table.

"Lie down," April says. "You have been drugged and should not attempt sitting."

Kendra salutes and stretches out, arms folded over her chest like a corpse. "Can I at least get a pillow?"

I grab two from the next room, and Kendra flips onto her side, hugging one pillow as she props onto her arm.

"I will be in my office," April says.

When April's gone, Kendra tells me her story. She'd gone to the Roc with Yolanda. Anders and Gunnar had joined them for a while. Then Kendra had invited Lynn over, and Gunnar slipped off, with Anders following shortly after.

Kendra had two drinks, which was one past her norm, so when she'd felt tipsy after leaving, she blamed the extra booze. The problem with being intoxicated—by booze or drugs—is that your brain isn't working well enough to assess whether "I just had too much to drink" is a valid explanation for what you're experiencing.

The memory holes start after Yolanda left shortly before closing. Kendra stayed until the end with Lynn—having invited the other woman to join them, she didn't want to abandon her. The next thing Kendra remembers is being on the deck of her residence, having apparently gone in and found the toilets occupied.

Unable to wait for a toilet, she'd headed for the woods. Time stutters there, as if she'd been blacking out. Someone attacked her, knocking her down and dragging her into the forest. She managed to scream, which is when Sebastian heard her—he'd been taking his dog, Raoul, for a bedtime walk. Sebastian came running, which scared off Kendra's attacker.

"I didn't see who grabbed me," Kendra says. "I can't even say for sure it was a man." She fusses with the pillows. "I know I might have been drugged, but I still can't believe I didn't take two seconds to look at who had me."

"Because you were fighting for your life, not thinking about making an ID. No one is going to wish you'd taken that risk to catch this person. That's my job."

Her eyes fill. "Thank you. I'm hoping I did catch a glimpse, and it'll come to me later."

I squeeze her hand. "Maybe it will, and if I'm a halfway decent detective, I'll have already caught whoever attacked you." I drop my voice. "While people think eyewitness accounts are the best kind of proof, they're actually one of the least reliable."

Kendra nods. "When I was doing social work, I had two clients who'd been wrongfully incarcerated because the victim saw an Indigenous person and ID'd them."

"Here it might seem as if it'd be harder to get it wrong, but add drugs into the mix, and you could end up accidentally ID'ing the last person you saw at the bar. Or even Sebastian."

Her smile softens. "Who is the one person I know did *not* attack me. I'm so grateful he was out there. He's proof that therapy can work, whatever someone's condition."

Kendra knows Sebastian's diagnosis. He insists on that for all staff, partly because he thinks they deserve to know and partly to expand his network of "monitors"; having people watching him helps compensate for what he lacks—the inner voice that tells us things we shouldn't do.

"Eric's talking to Sebastian now," I say, "and getting a look at the site to see whether he can pick up a trail."

"I'm sure you want to be out there getting a look yourself. My questioning can wait. The crime scene cannot."

"It'll be fine."

"So will I." She meets my gaze. "I'm shook, but I'm okay."

When she sees my expression, she sighs. "Yes, there are nightmares in my future, and I probably won't be drinking for a while . . . or peeing in the woods. But you know what I mean. Go dive into my crime scene, Casey. Find whoever did this before they try again. That's my real concern right now. That they'll try again with another woman . . . and there won't be a Sebastian to save her."

CHAPTER TWO

As I head to the scene, I think about what Kendra just said.

Will Kendra's attacker try again with someone else?

That depends on whether or not her attacker specifically targeted her.

If the intent was coerced sex, Kendra makes a prime target. She's an attractive and vivacious young woman. The fact that she's a lesbian might even be a factor. Some men can't abide the idea that a pretty woman is off-limits.

For a nonsexual assault, hate crime would be the obvious motive. Otherwise, I can't imagine anyone wanting to hurt Kendra. She's one of our most popular residents and rivals Anders for our most popular staff member. Like Will Anders, she exudes that rare combination of charisma and genuine kindness. They're the sort of people who never fail to ask how you are and actually care about the answer.

With Anders being our deputy, he's obviously going to piss off some people. Kendra, though? In Haven's Rock, she does social work—which is mostly problem-solving for residents who are struggling but don't require our resident psychologist or psychiatrist. That means she isn't dealing with those in crisis. She also does plumbing and leads hikes. While people are annoyed over the toilet situation, they all know it's a supply issue and even the drunkest resident is hardly going to haul her off and beat her for that.

Also, "drunk" is relative in Haven's Rock, where alcohol is strictly regulated. Getting seriously intoxicated isn't *imp*ossible— you could stockpile your booze allotments at home and consume them before hitting the Roc. But Isabel—resident bar owner and psychologist—has an eagle eye for that.

Thinking of the Roc leads me to another consideration. April is going to run a tox screen on Kendra, but it certainly sounds as if she was dosed. If so, it happened in the Roc. That means whoever did it was there. That might not narrow things down as much as I like—people come and go all night—but it does mean her attacker had to be from Haven's Rock.

We might live in the middle of the Yukon wilderness, but even up here, we are not alone. There are hunters and trappers and miners passing through, and most of them never know about our tiny hamlet. Structural and technological camouflage keeps us safe, but exposure threats do happen and we're always ready for them.

Could those hunters, trappers, and miners realize we have women here and drag one out? Yes. The one lone local we know is Lilith, a nature photographer, who is not dragging Kendra into the woods for any reason. The real danger is the group who set up camp *after* we built Haven's Rock.

As we were building, a prospector discovered gold nearby, and his claim is now run by a small firm that made camp a few miles away. We expected them to leave in the winter, and they did not, which is far from the first suspicious thing about them. We were on high alert for months after an issue with them rocketed our suspicion meter, but nothing has happened since. They've been perfect neighbors.

Could one of them have slipped into the Roc? No, our town is too small for strangers to enter unnoticed.

Yes, it's easier if our culprit isn't a stranger from the woods— or a miner from the neighboring camp. That gives me the fabled locked-room mystery, where Kendra's attacker must be one of us. But it also means I can't blame an outsider.

We are a town of refugees, of people who need sanctuary, of people who may have fled abusive partners, stalkers, or would-be killers. We promise them safety. And with this, we once again have failed to provide it.

I head to Kendra's residence first. Being the middle of the night means no one is outside, and as soon as I leave the clinic, I can pick up the murmured voices of Dalton and Sebastian. Nights out here are always quiet, but winter seems deathly silent, with each footfall crunching like the crack of a gun.

When I peer up, I can barely make out the quarter moon. It's a cloudy sky with no sign of the green that marks the northern lights. That sky makes me uneasy, as does the thaw. There's no way in hell a Yukon winter ends in March. Even in May, the ice on the lake will just be starting to break. It's much too early for a thaw, and there's a crackle in the air that warns of the calm before a storm.

The temperature has plunged overnight, crusting the melting snow. On the main thoroughfares, though, the snow is too well-trodden and slushy for that, and the front deck of Kendra's residence building is nothing but a puddling mass of footprints.

I snap a few photos on my phone. We don't have Wi-Fi or even a cell signal, but a smartphone is so much more than that, and I am relieved to be able to take pictures again, instead of sketching everything.

I search for signs of a struggle in that mess of footprints, but see nothing to indicate dragging or even slipping, which is consistent with Kendra's recollection that she wasn't grabbed there.

When I peer out toward the voices, I see Dalton looking over at me, and I wave. He takes a half step my way, stops himself, and waves back. He might want to help me in case I slip, but I'm fine and it's better to leave Kendra's trail as untouched as possible.

"Untouched" in theory, that is. In reality, I can't even see where she left the porch. It's just slush, and even in spots where the snow has crusted, there are a dozen trails from people returning late yesterday evening.

I whistle for Storm, and that is apparently also my husband's release signal. Sebastian stays behind with Raoul and only lifts a hand as if to let me know he'll wait for my questions.

"I could handle this," Dalton says as he approaches.

"But I'd like to."

"Which is why I said 'could.' How're you feeling?"

I haven't even considered that. At this stage of my pregnancy, I'm so accustomed to lumbering around like my dog that I suspect after the baby is born, I'll fall flat on my ass leaning backward for balance.

I won't pretend I'm not looking forward to that time—being able to wear my clothing, being able to fit into my boots, not getting up three times every night to pee, and having ankles. You never know how much you'll miss your ankles until they're gone.

I'm five foot two, which means at eight months, I'm basically carrying a beach ball under my shirt. Or more like a weighted exercise ball . . . that kicks. Overall, though, I haven't gained as much weight as I'd like, and I'm worried our baby will be small. Too small? My obstetrician says no, but I'm lower in that percentile than I want to be.

I assure Dalton that I feel fine, and then I get to work.

I brought Kendra's undershirt from the clinic for a scent sample. Storm finds her trail easily and tracks it in a perfect line toward Sebastian. We're far enough off the main thoroughfare now that I can pick up Kendra's footprints. She seems to be alternating between walking and staggering.

Then I see something that reminds me of a sight Dalton and I saw last week, when he grudgingly agreed to let me hike more than a hundred feet into the woods. An eagle had taken some small critter, and the memory of the attack remained emblazoned on the snow, with the wingbeats and the talon grabs and the violent struggles of whatever had been snatched. That's what I see here—a tableau of violence cast in snow.

What I *don't* see is anything I can use. Over here, a boot skidded. Here, a knee crushed the snow. Here, a hand smacked down, melted snow bloating each finger mark.

I follow the drag marks that skid over the crust with only the occasional deeper mark, where Kendra tried to get traction. They end where Sebastian heard her and came running. I can make out boot prints to the side, presumably his, though again, the melting and crusted snow means they're little more than ragged punched holes. The same, unfortunately, goes for the prints where Kendra's attacker retreated deeper into the woods.

I still take photographs of everything. Dalton helps with the close-ups. Being unable to put on my own boots means I'm also unable to crouch and take photos. Or measurements. Or to get down and examine the ground for other signs of trace.

This is the first time my belly has hampered an investigation, because this is the first actual investigation I've had in months. The last case was a missing heirloom watch that disappeared from a nightstand . . . and turned up under the bed. Someone else's bed, that is. That was three months ago, and quite possibly the last time I was easily able to drop to the floor. I've spent the intervening months on tasks that have not required deep bending.

I stave off my frustration by walking over to Sebastian, who is very patiently petting Raoul, the half-wolf dog he shares with Mathias.

"Hey," I say.

He looks up. "How's Kendra?"

"She'll be okay. You got there just in—"

"Butler?" Dalton calls.

I turn toward him as he rises from checking a print.

"It's late," Dalton says. "Let Sebastian go to bed. Interview him tomorrow."

My eyes narrow. I'm the one he wants to get back in bed . . . and not for the usual reasons.

Unfortunately, my husband has a point. He's already spoken to Sebastian, and the young man's story isn't going to change overnight, especially when—as Kendra says—he might be the only person in town who definitely didn't attack her. Well, I probably fit that category, too, if only because my current condition means I'm not dragging chairs across the dining room much less hauling people into the woods.

"In fact . . ." Dalton continues, and I turn slowly, my eyes narrowing to slits. "Sebastian, why don't you come by the house tomorrow at nine. Casey can interview you there."

"At nine?" I shake my head. "By then I'll be in town . . . investigating an attack on one of our residents."

"Fine. Sebastian? Come to our place at eight forty-five."

"I'll come over at eight thirty," Sebastian says. "And bring egg sandwiches from the café. That way you can interview me, eat breakfast, and still be in town by nine."

I thank him and give Raoul a pat before they leave. I take my time turning back to Dalton. I'm torn between being grumbly and being genuinely annoyed, which is par for the course these days.

For most of this pregnancy, Dalton and I have been fine, giddy even, as we prepare for the new addition to our lives. But the rest has been . . . less happily-ever-after, for both of us.

We knew this would happen. Throughout our relationship, Dalton has worked on keeping his protective streak in check and I have worked on reining in my fierce—okay, rabid— independence. Then came the pregnancy, which we both knew would set us back. His protective streak would soar, countered by my determination not to let this slow me down.

We're both in the wrong, and we know it. That doesn't mean he can help feeling frustrated by my insistence on working . . . and I can't help feeling frustrated by his coddling. The scare last month only made things worse.

So I don't turn around until I've stifled my annoyance and can look over without scowling.

"You good?" Dalton says from his crouch near a footprint.

"Yep. Before we go, though, we need to follow the trail. Can you help Storm and me with that? Then I'll go home while you two finish up."

His grunt is conciliatory, and when he comes over, he leans down to brush his warm lips over my forehead. Then he says, "I've already taken a stab at it. But yeah, she works better with you."

Newfoundlands are not tracking dogs, but that's what I've trained Storm for, and she does at least as well as any other non-hound. While I was at the clinic, Dalton would have tried having Storm follow the trail of Kendra's attacker. More importantly, he'd have tried to follow it himself, using visual markers. But as he said, Storm works better with me, and he held off on a proper search until I arrived.

Now we do that. Dalton had started by photographing and measuring the prints that clearly belonged to the attacker. That means we can walk over to the trail without worrying about destroying evidence.

I show Storm what I want her to track, and she gamely follows the trail. Sure, that's less helpful when we can see the footprints ourselves, but that isn't her fault.

She follows the trail into the woods and to the main path. When she loses it there, Dalton's grunt says it's where he lost it, too. That's hardly surprising. Once the attacker reaches that path, their trail will overlap with dozens of others, including iterations of their own. The wider path also means Dalton can't easily find visual cues. The trail is a solid mass of footprints, and broken twigs and disturbances could be from anyone.

The next step is to find where Kendra's attacker might have left the path. They don't, at least not as far as Storm or Dalton can tell. We follow the path all the way back into town and check every place where someone stepped off it. Storm reports none as being her target. Once we reach town, we turn around and follow it in the other direction. Nothing.

Kendra's attacker is from Haven's Rock, which means they know we have a tracking dog. They fled onto the path and followed it straight back to town, hiding their trail among dozens of others. Storm is tracking a ground scent, which is the smell a person leaves on their shoes and the detritus—skin, hair, and such—that falls as they walk. In winter it's easy to be so bundled up that you're hardly dropping any detritus at all.

Storm can follow a trail we set her on. She can also find a trail based on a scent marker. What she *can't* do is follow a trail and then lumber to the person who left it and woof like a witness with a police lineup.

The failure, really, is mine. I don't know how to tell her what I want, and I think to do that, I'd have needed to start much earlier. What we really wanted her for was finding people who get lost in the woods, so that's what she's trained to do. In the end, even if she could ID a suspect, I'd still need to make the case against them.

We keep searching for an hour before I give up. Kendra's attacker went straight to the path and presumably followed it to town. Finding them is up to me . . . starting tomorrow.

CHAPTER THREE

I don't bother going back to bed. It's nearly three. Trekking up the stairs and trying to get comfortable in bed again is an exercise in futility. Some nights, I don't even make it to our bedroom at all.

Three months ago, Kenny presented us with a rocking recliner, and it might be the greatest shower gift ever. Not only can I elevate my feet to rest, but it's the one place in the house I can comfortably sleep. It's well padded and extremely comfortable, and that's where I go tonight, while Dalton brews chamomile tea.

I'm still settling into the chair when he brings the tea and cookies. Then he pulls up an ottoman, sits on it, and starts to massage my feet.

Tears prickle my eyes. Yep, my hormones are still out of control, though I've started to fear this is just the new me. Constantly tired and stressed and on the verge of either frustrated rage or sobbing tears. At least these tears are ones of gratitude, even if they are touched with a hint of guilt.

"I love you," I say.

"I know." He shifts to get a better grip on my foot. "I also know that you need to investigate this, and I'm going to try not to get in your way." He lifts his gaze to mine. "But I need you to meet me in the middle, Butler."

I nod. "Try not to be frustrated by what I can't do, and try not to take it out on you when you slow me down."

"I know you don't mean it. Just like you know, if I'm slowing you down, it doesn't mean I don't think you can handle it. You just can't expect to operate at full capacity with a five-pound parasite hanging off your abdomen."

I place my hands on either side of my belly and lean down to whisper, "'Parasite' is a term of endearment. Daddy doesn't blame you."

"Not until they're a teen and start pulling the 'I didn't ask to be born' shit, and then I can pull the 'Do you know what your mother went through?' shit."

"That's supposed to be my line. Yours is 'Do you know what your mother put me through while she was having you?'"

He laughs softly and reaches over to gently kiss me. Then he stops as my stomach tents. His fingers go to the spot, and when the baby kicks again, the look on his face washes away all my exhaustion. Another kick, and he laughs with delight.

"She's going to come out fighting," he says. "Just like her momma."

I roll my eyes. "Or *he* is, like his daddy."

"*She*," he says. "Trust me on this. A little girl named Eric."

Another eyeroll. We don't know the baby's sex. I didn't ask because it doesn't matter for anything except names, and even then, our short list is gender neutral. We've narrowed it down to Quinn or Riley. Or, at least, that was what we'd narrowed it down to yesterday. By tomorrow, we might change our minds. Again.

Dalton pauses there, with his hand pressed to where the baby is kicking, until they shift around and settle again.

"Nighty-night," he whispers to my stomach. Then he looks at me. "That goes for both of you. If you get enough sleep, I'll be less likely to pester you to rest tomorrow."

"You know that threats aren't like warm milk. They don't help me sleep."

"It's not a threat. It's a promise. I could threaten to make you drink warm milk if you don't sleep, though."

I make a face. "Ugh."

"Then go to sleep." He pulls the blanket up, kisses my forehead, and returns to massaging my feet as I drift into sleep.

The next morning, Dalton "lets" me sleep until five minutes before Sebastian arrives. In other words, he fails to wake me in time to shower and such, but I'll give him this because I probably wouldn't have showered anyway *and* he has my clothing ready and a mug of hot chocolate waiting when he does rouse me. Then he helps me dress, which is very thoughtful and efficient but also humiliating.

Someday, I remind myself. Someday, in my relatively near future, I will be able to yank on clothing in thirty seconds again.

Sebastian doesn't arrive until 8:34, clearly finding the sweet spot between annoying Dalton by being early and annoying me by being late. We eat as we talk. The young man doesn't have anything to offer, really. Had he seen Kendra's attacker, he'd have said so last night.

As he told us then, his focus was on Kendra. He saw a figure, dressed dark, possibly wearing a balaclava, which is issued to everyone for the winter weather. If he had to guess, he'd say it was a man, though he won't rule out the possibility of a woman. The figure had been bent, dragging Kendra, so it was hard to tell sex or size.

Really, the most important thing he has to tell me is that he stopped by the clinic and Kendra is doing well. Sebastian might lack a natural conscience and struggle with empathy, but his brain has done an excellent job of filling in the blanks. He likes Kendra, therefore he is concerned for her well-being, and he knows I will be, too, and that it is considerate to check on her.

Dalton and I leave shortly after Sebastian does. Dalton heads to talk to Phil, as the town manager—we'd call him the mayor if that wouldn't suggest he was our boss. Yes, Phil is still here. It's been six months since he last reminded us that he's only staying until the town is settled. I'd love to think Haven's Rock and our mission have finally won him over, but I know the truth. He's accepted that Isabel isn't leaving, and as long as she isn't, neither is he.

I put off speaking to Kendra again—I don't want her to feel as if I'm hovering in hopes she'll remember something. First I'll talk to those who were with her last night, starting with Anders, who needs to know what happened as soon as possible.

Right now, we don't have overnight policing in Haven's Rock. At some point, we'll need it, mostly for the sake of having a town official available around the clock. With my pregnancy, we've decided to hold off. That means Anders—who often got the night shift in Rockton—doesn't start until ten. I should be able to catch him leaving his apartment over the town hall. When I get there, though, I can see his blinds are drawn, which means he's left for the day.

Storm and I pop into the town hall. No sign of him there.

Damn. We should have left him a report last night, so he'd know about the attack before he went out.

As chill as Anders is, the power dynamics are awkward. He was the deputy to Dalton's sheriff, just the two of them, and then I came along, wedging in with a newly created position equal to his . . . and then shacking up with the boss. Anders and I are still equals, two law-enforcement officers working under Dalton, but I'm the one with the direct line to the boss. I hate anything that might make Anders feel out of the loop.

I'm turning to go find him when the door opens. In walks a dark-haired woman with light brown skin, leading a snow-suited toddler by the hand.

"Storm," I say. "Look who's here."

The dog immediately lies down, and Nicole and I both laugh. At Storm's size, she isn't worried about being knocked over by a rambunctious two-year-old, but she knows the routine. As soon as she's on the floor, so is Stephen, as the toddler screeches loud enough to set Storm's ears back. He launches himself at her and drops onto her, mittened fists clenching fur as he buries his face in Storm's side . . . and hopefully doesn't bite her in his enthusiasm.

Nicole makes sure the door closes and lowers her voice. "I heard about Kendra."

"She's okay. Nothing happened."

"Good. I still—"

Stephen shrieks and strangles Storm in another hug. Nicole waits for the noise level to drop and tries again, only to have him shriek over her. Nicole slumps her shoulders with a deep sigh, and I try not to laugh.

There are many reasons why I love having Dalton's brother, Jacob, and his wife in Haven's Rock for the winter, but one of the best is that I get a preview of my life to come. Not having younger siblings—and having avoided babysitting whenever possible—I lack experience with small children.

With Stephen in town, I'm learning fast. He's recently learned to screech and loves the sound of his voice. He also has discovered the existence of the word "no," which can be used whenever his mother tells him not to do something like screeching. And from Nicole, I'm learning that even with toddlers—maybe *especially* with toddlers—you pick your battles. If she tells him to stop screeching and he doesn't want to, then she needs to enforce her decision, which means she might have to take him home when she wants to speak to me.

"Jacob took off this morning to get in some hunting while it's warm," she says. "Or that was his excuse. I really need to up my hunting—"

A shriek cuts her off, and she slumps again, her shoulders sinking dramatically.

"Hey, bud," I say to Stephen. "How about throwing Storm's ball for her?"

"Ball?" He perks up and looks around. "Where ball?"

I smile. "You need to find it. I think it's hiding."

He toddles off, snowsuit swishing.

I'm turning back to Nicole when the door opens tentatively. At first, it doesn't seem as if anyone's there. Then I see the head poke in about a foot below where I expect one. It's Max, our second-youngest resident.

"Sorry," Max says, looking from me to Nicole. "I was looking for—"

"Mac!" Stephen shouts. He can almost get Max's name, but the X is a little tough. He races over and Max smiles and crouches with his hand out for a high five, which Stephen enthusiastically returns.

"I was looking for Sheriff Eric," Max says. "We were going to walk Storm this morning."

"Ah," I say. "He'll need to give you a rain check. Something came up last night."

I don't fail to notice Max's gloved hand grip the door. I worded that as carefully as I could, but the last time "something came up," it was Max being abducted for four days.

"It's Kendra, right?" he says, his voice tight. "I heard something about that."

I wave for him to come in as Stephen bounces, waiting to snag the older boy's attention again.

"Kendra's fine," I say. "Someone knocked her down."

I'm sure as hell not saying someone tried to drag her into the woods. To my growing list of tasks, I add "tell Dana she needs to speak to Max about Kendra before he hears the full story from anyone else."

Max looks from me to Nicole again. "Do you want me to take Stephen for a while? So you guys can talk?"

I know "sensitive" isn't always considered a positive trait in boys, but Max's empathy always makes me smile . . . while hoping the world never drives it out of him. Not many eleven-year-olds would have realized that Nicole and I were trying to have a conversation, much less offered to help.

"Please," I say. "Just for a few minutes."

"I can take him for as long as you want. No lessons this morning." He taps Stephen's shoulder. "Wanna come outside with me? The bakery should have cookies, and then we can check out some feathers I saw in the snow. Figure out what kind of bird lost them."

Dalton has been teaching Max wilderness craft, which Max has been passing on to Stephen. Is the toddler too young for that? Sure, but no one's telling Max that when he obviously likes passing on what he's learned, and Stephen doesn't care whether he understands it or not. What matters is that this older boy is giving him his undivided attention.

Nicole makes sure Stephen's snowsuit is zipped up and his hood pulled over his hat. Then Max takes his hand. Storm rises with a questioning look my way.

Max sees Storm and says, "Can we take her?"

"Absolutely."

I give Storm the signal to follow, and she lumbers off with the boys.

As we watch them from the window, Nicole says, "He's so good with Stephen."

"He is. That also reminded me that I'll need to talk to Dana about what happened last night. Let her explain it to Max in whatever way she wants."

"I'll do that," Nicole says. "Talking to Dana, not Max. Though I'll also offer to talk to Max, being the resident expert on kidnapping trauma."

There's a lilt to her voice, and someone hearing her might be forgiven for thinking she's joking. She's not, and that lilt rings just a little bit false. Nicole recognizes she has trauma, and she'd really rather not. I get that. I get it so much, which is one reason we're such good friends.

By the time I arrived in Rockton, Nicole had been missing long enough that there wasn't even a case file for me to read, much less pursue. She vanished and evidence indicated she was dead. When we found her, she'd been gone over a year, kidnapped and held hostage in a cave. You don't get over that. You just don't.

"I can also talk to Kendra," she says, voice lowering. "That's why I came by."

There's a reason Nicole's captor held her in that cave, and it's the obvious reason a man holds a woman prisoner. If Nicole ever doubts how much progress she's made, I only need to point out where she is today—married to a man she loves with a son they adore. Life can't compensate us for past trauma, but in Nicole's case, I like to think it put in a good effort.

"You can speak to Kendra," I say, "but I'll take Dana."

"Why?"

When I give her a look, she says, "Oh, sorry, was that too blunt? Am I supposed to say you don't need to do that and then we dance around it for a while until I finally need to challenge you?"

I sigh.

"You like the direct approach, so I am being direct, Casey. I can speak to Kendra *and* Dana, and if Dana likes, I can also speak to Max. Jacob will be back by noon. He can take over toddler watch."

I want to argue, but her look won't let me, mostly because she's right.

"Fine," I say. "I'll get back to the investigation. I also have to call a town meeting—"

"Nope."

I cross my arms. "People need to know what happened."

"Yep, and we can handle that."

"'We' meaning . . . ?"

"Isabel and I will talk to the women. I might ask Yolanda, but I wanted your take on that. I don't know her well enough."

"Does anyone?"

"She likes you."

I snort. "Yolanda tolerates me. She likes most people here—she's just not obvious about it. Enlist her help. She'll want that, and she'll make damn sure everyone takes the threat seriously. But let me talk to her." I lift my hand against protest. "Not to take on more work, but because I already need to speak to her. She was with Kendra last night."

"Fine, I'll grant you that. I'll speak to Kenny about talking to the men. He'll know who to enlist."

"Have him speak to me first." I raise my hand again. "He isn't only warning men of possible attack, but almost certainly letting the attacker know just how seriously we're taking this."

"Okay. You can speak to Yolanda and Kenny. But that's it."

I arch my brows. "May I also speak to potential witnesses?"

"If you insist." Nicole puts her hat back on. "So how are you doing? And don't say fine. This is your chance to whine. Take it."

"I miss my ankles."

She lets out a choked laugh. "I remember that."

"Also booze, coffee, and sex."

Her brows rise. "You can still have forms of sex, Casey. Do I need to have the talk with you?"

I roll my eyes. "You know what I mean. The rest is fine and, at the risk of TMI, Eric is very attentive. I just miss the part that got me here in the first place."

"Just wait until you're in labor. I may have grabbed Jacob and told him if he brings that thing near me ever again, it better be wearing a rubber. Two, just to be safe."

I laugh and shake my head.

She puts on her gloves. "I always wondered why people seem to have babies three years apart. I figured it was to get the first one past the bottles and diapers stage. It's not. That's about exactly how long it takes to forget the horrors of pregnancy and birth."

"Does that mean another nephew or niece might be in our near future?"

Her cheeks color, just a little. "Not quite yet, but at the risk of jinxing it, efforts are being made."

"Anytime you want us to look after Stephen to help those efforts . . ."

"Uh-uh. You're focusing on that little one." She points at my belly. "We've got this."

"Glad to hear it," I say, and accompany her out the door. "Now, you wouldn't have seen Will around, would you?"

CHAPTER FOUR

I don't even make it off the town hall steps before I see Anders beelining my way. When I start continuing down the stairs, he makes shooing motions with both hands, and Nicole laughs.

"He's telling you to go back indoors," she says. "Before your baby freezes . . . inside you."

"Right?" I roll my eyes and try to keep descending, only to get more vigorous shooing.

"I need to talk to you," I call to Anders as Nicole takes her leave.

"You can do that from indoors," Anders calls back. "And while sitting."

I shake my head, but I retreat into the building and take a seat in front of the smoldering fireplace. Anders heads straight to it, adding a log before taking off his gloves.

"I heard what happened to Kendra," he says.

I wince. "I'm sorry. We should have told you last night."

"Uh, no, I was enjoying a very good sleep, and if you didn't need my help, I didn't need to know." He shucks his parka and lowers himself into the other chair. "Eric caught up with me and filled me in. He says she wasn't assaulted. Are we, uh, sure?"

"As much as we can be. There's no sign of it, and Kendra wouldn't feel any need to cover that up, especially with us. Whoever grabbed her didn't get her far into the forest."

"Good. I was feeling the spectral fingers of Rockton reaching out, reminding me of all the times I was pretty sure a woman had been fondled—or worse—and wasn't comfortable telling us." He knocks snow from his boot. "That got better after you arrived."

"It always helps having a woman on the force."

"Hell, it helps having an experienced *cop* on the force. There was plenty of sexual assault in the army when I was an MP, but I didn't have the proper training, and the higher-ups didn't seem particularly eager to provide any. Anyway, the point is that we've got a problem, and it's not just some asshole who can't hear the word 'no.'" He pauses. "Which isn't to say *that* wouldn't also be a problem."

"But I know what you mean. Dragging a woman into the woods means we're dealing with more than a guy who's been raised to think women just need convincing. However, we also can't be sure sexual assault *was* the goal. Drugging Kendra in a bar and dragging her into the woods suggests that, but I can't ignore the possibility it was a purely physical assault."

"Gay-bashing?"

"Let's hope not."

"Well, that I *did* deal with in the army. But stepping back a bit, I'm guessing you wanted to do more than just tell me we have a new case. I had a drink with Kendra last night. I'm a witness."

"You are." I struggle to untie my boots and feel a wash of relief through my already-sore feet. "Tell me about that."

"Not much to tell. Kendra was sitting with Gunnar and Yolanda. I came in. Obviously you aren't hanging out at the Roc these days, which means Eric isn't either. Isabel was behind the bar. There was no sign of Kenny or Marlon. So I joined Yolanda's table. Nursed a beer while Kendra and Gunnar one-upped each other telling stories. Then . . ."

"Lynn joined, and you left. You and Gunnar."

Anders makes a face. "That sounds bad. I just . . . Lynn is . . . Shit."

Together with her husband, Lynn was one of our first residents. It's been clear from the start that there's marital strain, and that it seems to originate with her husband. That puts the sympathy ball in Lynn's corner. Except Lynn has done a few things to deflate that ball.

She's also tried really hard to make up for those things, but the situation with her husband has led to her . . . looking for love—or sex—in all the wrong places. Like with Gunnar, who'd usually be the right place, but spotting the potential for trouble, he demurred, which humiliated Lynn. She'd then set her eye on our other most eligible bachelor, and Anders backstepped so fast it'd have been funny if I didn't also feel bad for Lynn. She's a woman trapped in an unhappy marriage who just wants companionship—in friends or a lover—and she can't seem to get either.

"I feel for her," Anders says. "I really do. Grant is an ass, and she's lonely, and she's a nice enough woman." He makes another face. "Which really sounds like damning with faint praise. A *nice enough* woman."

"No, I get it. I've come to enjoy her company in a group setting, but I wouldn't be inviting her to lunch. And if I did, it'd be a sympathy invite, which feels wrong."

He rises to poke the fire. "Anyway, so the four of us were

at a table when Lynn came in and did that thing—like I did—looking around for a group to join."

"Only in your case, people would be waving you over, and you get to pick the best option. Lynn's looking for *any* option, while ready to slip out if she doesn't get one. I know Kendra has been making an effort to include her."

"Kendra's good people. Yolanda grumbled but stayed. Gunnar took off before Lynn even got to the table, and we had to pretend he had somewhere to be. I finished my beer and pulled the 'look at the time' crap. I may also have blamed you, saying I needed to start early these days so you can sleep in."

"Feel free to do that whenever you need to. Even after the baby's born, it'll work."

He takes his seat again. "Yeah, but I did feel bad. Lynn wasn't ogling me or rubbing my leg under the table. She's never even *overtly* hit on me. But Grant's taken a dislike to me, and I don't have time for jealous-husband shit."

"Understandable. What time did you leave?"

"Eleven fifteen, which is the advantage of having done a fake watch check. I actually saw the time. It would have been just before eleven when Lynn came in and Gunnar left."

"Did Gunnar really leave? Or just move to a new table?"

"Left, I think. One of the women tried to catch his eye, but you know Gunnar. When he's on, he's good to go, but when he's off, he's very off."

I lean back in my chair. "His boundaries might be invisible, but they are rock solid."

"Yep. So he left when Lynn arrived, and I stayed about another half hour, finishing my beer. Lynn offered to buy us another round, but we're all lightweights."

"So she just got a drink for herself?"

He thinks and then shakes his head. "She didn't bother. She

said if we changed our minds, let her know. That didn't happen while I was there."

"It did happen afterward. According to Kendra, Yolanda talked her into another drink, and Lynn bought the round."

"Makes sense. Now you're going to ask how Kendra seemed, and the answer is absolutely fine. She was Kendra. Goofing around with Gunnar. Needling Yolanda. Chatting with me. I saw zero sign she was inebriated or dosed. It must have come in that second round."

"Or it was dropped into her drink by a passerby. Or it was injected during the closing bustle." I sigh. "With a town of seventy people, you'd think it'd be easy to figure out who dosed a resident in our only bar."

"It never has been. I'm guessing you'll want a list of everyone who was there?"

"Yep. If you can do that, I can get Yolanda, Lynn, and Isabel to check it over."

"Ask Gunnar, too. He might have taken off, but he pays attention. As for Yolanda, though . . ."

"Right. Her face blindness. I'll ask, because she'll be offended if I don't. But I'll be clear I know she might not have noticed who all was there."

Anders insists on fetching Yolanda, which makes me feel a bit like a queen on her throne, but it'll keep Dalton from fussing that I've been doing too much.

Yolanda built Haven's Rock. Okay, she had help, including Kendra and Gunnar, but she was in charge. Her grandmother—Émilie—is our fairy godmother. Émilie had been one of Rockton's earliest residents, and she and her husband had shown their appreciation by joining the first board. That was in the early and optimistic days when the town truly was a sanctuary run by idealists. Over the years, that changed, but Émilie and her husband stayed on to keep it from becoming a pure for-profit endeavor . . . and no one dared kick them out because they headed one of North America's biggest pharmaceutical companies.

So we have a billionaire backer, which would be more awkward if we didn't value Émilie's expertise more than her money. She truly is our fairy godmother—keeping us safe, finding us new residents, even securing a top-notch obstetrician for me—and we only want to be sure we never rely too much on her, however trustworthy she's been.

Her granddaughter Yolanda is successful in her own right as the founder of a company specializing in environmentally friendly construction, which of course made her perfect for Haven's Rock. But if the town is done, why is Yolanda still here? Because she won't leave and no one dares make her.

Part of that is protecting her grandmother's interests. Yolanda no longer suspects we're preying on an elderly billionaire; she just thinks we're naive idealists who might make a mess of Émilie's passion project. Also, Yolanda has early Parkinson's. She's dealing with that . . . and hiding out so she doesn't need to tell Émilie, who lost her husband to the disease.

The door opens, and Yolanda walks in. She's in her mid-forties, tall and curvy, with brown skin and dark curls.

Before Yolanda reaches me, she says, "I don't know who did this to Kendra, but she was fine when I left."

I inwardly sigh. "No one's accusing you of attacking Kendra."

"Yes, but I will be accused of not looking after her. Because Kendra is sweet and popular, and I'm a stone-cold bitch."

I lean back in my chair. "I see your point."

She crosses her arms. "Thank you."

"To alleviate it, I'm going to suggest you hold a town meeting. You can run it, and it'll give you a chance to be very clear that you did not abandon poor, innocent Kendra—"

"Fuck off. I'm not running your damn meeting." She slumps into the seat opposite me. "I'm just being clear that Kendra was fine when I left, which was a few minutes before closing. And I didn't abandon her. She was talking to Lynn about whether they should take advantage of the warm weather to run an impromptu hike. It was getting close to midnight, and the conversation didn't concern me, so I took my leave."

"When you say 'close to midnight' can you be more specific?"

"I was in the residence building at twelve, so I probably left at ten to."

"And went straight to your room?"

"Am I a suspect?"

I sigh. "Yolanda . . ."

"Fine. I went and sat on the toilet, okay? The one damn working toilet. The real reason I left early was that I had stomach cramps. Would you like details of what I did on the toilet? Maybe a sample from the tank to test for DNA?"

Kendra said she'd gone back outside because the one working toilet in their residence was in use. Now I know why.

I go to pull my legs under me, and my stomach muscles protest, so I settle in awkwardly. "Tell me about the round of drinks Lynn bought. That's the most likely source of the drugs."

Her eyes narrow.

"What?" I say.

"I did not dose Kendra's drink."

I thump my head back. "You are a bundle of paranoia this morning, aren't you? Why would I think you dosed a drink that Lynn bought?"

"Because I'm the one who picked them up from the bar." She catches my expression. "You didn't know that."

"I did not. Walk me through it."

"We were talking about drinking in college, and Lynn said something about black velvets, and Kendra had never had one and . . . Fuck." She shakes her head. "I may have unintentionally pressured Kendra. I teased and prodded her into having it. So if I'm on edge, it's because I feel guilty."

"Kendra is an adult. If she said yes, she wanted to say yes."

"I still feel like shit." She exhales. "So Kendra agrees to try one, and Lynn says she'll take one, too, and buy the round. I went to the bar and ordered with Isabel. Then . . ."

She shakes her head. "Reason two why I feel guilty. While I waited, I walked away to talk to Brian and Devon. It was probably five minutes before I came back, and the drink tray was waiting while Iz was in the back storage." She meets my gaze. "I was careless. I gave someone the chance to dose Kendra's drink."

"No, someone *took* the opportunity. To dose *a* drink."

Her brows knit at my emphasis on "a," then her lips form a curse. "A drink. Not Kendra's, because we all got the same thing. They had no idea which of us would drink from the dosed glass."

"Yep, though presuming they saw who ordered it, they knew it was going to be drunk by a woman."

CHAPTER FIVE

Yolanda agrees to help Nicole warn female residents. Up next on my list is Isabel, mostly to ensure she can also help with that. I don't get anything new from our resident bar owner and psychologist beyond echoing Yolanda's sense of guilt that the drink tray had gone unattended.

We've already become complacent in Haven's Rock. Yes, we got off to a rocky start with Max's kidnapping, but we've locked down even tighter, with new protocols and mandatory wilderness training, implementing our wish-list items faster than expected. It helps that things have been so quiet, giving us time to double down on resident safety.

Our complacency came from within. We've had only minor issues from the residents themselves, which reassured us that we'd fixed those problems from our Rockton days. Unlike Rockton, Haven's Rock isn't a refuge for criminals, not even white-collar ones willing to shell out handsomely for protection.

Émilie had decades to learn how Rockton worked and think about how she'd handle intake better, once she was freed from the council's need for profits. Everyone coming into Haven's

Rock is as much a victim as she and her husband had been when they arrived in Rockton fleeing political persecution.

Add in the fact that Haven's Rock accepts couples and families, and the vibe has changed significantly, especially as the staff settles in. Rockton had a tension to it we could never shake. Separated from their support systems, people acted differently. For some, it was like a trip to Vegas—go wild and be whoever you wanted to be, knowing none of it would follow you home. For most, though, arriving among strangers only added to their unease and anxiety.

Haven's Rock is different. The vibe is more wilderness-lodge getaway, which is exactly what we wanted. Or, maybe more accurately, it's like taking a job in a remote community for a few years, accepting the isolation in return for the rewards. In this case, the reward is safety.

We've been aware of the possibility of sexual assault, but we lowered our guard. Since we opened, we haven't had so much as a complaint of unwanted attention. That doesn't mean unwanted attention hasn't occurred, just that it seems to have been dealt with and never reached the stage requiring police intervention.

In Rockton, Isabel taught her bartenders to never leave drinks unattended. You filled it and you handed it over, and if the buyer wasn't around, it waited on the back counter. Take no chances.

Isabel hadn't intentionally left the drinks on the counter. She just didn't think about it. She made them, set them out for Yolanda, and then realized she needed to grab more beers to replace the ones she just used.

Feeling guilty means Isabel has started preparing for my questions before I can ask. She already has a list of everyone she saw that night, especially those she recalls seeing between eleven thirty and midnight. It's not a short list. It was Saturday night, and the weekends might work differently here, but people cling to those old patterns. Saturday is pub night, where you're pretty much guaranteed to walk in and find a table of people you know.

Of the sixty-seven adults in Haven's Rock, fifty are on Isabel's list, having been in the Roc at some point. Of those, at least half didn't leave until that final half hour, which means any of them could have dosed that drink. It's also possible that Kendra's attacker slipped in and out, and Isabel never noticed. A busy night means a busy bar.

I secure her agreement to do the rounds with Nicole and Yolanda. She wants to speak to them first, to solidify the message and include a warning about leaving drinks unattended. That's not blaming anyone. It's just a reminder of a rule every woman learns by the time she's twenty.

Three interviews down, two to go. I've moved Gunnar to the bottom of the list. He left first, and he's unlikely to give me anything new. Up next is my most important witness—the woman who was there when Kendra left the Roc.

It's just past eleven when I find Lynn at work in the general store. She's been working there for a few months, after spending some time at the restaurant. While we have some professional positions in Haven's Rock, most of the jobs are unskilled labor, and we rotate people among them to reduce dissatisfaction.

Anyone walking into the general store could be forgiven for thinking it's shutting down. Half the shelves are empty, with the goods all moved up to the front.

The store isn't closing—it just isn't fully stocked yet. In Rockton, even necessities had to be purchased. Ruined a shirt working in the kitchens? Lost weight and need smaller jeans? You bought them with the credits you earned at your job. In

Haven's Rock, your income is only needed for "extras." Kind of like going to summer camp and bringing tuck money.

Meals, clothing, and all necessities are included in your stay. Work isn't about survival; it's about supporting your community. You get paid, but your credits go toward luxury items. Your daily coffee is free. Your evening beer is not. Paper and pens are free. Fancy writing journals are not. Standard-issue black wool scarves are free. Pastel or plaid ones are not. You decide which items add joy to your stay, and that's where you spend your money. *Not* on essentials.

While you're entitled to that black wool scarf, we don't have a stack of them for residents to grab a new one every time they misplace theirs. If they do lose one, they need to requisition a replacement, and Phil will be examining those requisition lists to be sure this isn't the third scarf you've lost this winter. Yep, we want to be generous, but there *is* a budget.

While the general store fills requisitions, those items are kept in storage. The shop only displays the luxuries, which don't take up a lot of space. We might never need the full building, small though it is. For now, the empty space hosts private gatherings, for those who want to play a game of poker or hold a book-club meeting.

When I walk in, Lynn is on her stool with her inventory book. I grab a chocolate bar as I walk past.

"Add it to your tab?" Lynn says with a smile.

I don't have a tab. Staff are allowed to take what they want. Lynn makes the same joke every time I walk in, but I know it's just social anxiety and an eagerness to be friendly. We had a minor clash during Max's kidnapping—with a bit of casual racism tossed in—and she's been desperately walking it back ever since.

"Nah," I say. "Put it on Eric's."

Her smile broadens. I'm playing along, as I always do, naming a different staff member each time.

"What's our poor sheriff done now?" she says.

"The usual. Late-pregnancy hovering."

"That's very sweet." She quickly adds, "Annoying I'm sure, but still sweet."

There's a wistfulness in her voice that makes me regret my grumble. I've seen Grant hover over *her,* and it's a very different vibe.

She sets down her pen. "I figured you'd get to me this morning. I heard about Kendra. I popped by the clinic, but April ran me off." She quickly adds, "As she should. Kendra doesn't need a steady stream of visitors interrupting her rest. April did tell me Kendra was fine."

"She is, all things considered."

"I, uh, I know this is your investigation—obviously—but . . ." Lynn fingers the inventory book. "Are we allowed to tell what we did down south if it could be relevant?"

"You're always *allowed* to share that," I say gently. "We suggest that people don't give away too much for their own safety, but it's a personal choice. If you're offering to tell me something pertinent, it will be confidential. Within the police force, that is. I do share anything relevant with Eric and Will."

"Of course. And this isn't top-secret or anything. Although . . ." She chews her lip. "It's related to why Grant and I are here, but indirectly."

"I don't need to know any of that."

She nods. "Thank you. What I wanted to say was that I worked for a law firm specializing in civil litigation with sexual harassment and assault. I wasn't a lawyer myself. Just support staff. But I took a lot of training in working with survivors, and that was my specialty. So if you need any help . . ."

"That didn't happen with Kendra."

"Good. I hoped not, but since that was probably the intent . . ." She shrugs, looking sheepish. "I don't know what I'm offering." She taps the inventory book and then looks up. "Oh, but I do know a lot about dosing. The drugs commonly used, methods commonly used, and so on."

"That could be helpful. Would you be able to assist Nicole in writing up safety guidelines for residents?"

She perks up, face lighting. "Gladly."

"I might also consult with you. I know some of the drugs used, and we'll need to match them up with the tox-screen results and the drugs available in town."

"Anything you need, just ask. Until then . . ." Lynn rummages through a drawer. "Because Kendra seems to have been dosed, you'll want to know who was in the bar. I made a list."

She pulls out a sheet of paper. It's more than Isabel's simple list of names. It's in sections and color-coded. With notes.

"The sections are time based," she says. "I arrived just before eleven, so the first section is for those I saw when I first arrived. After that, it's divided into quarter hours. Now, the times aren't exact—I wasn't watching the clock. But I was paying attention to who was there."

She nibbles her lower lip again. "Grant was playing poker, and I didn't want to interrupt his game to tell him I was going to the Roc."

This might seem like a non sequitur. It isn't. She means she noticed who was in the bar because she was watching for Grant.

"The colors indicate how close people came to our table. Green for those who never got near us. Red for people who stopped by. Yellow means I noticed them walk past. Then I added notes for anything that seemed significant."

"That's very . . ." I'm about to say "thorough" when I realize that could sound as if she'd gone overboard. "Appreciated. It's very appreciated. Thank you." I take the page and carefully fold it. "You were also the last person to be with Kendra. How was she acting?"

Lynn's cheeks flame. "I . . . wasn't paying attention. That's awful to say, but Grant doesn't like me staying at the Roc until closing, so I was freaking out a little." A quick hand flapping. "Not that he'd, you know, do anything. He's never hit me. I just don't like fighting with him, and it's not worth it to stay five minutes longer. But Kendra and I were talking about setting up a hike and I lost track of time. When Isabel called closing, I grabbed my coat, said goodbye, and left."

Her hands clench on the countertop. "I wasn't a good friend. I was completely focused on myself. Kendra seemed fine, but I didn't pay enough attention and I didn't offer to walk her home. I realized I'd stayed too late, panicked, and took off."

I tell her that's understandable. It is. I grew up with parents who set rules and expected me to obey them. I rebelled by doing things like intentionally showing up five minutes past curfew in hopes . . . Well, as I realize now, I'd done it in hopes of eliciting an emotional reaction, because even a negative response was better than none. But I'd known other girls with overly strict parents who'd have a full-blown panic attack if they were running late.

Lynn would have been focused on avoiding fallout with Grant, and Kendra is as self-sufficient as they come. Haven's Rock at midnight isn't the big city at two in the morning. Lynn wouldn't worry about letting Kendra walk the hundred or so feet on her own, any more than Yolanda considered that when *she* left early.

I assure Lynn that she didn't do anything wrong. We'll all need to start being a little more careful. It's easy to get complacent, and I'm as guilty of that as anyone.

I thank her for the list. As I'm leaving, I'm mentally preparing to cross-reference it with Isabel's list, and I'm so engrossed in my thoughts that I smack into our newest resident, who jumps back as if I'd caught him breaking in after hours. He flushes, his freckled skin going bright red as he stammers something about needing toothpaste.

Maybe this should trigger alarms. New resident getting flustered at bumping into the town detective . . . who is actively searching for someone who committed an assault? But with Thierry, I might actually be surprised if he *didn't* seem flustered when I literally bumped into him.

Thierry arrived just before Christmas, and he's still finding his place here. He's a little older than me, pleasant looking and sweet natured. He's one of the rare professionals who can continue to practice his trade—an elementary school teacher who has taken over lessons for Max and his brother, Carson. That isn't a full-time position, but Thierry quite happily supplements it with some of the less attractive jobs, like the endless wood chopping and delivery needed in winter.

While Thierry is always a little awkward and overly quick to apologize, today's reaction seems like overkill, even for him. I realize why when Lynn hurries from behind the counter and starts listing the types of toothpaste we have in stock.

I glance between Thierry and Lynn, and I can't miss the looks that suggest something is heating up between them.

I should be happy for Lynn, finding someone open to receiving her signals, especially a guy who seems genuinely nice. But on the selfish side, a jealous Grant is not a problem we need right now.

Which is none of my business until it becomes my business.

Also, it will never be my business. If there's trouble in the next few months, it will go to Dalton and Anders, who can easily handle it.

I say another goodbye to Lynn and Thierry, but I don't think either hears it.

Next stop: Gunnar. He'd been on Yolanda's construction crew as a general laborer, so that's what he continues to do in Haven's Rock. He assists Kendra or our carpenter, Kenny, with post-construction projects. Winter means any construction needs to be indoors, and if I'm right, his latest assignment is retrofitting a loft storage area we've decided to convert to a "playroom" for the kids. Yes, we haven't been open even a year and we're already making changes. No matter how carefully we planned, there is no substitute for living in a space. It's only after we got here that we started realizing that particular storage building would always have an abundance of space . . . and our younger residents lack an area where they can play. Granted, being eleven and thirteen, Max and Carson would be insulted by the use of the word "play-room," but they can make what they want of it.

The loft had actually been Gunnar's idea. He has his own loft space, which we'd also set aside as storage but haven't needed. There can be a childlike side to Gunnar, which had struck me as odd until he gave me his backstory, albeit very brief and very reluctantly, offering it only because it pertained to a case. That backstory has nothing to do with why he's here, but maybe it has everything to do with why he *stays* here.

As a child, Gunnar saw his father shoot his mother, and he fled before catching the next bullet. His father then turned the gun on himself. That kind of trauma can arrest development in subtle ways, like making a twenty-eight-year-old man seek out a hidey-hole of his own, where he can sit and watch life unfold below him and feel safe.

I'm heading to the playroom construction site when I spot my target outside, talking with Anders and Marlon. Marlon is another recent arrival, having come in early December, and he's been another excellent addition to our little town. Like Anders, he's former military, which means he's also a good hunter, and we can always use more of those. We can also always use additions to our militia.

These days, security in Haven's Rock is mostly about keeping the outside world outside—watching for anything out there that gets a little too curious about what's in here. That can be animals or it can be humans, and a resident with military and hunting experience is suited for both. Marlon's easygoing personality means Anders and Kenny were happy to add him to the militia.

Right now, Marlon is deep in conversation with Gunnar, and I'm glad to see that, too. Gunnar is more comfortable around women. That isn't always obvious, because he has the kind of gregarious personality that masks discomfort. But he does gravitate toward women, and I suspect that's another lingering effect of his background. Having a father who killed your mother—and tried to kill you—is going to taint your relationships with adult men, even if Gunnar himself might not realize it.

Gunnar really doesn't care for Dalton, and without going too amateur-shrink, I suspect there's some unfortunate overlap in personality between Dalton and his father. He likes Anders, though, and now seems comfortable with Marlon, too.

I'm heading their way when I see Grant. It's only been a few minutes since I left Lynn, but my mind has traveled down these other tracks—Gunnar and then Marlon—and it takes a moment to realize why seeing Grant sets me on alert. Right. After talking to Lynn, I'm all the more annoyed with Grant's behavior toward his wife, especially when it meant Lynn had been too worried about his reaction to walk Kendra home last night.

Then I see where Grant is heading, and I have a whole new reason to be concerned. He's on course for the general store, walking fast, clearly wanting to speak to Lynn . . . who is inside flirting with Thierry.

Damn it.

Some residents love the soap-opera drama of life in a very small town, but I am not one of them. Especially when "drama" means "trouble."

"Yo!" Anders calls. "Case!"

I lift a hand without looking his way, my attention still on Grant.

Should I find an excuse to pop into the general store again? One more question for Lynn?

I shake off the impulse. Lynn and Thierry were barely at the flirting stage. Grant isn't going to walk in on anything more than shy glances, and if Grant hasn't realized how hard his wife's been looking for love, that's certainly not going to tip him off.

As I head toward the trio of men, I catch at least one passing female resident glancing their way as if she'd like to join that little group. It really is a gathering of Haven's Rock's finest straight single guys. Based on appearance alone, Anders and Gunnar are obvious choices; Anders for his head-turning good looks and Gunnar for his strapping Nordic appeal. Marlon is older—in his mid-forties—but if it wasn't for the gray in his short dark curls, he'd seem no older than Anders, without a wrinkle on his dark skin. He's not nearly as good-looking, but his average face has an openness and a genuine smile that makes it impossible not to smile back.

"How long have you been on your feet, soldier?" Anders calls to me.

I check my watch. "Twenty-two minutes, sir. I have eight more before I'm under strict orders to sit my ass down."

"Mmm, if you say twenty-two minutes, it's actually been thirty-two, meaning you're overdue."

Gunnar laces his hands in a makeshift seat, but I only roll my eyes.

"I'm going to steal this one." I wave at Gunnar. "And yes, we'll sit." I turn to Gunnar. "Let's go to the town hall. I need to talk to you about last night."

"Café's closer," Anders says. "Or the clinic."

"I can walk the hundred paces to the town hall for privacy."

"What you need is a palanquin," Marlon says.

Gunnar screws up his face. "A what?"

"Don't look at me," I say. "I'm hearing 'paladin' or 'pango-lin.' I'm not sure I need a guy with a sword, but pangolins are nice. Not really cold-weather animals, though."

Marlon laughs. "A paladin could carry you on his shoulders. Pangolins are a bit small for transport duty. And I might be say-ing 'palanquin' wrong, too. I mean those litter things that people ride on, carried by others."

"Ah, yes," I say. "I know what you mean—I've just never heard the word."

"Which I might very well have wrong. I'll ask Eric. That man is a walking encyclopedia. But a litter would work. Gunnar and I could whip one up from spare materials, carry you around."

He pantomimes it, and I roll my eyes again.

"I'm pregnant," I say. "Not an invalid. And, technically, my doctor—the one who is not my sister—says it's fine to be on my feet for an hour at a time. It's my lovely husband who cut that in half. Now—"

"Butler!" a voice bellows from clear across town. "Didn't I see you leaving the town hall a half hour ago?"

"Speak of the devil," I say, and I may add a few more choice words that have the men laughing. I turn around and shout back to Dalton. "Gunnar and I are going to the town hall for his interview."

Dalton—appearing from behind a building down the road— opens his mouth, undoubtedly to say something about how far that is, but I cut him off with, "I could really use a decaf coffee. And cookies. I was going to stop by the café—"

"Got it!" he calls. "Meet you at the town hall."

"Smooth," Marlon murmurs.

"Thank you."

"Sure you don't want that litter?"

"Yes, and if you mention it to Eric?" I draw a finger across my throat. Then I say to Gunnar, "Ready for that interview?"

"I just need to tell Kenny I'll be late helping him with the playroom."

"I'll tell him," Marlon says. "I offered to help out anyway."

"Isn't it your half day off?" Anders says.

Marlon shrugs. "It's a playroom for kids. Like volunteering for Habitat for Humanity."

"Except there's beer," Gunnar says.

"Why do you think I offered?"

Gunnar and Marlon high-five. Anders laughs, and I usher Gunnar away for his interview.

CHAPTER SIX

Gunnar's story mostly matches Anders's. He left the Roc as soon as Lynn joined the group, and I understand that. He didn't avoid her because she'd once hit on him. He'd made it clear to all that he was open to that, and he wouldn't want any hard feelings if he turned down an interested party. But Lynn hadn't taken no for an answer. While Gunnar handled it on his own, he was understandably wary around her, as if even friendly attention might be misinterpreted as a sign that he'd changed his mind.

Last night, though, despite what Anders thought, Gunnar hadn't left right away. He'd been heading to the door, but then he'd seen Marlon and Kenny coming in. Gunnar, Marlon, and Kenny had chatted for a few minutes, and then a table of people tried to call them over, and Marlon and Kenny accepted while Gunnar went home for the night.

As promised, Dalton shows up mid-interview with my decaf coffee and cookies. Technically, my baby doc says one cup of regular coffee a day is fine, but however much I miss a solid hit of caffeine, it's not a chance I'm comfortable taking.

I can grumble about Dalton cutting the doctor's "on my feet" time in half, but today is the first time I've gone over it since the premature-delivery scare. No matter how much my doctor insists that if something does go wrong, it'll be Mother Nature's decision, I'd still feel as if it could have been something I did. Was a sip of champagne at New Year's worth it? A daily cup of coffee? Regularly standing for an hour at a time? No. So I have my one decaf coffee a day, plus one hot chocolate, and after that, it's herbal tea and water. And I get off my feet after thirty minutes.

Dalton brings extra cookies, and a coffee for himself, while pointing Gunnar in the direction of the fire and kettle and French press. Even in more laid-back Haven's Rock, Dalton has a rep to maintain. He's the hard-ass sheriff, Anders is the nice guy, and I get to swing between good cop and bad cop, depending on the situation.

Dalton brought extra cookies because he knows Gunnar is wary of him, and he also knows why. I told him Gunnar's backstory, having deemed it important information. But he can't let on he knows, because Gunnar would hate that. So Dalton walks a line here, bringing enough cookies for all but making Gunnar brew his own coffee.

When the interview's done, Gunnar takes his leave. He may also snatch the last cookie, and Dalton may also grumble about that, but once Gunnar's gone, Dalton only shakes his head.

"That help any?" he says.

"The interview or the cookies?"

"The interview."

"It does. He didn't leave as soon as Anders thought, but he did leave."

"Before we're presuming Kendra's drink was dosed."

I nod. "Speaking of dosing, I need to stop by the clinic and see whether April's tox screen—"

"I'll bring her to you."

I open my mouth. Shut it.

Dalton crouches in front of me, his hands on my knees. "Remember a few years ago, when I tore a ligament slipping on the mountainside? April wanted me off that leg for two weeks, and I was a *bear*. Also unbearable. Snapping and snarling at everyone who dared remind me to rest. Including you."

"It was frustrating for you. We were preparing for winter, and there was a lot to be done."

He shakes his head. "No excuse. I fell on that path. You didn't push me. But I felt like I was being a lazy bastard, and I vented my frustration on you." He squeezes my knees. "You're dealing with this much better than I did, and I know that's not because you aren't just as frustrated. Especially now with this case."

I sigh. "I'm taking it out on you."

"No, you're taking it out on yourself. You're torn between feeling like you're shirking your duties and knowing, if anything goes wrong after you overdid it, you'll blame yourself, even if that had nothing to do with it."

"It's just . . ." I shift on my seat. "Lousy timing. I *want* to be off my feet. In bed if possible. Whatever it takes to protect . . ." I put my hands to my belly.

"You are already doing everything—over and above. Like Dr. Kapoor said, staying off your feet is just extra. But you need to let others help you, as hard as that is. It's no imposition for April to come here and talk to you. Or, on second thought, to come to the house. I've done what I needed to do, and Will can handle the rest. Consider me your personal gofer. Anything you need, including rounding up witnesses, I will do." His lips quirk. "After all, this baby *is* half my fault."

I push aside the urge to negotiate, to say that I'll stay here, that I don't want to feel like a queen holding court. But that's exactly what he means. Don't make him negotiate. Don't make him my captor, taking away my freedom. That's especially loaded for a man dealing with his wife.

"Can we go for a walk later?" I ask. "In the woods? While it's warm?"

When he hesitates, I sigh and say, "I'll take the sled."

He smiles and leans in to kiss me. "Then we can go as far as we want. Get out of town for a while. Discuss the case if you insist. Or just be glad Kendra wasn't hurt, know that we're locking down as best we can, and relax."

"We probably should discuss the case."

He exhales a long, dramatic sigh. "Of course."

"But I'll stay in the sled."

"And won't complain about it?"

"Asking a lot, aren't you?" I look up at him and shake my head. "Fine. I'll stay in the sled and not complain about it."

I'm settled in at home. Max has returned Storm, who's stretched out at my feet, forgoing her bed for the cooler hardwood floor. She's panting softly, which means the boys must have been running around with her.

I can say she's just tired because she's such a big dog. That's part of it. She's good at endurance, thanks to hikes that can last all day, but running around takes its toll, and it's doing so more and more as she ages. She's only four. For another breed, that'd be young adulthood. For a Newfoundland, it's middle age.

I try not to think of that. Middle age isn't old . . . says the person approaching the middle of the average adult life span. Storm is healthy and happy. I just have to keep an eye on her exertion levels. Both of us need the occasional reminder that we aren't pups anymore.

"I have the results of the toxicology screening," April says, by way of greeting as she enters our chalet. "And I am not satisfied with them."

"They misbehaved?" I say.

She takes off her boots, marches in, and stands by the fireplace.

"Can you sit, please, April? I know you're upset, but if you stand, then having me sit feels awkward."

She lowers herself to a chair. "Eric wanted you to know he is speaking to Kendra about your list of names from the Roc and obtaining her own recollections. He will be here shortly. As for the toxicology screening, I am displeased by the results. They are unsatisfactory, and the blame lies with the tests. We need ones specific to this purpose."

"Then we'll get those. Which doesn't help right now. I wasn't properly prepared for this. I haven't been reminding residents of safety precautions at the bar, and I didn't think to get specific tests for drugs used in sexual assault."

"*We* didn't do these things, Casey. Not you specifically. I did not obtain the correct tests. Isabel was not cautious enough at the bar. We all forgot to remind residents—and staff—of the dangers."

I stretch out my legs on the recliner. "I'm just glad Kendra wasn't hurt. This was our wake-up call to fix things. We'll give the warnings, and we'll lock down opportunities. We also need those coasters that test for dosed drinks."

I pull over a pillow from the chair beside me and use it under my feet. "Of course, all that presumes Kendra was dosed, which the tests didn't prove."

"I never said that."

I arch my brows.

April shakes her head, as if I'm suffering from a terminal case of baby brain. "I said they were unsatisfactory. I have two types of screening—blood and urine. The urine test showed alcohol, which we know. Also trace amounts of THC, but that is as much Kendra's business as the alcohol."

Kendra did ask for edibles the last time we went south. We already get medical marijuana for Yolanda's tremors. Recreational marijuana is legal in Canada, but we haven't decided whether to stock it. While we got some for Kendra, that wouldn't explain her blacking out, especially since trace amounts suggest it'd been days since she took any.

"And the blood test?" I ask.

"It showed evidence of a benzodiazepine."

"That makes sense. Benzos are one of the most common types of drug used in sexual assault."

"Yes, but this is an advanced test, from Émilie's company. It can narrow that down further and the specific drug it detected is temazepam."

I frown. "I'm not familiar with that. Mostly, I know the drugs by their common names. Rohypnol, GHB, and generic benzos. But temazepam is a benzo, and if it was in Kendra's bloodstream, that's the smoking gun. So what's the problem?"

"There is no one in this town taking temazepam, which means Émilie's test is faulty. All prescriptions come through me. No one is permitted to bring their own. Unless your entry searches have become lax . . ."

"They haven't. We've found people bringing in recreational drugs, and they're confiscated." I reach for the table and take my papers. "Hold on. Someone gave me a list of drugs used in sexual assault, from work they'd done down south. It's very thorough."

I hand Lynn's list to my sister.

"Very thorough indeed," she murmurs. "Impressive. And here is temazepam."

"So that tracks."

"Yes, but again, no one here has it." She points to the page. "It's a strong sleep aid, used to treat severe insomnia. We have people on various benzodiazepines, but even if the test incorrectly identified the subtype, no one is taking benzodiazepines in a high enough dose to drug anyone's drink without them detecting the taste."

"So we have no residents with severe insomnia? None of the staff?"

"Even staff are required to register drugs with me, and I have checked my list. We only have one person with severe insomnia, but he is not . . ." She trails off.

I lean forward. "Is he taking something similar?"

"I presume he is taking something for his insomnia, but I play no role in that part of his care. I am not the one who prescribes his medications."

I frown. "Someone else is prescribing . . . ?" The answer hits. There's one other person in this town qualified to write prescriptions. But his only patient right now is Max's older brother, Carson, and Mathias wouldn't be prescribing a strong benzo to a thirteen-year-old boy.

Yet that doesn't mean he couldn't write them for himself and fill them on his trips out of Haven's Rock. And, while they should be registered with April, this is the one person she wouldn't insist do that. No one would insist he do that.

"Mathias," I say.

"Yes but . . ." She clears her throat. "The prescription would not be for him."

I'm about to ask who else Mathias would prescribe for. Then I realize the answer.

"Sebastian."

I need to handle this on my own. That's not me being territorial or obstinate. It's the fact that it involves Mathias.

We have three mental-health professionals on staff. Kendra is a social worker, and Isabel is a psychologist. But we also have a psychiatrist—a medical doctor specializing in mental health. That would be Mathias.

Kendra and Isabel both have other jobs, and so does he. Mathias is our town butcher, and one could argue he's not the sort of person you want having access to large knives, but again, no one refuses Mathias. Dalton grumbles that he's not even sure how Mathias ended up following us to Haven's Rock. Of course he knows the reason—no one dared tell Mathias no.

Okay, if we really didn't want him here, we could have kept him out. But despite Mathias's . . . quirks, he's an excellent butcher. And a decent psychiatrist.

As Dalton and I approach the butcher shop, Storm perks up, looking for Raoul.

"I think he's with Jacob," I say, patting her head. Raoul has proven a fine hunting dog, and there are a very small number of people Mathias allows him to go out with, Jacob being one of them.

Dalton and I find Mathias inside the shop making sausage, which is never an auspicious moment to confront a man rumored to have done terrible things to his victims. Yes, his "victims" were killers, but still . . .

"Casey," he says, and then continues in French, which of course excludes Dalton from the conversation, but that's nothing personal. Mathias likes me because I speak fluent French, and so that is what he uses with me. Otherwise, why talk to me at all?

"You look tired," he says. "You are not resting enough."

I ignore that. "This is a professional courtesy call."

His brows shoot up. "That sounds ominous."

I take a seat on a wooden crate as Dalton stands beside me. "Have you heard what happened to Kendra?"

"Of course. Sebastian told me. Ah. She is in need of my professional services." He lays down his cleaver, and I may exhale a little at that. "I would strongly suggest Isabel is better suited, but I will see Kendra if she prefers. I like her. She brings the best game. Always perfectly shot and field dressed. You could take notes, Casey. You are the worst for birds. Your husband here is adequate, but Kendra is better."

"It's not about therapy. It's about what was used to drug her. Temazepam."

There's only a split-second hesitation before he makes the connection and his lips press together. "*Non.*"

"I take it you're prescribing temazepam for Sebastian's insomnia?"

"Sebastian's psychiatric care is not your—"

"Yes," says a voice from the back room. As Sebastian steps through, I try not to wince. I hadn't thought to make sure he wasn't around. Sebastian's French was decent when he arrived in Rockton, but he quickly realized that if he wanted Mathias's full attention, he needed to be fluent.

"I take temazepam," he says. "Restoril, to be exact. That's what was used to dose Kendra?"

"According to what test?" Mathias says. "And who interpreted the results? To say it is a benzodiazepine is one thing, but to know which one?" He shakes his head. "I am sure that trick works on others, but I know drugs and their tests, Casey."

"Since the person filling our medical supplies owns a drug company, we get only the best—and most cutting-edge. April said temazepam."

"No one's accusing me, Mathias," Sebastian says. "Obviously, if it was temazepam, and I'm the only person taking it, then Casey needs to investigate. I know I didn't drug Kendra, and I trust Casey to verify that." He turns to us. "I'm guessing you'll need to see where I keep the pills?"

"If you can just tell us, we'll conduct the search." I raise a hand to ward off Mathias's protest. "If either of you is there, someone can say you hid the pills to pretend they'd been stolen."

Sebastian nods. "Sure. I can tell you where I keep them. I can also tell you how many there should be. I don't take them often—they're really strong stuff. But I do get severe insomnia, which can mess with my brain and that's never safe with me."

"You do not need to explain," Mathias says. "I prescribed what you needed. The rest is confidential."

Sebastian looks at us. "Ignore him. Anything you need, just ask."

CHAPTER SEVEN

Sebastian and Mathias live in an apartment over the butcher shop. When Sebastian first arrived in Rockton, Mathias had balked at taking any responsibility for the young man. Now, obviously, things have changed.

It's a platonic relationship—both men are straight and Sebastian has a girlfriend who lives back near Rockton. Mathias has taken Sebastian under his wing, as much as he'd hate that description. They get along well while giving each other as much space as they need, which can be "a lot" on both sides.

While Dalton and I conduct our search, both Mathias and Sebastian stand outside the butcher shop. People are bound to notice that, which is what I want. If someone later discovers we searched their quarters, witnesses can confirm that the occupants were outside while it was being done. One issue with such a tiny town is that residents are, unfortunately, quick to decide the police don't know what they're doing . . . if they're even trained police at all.

We find the pills right where Sebastian told us to look—in a small box under his bed. There are other pills there as well, in bottles with only the drug name and directions on the front. I don't look at the others. As Mathias said, that's none of my business.

I took photos of the box while it was under the bed, and I take photos of the contents. Then I lift out the small bottle marked Restoril. While the fact that the bottle is still here—and contains pills—suggests this isn't the drug used on Kendra, I still wear gloves as I work. I take more photos. Then I open it, shake out the capsules, and . . .

I look over at Dalton, patiently waiting. "He said there were sixteen, right?"

Dalton nods. "It was a bottle of twenty, and he's only needed four since he rejoined us last fall." Sebastian had spent the summer with his girlfriend, Felicity.

Sixteen pills. I only count fourteen. That could be a mistake—it's easy enough to forget how many you've taken over five months—but Sebastian said he tracks them. These aren't over-the-counter sleep aids. They're serious stuff.

From what Mathias said, half of one in a drink would be enough to cause what Kendra experienced. So there would be no need to take Sebastian's entire bottle. Two would be plenty . . . and the thief would likely expect they'd never be missed. Like I said, people don't usually keep quite that careful a count of drugs they rarely take. They only notice when they're low, and Sebastian isn't.

I bag the bottle. Then I head downstairs to speak to Sebastian again.

While I believe Sebastian's pills were stolen, I certainly can't declare that as truth without proof. We're back in the town hall, where I have my feet up, Storm by the fire, and Dalton at the desk doing paperwork. Sebastian sits across from me.

Mathias wanted to come, of course, but Sebastian shut him down, telling Mathias that he could handle this, and having his shrink present looks as if Mathias thinks his services will be needed. Looks as if Mathias thinks Sebastian might have done this and will require a psychiatric defense. That backed Mathias off fast, though not without grumbling.

As we settle in, I say, "I'm going to need a complete list of your whereabouts last night, from nine in the evening until you saw Kendra being attacked."

"I was making fishing lures most of the evening. For Felicity and her settlement." He shrugs. "They like my lures, and it's an easy way to score points." He pauses. "With her settlement, not with Felicity." Another pause, head tilted. "It doesn't hurt with Felicity either. I'm still a half-assed hunter, and I'm not much better at trapping and fishing, but I'm good at making lures and traps, so that keeps them from deciding I'm completely useless."

I don't point out that Felicity's settlement thinks he's far from useless. He's young and strong, but mostly his appeal comes from his genetic material. A healthy young man who isn't in any way related to anyone in their settlement. There is the sociopathy, of course, but that's not considered hereditary.

Felicity's grandfather—Edwin—would be thrilled with Sebastian even if he couldn't hit a moose from two feet away. Sadly for Edwin, Felicity is in no hurry to get on with marriage and babies. She's poised to take over leadership of the settlement, and that's all she cares about. Well, no, she cares about Sebastian . . . as a romantic partner, not as a baby daddy.

Sebastian continues, "I can show you the lures, but that won't prove when I made them. I was alone in the apartment—Mathias was off doing Mathias things. The shutters were closed, by regulation, so I can't even hope someone saw a light on. Which also wouldn't really prove I was there." He glances at me. "None of this is helpful, I know."

"When did you take Raoul out?"

"Ah, right. This might be more useful. Mathias came home before I left, and we talked for a few minutes. That was just after eleven. Then he went to bed at eleven thirty, and I took Raoul for his bedtime walk. That's my usual routine. At that hour, the town's quiet. Everyone's in bed or at the Roc until last call. We took the perimeter trail. Again, that's our usual. I was heading back to our place when I heard Kendra call out."

"Did anyone see you?"

He considers. "I passed Grant. Well, actually, I avoided Grant. Not Raoul's favorite person."

There'd been an incident earlier this month, where Raoul had growled and lunged at Grant. It'd been a warning feint when Grant came near the butcher shop. Understandable from Raoul's point of view, because Grant's last visit had involved an altercation with Sebastian.

Mathias is responsible for the meat, but Grant decided he'd rather complain about the nice young man instead—by shouting and getting in Sebastian's space. Raoul had taken exception to it and apparently decided Grant had lost his butcher-visit privileges. That would be fine . . . if that weren't the only place to get meat.

After the lunge feint, Sebastian had asked Grant to help him with a bit of training, to teach Raoul that the dog can't decide who does and doesn't enter the butcher shop. Instead, Grant went off on a rant about the dangers of having a half wolf in town with children. Never mind that Raoul adores the kids. Clearly we had to get rid of the dangerous canine.

The upshot was that we refused, and now Lynn picks up

the couple's meat orders, and Sebastian understandably avoids Grant while walking Raoul.

Understandable . . . but a problem when Grant would have provided a partial alibi.

"I can't prove it wasn't me," Sebastian says finally. "But I'll give you whatever you need to help with that. Ignore Mathias's growling. I will fully cooperate."

"I know. Just like you know I need to consider you as a suspect for the dosing part." I make notes. Then I say, "If you didn't do it, then someone stole those two pills. You last took one on February twelfth, right?"

"On the eleventh and again on the twelfth."

"And when did you last touch that box?"

"This morning. It has my regular prescriptions in it. I take it out daily. I don't remember ever thinking it wasn't exactly where I put it, but honestly? I just pull it out and shove it back under. Half the time, I'm still in bed. I don't have a nightstand yet—I'm on the list for having one built—so my med box goes under the bed."

He shrugs. "Not the most secure place for pills, but I never really thought of that. Usually, living with Mathias is security enough. Then there's Raoul, obviously."

Storm might be nearly twice Raoul's size, but the Australian-shepherd-and-wolf blend makes Raoul a better guard dog. He's very protective of his home and his people, as the incident with Grant proved.

"No one is going into your place while Raoul's there," I say. "Even if he was down in the shop, he'd hear someone break in upstairs."

"And everyone would hear *him*."

"When's the last time someone took him hunting?"

Sebastian shrugs. "Before today? It's been a few weeks.

Sometimes he's with the boys, but Mathias and I would both need to be away for anyone to break in. Even going upstairs while we're in the shop would be risky."

I tap my pen on the pad. "Let's say you got back from a walk and someone had been in the apartment. Would Raoul alert you?"

Sebastian thinks about it. "I don't think so. Remember how territorial he was as a pup?"

I smile. "He decided only the people he liked were allowed into the butcher shop, which made a very small list. Your dog is much pickier than mine."

"He is. But we worked on that through training. He defends people, not turf. When we had the incident with Grant, that's because I was in the shop. It wasn't that Raoul didn't want Grant going in—it was that he didn't want him near me. If someone broke in while Raoul was alone in the apartment, he'd go after them. But I don't think he'd react much if he came home to discover someone else had been there."

Sebastian goes quiet, still considering. "We've definitely had people in while we're gone, especially with the final construction touches. Raoul has never seemed bothered by it. Of course, I *could* be saying that to support the theft theory. I'd need to explain why Raoul wouldn't have reacted if we had a break-in."

I shake my head. "I appreciate your honesty, Seb, but you really don't need to play prosecution against yourself."

He only smiles. "Covering all the bases. Also, because I know you'll ask, we don't use any other security measures. Like most people here, we don't lock our door when we're out. Nothing for anyone to steal."

"Except very strong prescription drugs."

He makes a face. "Yeah. I never thought of that. We should start locking it."

"On that note, in order for someone to steal that particular drug, one that's used in sexual assaults, they need to know you had it. Even April didn't."

He leans back. "You're right. The only people who know are me and Mathias."

"You're taking them for insomnia."

"Yeah. It's a . . ." He makes a vague gesture. "A holdover from when I was incarcerated. I had problems with other inmates. I got into the habit of napping rather than sleeping. I'm mostly back on track, but I go through spells."

"It's not an uncommon problem up here," I say. "The summer's worse, when the endless sun doesn't help anyone sleep, but winter can be bad, too."

"Twenty hours of darkness also screws with sleep schedules," he says.

"It does. Which leads to my question . . . Have you discussed your sleep problems with others? In casual conversation?"

"You mean someone says they're having trouble sleeping, and I say I do, too? Sure. That's one way of showing empathy. A cornerstone of my therapy. Learn to show it and eventually it becomes second nature. Whether that's actual empathy or just faking it, I don't know, but it does help me connect with people."

He pulls one stockinged foot under him. "The trick is to find the right balance. If someone says they're having trouble sleeping, and I say I suffer from severe insomnia, that's not empathy. It's one-upmanship. If someone says they're having serious insomnia, and I say I understand because I sometimes have trouble sleeping, that's downplaying their experience." He gives a wry smile. "I know all the tricks. Which means, in most cases, it's just residents saying they have trouble sleeping, and I just say I do too, and we exchange tips."

"Would you ever have mentioned the Restoril?"

He shakes his head. "If they were suffering from real insomnia, I'd say to speak to April, and I'd never mention Restoril. It's like someone saying they have a headache and I suggest morphine. It's way more than they need."

He pulls up his other foot, cross-legged now. "I can guarantee I've never mentioned Restoril specifically. But in a conversation about sleep problems, could I have admitted I take something? Yes."

"If you can think of anyone you mentioned sleep issues to—at all—that's really what I need."

"The only thing that comes to mind is a conversation over dinner, maybe a few weeks ago. It was a full table in the restaurant, a six-seater, and we got talking about how it's nice that the days are getting longer. Someone . . . Oh, wait. It was actually Kendra. She said she sleeps better during the longer days, because she can close the shutters at night and open them in the morning, simulating a regular sundown and sunup. We all got to talking about sleep strategies. A few people said they need a little chemical help now and then. I probably said I do too, and there was some comparing of sleep aids, but I pretended I don't know what I'm taking."

"So Kendra was there, and . . ."

"It was all staff. Kendra. Me. Gunnar. Brian and Devon. Maybe Yolanda? If not Yolanda, then Kenny, but he usually eats with April, so I think it was Yolanda."

"Anyone sitting nearby?"

"Close enough to overhear us? I didn't pay any . . . No. We were talking about the longer days because it was a late dinner and it was still light outside. There'd been a staff meeting, and Phil asked the restaurant to stay open. You and Eric and the others ate at your place. At the restaurant it was just us. Even the servers were gone."

"And that's the only time you mentioned taking something to help you sleep."

"As far as I know."

Time for our walk. Or, in my case, drag. The most annoying part of that is that if I weren't only in the sled because I'm pregnant, I'd have enjoyed it, relaxing and indulging in the ridiculousness of it. In other words, I'm just being cranky.

I'm riding in an adult version of a toddler sled, with a curved back for me to rest against. The interior is piled high with furs, and Storm is moving briskly, having recovered from her temporary exhaustion. Pulling me—even with my added weight—is easy on a trail that's practically an ice-sled run, the well-trodden snow having partly melted and refrozen.

Dalton and I are quiet as we leave town. We plan to discuss the case, which means we need to be out of earshot. I hunker down into the furs and lean back to gaze up at the endless canopy of evergreens with a gray sky above.

Kenny and Dalton might have designed this sled for me, but it will be perfect in the years to come. It'll let us take our child out on long winter walks, with Storm having no difficulty pulling the lighter weight. My mind shifts to next year, when I'll be in this sled again, holding a bundled baby.

Will our child be content to relax against me and take in the nature around them? Or will they be squirming to get out and crawl through the snow?

With Dalton and me as parents, the answer is probably that it'll depend on their mood. We can both be still, lost in our thoughts and in the world. And we can both be restless, wanting to get out and interact with that world.

I struggle to indulge in dreams like this, especially after two miscarriage scares. Dalton and I have pored over the books, and we've tracked exactly how far along our baby would be if they were born this week, next week, two weeks from now. We're so damned close now that I want to relax. In mere days, the baby wouldn't even be considered premature.

But that presumes the baby has developed properly, and I worry that I haven't gained enough weight for that. It also presumes a normal delivery, and that's never a guarantee, especially if they come early.

Deep breaths. I'm going to let myself dream of next winter, when I'll have a baby on my lap and it'll be Dalton pulling the sled, whipping us along with Storm bringing up the rear—

Dalton grabs the ropes, tugging Storm to a halt. We go still and listen. A sound comes. One that sounds remarkably like our sled, whooshing along the icy snow.

"Jacob!" Dalton calls.

"Here!"

Dalton relaxes and gives Storm the signal that she can take a break. In a few minutes Raoul appears, pulling a flatter version of our sled, with the morning's hunting catch under a secured tarp.

Bringing up the rear is a man with long light brown hair, a thick beard, and steel-gray eyes. Two years younger than Dalton, Jacob is, as everyone jokes, "the nice brother." He has his shadows—trauma from life after their parents died, before he reunited with Dalton—but in Jacob, it mostly manifests as shyness and a preference for forest life. Both his personality and his past make him a perfect match for Nicole.

"Good hunting?" Dalton asks as he peeks under the tarp.

"Nothing big. Mostly just cleaning up the snares. Hare, grouse, ptarmigan. Oh, and an ermine that was sniffing around the snares. It'll make a good baby blanket."

"Nice," Dalton says. "Can we grab one of those grouses, too? Before Mathias gets hold of it?"

"I'll drop it at your place." Jacob glances up and over his shoulder. "I don't know how far you guys plan to go, but I'd suggest sticking to the path around town."

Dalton's answer is a grunt that his brother knows is a request for more information. Jacob waves at the sky, as if this is information enough.

Dalton peers up.

"Snow's coming," Jacob says when Dalton doesn't respond.

Dalton shrugs. "Eventually. It's too early for a thaw, and yeah, the temperature has dropped, but the wind's still blowing from the south."

"I don't like the look of that sky."

"It's been overcast all day."

Jacob lifts both gloved hands. "Not arguing. I'm just saying that if you don't need to go farther, maybe stick close to town. I was over by the mountain and decided to head back early. I didn't like the air there. Felt like a storm."

"We will take that under advisement," Dalton says.

I quickly add, "We're not going far. We just have business to discuss, and we can't do it on the town loop." I pull the sat phone from under the furs. "We have this, too."

"But we won't go far enough to need it," Dalton says. "Give us an hour, and we'll be back." He looks down at the two dogs, snuggled together as they rest on the path. "The real problem is separating these two and deciding who's making way for whom on this path."

CHAPTER EIGHT

I don't ask whether Dalton thinks a storm's brewing. Yes, his brother can be overly cautious—living most of his time in the wild means he's more concerned about storms than Dalton, who's accustomed to a solidly built town full of resources. But if Dalton thought there was a chance of trouble, he'd get us back home. Asking might make him second-guess and cut our walk short.

"Regarding Sebastian," he says, a few minutes after we part ways from Jacob. "Since the drug used was one he takes, and there are capsules missing, logically, it came from his stash. Either he did it or someone stole them. Those are the only options."

"They are," I say.

As the path narrows, Dalton falls back behind the sled. "I'd like to jump on theft as the answer, but that's complicated."

"Because it requires someone knowing Sebastian has the pills, and it seems the only people he told are staff members. Of course, while I'd love to say none of them could have done it, we know that's not true."

In Rockton, we had several cases where the culprit turned out to be a trusted staff member, even a good friend.

"Could be that someone from the dinner party told someone else," Dalton says. "Casual conversation. Talking about sleep aids. Names come up, including Sebastian's."

"True," I say. "It's still a leap from Sebastian mentioning he takes 'something' to Kendra's attacker realizing he's taking seriously strong medication. If the person only wanted sleep meds, others at the table said they also have some. I'll need a list of who said that, but I can't see anyone deciding, from that list, that the person whose place they want to break into is Mathias."

I adjust a fur that's slid down behind me. "Unless Sebastian was the *only* name mentioned in a secondhand conversation."

"Could be. I can't see someone listing off everyone who's taking meds so they could just give one example, and it's him. But yeah, the theft answer isn't an easy one."

"Which leaves Sebastian as a suspect."

We continue on in silence until Dalton says, "You want me to play devil's advocate on that?"

I smile over my shoulder at him. "Please."

"Okay." He rubs his hands together, gloves swishing. "I am now an advocate for the devil, arguing why the nice young man who rescued Kendra could actually have been her attacker."

"Because that nice young man is also a sociopath who murdered his parents?"

Dalton moves up beside me. "Strange how that should be the obvious answer, and yet it isn't. You ever get the feeling we have some skewed ideas of what constitutes 'nice people'?"

"I killed a guy and got away with it. I don't think I'm the audience for that question."

"But that only means you're very unlikely to do it again," Dalton says. "You slipped up and spent half your life drowning in guilt. In Sebastian's case, he knew what he was doing. But he didn't get away with it either."

"He didn't try, from what I understand."

Dalton sighs. "We got the strangest people in Rockton, didn't we?"

"Yep, and then we hired them all on as staff for our non-evil new town. But yes, Sebastian didn't try to get away with killing his parents. He knew the price. He decided it was worth the risk. Same principle here. If he attacked Kendra and got caught, he'd be sent south, which he really doesn't want. He could take off back to Felicity and the First Settlement, but if we told her what he did, she'd kick his ass out." I readjust the furs on my legs. "Which is talking about why I think he couldn't do it, and I want ways he could have."

"That's my job, advocating for the dark side. Okay, possibility one. Sebastian attacked Kendra and then, with her confusion, made it seem as if he was rescuing her."

I shake my head. "She spotted him *while* she was being dragged. There's no confusion about that."

"Yeah, also, why drug her and then rescue her? I can see some twisted fuck doing that for hero points. I can even see Sebastian manipulating a situation to get something out of it."

"Sociopathy 101."

"But what would he want from Kendra? Nothing I can see. Maybe something from the town? Again, not that I can see."

"Sebastian doesn't want anything except to stay for as long as he chooses, and he's in no danger of being kicked out. So there is no plausible chance that he was both attacker and rescuer."

"Possibility two. He was the one who drugged Kendra, and that's why he was outside. He was waiting for her to come out."

"And someone else took advantage?"

Dalton throws up his hands. "Maybe? I'm playing advocate without a law degree here. Cut me some slack, Butler."

"He was outside walking Raoul. Kendra saw the dog, so that part is confirmed."

"Raoul could have been the excuse, in case Sebastian was caught."

"No one saw Sebastian in the bar that night." I pull more furs over my legs. "Overall, while 'drugged her and someone else claimed his prey' is a possibility, it's very remote because, again, we can't see a motive. So let's set it aside. The related theory would be that Sebastian was working with her attacker. He supplies the drugs. The other person doses Kendra. They're both hanging around to grab her. His partner gets to her first. But Kendra sees Sebastian, so he has to play rescuer."

"Could work," Dalton muses. "Even better if his partner doses Kendra, and when Sebastian sees who the prey is, he changes his mind. He likes Kendra. As a person, that is. The problem still goes back to the first issue, though. What would be his motive and could we imagine him doing this?"

I shake my head. "I really can't. I hate saying that about anyone. I've been wrong before."

"We both have. But if we combine not being able to imagine it with the complication of him being the one who rescued her?"

"The chances it's him seem next to nil. So we presume the attacker found out about the temazepam and stole it. That's easily done while the apartment is empty, and the pill box wasn't exactly well hidden. We . . ."

I trail off as I see I've lost my husband's attention. He's turning slowly, gaze up.

"Eric?"

"Fuck."

I notice it then. I've been fussing with my furs without realizing why—because the temperature has plummeted. My cheeks are cold, and I have every fur wrapped around me. I follow Dalton's gaze to the nearby mountain. The top is gone, lost in dark clouds.

I echo Dalton's curse. This is one thing about living near mountains. The weather can seem fine, and then it's as if the storm peeks out from behind it. The wind has also shifted to the northwest, blasting cold through the thick forest.

"We okay?" I ask, trying to sound calm while being very aware that I'm stuck in a sled pulled by a dog.

"Yeah, we're fine," he says. "But it's time to get back. Come on, pup. No rest break today. I'll help with the pulling."

We beat the storm to Haven's Rock. Dalton doesn't exactly run, but he does move faster. While the danger of being caught out is minimal, he doesn't want anyone—mostly himself—thinking he'd taken a risk with his heavily pregnant wife. It's a reminder to me that I'm not the only one living under the looming shadow of future guilt. There's a rock precariously poised above us both—the chance that something will go wrong and we'll blame ourselves.

By the time we reach Haven's Rock, snow is falling. It's light, but carried on a sharp wind that warns of worse to come. Once we see our chalet, Dalton picks up the pace even more, leaning into the rope and pulling hard enough that I need to hang on tight.

When he opens the front door, it whips out of his hand, and he curses. I turn around to squint into the woods. It's dark enough that I need to check my watch. Four fifteen. Yes, in midwinter, this would be dusk, but in late March, we should have another few hours of sun.

"Coming in fast," I say, and I need to raise my voice over the howl of wind.

Dalton only grunts and waves me inside. The fire is out—we don't waste wood when we're not home. I shuck my outerwear and head for the fireplace as Dalton slams the door behind me. Then he bangs on it, and I head back to help secure the heavy latches that will keep it snugly shut against the wind.

By the time the fire is roaring, that's the only light in the house. Dalton has closed and latched all the shutters. I turn on the living-room light. In Rockton, we used a combination of battery lanterns, oil, and candles. While we have oil and candles here, innovations have made higher tech more energy efficient. We have solar panels on the house—ones that won't reflect and alert passing planes. That means electricity. We don't always use it, but being able to flip a switch and get light feels like a minor miracle. It's a reminder of just how outdated Rockton had become. Solar could have worked. So could tech like tablets and cameras. But that cost money, and there were investors to feed.

Haven's Rock is what Rockton should have been all along. The philanthropic project of a billionaire who doesn't give a damn about the tax-deductible status of her donation. Haven's Rock helps Émilie give back, and we accept that. We also accept a modest salary because, when Rockton shut down, people who'd devoted years of their lives to it realized they were being thrown into the world with the equivalent of pocket change.

Having all expenses covered means we don't need much income, but it's important to know that if this town fails, our staff will be in a financial position to reestablish in the real world.

I don't really have that concern. I came to Rockton with a

sizable inheritance, and while April and I contributed to re-
building, we have plenty left.

The main advantage to a lack of greedy investors is state-of-
the-art construction. Our fireplace will heat our whole chalet through a snowstorm. The solar battery will give us light
even on days with limited sunshine. And our very solidly built
house will withstand Nature's beating. While I putter about,
Dalton heads off to literally batten down the town's hatches
with others.

I can only faintly hear the wind outside, and with the windows shuttered, it's easy to forget what's happening there. I'm
reminded when Dalton bangs on the front door and shouts for
me to unlatch it and stand back.

I do, and when the door flies open, a bucketful of snow
rushes with it. I peer out into what looks like a night scene, the
sky dark, snow blasting in on a wailing wind.

Dalton has to lean on the door to keep it shut as I latch it.
When we're done, he exhales and leans against it.

"Hot chocolate?" I say.

"Please."

He shakes off the snow, making me yelp as it hits my bare
feet.

"Toasty in here," he says.

"You complaining?"

"Nope."

He heads for the kitchen, but I shoo him into the living
room. I've been off my feet for hours. I can handle making him
a hot drink.

We sit and drink our cocoa and listen to the whine of the
wind.

"Sounds like a bad one," I say.

"Worse than I expected. Definitely a blizzard."

"Everything okay in town?"

"Yeah. I just don't like . . ." He shakes his head. "Shitty timing."

It takes a moment to realize what he means. Shitty timing because it means we'll be grounded for a few days. While flying south is never as easy as calling an ambulance, it's nice to know we have that option. We don't right now.

I get off my recliner and snuggle down beside him on the sofa. "I feel fine."

"Good."

I reach and take his chin to turn his face toward me. "Really. I feel fine. My biggest worry is how the storm's going to delay my investigation."

"At least we don't have to worry about anyone else getting dosed at the Roc," he says. "Storm like this means it'll be closed for a day or two."

"Which might not be such a bad thing." I lean in to kiss him. "Let's take advantage of the fact no one can come banging on our door tonight."

He arches one brow.

I laugh. "Yes to that, later, but for now, let's stick to the time-honored storm tradition of eating junk food for dinner and playing board games."

"Sounds like a plan."

When I wake with cramps, I grumble at myself loud enough for Storm to lift her head from the floor and whine. I'm still downstairs, having fallen asleep in my rocker recliner.

I stretch my legs and tell myself I hallucinated the cramping. There's no way I can actually be feeling contractions. It's hypochondria. Realize I'm trapped in Haven's Rock, and I start thinking I'm going into labor. The last two times I had a scare, there'd been plenty of warning signs, and I really had felt fine earlier. No aching in my abdomen. No weird sensation that something just wasn't right. Definitely no cramping.

I'm fine.

Of course, as soon as I think that, my thoughts swing to *Is the baby fine?*

When's the last time I felt movement? The last kick or punch or—?

The baby shifts, and I swear there's a grumble in that shift.

I'm trying to sleep, Mom. Can you stop worrying? You're keeping me up.

I smile and lay my hand on my stomach. "Sorry, Quinn."

I sometimes test the names for size, seeing how they feel, even if I have a sense we'll need to see our baby before picking.

"Riley?" I try.

My stomach moves as they shift again.

"Is that a yes to Riley?" I say. "Or another 'let me sleep, damn it'?"

A bump appears in a kick, only to vanish again.

"Sorry," I say. "Go back to sleep . . . Avery." I purse my lips. "I kind of like that one."

"Sure," mumbles a voice beside me. "Avery works. Sleep works, too."

I reach over and pat Dalton's head. He's on the sofa, stretched out with his head next to my recliner.

"Sorry," I say. "To both of you. Sleep it is. I'll see you—"

A cramp hits, strong enough for me to catch my breath.

"Casey?" Dalton twists to look at me.

"Seems I have a case of indigestion or paranoia," I say. "Probably both, between the storm and our very unhealthy dinner.

My stomach's a bit off. That's what woke me up. It's fine." I rub my stomach. "Sorry about the two cups of hot chocolate, kid."

Dalton still sits up and flips on the side table lantern. "What does it feel like?"

I want to lie to reassure him, but I won't do that. "Cramps. But they could be stomach ones. It's hard to tell. Stomach, uterus . . ."

He peers at me.

"*Honestly,*" I say. "I can't tell, and I really was fine all of yesterday. Whatever this is, they're not coming close enough together to be contractions."

"Uh, don't contractions start farther apart and get closer?"

Another hits, and I try not to make a face, but they're strong enough that I can't help it. Dalton scrambles up, and in a blink, he's hovering over me.

"I really think it might just be my stomach," I say. "I can't remember my last bowel movement. I bet that's it. Can I get some help up the stairs?"

Dalton crosses his arms. "I'd rather not add to the tally of babies who've been born in toilets because Mom thought she had to poop."

"But the fact that it happens proves I'm right that it's hard to tell the difference between stomach cramps and contractions. I—"

Another one hits. This one lasts long enough that I have to grit my teeth through it.

"Those seem a little too regular to be digestive cramps, Butler," Dalton says when it passes.

"Fuck."

Dalton laughs under his breath. "Well, at least we're both remaining calm about this. Despite the fact there is a raging storm outside. I just hope we're not in shock and are going to freak out in five minutes."

"You're in shock. I'm in denial. Whole different land." I put both hands on the seat and push myself to standing. "Damn it. I don't know what this is. I really might just need to use the—"

Another one hits, hard enough to almost double me over.

Dalton catches me. "I think the shock is fading, Butler. Panic imminent."

"They could be Braxton-Hicks contractions."

"Which you have had, and we know all the signs of, including that they don't come closer than five minutes apart."

The fact that I forgot that shows I'm *deep* in that land of denial.

"Tell me I can at least call your sister," he says.

I nod. "This is one case where she won't give me shit for waking her up."

Dalton goes for the sat phone on the mantel as I stretch. I'm really not panicking, which is good. Yes, there's a storm, but even if this is labor, it feels normal. No sudden stabs of pain. Just those strong cramps a few minutes apart.

If Quinn/Riley/Avery is coming early, it'll be okay. They'll be far enough along. We're prepared. Everything is fine.

I keep repeating that mantra until Dalton curses. Then my whole body convulses, proving I'm not as calm as I'm pretending.

"Phone won't connect," he says. "Damn storm. Are you okay if I run over— No, April has everything there. I should take you— Snowstorm. *Fuck.*"

He lifts his hands to run through his hair. I catch his arms and pull them down.

"I'm fine, Eric. Even if this is true labor, I really do feel fine. Yes, April has everything she needs there, so that's where we should go. It's five hundred feet."

"In a snowstorm."

I tilt my head to listen. "The storm actually seems to have died down."

His lips tighten, as if I'm being difficult, but he doesn't argue. It really has gone quiet.

"Get dressed and go out," I say. "If it's bad, we'll rethink this. Otherwise, the sled is right there."

I catch his hands again and squeeze.

"I feel fine. If this is it . . ." I look up at him. "We'll be okay. Nothing is wrong. Just a potential early arrival. Okay?"

He nods, and I nudge him toward the front to get on his outerwear.

CHAPTER NINE

The blizzard has not abated completely. It's just no longer gale-force winds and whiteout conditions. We got a dumping—at least a foot. Snow still whips around on a bitter wind, but we can see where we're going, and we're fine.

We're fine.

That's what I keep telling myself the whole way there, with Dalton running while Storm lopes beside the sled, glancing over as if picking up on the vibes I'm giving, the ones that say I'm *not* fine.

Dalton swings around to the back of the clinic. The building shelters us from the storm, and I wobble up as he bangs on the door. Then he sees me and lunges to help. I let him, and we move carefully onto the snow-slick deck.

The back door is unlocked. I'm never sure how I feel about that for my sister's sake, but I'm grateful for it now. Dalton bustles me in and then raps hard on the door up to my sister's apartment. That one is locked, though he has the key and if April has her earplugs in as usual, he'll need it.

Dalton helps me into the exam room first.

"Go get April," I say as I unzip my parka.

When he hesitates, I add, "Please," and that gets him moving. April must have heard the noise downstairs, because I'm still in the midst of sitting to kick off my boots when she appears with Dalton.

"On the table," she says. "Eric?"

Dalton boosts me up even as I protest that I haven't removed my boots. Once I'm on the exam table, he does that and April moves in to lift my voluminous nightshirt.

"Can I explain what I'm actually feeling first?" I say.

"Contractions." She presses cold hands to my abdomen, and I jump and swear.

"Stay still, Casey," she says.

I glare. "Your hands are like ice. I'm not screaming in pain, April. Can we slow down? Please." I pull my nightshirt over my stomach and shift backward onto the table.

"I seem to be having contractions," I say. "I've had no other symptoms. I feel them here." I point. "They're a few minutes apart, and they're lasting maybe thirty seconds."

"Eric?" April glances over her shoulder. "There's a timer in the drawer. Would you get that out please?"

He's still doing that when the next contraction hits.

"Hit start," I grunt, wincing.

"There are two timers on that," April says. "Use both. One for the length, and one for the interval."

He does, and I grit my teeth as I wait it out. Once it passes, I let April help me remove my sweatpants. Then I lie back on the exam table while April checks for dilation. I try to be patient, but when another contraction comes, I can't wait.

"April?" I say, panting. "Anything happening down there?"

It takes her a moment to say, "No."

I lift my head. "Nothing?"

"I don't see any signs of dilation."

"So it's a false alarm?"

"I don't know."

She moves her hands to my belly and begins to feel around. I study her face, but it's Dalton who speaks first.

"April?" he says. "What's wrong?"

"I am not an obstetrician," she snaps. "That's what's wrong. I—" She takes a deep breath, air sucking between her teeth. "That was uncalled for."

"It's fine," I say. "I know you're not an expert, but we can both see you're concerned."

"She's in breech," April says.

Any other time, I'd give her shit for gendering the baby. With Dalton, it's him teasing that he's sure we're having a girl. With April, it's that she balks at the nongendered pronoun. Now, though, I let it pass, far more intent on what she just said.

I swallow. "So the baby is feet-first?"

"Buttocks," she says.

"Bum first?" I say, and I can't help sputtering a small laugh.

April gives me a sharp look. "Yes, and that would be far more amusing if it didn't pose a problem that I am not sure I can solve."

Dalton cuts in, "But if Casey isn't dilating, that's okay, right? The problem would be if the baby was coming fast and in the wrong position. This gives you time to move her or prepare for a C-section."

"I'm not dilating at all?" I say.

My sister snaps, "Do you *want* to be, all things considered?"

"April . . ." Dalton says.

April mutters something and stalks off to yank a book from the shelf. Dalton moves up beside me as I lower my hands to my abdomen. The baby shifts, and I can feel the head up high. Another shift, and Dalton rubs my belly, as if to soothe the baby.

"How long has it been?" I say.

"Hmm?" He follows my gaze to the timer. "Shit. Right." He frowns as he picks it up. "Seven minutes." He looks at me. "Nothing since the last one?"

I prop onto my elbows. "Nothing."

April comes over and checks again for dilation. I rest back on the table, holding Dalton's hand. Minutes tick past. No dilation and no more contractions.

"False alarm?" Dalton says.

"False labor," I say.

"No," April says. "Prodromal labor. Which your obstetrician warned us to watch for."

I wince. "Right."

During my last scare, Dr. Kapoor had considered it might have been prodromal labor, but the symptoms had resembled a possible miscarriage, which is what put us all on high alert.

I continue, "Prodromal labor can be caused by abnormalities with the pelvis or uterus, which I might have."

April brought over the book. "It can also be caused by the baby being in breech. Your body may be attempting to reposition her, in preparation for labor."

"Does it mean we're getting close?" Dalton leans over the book.

"Not necessarily," I say. "But it does mean we should contact Dr. Kapoor as soon as we can."

It's good that I'm not in actual labor, given that the baby is in breech and we're in the middle of a snowstorm. However, I'd feel a lot better about that if not for the "baby in breech and also snowstorm" part. It's a reminder of just how many things can go wrong and just how isolated we are here.

And I'm bringing a baby into this life?

I shove away the thought. It's my parents' voices, telling me I'm being careless, selfish. People have children in far more remote situations all the time. The Yukon itself is dotted with dozens of tiny settlements, many without the resources we have. Dalton and Jacob were born and raised in the wilderness here—with a multiday walk to the nearest source of medical attention—and no one would ever accuse their parents of being uncaring.

We bring Storm over but stay at the clinic—none of us are getting any sleep while waiting to make that call. When morning comes, the first time we try, the satellite phone doesn't connect. A half hour later, it does, and we reach Dr. Kapoor before she heads off to work.

"Dr. Butler's assessment is correct," she says as we gather around the phone. "It sounds like prodromal labor, which is not a concern in itself."

"But the baby being in breech is," I say.

"I can provide suggestions for how to facilitate a shift in position. The prodromal labor suggests your body is already working on rectifying that, and in the worst case, we'd be looking at a Cesarean section. Dr. Butler is, I understand, an accomplished surgeon."

"She is," I say before my sister can point out, again, that she's not an obstetrician.

"All this is to say that if things go wrong, you should be fine," Dr. Kapoor says. "However . . ." Her exhale sounds against the phone. "There are too many factors making me uneasy, Casey. I would like you to finish your pregnancy in Whitehorse. I understand you have a personal small aircraft, which alleviates the issues of late-pregnancy travel. Once you are in Whitehorse, you'll be close to a hospital, with everything you might need. I've also been cleared to fly there myself, by private jet."

By "cleared" she means that Émilie has assured her any cost will be covered.

Dr. Kapoor continues, "That means I would be there in a few hours to assist, although I have contacts at the Whitehorse hospital and know you'd be in good hands."

When we're quiet, she says, "I understand this isn't what you want, but we really have reached the stage where it is the best option."

"The safest option," Dalton says.

"Yes."

"And we'd agree," I say. "The reason I'm hesitating is that we just got hit by a blizzard. We can't fly out today."

I look at Dalton, who hesitates, but then reluctantly agrees. He might want to get me south, but he's already assessed the conditions.

"Tomorrow then?" she says. Before we can answer, she says, "It isn't an urgent situation. Tomorrow or the next day would be fine. I'll tell you what to watch for, and we can monitor it until you're able to leave."

We are not going to panic.

The baby is fine, active and moving about. I'm in my thirty-seventh week of pregnancy. All my vital signs are good.

I've made it further than I dared hope, and we are in a holding pattern that means, for now, everything is fine. The contractions have stopped. If they resume without dilation, it just means my body is attempting to get the baby ready for birth.

I am in Haven's Rock, and I am safe. April can deliver a baby, either naturally or by C-section. She's prepared. I'm prepared. Dalton's prepared. Anders—who has medical training—is prepared to assist. Even Mathias would bring his training to the table if needed.

I tell myself that I'm lucky. Every possible resource is at my disposal here, and I'm not in labor. I have time to get to Whitehorse if that's what my doctor wants, and even that is only a precaution.

Yet I can't help but feel trapped by this storm. We leave the clinic to head home, and we're both staring into the sky, assessing.

The morning is quiet enough to hear people moving inside buildings, and the layer of snow only adds to the muffled hush. It's beautiful, too, every surface draped in pristine white.

But that sky. That damn sky.

"The storm isn't over, is it?" I say.

Dalton hesitates, and I know he wants to say it is, but after a moment, he shakes his head. It's unnaturally quiet with the wind gone, but the clouds overhead aren't just gray—they're practically black. We're enjoying a brief respite, enough to catch our breath—and make that phone call. But that's it. More is coming.

"We need to pull out the two-way radios," I say as we walk. During a storm, as long as we're in town, we'll get more reliable reception on those than a sat phone.

"I'd like to have one at our place tonight, and one with April, in case of an emergency. Then I'd like to leave first thing in the morning."

"Agreed," I say, and I don't miss his exhale of relief.

I slide my gloved hand into his. "I'm not going to argue, Eric. Part of me freaks out a little at the thought of being in the air, away from April, but it's only a couple of hours. Then I'll be in the city. We'll ask Émilie to find us a place to rent. I know that's not easy in Whitehorse but . . ."

"Easier in winter than summer," he says. "And easier if you're willing to pay a premium."

I nod. "In the meantime, we'll keep that two-way radio close, just to be sure I don't suddenly go into full-on labor in the middle of a whiteout. We—"

A figure appears, running toward us, and we both tense, clasped hands tightening. A gloved hand knocks back the parka hood. It's Gunnar.

"Trouble at the kitchen," he says. "Someone left the chimney open."

"Fuck," Dalton says.

"Yeah, it's a mess, and people are looking for their breakfast."

Dalton glances at me.

"Doesn't need our personal touch," I murmur.

Dalton nods and turns to Gunnar. "Grab a few people for cleanup. Get Kenny in to see if any repairs are needed. Maybe grab Marlon too."

"He's already there helping deal with the grumbling."

"Excellent," I say. "We'll swing by Brian and Devon's place and see if we can get the café open early."

Once Gunnar's gone, Dalton turns to me. "You can go on home if you want."

I shake my head. "Their place is on the way. We'll stop by and then go home, get a bit of rest. If snow in the kitchen is the biggest emergency we have, we'll count ourselves lucky."

We don't end up going home. There are other minor emergencies to be handled. I do, however, agree to let Dalton and Anders oversee those while I rest in the town hall. Being there also means I can feel moderately useful—any problems can be reported to me, and I'll assign duties as needed. Nicole is out with the boys, walking Raoul, so they take Storm. We're not going to be in any shape for long dog walks today.

I'm in the town hall, with my feet up, when Yolanda stops by. She walks in, shakes off the snow, and drops onto the chair across from me.

"How are things going out there?" I ask.

"Too many cooks, too little broth," she says. "It's nice that everyone wants to help, but the damage is minimal. I decided to come keep you company."

"Keep me company? Or keep yourself from telling people to go the fuck home and stop getting in the way?"

"Will may have suggested you could use some companionship."

I laugh under my breath. "Don't worry. Eric is more than capable of delivering the 'go the fuck home' message on his own." I shake out one foot that's falling asleep. "I know we can't focus on Kendra's attack right now, but did you get anything interesting yesterday? I never had time to check in."

"If I did get anything, I'd have told you. It was just passing along the message without working folks into a panic. We did have some starting to fret, but the storm will distract from that. It should also, I hope, stop Kendra's attacker from trying again."

"Yep. That's one good thing about storms. Even the predators lie low."

"The other good thing?" Yolanda spreads her arms and slumps back in her seat. "Snow days."

I yawn and reach for my rapidly cooling tea. "Not to bring up business while you're enjoying some time off . . ."

"Then don't."

"Eric and I will be heading to Whitehorse once this clears. We'll probably be staying until the baby comes."

She sits upright. "What?"

"I know it's shitty timing. A few days ago, it'd have seemed just fine, but with what happened to Kendra, having both of us leave is a problem."

"It's actually not, Casey. Everyone's been warned, the perp must know by now and will be lying low. Whatever happens, Will can handle it. My surprise was because you wouldn't leave if it wasn't urgent." Her gaze drops to my stomach. "Is everything okay?"

"We had a scare last night. It turned out to be a false alarm, but it did alert us to a potential issue—the baby's in breech. Again, I'm fine and the baby seems fine, but enough small things have piled up that it would be negligent not to get to a hospital as soon as we can."

"Once this damn storm passes." She lifts her eyes to the ceiling. As if on cue, the wind whines. "And here it comes again."

"Yeah, Eric and Jacob figure it'll come and go for a day or two. Our biggest issue for flying out isn't the snow—it's the visibility. Once that clears—"

Bootfalls tramp on the wooden deck. Then the double bang of someone knocking snow off before the door opens, only to catch the wind. Yolanda rises as the newcomer wrestles the door shut. We still can't tell who it is. The lighting's fine in here—it's the fact that like most people, the newcomer is bundled in standard-issue winter wear, from a parka with a tunnel hood down to heavy boots.

A gloved hand rises and pushes back the hood.

"Kendra," I say, pushing up.

"Tell me you brought a hot lunch," Yolanda says. "Delivered

right to my table here, so I don't need to get up, much less put on my . . ." She sees Kendra's expression.

"Something's happened," I say.

"It's Lynn," Kendra says. "No one's seen her since last night."

CHAPTER TEN

I start heading for Kendra, still standing just inside the door, but Yolanda catches my arm and points to the seat.

"At least sit while she talks," Yolanda says. "We both know that this might not be an emergency."

When I hesitate, Yolanda lifts her brows, and I get it. What has Lynn been looking for since she got here? A night—or at least an evening—in a bed other than her own. I remember seeing her in the store with Thierry. Was that only yesterday?

I lower myself into my seat and wave for Kendra to come in. "Lynn's missing," I prompt.

Kendra nods as she unwinds her scarf. "The general store wasn't open, and a couple of people were milling around, hoping to get supplies. They figured it was closed because of the blizzard. I was walking past with Nicole and the boys. We were taking the kids and the dogs for a walk before the storm hit again. I said I'd check on the store situation while Nicole took the kids. They weren't going far anyway."

She moves farther into the room. "I went to talk to Lynn first. I don't know whether it's even her shift, but I figured she'd know what was going on. She wasn't in her apartment, so I had to keep looking. No one had seen her. Finally I bumped into Grant helping with a tree that fell in the storm. He said he hadn't seen Lynn since last night."

I have my pad and pen out, already making notes, even as Yolanda's look says I'm overreacting.

"When last night?" I ask.

"Before the storm."

I frown. "Grant didn't raise an alarm when Lynn failed to come home during a storm?"

"Grant is a fucking asshole, pardon my language."

"Agreed and seconded," Yolanda says. "I'm not sure how I feel about Lynn, but if she gets any sympathy points from me, it's because she's married to that dick."

"Did he say why he wasn't concerned?" I ask.

"He snapped something about checking Thierry's bed and stomped off."

"Shit," I say.

Yolanda looks at me.

"Thierry came into the store yesterday when I was leaving," I say. "There was definitely some tension there. Positive tension. Then I saw Grant heading for the store, and I considered intervening but . . ."

"They're all adults," Yolanda says. "Your police duties don't extend to enforcing marital vows."

"Yes, but this might fall under general peacekeeping." I look at Kendra. "Have we found Thierry?"

She nods. "He's been helping with the kitchen for the past hour. He says he hasn't seen her since around noon yesterday."

"Any chance he's lying and Lynn is in his room? Waiting for him to come back?"

She hesitates. Then she says, carefully, "I really don't think so. I know Lynn can be . . ." She clears her throat. "A bit of a joke for some people."

"Not for me," I say. "It's awkward, because it's such a small town."

"And she's not exactly discreet," Yolanda mutters.

"She's just really lonely," Kendra says. "And she's obviously never done this sort of thing before."

"*Is* she lonely?" Yolanda says. "Or trying to get Grant's attention? Because in my experience, cheating isn't always about finding someone new. It can be about getting the attention of the person you have. The totally wrong way to go about it but . . ."

"All I can say is that she's unhappy," Kendra says. "I know she hasn't been discreet, but she, uh, believes she is. She's trying to be. I don't think she wants to hurt Grant, and I really don't think she wants to upset him."

My hands tighten on the chair arms. "Has he been physically abusive? We've been watching for signs. Like Yolanda said, I can't enforce marriage vows—or interfere in unhappy marriages—but if there's abuse, that's grounds."

"If I saw it, I'd say so. That's the reason I started being friendlier to Lynn in the first place. I don't know what's happening there. I don't see any signs of physical abuse either, and that's really the only grounds we can use to get involved. All I can say is that I can't see her intentionally provoking Grant by staying out all night."

"But the storm could provide an excuse," Yolanda says. "She can say it hit, and she had to hole up somewhere, maybe the store." She shrugs. "No one would know any better. She fell asleep at Thierry's, and now she needs to find a way to sneak back to the store and come out saying 'Whoops, I drifted off and lost track of time.'"

I push to my feet. "Whatever has happened, I shouldn't be sitting here debating possibilities. I need to look for her."

"Yolanda and I can do that," Kendra says.

"I spoke to my obstetrician this morning, and I'm still cleared for walking and standing in one-hour stretches. Just no hikes or runs, which are impossible in this weather anyway." I turn to Yolanda. "Do you want to help? Or stay here and man the station?"

She sighs. "What I want is a snow day, but the sooner we find Lynn in Thierry's apartment, the sooner everyone can admit I was right."

This might be the most awkward search I have ever undertaken. We conducted scores in Rockton and already a half dozen in Haven's Rock. Someone's reported missing, and we need to look for them. They could turn up in someone's bed. They could turn up passed out drunk. They could turn up in the forest, having lost their way *while* drunk. Most situations are resolved so quickly that they never become an actual missing-person case. This is the first time, though, where the most likely answer is that our missing resident is in someone's bed *and* really doesn't want to be found there. Add in the fun of her husband hovering nearby, feigning disinterest in the search while constantly finding excuses to come close.

I've quietly spoken to Dalton and Anders, but I've asked them to keep working on storm damage. If Lynn is in someone's bed, we want this handled with an absolute minimum of embarrassment for her and Grant. Not that I care about Grant—I just care that he could vent that humiliation on her later.

Dalton has given me his skeleton key, and we're very discreetly using it. Yolanda stands guard outside the building, mostly keeping Grant at bay. Kendra stands guard in the hall. I knock and then enter.

For Thierry's apartment, I check everywhere, including under the bed. Same goes for a few other bachelors. For guys much lower on my list—like Gunnar and Anders—I only pop open the door, listen for the sound of someone scuttling away, and take a quick look. Yes, I check Anders's apartment. I have zero expectation of finding Lynn there, but I must to avoid later accusations of bias.

"Nothing," I say when I come out of Kenny's apartment, holding shut the door against the wind.

Yolanda shakes her head. "You realize the only person you'd find in there is your sister."

"I keep hoping," I say.

Kendra and Yolanda move in to block the wind. Snow swirls about, but it hasn't reached storm status again yet.

"That's everyone," I say. "We have now checked every single guy's apartment, as well as the general store."

"Time to panic?" Kendra says.

"I hope not," I murmur. "Let me talk to Eric first."

I'm having trouble reaching panic status. My head keeps insisting this is just a misunderstanding. Lynn is safe and holed up somewhere, and the problem with turning this into a full-scale search is that the one who panics could be her.

Exactly how scared of Grant is she?

Scared enough to go into defensive overdrive when she hears we're all looking for her? Scared enough to set up some kind of elaborate explanation? Lock herself in a storage area and pretend she'd been there all night? Play possum in the forest, as if she hit her head?

Dalton and I are on the edge of the forest with Storm. We left Anders at the kitchen, and we're trying to look as if Dalton and I are just taking the dog for a walk.

"No point searching out there," Dalton says, peering into the woods. "We should still circle the town, in case she went out and happened to choose a spot that hasn't been covered in snow, but . . ." His gaze scans the area. There are no spots left bare enough for footprints or scent trails.

"A long shot," I say, and we head out to make that sweep as we talk. "The only way she's ending up in the forest is if she lost her way in the snow."

Or she was dragged in. Drugged and abducted. Like Kendra.

Neither of us says that. Of course, we can't help thinking it, but we also can't imagine anyone doing that in the middle of a snowstorm.

"I'd like Kendra, Yolanda, and Will conducting discreet inquiries," I say. "Asking around to see if anyone's spotted her. I don't want to raise the alarm yet. In the meantime, I need to figure out when she disappeared."

"Who saw her last, where she was, what she was doing."

I nod. "I know I'm going to push it over an hour on my feet, but I don't feel right taking a break. This isn't Kendra, safe in the clinic. We have a missing person. I'll sit whenever I can, but I need to power through this."

"Can I come along?" He glances over. "To help, not to nag."

I lean my head on his arm. "If I need the nagging, go ahead. But I'm still hoping we can wrap this up fast."

★   ★   ★

The first person we need to interview is the one I least want to interview. Dalton asks me to rest at the town hall while he tracks down Grant and brings him in.

I expect Grant will be easy to find. He certainly was while we were searching the residences. But it takes twenty minutes for Dalton to return with Grant, both of them scowling and grumbling.

Grant doesn't make any attempt to remove his outerwear. He starts barreling toward me until Dalton grabs his parka. Grant wheels, hand lifted. He thinks better of that and settles for yanking from Dalton's grip and kicking off his boots.

"Happy?" he says. "Or will you be happier when you find my wife and publicly humiliate me by having let everyone know she spent the night in another guy's bed?"

"You seem very sure of that," I say.

He turns a hard look on me. "I am, because I'm not as clueless as everyone here seems to think. My wife is hell-bent on cuckolding me, and I just wish she'd get it out of her system."

"That's an . . . interesting approach."

His glare sharpens. "Don't patronize me, *Detective*. My marriage is none of your business, but I'm going to get this over with, so we can move on to finding Lynn. I screwed around, okay? She found out right before we came here, and she wants revenge. I'm letting her have it."

I bite my tongue against saying that's very generous of him.

Grant slumps into a chair. "I don't expect you to understand. What happened to us back home is confidential. Let's just say my wife got herself in trouble, and she was so wrapped up in it that she started forgetting she had a husband. I got frustrated. I stepped out. She wants her turn, and then we'll be square."

There's a lot to unpack there. I really *don't* know why Grant and Lynn are in Haven's Rock, but that doesn't seem germane to her disappearance.

"You and Lynn had agreed she was entitled to a fling."

"What kind of guy do you think I am? I'd never have *agreed* to it. I'm just looking the other way until she's done. Apparently, she picked the worst possible time—middle of a fucking blizzard—and instead of her just getting it over with and us moving on, I have to deal with this bullshit."

"Has it occurred to you that she could actually be missing?"

His jaw sets. "She's not."

"We've checked all the apartments. You saw us checking."

"How does that prove anything? She just ducked out before you got there, and now she's lying low until she can come slinking back."

"When's the last time you saw her?"

He crosses his arms. "I don't know."

I turn to Dalton. "Please note that if Lynn *is* actually missing, her husband refused to cooperate—"

"Yesterday," Grant spits.

"Any chance you can be more specific?"

"I went to the store to see her. It was nearly noon. I caught her with Thierry."

My chest tightens. Damn it, I should have followed my gut and interceded. "You caught her with Thierry doing what?"

"Giggling."

I stare at him. "Giggling?"

"My wife is thirty-six, Detective. She doesn't giggle unless she's flirting."

That's a fair point, but I keep any acknowledgment out of my face and only busy myself making a note. "You found her in a conversation with Thierry that you deemed to be flirtatious and you did what?"

"Walked out. Like I said, I'm giving her space to get this thing over with. Better Thierry than . . ." He waves a hand that might be indicating Anders's apartment above. "Seems she's finally scraping the bottom of the barrel."

My jaw tightens on Thierry's behalf, but I say nothing.

"You left the general store shortly after entering," I say. "Did you see Lynn later that day?"

"No."

"Communicate with her in any way?"

"No."

I watch him for a moment before continuing, "Where were you when the storm hit?"

"I was at work when Will came by with Marlon. They were rounding up help to close shutters. I did that, and then we were sent home."

"We," I say. "Who else was helping?"

He waves at Dalton, still standing inside the door. "Ask your husband, he was there."

"I'm asking you."

He reels off the names as fast as he can. "The sheriff, Will, Marlon, Kenny, and one of the guys from the bakery—I forget his name. We all paired up. I worked with Kenny."

"What time did you get home?"

"Around six."

"Lynn wasn't there?"

"No."

I make notes, stretching it out before asking, "You weren't worried?"

"We went from a little blowing snow to whiteout conditions within minutes. I barely found my way back. I figured she was at the store. Around nine, when the wind died down, I went to check on her. She was gone. Someone said they saw her walking with Thierry just before the storm."

My head jerks up. "Who said that?"

"A guy in a parka. That's all I know. I was peering in the windows of the store, and he was walking maybe twenty feet away. Shouted that if I was looking for Lynn, Thierry had escorted her home before the storm hit."

When I don't comment, Grant crosses his arms. "Let me guess. Thierry didn't mention that little tidbit when you questioned *him*."

I haven't officially questioned Thierry. Before we checked his apartment, I'd asked whether he'd seen Lynn, and he repeated what he told Kendra—that he hadn't seen her since yesterday. She'd believed him. So had I. Time to take another run at Thierry.

CHAPTER ELEVEN

Do I like Grant's story? Of course not. Even if he's telling the truth, it means he heard Lynn had last been seen with Thierry, concluded she was screwing around, and went home. During a snowstorm. When she didn't return by morning, he just continued on with his day. Presuming she was still screwing around. In the aftermath of a snowstorm.

I'm not saying Lynn *wasn't* screwing around during a snowstorm, but there is another explanation, one that should be worrying Grant at least enough to have checked on his suspicions. Someone saw Thierry escorting Lynn from the store, apparently taking her home. Grant said it went from a flurry to a whiteout in minutes. Imagine Thierry starts to walk her home, and they separate once her goal's in sight. Only, within seconds, that goal could have disappeared, leaving her wandering into the forest instead.

Did Grant really never consider this?

Or is it that—despite his insistence he's fine with her marital bookkeeping—he's so furious that he's decided he doesn't give a shit what happened to her? Got lost heading home after walking with Thierry. Got lost heading home after being at Thierry's apartment. Whatever. She fooled around, and so she deserves what she gets.

I cannot fathom that sort of thinking about a life partner, even if it's someone you've fallen out of love with. You might not be willing to cook breakfast for them or wash their laundry or all the dozens of small things couples do for each other. But to presume if they didn't come home during a blizzard they were just screwing around . . . and not check? Even the next morning?

I don't like it on a visceral level, the one that whispers there's more to this story. Grant establishing his alibi? God, I hope not.

Before I analyze that any further, the obvious next step is to interview Thierry. I don't have Dalton bring him by. My danger meter is too high for that now, and it really is starting to feel as if I'm just lounging around, casually investigating while a resident is missing.

Dalton must sense my unease, because he doesn't argue when I want us to find Thierry together. We track him down outside the now-fixed kitchen complex, where a lineup awaits the first hot meal of the day.

We don't even get as far as that line. Thierry sees us and comes over at a lope, his face drawn with concern.

"Lynn hasn't turned up?" he says when we draw near.

I shake my head and motion for him to join us. We walk around the building and find a sheltered spot to speak. Snow continues to swirl around us, still threatening a storm but not delivering on the promise.

"When did you last see her?" I ask. "I know you said yesterday, but you'll need to be more specific."

"At the store. When you were there."

"Then I left, and Grant showed up."

Thierry's cheeks color. "Um, yes. He popped in to tell Lynn that he was going to the Roc that night with some guys, and he'd probably skip dinner. That was before the storm, of course."

"Then he left?"

Thierry nods.

"Did Grant speak to you?"

More flushing. "No. He doesn't, really. He's . . ." Thierry shrugs. "That type, you know? Very high-school."

I lift my brows. "High-school?"

"There are guys he talks to and guys he ignores. I'm one of the latter."

I want to press, but I need to get back to the more important part of what he said.

"What time did you leave the store?"

"About . . . eleven forty-five?" he says. "I talked to Lynn for a bit and then I had lessons with the boys."

"Did you see her again after that?"

He shakes his head.

"Are you sure?" I press.

That flush returns, but his tone is measured. "I'm sure. I heard someone apparently thought she was with me later, but she wasn't. I left the store and went to Dana's house to teach the boys. We were finishing up when the storm hit. I stayed with the boys until Dana came back. Then I headed out. I saw people closing shutters, and I offered to help, but they had it under control. I returned to my apartment." He meets my gaze. "Alone."

I hold his gaze. "And if someone says they saw you escorting Lynn from the store during the storm?"

He hesitates. Then he exhales, relaxing back in his seat. "Is that why someone thought she was with me? No. I did not escort anyone home. If I'd seen someone struggling, I'd have stopped to help, but by the time I made it to the residence, I could barely see two feet in front of me."

"The last time you saw Lynn was at the store, hours before the storm started."

"Yes."

I ask more questions. I need to nail down Thierry's timeline. The most important part is when he started giving the boys their lessons and when he stopped. That can be verified. I also ask who he saw closing shutters, and the answer is Brian and Anders. Again, easy to confirm. And after that? Did he see anyone from that moment on? In his residence building? Outside it?

No. After leaving Brian and Anders, he made his way through the whiteout and into his building. No one was in the halls. His apartment is on the second floor, right off the stairs. He went inside, where he remained until morning.

Under the circumstances, he did exactly what we'd want all our residents to do during a blizzard. He got someplace safe and stayed there. The problem, of course, is that it doesn't provide him with an alibi.

Does he *need* an alibi?

I hope not.

With this interview, the search changes. Lynn did not come home last night, and it's past noon the next day. It's still possible she's lying low after spending the night with a man, but that's seeming increasingly unlikely as time goes by.

And as time goes by, we become increasingly negligent if we don't start looking at other answers—namely that she might have gotten turned around during that whiteout. Multiple people have mentioned how bad it was, and Dalton can confirm. In retrospect, we probably should have conducted a door-to-door search last night and been sure everyone made it home.

We need to institute a buddy system for storms. When one hits, you must check on your neighbor and make sure they got in okay. These are all things we should have been doing even in Rockton, and maybe it's a miracle that we haven't lost anyone before, but we haven't even had a close call, so it hasn't occurred to us. Until now.

We find Anders joining the line to grab food. I hate pulling him out of it, but the truth is that we don't need to wait in line—we only do it because cutting to the front is awkward.

"We have to start looking for Lynn," I say as we take Anders to the same spot where we'd spoken to Thierry.

"Shit."

"At this point. we don't even know who saw her last," I say.

"It wasn't Thierry," Dalton says. "And it sure as hell wasn't her husband."

"We have a report that Thierry was seen escorting her," I say. "But he says he didn't."

Anders looks back toward town. "Who made the report?"

"Grant says someone hailed him," I say. "Male. That's all he knows. Also, Thierry says he spoke to you and Brian while you were closing external shutters."

Anders nods. "He offered to help, but we were finishing up."

"Right now, though, straightening all that out is secondary," Dalton says. "Our main concern is that we have a missing resident." He looks into the darkening sky. "And a storm that's going to hit at any moment."

"Organize a search team?" Anders says.

"Militia only for now. Everyone in pairs. No one goes more than fifty feet from town. Get their asses back as soon as that snow hits."

Anders gives a humorless smile. "Or we'll be looking for multiple missing people."

"Exactly."

"I presume you're taking the pup out?"

"Yep."

Anders gives a quick glance my way.

"Casey will be with me for as long as we can stay out," Dalton says. "I'm not even going to try to make her stay behind. Storm works best with her, and we need to know we did *our* best to find Lynn."

CHAPTER TWELVE

Dalton doesn't need to worry about me being out here for long. The storm is coming fast. The sky seems to darken with every step we take, and the wind whips around us even once we're in the forest.

I can't use the sled now. This is work, for us and for Storm. I've set my watch timer for forty-five minutes, in hopes I can get back not long after my allotted hour.

Earlier, I'd retrieved a scent marker for Storm. She knows who she's looking for. But there's no real chance of finding a trail heading into the woods. Not unless Lynn went in this morning, breaking through the fallen snow. We'd checked for that earlier, and the only trail we'd seen going in had been accompanied by paw prints.

Even those only went about ten feet in. Just enough to get any doggie business done out of town, which almost certainly means it was Sebastian—Mathias would have let Raoul take a crap on the main street.

We circle again now, in case we missed something. We didn't. It's unbroken snow. Newly fallen snow, too, but we can still see where Sebastian went in, snow-filled divots indicating his boot prints.

Next we take the perimeter trail. It's just past the edge of the forest and encircles the town. It's used for patrolling but also for strolling. We've deemed it close enough to town to be safe even without escorts. No one could step off it and be unable to find their way back.

Unless it's during a snowstorm.

We walk that path and, again, find nothing. Then it's on to the second perimeter path. Yes, we have multiples. Having lived in Rockton means we have a long list of things we wanted to do in Haven's Rock. One perimeter path close enough for residents to safely use. Another one deeper in, both for patrols and a slightly better walk, for staff and for short guided hikes.

This path also meets up with the lake and skirts along the edge closest to town. We start there and go clockwise. Keeping this path clear is extra labor, but right now we're running efficiently enough to have a shortage of work, especially in the winter, when hunting, fishing, and logging are at a minimum.

What we don't have a shortage of? People happy to do this particular job, because of the method we employ—a narrow-bodied ATV with a snow blade. Gunnar, Kendra, and Sebastian draw straws to see who gets to do it. This means that the path had been cleared down to a few inches before the storm, and it's only ankle-deep. That should also mean that we'd see tracks if anyone came out here last night. We don't . . . until we do.

Other trails intersect with this one, trails that head deeper into the forest, and we find footprints at one of those intersections, where trees do an excellent job of sheltering the path. There are deep divots, like the ones we saw from Sebastian.

"Storm?" I say, pointing at the tracks.

She side-eyes me.

"What's *that* look for?" I say as I tap one print. "Is this Lynn?" I shake the bag containing the scent samples. "Is it this?"

Storm lowers her head and whines.

Dalton starts toward us. Then he stops and shakes his head. "You're trying to decide whether this is a joke, huh, pup? And if it's not, you really don't want to insult our intelligence."

"Huh?"

The word barely leaves my mouth before I see what he means. There are other, much smaller divots near the first ones. And one reason those divots show up? Something had been dragged along the path, compressing the snow around them.

"Shit," I say, rocking back. "These are our prints, from yesterday."

"Yep. From us heading back. Storm and me walking, and you on the sled."

I ruffle Storm's fur. "Sorry about that. Okay, let's keep going."

We continue along the path until Storm goes rigid, head swinging up. She sniffs the air. Then she practically bounds off the path into snow up to her belly. Dalton waves for me to stay where I am, in the much shallower snow. While the recent warm temperatures started melting snow in town, it's different here in the thick woods, where we'll find patches clear into June.

When my alarm vibrates, I discreetly turn it off. Dr. Kapoor said the one-hour limit was out of an abundance of caution. I'll take another half hour and then get home.

Dalton steps off the path and sinks past his boots. That doesn't seem so bad . . . until you try walking in it. I've had to go off trail and accidentally stepped in almost to my waist. Try lifting your foot when you're thigh-deep in snow. I'd had to practically swim out, all the while imagining myself falling face-first and being unable to rise, trapped under snow.

The answer is snowshoes. We didn't bring them on this walk,

which means Dalton's left doing a lot of grunting and grabbing for trees to lever himself along. Meanwhile, our dog has nearly disappeared through the swirling snow.

"Stay there," Dalton says, and I'm not sure which of us he's speaking to. Probably both.

A gust whips the snow thick enough that I lose sight of them both for a moment. Then it dies down, and I spot Dalton's jacket with his bright orange scarf. Yes, we kept the high-visibility staff scarves I instituted back in Rockton. Dalton's wearing one and so is Storm, with a kerchief around her neck. With this weather, though, I'm starting to think we need full high-visibility vests, too. For both of them.

"Got something!" Dalton shouts back. "Stay there!"

My heart pounds. "Is it Lynn?"

A fresh gust of wind—and accompanying whine—cuts off his next words, and I need to ask him to repeat himself.

"It's a glove," he shouts back. "Storm says it's hers."

I lift one foot, ready to barrel over there until common sense kicks in. I grit my teeth against a surge of frustration.

"Can you keep searching?" I say. "In that area?"

"That's what I'm doing."

"What's Storm indicating?"

A pause, and I know I'm being a pain in the ass. Dalton is trying to work, and I'm that annoying supervisor asking for a running commentary.

"Nothing," he says. "She's snuffling around, but she doesn't smell anything. I don't see any sign of passage either. It's thick brush."

"Where was the glove?"

"Caught on a tree. As if it blew there."

Shit. Not helpful.

"Okay," I call back. "I'll shut up now."

I swear I hear a chuckle, even over the sound of the trees groaning in the wind.

I rock back on my heels and look around. The glove suggests Lynn was out here.

She could have crossed the first perimeter trail and had her prints fill in. Being so close to town, if she'd happened to cross in a more open spot, snow would have fallen thick enough to hide her tracks. Also, we're only two-thirds of the way around this outer perimeter trail—maybe her tracks are just up ahead.

I tap my boot as I wait for Dalton. I want to get moving, but I also need him to be thorough. To temper my impatience, I sit on a nearby fallen log. At least I'll be off my feet for a few minutes.

It's at least ten minutes before Dalton finally comes out, and when he does, I don't even see him until Storm thrusts her snowy head in my face, checking to be sure I'm okay. I glance up to realize I can barely see Dalton, even though he's only a few feet away. I'd been so lost in my thoughts that I hadn't noticed how bad it'd gotten.

Seeing Storm's alarm, he crosses those last two steps at a run.

"I'm fine!" I say, shouting to be heard over the wind. "Just sat down to rest."

I put out my arms, and he pulls me to my feet.

"Nothing?" I say.

He shakes his head and waves toward town.

I motion for him to bend down. When he does, I say in his ear, "Can we finish the trail? Go back to town that way? I want to be sure, and we only have a few hundred feet left."

He nods and motions that he'll move in front. The wind is coming from that direction. He puts Storm in front of him so she can keep sniffing. Then he ties his scarf around his arm and hands me the end.

I do not roll my eyes. Oh, I want to, and I doubt he'd notice with the snow blasting between us, but I still don't. I take the end and try not to feel like a toddler on a day-care expedition. Then he sets out, and I must admit—with my belly and my snowsuit—I *do* toddle along behind him.

I'm soon grateful for the scarf. If I get even a step behind Dalton, a gust of snow swallows his dark figure. More than once I feel a tug and realize I've started veering off the path.

Thick conifers should line the trail, but I can't see them even when I squint. When a snow-laden branch appears at my shoulder, I jump as if it sprang at me. Wind blasts my face, and I duck my head down to focus on my boots, as if I can see them between my stomach and the snow.

I truly am a child in those moments, trundling along with that scarf in my hand. I said I wanted to watch for spots where Lynn might have crossed the trail, but I wouldn't see blazing neon footprints.

My nose goes numb, and I use my free hand to pull up my own scarf. That reminds me Dalton doesn't have his on. His face is exposed to the wind. I want to tell him to put the scarf back on and I'll hold his coat, but I can't get his attention. He's plowing forward, just like me, both of us trudging along, as if there's a hope in hell of seeing—

I smack into Dalton's back. He's standing there with his hand out as he points off the path. I have no idea what he's indicating. I only see a wall of white.

Dalton motions for me to wait as he takes one step off the path. I can dimly make out him reaching forward. When his hand comes back, it's holding something bright red.

Something soaked in blood.

My heart picks up speed, and I start toward it, but he's already moving it my way. I reach one gloved hand out . . . and realize it's not blood. It's red fabric.

No, it's red knit. A scarf? I take it in both hands, feeling along it as I try to make out what I'm seeing through the damn snow.

Not a scarf. A . . . sweater?

I hold it up by the shoulders. It's a woman's sweater.

In my mind, I see Lynn yesterday in the store. Dressed in dark chinos and . . .

A red sweater.

My heart hammers. I keep running my hands over the thick wool, as if I'm seeing wrong. I'm not. This is a sweater, and it looks like the one Lynn was wearing yesterday.

Dalton's gone back to root around where he found it. I hold out the sweater to Storm, who's come over to see what I have. I lower it, and she takes a deep sniff, as if it's hard to catch the scent with the wind. Then she signals. Yes, this belongs to her target.

As soon as she signals, she goes still. Then she whips around and dives off the path the other way. When she returns, she has a sock in her mouth, as if she grabbed it flying past.

I stand there, struggling to comprehend what I'm seeing. If Lynn removed a glove, the wind could have stolen it. Even the sweater *might* be explained. It'd been warm yesterday. She could have taken it off in the shop because she had another shirt on and then left carrying it.

There is no logical explanation for a sock.

I hold it up as Dalton returns. He grimaces and shields his eyes as he peers around. Then he lowers his mouth to my ear.

"We need to get back," he says.

I nod. Everything in me screams against that. We've just found three pieces of clothing belonging to our missing woman. She was out here. She may still be out here. If she is . . .

All I can think of is Kendra being dragged into the woods.

Why would Lynn's clothing be off?

Yes, the answer seems obvious. I presume sexual assault had been the motive of Kendra's attacker. But that makes no sense. It was a freaking snowstorm. Who is going to drag a woman into the forest and assault her during a blizzard?

And if I'm seriously asking that then I learned nothing in my years on the force. I will never be able to put myself in the mind of someone who would do that to another person, and so questioning whether they'd do it in bad weather is ridiculous.

This isn't about finding a cozy place to have sex. The storm could make things even more exciting for Lynn's assailant, heightening their victim's terror.

Still, the logistics make me question that theory.

So what else could it be? Lynn was leaving the store with an armload of dirty laundry, and it went flying into the woods?

I'm behind Dalton again. I've had him put his scarf back on, and I'm holding his jacket. I don't know if he's going to insist we cut back to town rather than finish the full perimeter path. I don't know if there's any point in finishing it. Snow blasts from every direction, and my toes and fingers are numb. So are my cheeks. I think about Storm out in front, with her equally delicate nose. Much more of this, and we'll be treating frostbite.

When I lift my head, snow coats my lashes, and that's all I see. I blink hard. Then I stuff my free glove into my pocket and press my semi-warm hand against my cheeks. I go to take the glove out again and fumble it.

I tug on Dalton's jacket. He looks back and sees me trying to bend. Somehow he manages to spot my glove and scoops it up. Then he goes still. His hand taps something beside the path. My gut chills, and I carefully lower myself on one knee to see what he's touching, terrified it'll be Lynn.

It's not. He's touching an outcropping of rock.

I frown. Then I realize why that stopped him.

Because there are no outcroppings of rock on the trail.

We've lost the path.

CHAPTER THIRTEEN

Dalton motions for me to stay still and then he circles wide around me, shading his eyes. When he comes back, his gray eyes are clouded with worry.

"We left the path," he says in my ear. "Where it comes close to the lake."

That would be the one spot where Storm—or Dalton—could wander off the trail. It opens up enough that the snow would be less deep. That might seem counterintuitive—wouldn't "open" mean less shelter and more snow?—but open ground near water allows wind, which sweeps the snow out over the lake.

The snow on the path meant Storm couldn't always follow her nose. When the trail curved to skim the lake edge, she kept going straight.

Dalton bends to examine the outcropping again. As he does, I recognize it. Not rock along the shore, but an outcropping *in* the lake.

We're out on the frozen lake. Where the ice had begun to weaken in the unexpected warm spell.

"We need to spread out," I say. "We're concentrating too much weight."

Dalton shakes his head. "We're in greater danger of getting separated. The ice will hold until we get back to shore."

Which is where?

I turn to look around, and the wind slams the air from my lungs.

"I've got this," Dalton shouts near my ear. "Let me figure it out."

I turn my face from the wind and bend to hug Storm, both of us sharing our warmth and shelter. If I hadn't known we were on ice, I'd think it was solid ground. All I see underfoot is snow.

My heart hammers as a little voice whispers we need to move, we're putting a strain on this piece of ice. Yet I know Dalton's right. Last time we checked, it was nearly three feet thick. We walk on it. We ice fish on it. We even have bonfires on it, with no worries that the heat would melt that much ice. What's happening now is small fissures. We wouldn't intentionally walk across it, but the ice is still thick.

We're fine.

We just need to get the hell back to Haven's Rock.

Dalton's hand grips my shoulder, and he points. I don't know what he's seen to tell him the town is this way, but I trust him enough not to waste energy asking.

I push to my feet as he helps me up. Then he puts his arm through mine. Since we're on the lake, we don't need to worry about walking single file down a narrow trail.

How long have we been off the path? The fact that we had no idea we'd left it tells me exactly how much danger Lynn was in out here.

How much danger she *was* in?

Past tense?

What if she's still out there, having found shelter, knowing to stay where she is and wait for rescue.

Isn't that what we teach? What *every* wilderness safety program teaches?

Stay put. Wait to be found.

Wait to be found . . . while your would-be rescuers are sleeping soundly in town, having no idea you're missing because your husband didn't bother mentioning it. Wait to be found . . . while your would-be rescuers question people on your whereabouts instead of getting off their asses and looking for you.

I can't think of that. Right now, Lynn could be literally inches from us, and we'd never know that. It's a miracle we found that clothing.

No, not a miracle. Storm scented Lynn on the glove because that's what she does. Dalton spotted the sweater because that's what *he* does. It was luck that we got close enough for them to do that, but we can't keep looking until this blizzard dies down.

Find town. Get indoors. Rest and be ready to go out again with Anders and others to help search.

I walk with my head lowered and one arm raised against the snow, as if that will help me see. When Storm stops suddenly, I smack into her and would fall if it wasn't for Dalton's arm through mine. I lower my hand to Storm's back and feel it vibrating.

She's growling; I just can't hear it over the wind.

I move up beside Storm. She has her head up, as if sniffing. Then she starts forward. Stops. Growls. Looks at me.

"Something's wrong!" I shout to Dalton.

He moves up to Storm's other side, where he bends. The wind changes direction, and I catch a deep musky smell. My hand tightens on Storm's fur, and I move toward Dalton. He's already rising. He smelled it, too.

The smell is gone, but my brain holds on to it and whispers, "Bear."

I want to laugh. It's March. Bears are hibernating for another month. The problem with that, as I've learned, is that bears don't know the schedule. Mother Nature tells them when they should go to sleep and when they should wake, but a dozen factors can influence that, and we've seen bears in March, woken by unseasonably warm weather or a grumbling stomach, if they didn't get enough to eat before they went to bed.

Whatever woke it, a bear out of hibernation in March would be hungry and angry, confused by the storm.

Something is out there.

It might be a bear.

And we can't see anything.

I grit my teeth. Yes, we can't see a foot in front of our noses, but we're with a companion who has a very good nose, one that scented danger before we did.

I lower myself to one knee beside Storm. She's staring slightly to the right. Whatever is out there, it's in that direction.

I wrap my hand in her high-visibility kerchief to lead her to the left. That'll keep us roughly on track with where Dalton was leading us. I'd like to also stay downwind from whatever's out there, but that's impossible with how the wind is blowing, like a snake striking from every direction.

Dalton's hand tightens on my arm as he rises. I tug Storm's collar. She stands her ground. I frown down and give another tug.

Dalton peers the way we were going to head. Is there something in that direction, too?

A whine reaches my ears, and I squint down to see Storm looking at me. Her lips move as she whines again, my head close enough to hers for me to hear it.

She doesn't like this.

She really doesn't like it.

Neither do I, girl. But I don't know what else to do.

When I glance over, I see Dalton's free hand raised. He's holding his gun, because of course he is. We're always armed out here. I've just been too focused on the blizzard—a threat where weapons are useless.

I take out my gun.

Storm tugs to the left . . . where she's been staring.

I look at Dalton. He reaches to grip her collar and then motions for me to stay behind the dog. I do, and they take a careful step forward.

I aim my gun, very aware that I'm pointing it into a wall of swirling white, and my brain screams that I can't take this chance. As a police officer, I had trigger control drilled into my head, but all the teaching in the world doesn't compare to the real-life experience of fucking up. I once killed someone because I took a gun to an argument. I do not even like to *draw* my gun in these whiteout conditions. What if Lynn came staggering from the snowstorm and my brain screamed "Grizzly!"?

I tamp down the fear. I will never again fire blindly. I don't know what's out there, but I will be absolutely sure of what I see—and that we are in danger—before I pull the trigger.

Another step. Then another.

Dalton is letting Storm lead the way, one hand on her collar, the other on his raised gun.

I can't see a damned thing. I know I keep saying that, but my mind won't stop snarling that I need to do better. It's not dark. It's just snow.

I *can't* do better, and I've endured enough storms to know what a whiteout is. I'm just frustrated because something is there, right there and—

The wind swerves and snow blasts my face. A scent smacks into me, that musky smell, clearer now.

That isn't bear, it's—

I lunge for Dalton just as a shape flies from the snow. It's low to the ground, only coming as high as Storm's chest, and that might seem safe. What creature that size could pose a serious threat to two people and a dog?

One creature.

"Wolverine!" I shout, even as the wind whips my words aside.

Dalton kicks. I catch a glimpse of a dark brown face with tiny eyes and teeth. Mostly what I see is the teeth.

Dalton's blow catches the beast under the jaw and sends it flying backward. Only then do I see the true size of it. Wolverines are weasels, and I've learned just how misleading that is. The creature's short legs keep it low to the ground, but this one has to be at least thirty pounds. Even that might seem small . . . if it weren't a freaking wolverine.

The beast disappears into the snow, only to come charging out as if thrown back by some unseen hand. That's when I see Storm hunkering down to lunge, and I let out a yelp as I launch myself at her.

Dalton fires. The bullet hits the wolverine in the shoulder, but it keeps coming at him. He steps back, and his foot must slide on the ice because his gun swings up. Storm wrenches against me, wanting to leap to his rescue, but I yank her with as much force as I can muster, startling her enough that she yelps. Then I fire.

My bullet hits the wolverine in the flank, knocking its rear quarters sideways, but it's still charging at Dalton, even as its whole back end whiplashes.

I fire again, and so does he. His bullet hits the wolverine right in its open mouth, but he still jumps aside, as if that might not be enough.

It is enough. His shot penetrates the central nervous system, and the beast finally goes down. We both stay where we are, shuddering in relief.

When Storm glances at me, I nod, and she approaches the dead wolverine. She moves slowly, as if it might spring back up, and I give a choked laugh at that.

"Good call," I murmur, even as the storm swallows my words.

Storm has never encountered a wolverine, but she's scented them, so she's curious. Having seen how we reacted made her anxious. After all, it was just an oversized weasel, right?

No, wolverines are something else altogether. They are killing machines, predators who seem to lack the ability to tell when they're outnumbered and should give up. Or, maybe, what they lack is the ability to give a shit.

I've heard stories of them fighting entire packs of wolves, and even when it's clear they can't win, they don't stop. Fortunately for us, they might be the most elusive predator out here. I've heard there are as many wolverines as grizzlies, but I've spotted dozens of grizzlies and only two wolverines, both of whom thankfully took off.

So why didn't this one?

The answer can be seen on the beast's muzzle, coated with blood.

Dalton bends to pick up the wolverine. I'd say that with four shots in it, even that prized pelt won't be much good, but he'll try to do something with it, out of respect.

Storm has moved back ahead of us. She glances over her

shoulder, and while I can't hear it, I know she whines. I gesture for her to continue moving, slowly, and she does.

We follow right behind her, and we only get three steps before we see dark brown hair splayed on the ice, and a woman's face staring sightless into the sky.

CHAPTER FOURTEEN

I run forward and lower myself beside Lynn. She's on her back. I don't need to check for a pulse. If those staring eyes, frozen open, didn't tell me she was dead, the gaping wound in her stomach would. This is what the wolverine had been protecting. What it'd been eating.

I kneel there, and I know I should feel something, and when I don't, guilt floods me. But it's not that I don't grieve for Lynn's death. It's that so much else spins through my brain that this isn't fully processing.

Caught in the storm, realizing we are on ice, the wolverine charging. It's too much in quick succession, and when I find Lynn, there's a confused and exhausted piece of my brain that doesn't know what to do with this information. We have been searching and searching, growing discouraged and even panicked, and now we've finally found her . . . and she is dead.

Was she killed by the wolverine? Almost certainly not. It could do the job, but at this time of year, it'll only be scavenging.

There's another reason why I highly doubt the wolverine killed Lynn.

She's naked.

Lying on the ice, frozen stiff and naked.

The grief hits then. Grief followed by rage. I see Lynn yesterday at the general store, so eager to help find Kendra's attacker. I see her light up when Thierry walks in.

After our early negative interactions, I haven't known what to make of Lynn, but yesterday, I got my first glimpse of the woman I could have gotten to know, if not for the rest. That doesn't negate the rest—she'd judged other residents and interfered with an investigation—but she'd realized her mistakes and tripped over herself to do better.

I should have done better, too. We all should have, and if Lynn's loneliness somehow led to this, if she trusted someone she shouldn't have . . .

"We need to mark the spot," Dalton says in my ear.

His voice startles me from my thoughts. The storm rages around us, but he has let me kneel here beside Lynn without comment, because he knows I must.

"I can carry her back to town," he says. "But we can't stay out here."

He's right. Whether she was led out here or drugged like Kendra, her lack of clothing means I can't imagine it's *not* a crime scene, so I need to investigate. Right now, though, that's impossible. Even getting Lynn's body back to town will be tricky. But we have to do that . . . or there might not be anything left to take back. It's late winter, and even in a storm, that wolverine won't be the only creature who'll come at the scent of easy scavenging.

In abandoning a likely murder scene—and taking the body before I've examined it—I am committing unforgivable law-enforcement crimes. But leaving her body here would be a crime of a higher order.

Dalton helps me to my feet. Then he takes the wolverine over to a tree, and I frown in confusion, especially when I see he's attached a rope to its thick tail. He hoists it up and ties it there, and my brain spins, baffled. It's not even a good hide. Why is he—?

He's marking the spot, like he said. The wolverine is hanging far enough from Lynn's body that if it attracts scavengers, they won't leave tracks over my scene. But that corpse will make it easy enough for Storm to find the spot again.

Once the wolverine is in place, we wrap Dalton's scarf around Lynn's torn abdomen. Then he lifts Lynn over his arms. Firefighter's carry would be easier, but I don't suggest it. He's chosen the more awkward maneuver because it is more respectful.

He has to take a moment to adjust, and he moves back and forward, testing Lynn's weight and finding his footing. As he does that, Mother Nature finally decides to give us a break. The wind dies down so fast it's eerie, and I peer about, half expecting that when the snow stops swirling, we'll find ourselves in some alternate dimension.

Even Storm whines, and now I can hear her. She moves against me, and I pet her head. Then I remember *why* she would whine, and I awkwardly drop to one knee and hug her.

"You found her," I say. "And I'm sorry."

She leans against me and exhales, and I hug her tight.

"Thank you," I say. Then I use her bulk to help me rise, and when I look out, I can see smoke rising ahead and slightly to our left.

Haven's Rock.

I reach over to squeeze Dalton's arm. Then I set out with Storm, and he brings up the rear with Lynn's body over his arms.

★ ★ ★

With the storm abating, we decide to veer a little more and take the perimeter path to our chalet rather than get close to town with Lynn's naked body over Dalton's arms.

I go inside first and grab a blanket to lay on the kitchen floor. It's not the most ceremonious place to put her, but it has the best lighting.

Dalton sets her on the blanket, and she's still in the position we found her in. I don't know whether she's in rigor or literally frozen.

"I'll get April," Dalton says.

I shake my head. "Warm up a bit first."

"And let you have a look first?"

I glance up at him. "Please."

My sister is an amazing doctor, and she's become a good medical examiner, but if I have the chance to examine a body first, I want it. And after being out in that wind, Dalton really should warm up. When I start to bend beside Lynn, though, he shakes his head. I think he's going to insist I sit down, but he only unzips my coat.

Right. He's not the only one who needs to warm up. I can't feel my toes, and my cheeks have long since gone numb.

I shrug out of my parka and sit to let Dalton take off my boots. The process seems obscenely slow when there's a dead woman on our kitchen floor. I should be on my knees examining her without a thought for my personal comfort. But it's not comfort—it's safety. My toes are indeed numb, and they burn enough to make me hiss in pain as Dalton gently warms them with his hands. The chalet is maybe fifteen degrees. Hardly cozy, but a roaring fire wouldn't be safe for potential frostbite or for examining Lynn's partially frozen corpse.

As Dalton warms my toes, I do the same for my cheeks. Then I insist he remove his outerwear. Thankfully, his feet are fine—I'll blame poorer circulation from my pregnancy for my brush with frostbite.

Just when I think I'm ready to get to work, Dalton wordlessly plucks at my sweatshirt. It's wet from snow and sweat. I pull it off as he goes upstairs to get dry clothing. Only once I'm changed does he let me finally get down beside Lynn's body.

"If I make you hot chocolate, will you drink it?" he asks.

I want to say no, of course not. I have a corpse to examine. But I'm still shivering and as I warm up, I'm getting sleepy, and part of that is low blood sugar from not having eaten for hours.

I nod, and he sets to work on that while I take my first good look at Lynn. When Dalton returns with my phone, I smile weakly at him.

"Thank you," I say, and I hit Record on the voice memos and turn back to Lynn as I give the date and time.

Then I continue, "The deceased is known as Lynn Williams, resident of Haven's Rock. Lynn was definitely seen by customers at around one thirty yesterday afternoon, although we have a secondhand account of her being seen with another resident after the storm hit. We still need to interview all residents to secure a complete timeline. For now, it is possible she had been missing for as long as twenty-four hours. Victim was found south of town near the edge of the lake. On-site examination was impossible due to the weather conditions. She was lying on her back. All clothing had been removed. The body was disturbed by a wolverine who seems to have . . ."

I hit Pause and move closer. When my small medical kit appears from nowhere, I look up at Dalton and murmur my thanks.

My fingers still sting from the cold, but any numbness has faded and I pick up the metal probe easily. I use it to prod around the wolverine damage. Then I start recording again.

"I count three distinct bites on the abdomen where the wolverine had begun feeding. Each chunk is . . ." I measure. "No deeper than an inch and a half. There's some damage to the internal organs from the bites, but I'll tentatively say none should be the cause of death. They're all shallow and, at the scene, I confirmed that the interior of each wound was unfrozen, suggesting they had been made very recently. The deceased is in full rigor and partially frozen. With the cold, the onset and the speed of rigor would be slowed. While I need to run calculations based on the weather, the cold and the exposure means she likely died at least eight hours ago."

I pause and take a few temperature readings, internal and external. Considering we moved Lynn's body, a defense attorney would jump on any conclusion that involved those readings, but that isn't something we need to worry about here. Even if it's murder, there will be no trial. This is to help my own investigation.

Is it murder?

The lack of clothing would certainly suggest that. But while a storm might not keep someone from sexually assaulting her, would he strip her entirely?

I make the briefest examination of her inner thighs. That part I really do want to leave for April. For now, I'm just looking for blood or obvious contusions. There are none.

I report that on the recording. Then I say, "I will turn the subject over in a moment, but I did get a good look at her back before she was set down, and I saw no sign of injury or blood there. Nor is there any on her front, other than the scavenger damage. No stab wounds. No bullet holes." I stop and curse under my breath.

Be more careful. Do not jump to conclusions. There could be bullet holes or even thin stab wounds in one part of her body.

Using the probe, I examine those wolverine bite marks. If she's been stabbed or shot in the stomach, the bites would hide it. While the tender belly is an obvious place for a scavenger to start feeding, blood could also have drawn it there.

I pull apart the wounds and shine a light in. The wolverine had bit her after she'd been frozen and her blood had settled into her back. There was no bleeding.

I resume the recording.

"I'll need April to make a closer examination, but I see no sign that any of these bite wounds cover a deeper injury. Even if the deceased had been fatally wounded in the stomach, the location of the bites would have meant a slow and painful death, and she was found lying on her back with her limbs slightly spread, abdomen exposed."

I move up to her head and run the probe through her hair. "No obvious contusions on the scalp, nor any blood in the hair, though again, April will need to confirm. Poison is another possibility, but again, I see no signs of it in her posture." I check her mouth. "Nor any signs on her lips or mouth. There are no ligature or other marks on her throat. Her eyes are open and display none of the hemorrhaging I'd expect to see with strangulation."

I move back on my heels and run my gaze up and down Lynn's body. "There's the possibility of a pinprick injection. We'll need to run a tox screen for both poison and drugs—if this is the person who attacked Kendra, he likely drugged Lynn. At this moment, though, I don't see any indication of how she died. The obvious answer would be hypothermia, but she isn't going to remove her own clothing in a . . ."

I slow, something nudging at me. When Dalton clears his throat, I turn to see him holding out the hot chocolate, but his expression says that's not the cause of his polite interruption.

"She might have removed her own clothing," he says.

I stare at him. Then that nudge cracks open a box in my memory. "Paradoxical undressing," I whisper as I wince. "Of course."

A few years ago, Dalton and I had read an article on two strange things that can occur in extreme hypothermia. One is "terminal burrowing," where someone about to die from the cold finds a small spot to curl up in, even digging into the earth. It's something animals do in extreme cold, the tight quarters helping to produce body heat, and it could be our brain-stem instinct overriding everything else in our final moments.

Before that, an even stranger phenomenon has been observed. Victims of hypothermia have been found naked—or in states of partial undress—as if they threw off their clothing *while* freezing to death.

That does indeed seem paradoxical, until you look at what happens during hypothermia. When I started losing heat from my extremities, my body would have induced vasoconstriction—the blood vessels reflexively constricting to stop the heat loss. Vasoconstriction consumes a lot of energy, though, and at some point, the body gives up. Blood rushes to the extremities, and it feels like a hot flash. Anyone in their right mind would know better than to strip when they're freezing to death, but by that point, the victim *isn't* in their right mind. They take off their clothing, and they never regain the mental capacity to put it back on.

So what happens when a hypothermia victim is found naked? Or wedged into a tight space? It doesn't look like death from exposure.

It looks like murder.

I push up to sit on a kitchen chair and drink my hot chocolate. Dalton refills it, and I'm still sitting there, staring down at Lynn.

"Hypothermia," I say.

He doesn't answer. It's the obvious solution.

Do I want Lynn to have been murdered? Of course not. That would mean a killer in our midst, and a murder to solve when I am in no shape to solve it.

So why am I not dissolving in a puddle of relief? Because this feels like negligence. A resident disappeared during a storm, and we didn't even know she was gone, and she died barely a hundred feet from town.

Exhaustion sweeps over me, the exhaustion of feeling as if we're constantly running uphill. We built this town confident in the fact that we could do better. We saw all the issues with Rockton and vowed to fix them. Yet every time something goes wrong, we realize we failed to fix something else.

We're supposed to be doing better.

Better means that we make damn sure everyone is safe when a storm hits.

"They aren't sheep," Dalton says as he pulls another chair over beside me. "I know it can feel that way. They're the sheep, and we're the shepherds, here to keep them safe, but they're grown-ass adults."

He's right, of course. He's been wrestling with this from his earliest days as sheriff in Rockton. At what point do we need to stop herding and say "they're grown-ass adults"?

I'm not saying it was up to Lynn to stay safe in a blizzard. But it *was* up to her damned husband to tell us when she didn't come home during one.

A buddy system is a good idea, and we will institute it for all emergency situations. But even that wouldn't have saved Lynn. Her buddy would have been Grant, who wouldn't have behaved any differently.

I stare down at Lynn.

We may not have failed her, but we'll still feel as if we did.

"Time to get April?" Dalton asks.

I shake my head. "Time to get Will or someone else who can help you carry her to the clinic. If this isn't a murder, we can get her body where it needs to be. There's no rush for an autopsy."

CHAPTER FIFTEEN

I'm upstairs when Anders arrives to help Dalton with Lynn. I'll meet them at the clinic. Part of me doesn't want to. Part of me actually wants to use the excuse that I need to be off my feet. Which *would* be an excuse. I'm fine, and I can sit at the clinic. I don't want to go because exhaustion is tripping my mental circuits, and I'm caught in a loop of self-blame.

If only we'd known Lynn was missing sooner.

If only we'd started searching sooner.

Logically, I realized that the first thing wouldn't have happened because of Grant, and the second wouldn't have saved her, because she'd been dead before anyone realized she was missing. But, like I said, I'm exhausted, and when I get tired, my brain can revert to old habits.

I screwed up.

I wasn't good enough.

I need to do better.

So, yep, what I want is to stay home and huddle under the blankets and feel sorry for myself, as shameful as that is to admit. Fortunately, I know April needs me. While Anders can help with the postmortem examination, I'm the one who did the preliminary one, and so she needs to speak to me.

Anders and Dalton carry Lynn through the forest, in hopes they still won't be spotted. I suppose we really should tell her husband she's dead, but considering it's his fault we didn't search for her in time, I'm in no rush to notify Grant.

I head straight through town to the clinic. A few people are out, mostly shoveling the road, and the distant rumble of the ATV says someone is already clearing snow. Someone does head my way, but apparently, my gait says I am on a mission, and since the pregnant chick is beelining for the medical clinic, no one is going to stop her.

I enter through the front. April is with someone, her muffled voice audible through the closed door. A moment later, the door opens and Grant steps out. Seeing me, he stops short. I brace for him to ask about Lynn. I won't lie to him. That crosses a line. But he only lifts a bandaged hand and says, "Ax slipped." Then he starts to pass me before stopping and turning.

"Any sign of my runaway wife?" he says.

My jaw clenches, and I know I should tell the truth, but the flippant way he asks—and the fact that it seems an afterthought—means I can't bring myself to do it. If I do, I won't deliver the news with an ounce of compassion, and I'd regret that later.

"We'll have an update soon," I say, and brush past him.

"I still think she's with Thierry," he calls as the door shuts behind me.

I walk into the exam room and take a deep breath. April is putting away a gauze roll and doesn't turn as she says, "He will be filing an accident report. I suspect he wants a few days off work. Do not give it to him. It is a minor cut, and he did not even bother to seek medical attention until now, when he seems to have realized it could earn him time off."

I open the door to check the waiting room.

"He's gone, Casey," April says. "I would not have said any-thing until I heard the door shut."

"It's not that." I head past her to unlock the rear door as I hear a boot on the back steps. "We found Lynn."

She jerks up. "She's injured? Why didn't you radio—?"

"Because she isn't injured, April. She's dead." I steel myself. "Hypothermia."

I'm braced for comment, because that voice of recrimination in my head doesn't come from nowhere. It's from our parents, particularly my father, and . . . it's also from my sister.

It's easy to blame the autism. She doesn't realize when she's being painfully honest. But when it comes to how children treat younger siblings, they pick up cues from their parents, and the autism only kept April from realizing that it wasn't her job to teach me by forcing my nose into my mistakes.

Yet part of that damaged relationship lies on my shoulders, too, especially when I struggle to acknowledge that she's no longer the girl she had been. So I'm braced for her to say we should have been searching for Lynn sooner, and she only says, "I'm sorry."

I nod, and my eyes dampen. I shake it off and open the back door just as Anders reaches for the knob on the other side. He meets my eyes and gives a tight nod, acknowledging what we found and understanding how I'll feel about it. No, under-standing how Dalton and I will *both* feel about it, because Dal-ton might be quieter in his self-blame, but he's asking himself the same questions.

What did we do wrong?

How can we do better?

I back up, and the two men bring Lynn in. She's wrapped in a sheet, and April makes a noise of obvious disapproval.

"I wrapped her once we knew it wasn't murder," I say. "I wasn't concerned about fibers."

"I believe," she says, struggling to keep her tone gentle, "that making the determination regarding murder is my job."

"Agreed, but I still made the call on the sheet. There was a chance someone would see the guys carrying her, and given her state, I didn't want that."

April frowns. "Because she's dead?"

"That and . . ." I motion as Dalton unwraps the sheet.

"You undressed her?" April says.

"No, we found her like that. We first found a few pieces of her clothing." I explain our theory of paradoxical undressing.

"Oh," she says. "I have heard of that. The science is sound, I suppose."

"So can we stop judging how I chose to transport her and move on to the examination?"

"I apologize." Her tone is not exactly apologetic, but I've learned to live with that. There are many things about my sister I'm learning to live with, because forcing her to act in a way I understand is as wrong as her forcing me to act in a way *she* understands.

Dalton carries over a stool as I move up to the exam table. I accept it along with his help getting up. Then he melts into the background, and Anders begins preparing April's implement tray as I explain my findings.

The first thing April does is check those wounds. She repeats the same process I did, pulling apart the edges and peering down. She also uses a light and a magnifier to be sure of what she's seeing.

"Minor damage to the intestines," she says. "Consistent with a bite. For such shallow wounds to have caused death, they would have needed to be septic, but the wounds were clearly inflicted postmortem."

She moves to Lynn's scalp, the next most likely place for me to have missed something. She takes more time than I did here, but comes away with the same conclusion.

"No evidence of contusions," she says.

"And if we did find one, it could be related to hypothermia," I say. "She becomes disoriented, trips and bangs her head."

"Yes. I will accept that I see no signs of trauma. Concluding hypothermia is difficult. There are signs I would expect to see in an autopsy, but the lack of them doesn't preclude hypothermia. I presume you will still like the autopsy conducted."

I nod. "Can you start by checking for Wischnewski spots? If we find them, we have our answer. If not, we'll need a full autopsy."

I turn to Dalton. "Are we notifying Grant first?"

"Can he stop us from autopsying her?" Dalton asks.

"He can try, and ethically we might need to listen, but they signed away those rights when they came here. We are allowed to conduct an autopsy, just as we would down south if we had reason to suspect her death wasn't from hypothermia."

"Go ahead then. I'll deal with Grant."

Wischnewski spots are black dots on the gastric mucosa—a layer of mucous membrane in the stomach. They're found in many cases of hypothermia . . . and not often found otherwise. That's what April starts with, partly because the wolverine damage means Lynn's abdomen has already been opened.

April finds the spots, and we take turns looking at them.

"Hypothermia, then," April says. "I do not see any reason to continue the autopsy, unless you have concerns."

"I don't," I say.

Anders clears his throat. I glance over.

"You . . . might want to look at her left wrist, Case," he says.

I frown. We all look toward Lynn's wrist. At first, I see nothing. Then, as I move closer, I pick up what looks like a very faint abrasion on the tender underside.

"Shit," I say. "I didn't see that."

"Neither did I until a moment ago," Anders says. "I suspect something about the lighting—or maybe the body warming up—made it show up."

It really is faint. Only a thin line along the underside. It could be nothing more than the cuff of Lynn's glove chafing the skin, but I quickly move to her other wrist. While I don't see anything on the underside, when I lift it and use a light, I can make out an abrasion along the bony part where something rubbed enough to scrape the skin.

I hurry to her ankle.

Anders is already there with another light. "I don't see anything. Take a look."

I do, with both the light and a magnifying glass. Lynn had shaved her legs recently, and there's a small cut, but it's scabbed over.

I check her other ankle and find another faint abrasion.

"Three out of four," I say. "That's not tight winter clothing."

"Signs she was bound?" Dalton says. "With something soft?"

I don't answer. I keep shining the light. When I pull a fiber from the ankle abrasion, I lift the tweezers.

"Of course, I can't be sure this came from a binding," I say. "Since I made the decision to wrap her in a damn sheet."

Dalton takes tweezers and moves to April's microscope. After a moment, he says, "It's pale. The sheet is dark."

All of our sheets are dark, which helps when you have a black dog and you can't wash them more than once a week. Out of sight, out of mind.

We check the other abrasions. No fibers at her left wrist, but we pull two from the right, and one is also light.

"But the Wischnewski spots mean hypothermia, right?" Anders says.

April taps her probe as she thinks. "They can also indicate chronic alcoholism, I believe. Lynn showed no signs of that—it would have been on her intake forms. I will check her liver as well. While I cannot say, with certainty, that you wouldn't find Wischnewski spots in any other situation, they are considered a classic sign of hypothermia."

"And since she was found outdoors in a storm, naked, hypothermia makes sense," I say.

"Yes. However, in light of this new evidence, I would suggest a complete autopsy."

I nod. "Do that, please, along with a tox screen. I'm going to sit in the other room. I need to think about this."

Dalton glances over. "Think alone? Or would you like a sounding board?"

I manage a faint smile. "I would love a sounding board. Thank you."

CHAPTER SIXTEEN

I ask April to check one more thing before she begins the autopsy. Then I wait for her answer before Dalton and I head into April's office. I sit there, thinking, for at least fifteen minutes. Then I turn to Dalton, and even then, I only say, "I don't understand."

He nods, saying nothing, just waiting for me to continue.

"I'm afraid to speculate," I say. "The obvious answer is that the abrasions and the hypothermia are connected. Whoever tried to take Kendra succeeded with Lynn. He could have drugged her, but he wouldn't even need to. There's a storm, and he offers to help her get home, and instead he leads her into the forest, and by the time she realizes it, she's too far away for anyone to hear her scream. The storm would have made that easy. He binds her and rapes her and then lets her go, but she dies before she can make it back."

Dalton grunts. He knows there's more coming, after what I just asked April to check.

"But that's not what happened, is it?" I say. "There are no signs of forced penetration. No signs of semen. Consensual sex wouldn't show, but is anyone going to do that outside during a blizzard?"

I pick up one of April's pens. "I can't say that would *never* happen. Or that it's impossible for rape to occur without physical evidence. But what am I saying then? That Lynn had consensual sex in a blizzard, with temperatures below freezing, while totally naked, and then got separated from her partner and died of hypothermia? Or that she was assaulted but shows no signs of trauma and just lay down afterward and froze to death?"

"Could the wrist abrasions still be connected to sex, but not to whatever happened out there?"

I consider that. "They could come from light bondage. Very light, with soft materials. That could have happened earlier in the day, unconnected to her death."

I spin the chair to face him. "The abrasions make it look as if we're back to the kidnapping scenario, but my brain keeps wanting to make that mistake because that's where it started. If Lynn went missing, then the same fate that almost befell Kendra must have befallen her. If we found her naked and dead in the forest, that *must* be murder, probably following rape. When the cause of death seems to be hypothermia, it could still be that scenario—she froze to death afterward. Now we find abrasions on her wrists and ankles? Clearly her killer tied her up. Except there's no sign of rape so . . ."

I roll my shoulders. "This doesn't need to be connected to Kendra. Yes, Kendra was drugged and dragged into the forest and, yes, a day later, Lynn died out there, but that doesn't mean it was the same situation."

I pick up my pad and jot notes. "Abrasions on the wrists and ankles. Very light, almost invisible. Found on a woman who was known to be seeking sex outside marriage." I pause and shake my head. "Which doesn't mean she *had* sex outside marriage."

"The bondage could be with Grant."

"So the sex and marks happen earlier in the day. Later, when the storm hits, she tries going home during the storm and gets lost." I press the pen tip to the paper. "But we still have a second-hand report that Thierry was seen leading her home, which he denies. I need to find out who said that."

Dalton rocks back on his heels.

I look up at him. "We can't fly out today anyway. I can answer this question first."

"Not arguing. I was just going to ask if you'd let Will and me handle making the rounds. When we find the person who hailed Grant, we'll bring them in to speak to you."

I glance at the closed door. "If you want Will, I'll need to take over assisting in the autopsy."

"Can you do that while sitting down?"

I manage a faint smile. "I can try."

April hasn't found anything new in the autopsy. There's no sign of liver disease, which would argue against alcoholism as the cause of those spots. Nor is there anything that argues against hypothermia as the cause of death. In short, if we'd found Lynn fully dressed in her apartment, we'd have been stumped. Hypothermia is a stealthy killer, leaving few traces behind, and none we'd normally look for.

April is stitching Lynn up when a knock comes at the door. Then a voice follows.

"Casey? Eric said you needed to speak to me."

The heavy door muffles the voice, and my first thought is that it's Grant, and I hop off my stool and move quickly to the door. Then I replay the words. Grant doesn't call me Casey.

"Hold on," I say.

I quickly wash up, and hurry back to the door and ease it open just enough to slip out, which isn't easy while eight months pregnant. Luckily, the person waiting is considerate enough to back up and give me room. That lets me get the door closed before he can look inside.

The waiting-room light is off, the shutters still closed, so I need to light the lantern to see who's there.

"Marlon," I say with a smile. "How are you holding up?"

"Good. Eric says you're looking for the person who called out to Grant last night, saying they saw Lynn."

"I am."

"Well, that'd be me."

I wave him to one of the waiting-room chairs. Then I lower myself into the other.

"You hailed Grant?" I say.

"I did, and I only just discovered that Lynn was missing or I'd have spoken up sooner. After we got the shutters open this morning, Phil put me on inventory duty. I didn't know anything was wrong until Will asked me to help find the guy who hailed Grant . . . which was me."

"You saw her with Thierry?"

"Thierry?" His brow furrows. "Is that who she was with?"

"Isn't that what you told—?" I wave it off. "Let's back up. Yesterday, when the storm hit, Grant figured Lynn was waiting it out at the store. As soon as it died down a little, he went to check on her. He was outside the store when someone passing by shouted that they'd seen Thierry helping Lynn home during the storm. Was that you?"

"I was out doing a quick patrol. I saw Grant peering in the store window and so I called that I saw someone helping Lynn home during the storm. *Someone,* not Thierry."

"So who *did* you see with her?"

Marlon shrugs. "I don't know. The storm was going strong. I'd just gotten back to my residence after helping Will and others close the shutters. I saw what looked like Yolanda going past, alone, so I headed back out. I was worried she might be lost in the whiteout—she seemed to be heading the wrong way."

I've suspected Marlon has an eye for Yolanda. It's not reciprocated . . . yet. But he would definitely have braved the storm if he thought she could use help.

"Anyway, if it was Yolanda," he says, "I never caught up with her. That's when I saw Lynn. Someone was helping her through the whiteout. I considered going over to them, but I really wanted to be sure Yolanda was okay, and whoever was with Lynn seemed to have it under control. I did a circuit of the town, and I noticed Yolanda's light on, which meant she got home fine. I finished my circuit, and got myself inside."

"And then you went out later."

"Just when the storm was dying down. Maybe seven o'clock? I came out and did another patrol. After thinking I saw Yolanda and then seeing Lynn, it made me realize someone should go out every now and then and do a quick circuit. That's when I saw Grant peeking in the store window, and I figured he was looking for his wife. I called out that I had seen someone taking her home during the storm."

"The person you saw being helped. Are you sure it was Lynn?"

Marlon nods. "She has a multicolored scarf. That's a giveaway. I've seen it before, and it made me think we should all have different scarves. Like you and Eric do." He smiles. "It'd be easier to tell people apart in winter, when they're all bundled up."

"And the person with her?"

"No distinctive scarf, or anything else." He leans back in

his seat. "When Eric said you wanted to talk about that, I thought back to what I could tell you. Not much, I'm afraid. With the whiteout, I really needed something distinctive—like that scarf—to tell people apart. The person with Lynn was maybe four or five inches taller than her. Average build. Slender, though it's hard to tell with the parkas. My impression was that it could be a man slightly under average height or a tall woman."

"The person seemed to be leading her back to her apartment?"

He nods. "That was my impression. I know she's in the family residence with Grant, and they were headed in that direction."

"Can you hold on for a second?"

"Sure."

I slip into the exam room, where April is still finishing her post-autopsy cleaning. I take my tablet from the counter and return to the waiting room.

I tap the tablet and bring up a map of Haven's Rock. "Can you show me where you saw Lynn?"

He pulls off his glove and points. "Right here. And I was over here." Another point.

I mark the spots. "And which direction were they heading?"

He indicates, and I put an arrow on the map.

Then I look at it, and my heart drops. Yes, they were heading toward the family residence . . . but if I extend that arrow further? It goes straight to the lake.

"You said this person was helping Lynn?" I say, as I realize why that's significant. "Not walking *with* her? Not Lynn helping this other person find *their* way?"

He frowns. "I presumed Lynn was being helped, and now I'm not sure why. Because she seems like someone who might need help, and I jumped to conclusions?" He drums his fingers on the chair arm and then snaps them. "No. It was the posture. Whoever was with Lynn had her by the arm, as if helping her walk."

"Show me."

I stand, and he does the same, moving in beside me. He takes my arm closest to him, holding it by the upper arm. Then he reaches the other hand over to hold my lower arm.

"Like she needed to be steadied?" I say.

"Exactly."

Marlon steps back out of my personal space. "I really don't like where this is going, Casey. You're saying Lynn is missing, and I'm probably the last person to see her. Except I didn't see her alone. I saw her being led by someone with a good grip on her." His voice drops. "I know what happened to Kendra. Please tell me I didn't make a very bad mistake here."

What do I say to that? If he mistook Lynn's killer for a helper, that wasn't his fault. It was a blizzard and the person *seemed* to be helping her. But that won't make things easier, will it?

"I'm still checking things out," I say. "Thank you for all this."

"Is there going to be a search party? The storm's died down. I can help Will or Kenny arrange one."

I squeeze his arm. "I'll let you know. Thank you, again."

When he's gone, I hurry into the exam room. April looks up from her note-taking.

"We definitely need that tox screen," I say.

An hour later, Dalton and I are back where we found Lynn. We don't have the toxicology report from April, and we won't until tonight. That takes time. But the storm has died, with no sign of returning soon. We have another couple of hours before it's too dark to check that crime scene, and if I can do it tonight I must or I fear waking to find it covered in fresh snow.

Dalton doesn't argue. It's hardly a mile trek into the forest. It's literally steps past the town border to the lake, with the site maybe a hundred and fifty feet away.

A hundred and fifty feet from Haven's Rock. That's the equivalent of being on the other side of a four-lane highway. Lynn died of exposure so close to town that, in good weather, she'd be able to smell smoke from our chimneys. She'd be able to see it too, spiraling over Haven's Rock.

She'd died so close that we'd have been able to hear her screams.

Had she screamed? She might have. But we wouldn't have heard them last night, over the wind, and she wouldn't have seen or even smelled that smoke.

The storm meant that we couldn't have heard her and she couldn't have seen Haven's Rock. She might have died never knowing how close she'd been to safety.

Having been out here earlier helps ease my conscience, because I saw what those conditions were like. It seems ridiculous, how much we'd struggled to cross the distance between her body and town. I remember the relief of finally seeing Haven's Rock ahead. It really had felt like trudging a mile in a blizzard.

The fact that we took such pains to mark the spot proves how far away we'd felt. Returning, we don't need that hanging wolverine corpse or Storm's nose. We know right where to go, and we head directly there. Dalton pulls down the wolverine— now that we can see how close it is to town, we really don't want to attract scavengers.

With the wind having died so soon after we left, the hollow

where we'd found Lynn's body is still there, an impression in the snow.

As Dalton holds Storm back, I accept his help and lower myself to my knees. Then I feel around in the snow. My touch is light, looking for something in particular. I find it easily. Beneath the thinnest blanket of snow, there's a frozen layer. When I brush it off, the shape comes clear. The shape of Lynn's body.

She'd died here, her body still warm when it melted snow that then froze under her as she cooled. I find the divots of her head and hands. The wolverine had done little to disturb her. She'd died on her back, looking up.

There is, however, something wrong with the shape. There are narrow protuberances from where her shoulders had been. Those look like marks of her arms, but when I found her, they'd been at her sides.

I check where her legs would have been. I found her flat on her back with her legs straight down, but that ice suggests they were parted. She'd died with her arms wide and her feet nearly a meter apart.

My breath catches, and I look up at Dalton. I don't say anything. I'm just making contact, grounding myself and slowing my racing heart.

Then I put out my hand. He wordlessly helps me to my feet, and I survey the site.

"Can you do me a favor?" I say.

"Name it."

I tell him what I need him to check for, and he does it while I stand with Storm. He picks his way carefully over the ice and bends in two spots. He clears away snow. Then his gaze lifts to mine in a grim nod.

I head out, and I see what he found—what he'd been able to bend easily and search for.

Two small holes in the ice, where something had been driven deep. Two spots the size of bolt holes, now empty.

Dalton leaves them and moves to two trees I'd indicated. He digs into the snow, checks one and shakes his head, but at the second, he nods. I walk over and bend as well as I can. There, where he's cleared away snow, there's a rub mark on the bark.

"So . . . yes?" I say.

Another grim nod, and I stand in that spot and look out at the scene now coming to life before me. Faint abrasions on Lynn's wrists and ankles. Holes where bolts had been driven into the ice, about six inches from where her feet would have been. At least one mark on a tree, about the same distance from her extended arm.

She'd been staked out. Tied on the snow, presumably naked, and left to die.

"There's something else," Dalton says.

When I look over, he's rubbing a bare hand over his beard as he looks at something to our left. I only see a fallen tree, stretching along the side. He walks over, circling wide as if to avoid contaminating a scene. Then he bends at the fallen log, leaning right over it to point at the snow.

"That's been moved," he says. "Someone filled in snow. Probably covering footprints."

I ease back for a better look. I can see it now. There are obvious disturbances in the snow all around. There'd have to be—whoever did this would have left footprints and wouldn't have relied on the blowing snow to cover them.

But that wouldn't be cause for concern. It's expected behavior.

Dalton points again. "They missed a spot here. It's lightly covered, but I can still see impressions."

"Boot prints?" I ask, and then I see what he means, which

is far too high on the snow to be boots. It's two impressions in the snow, less than a foot wide, just over a foot long, almost forming a V before they reach the log.

I scan the log. Then I reach out and pull a trapped fiber from the bark, and I know for certain what I'm seeing.

Those impressions are from thighs. From someone sitting on this fallen tree.

Sitting here . . . and watching Lynn staked out on her back and naked, as she slowly died of exposure.

CHAPTER SEVENTEEN

We stay at that site until even our flashlights aren't enough to illuminate properly, and when we do need to leave, I try not to grind my teeth in frustration. I have a new theory, which means a new way of looking at the scene.

That frustration is an excellent way to displace the horror of my new theory. Don't think too much about it. Focus on the crime, not what occurred here to a living person. To a person I knew . . . *by* a person I know.

Pregnancy has been an emotional roller coaster for me. I've blamed the hormones, but I think, in some way, those hormones have only eroded long-erected walls. In my family, I was "the emotional one." Is it possible, even in a moderately functional family, for that to be a good thing? For a child to be told they're emotional or sensitive, and not hear it as a criticism? Being emotional or sensitive is considered a feminine quality. If you're a boy, that's bad. Even if you're a girl, coached to be strong and independent, it's bad.

I learned to box up those parts of myself, and now hormones

have exploded those boxes. I cry easily. I get angry and frustrated more easily. But I'm also quicker to hug Dalton or tell him how much I appreciate him. I'm quicker to show affection and gratitude with everyone in my life.

Going forward, I'd like to stanch the tears and dowse the anger and control the frustration but retain that ability to show people that I love and value them. And if it's not possible to have all that, then maybe keeping the tears and the rage isn't entirely a bad thing.

Right now, though, I can't use the rage or the tears. I need to set them aside or I'll get caught up in the horror of what Lynn endured.

Once I had my theory, I was able to find more evidence to fit it. More fibers on that log. More marks in the snow where Lynn had lain. Marks that do nothing to keep the horror from seeping in, because they do not indicate a woman who'd been drugged senseless and died without regaining consciousness.

Stripped naked. Staked out on the ice. Screaming for help that would never come. Dying slowly and horribly . . . as her killer sat there and watched.

I might manage to process that scene. But I do not manage to squelch my horror or my rage.

Not for a second.

We're back at the clinic with more questions for April. She's run the tox screen, and it's inconclusive. Was Lynn drugged and led out there, waking only after she'd been staked out? Or did Lynn trust her killer and let them lead her onto the ice before she realized they weren't taking her home?

I'd expect to see signs of a fight once she understood she

was in trouble, but that's as wrong as assuming rape will always show physical trauma. She could have stripped willingly, certain if she just listened to her captor, he'd get it over with and she'd be released. But I can't say—even knowing what I do— that I wouldn't feel the tug of that solution.

Be a good girl. Do as you're told, and this will all be over soon.

April does another, even more thorough check for sexual activity, but still finds none, and I don't think she will. We made a mistake with Kendra. An understandable mistake. A woman was drugged in a bar and dragged into the woods. That means sexual assault, right? Usually, yes. But it could also mean that Kendra avoided Lynn's fate.

Someone wants to commit a horrible murder. To watch someone die of hypothermia. They put drugs into one drink of a tray going to three women. Russian roulette. Whoever gets the dosed drink dies. That fails, but then a storm allows them to lead a different woman out of town the next night.

One new question for April is whether there's any sign that Lynn was gagged. There isn't, which takes this to another level of cruelty and confidence.

Whoever killed Lynn knew that if anyone heard her screams, it'd be mistaken for the wind. Was that even more exciting for them? Knowing someone might later realize they'd heard Lynn screaming for help and ignored it?

Leaving her free to scream might also have kept her from fighting as hard as she could. After all, town was *right there*. Surely someone would hear. Someone would come.

While it's possible she was gagged and it left no physical evidence, I don't think she was.

And that tells me a lot about the person I'm hunting.

★ ★ ★

I know what I need to do next, and I am physically, mentally, and emotionally incapable of doing it. That is excruciating for me to admit. I always thought motherhood would mean I'd need to be tougher, stronger, even more capable and independent than I already am, but I'm coming to wonder whether it's going to require me to change in even more difficult ways. To become softer, letting those emotions in, and to be able to recognize my own limits and accept help. Even *ask* for help.

I do that today. I'm exhausted, and every ounce of energy I have left has been diverted to sorting out all the implications of what has happened. I need to find someplace dark and quiet so I can think. Yet someone also needs to tell Lynn's husband that his wife is dead. So I ask Dalton to do that for me.

I hate giving him an ugly task, and I hate surrendering a vital interview. Who is the person most likely to have murdered Lynn? Her husband, and that has nothing to do with the state of their marriage. It's pure statistics.

I should be there. But do I *need* to be there? Or can I trust Dalton to do this? I can, and I will.

He suggests videotaping the interview for me. He'll have Anders bring Grant to the town hall, where Dalton will be waiting with a tablet set up to record video. I appreciate that so much I burst into tears, more proof that I desperately need a break.

I stay at home, jotting notes and making voice memos, curled up in my chair with Storm at my feet. When Dalton returns an hour later, he brings dinner . . . and the recording. He plays the video as we eat in the living room.

On the screen, Grant walks into the room and looks around. "Where's the little woman? I thought that's who I was talking to?"

Anders's voice comes from the background. "I said Eric needed to speak to you about Lynn."

"I figured you meant Casey did. Okay then." He turns to Dalton, who must be off camera. "Since I haven't seen my wife, I presume this is just to tell me she hasn't turned up yet."

"Actually, she has," Dalton says. "Sit down."

"Is that an order?"

Dalton had said it without any hint even of his typical brusqueness, and I note Grant's reaction. On the defensive already? Or just being bristly, as usual?

"Please sit," Dalton says. "I have bad news."

I zoom the screen on Grant's reaction. He goes still and then slowly focuses on Dalton.

"Bad news meaning you found her with Thierry after all?" Grant says.

"Your wife is dead."

I hide my flinch at the bluntness of that, but I'm not sure I'd have made any other choice. Grant clearly wasn't going to let Dalton ease into it.

I rewind ten seconds and zoom again to watch Grant's face when he gets the news.

He just stares. Then he says, "What?"

"I'm sorry, Grant. Lynn is dead."

"What the fuck does that mean?" Grant steps toward Dalton. "Is this a joke?"

"She's—"

"This is a prank, right? No, it's a punishment. You think I'm a dick for not caring that my wife is missing, so you're telling me this to scare me. Shock treatment. Teach me to give a damn. Well, I *do* give a damn. If I didn't, I wouldn't be in this town."

"Please sit—"

"I didn't need to come here. She's the one who got herself—" Grant bites off the words. "She's the one who was in trouble. I *chose* to come with her, even after she found out I'd screwed around and told me I didn't need to come. She said I could stay and keep the house and everything. I *chose* to come with her. And if it seems like I'm being a dick, maybe that's because I don't know how else to handle this. She wants revenge because I screwed around, and she deserves that. Doesn't mean I need to like it. And it doesn't mean I deserve this shitty prank—"

"It's not a prank, Grant."

"What?"

Dalton's voice drops as if he's trying for even more empathy. "Lynn is dead. Casey and I found her body."

"What?" Grant shakes his head sharply. "No, you're trying to scare me straight. Scare me into caring. I didn't report her missing, and now you want me to realize what could have gone wrong."

"I'm not, Grant. I'm really not."

Anders speaks up. I thought he'd left, but he must have lingered in case of trouble.

"Eric wouldn't joke about this," Anders says. "He wouldn't say something like that to scare you. No one here would. Casey and Eric found Lynn's body. She's in the clinic now."

Grant only stares for at least ten seconds. Then he says, "I don't understand. He . . . He killed her?"

"We don't entirely know what happened at this point," Dalton says. "If you mean Thierry—"

"Who else?" Grant's voice rises as he rocks forward. "She was with Thierry, and now she's dead. Obviously he killed her."

"We have no—" On the video, Dalton cuts himself short. At the same time, beside me, Dalton hits Pause and turns to me. "I wasn't sure what to do here. We'd agreed we wouldn't say it was murder just yet, but I wasn't sure whether I should get into what Marlon said—that he never claimed it was Thierry with Lynn. I decided I should leave that for you."

"Good call."

Dalton hits Play on the video. His off-screen voice says, "We are not entirely certain how Lynn died, but we have not eliminated any theories or suspects."

"What happened? Where was she?"

There's a pause, and beside me, Dalton's jaw works as he mutters, "It was so tempting."

I know what he means. So tempting to answer that with a lash of blame.

What happened? Your wife froze to death the night of the storm, because you didn't bother telling us she never came home.

"We found her outside town," Dalton says on the video. "We believe she died of hypothermia, but that's still being investigated."

"Hypo . . . ? She *froze* to death?"

Another pause. This time, it's Anders who answers. "In a manner of speaking. In these temperatures, hypothermia can set in quickly."

"So she went with Thierry, and then tried to get back to our apartment and got lost? Froze to death in the forest?"

"We are continuing to investigate," Dalton says. "We're putting together a timeline now, and we hope to complete that soon. Casey will speak to you later."

"Later?" Grant looks around. "Where the fuck is she? Isn't she some kind of detective? My wife is dead and she's, what, taking a nap?"

I flinch, even as Dalton's hand squeezes my thigh.

On the video, Dalton answers with extreme care, each word clipped. "Casey was out searching for your wife after having a pregnancy scare. She is currently investigating. I decided to be the one to tell you, which isn't part of the investigation." A pause that extends a moment past comfort. "Unless it is. I'll need you to account for your whereabouts last night and early this morning."

"You're asking me for an *alibi*? What do you think I did? Dragged my wife out there to freeze to death?"

I hit Pause and rewind to watch Grant's face while he says that. It's all outrage and flashing eyes, but I make a noise deep in my throat, and Dalton nods.

"Little too close to what actually happened," he murmurs.

"Hmm."

I hit Play. There's some back-and-forth, Grant indignant that Dalton would think he'd done this, while Dalton dives in hard.

"Home," Grant says finally. "I was in our apartment all night, because there was a damn blizzard, and my wife was out screwing another guy. Was I sulking? Maybe, yeah." He glances to one side. "But was I also thinking that it was my own damn fault? That I'd screwed around first?" He looks back at Dalton. "Yeah, I was. So I sat in my apartment, and I drank a couple of beers. The bottles are still there, if you want to check. And before you ask, no one saw me, because I was . . ." He meets Dalton's gaze. "In my apartment."

"When did you leave?"

"Eight o'clock this morning. I got up at seven, and Lynn wasn't there, so I sulked for a bit. Then I went to have a shower. There was a lineup. I was behind Frank. He wanted to chat about the blizzard. Typical weather small talk. Some storm, huh, blah blah. I let him talk. By eight, I was joining another line, this one at the commissary, for breakfast that wasn't coming because someone forgot to close the damn chimney. I was behind Dana and the boys. Didn't say much more than hello. I left when it was clear we weren't getting breakfast." He stops. "How much more of this do you want?"

"That's enough." Dalton looks down at the bandage on Grant's hand. "Remind me how that happened again?"

His jaw tenses. "Cutting wood." He yanks back the bandage. "See? Not scratches from my wife trying to escape as I murdered her."

I pause to look at the mark. It's a cut, maybe an inch and a half long.

When I resume the video, on it, Dalton says, "Explain to me how you got that with an ax."

"Putting it away, okay? I was careless."

Dalton nods slowly, as if assimilating this, giving Grant time to worry that his explanation isn't being accepted and embellish it. But Grant only says, "What about my wife? Do I get to see her?"

Silence as Dalton must be mentally shifting gears. This is the part that we've lost in all the chaos. When the husband is a suspect, it's easy to forget he might be another victim—a man who just lost his wife.

"There needs to be an autopsy," Dalton says, skimming over the fact that there's already been one. "You can see her after that."

"Autopsy? For what? She froze to death."

"I said that *seems* to be the cause of death. The autopsy is underway to confirm that."

"Underway?" Grant says. "What if I don't want that done to her?"

"If we even remotely suspect foul play, we don't give suspects the right to determine whether or not the victim is autopsied."

"But she didn't want that. For . . ." He seems to struggle for an excuse. "Religious reasons."

"Then that would have been in her file, which it was not.

Is there a problem here, Grant? Something you maybe want to tell me before we find out?"

Grant sits back abruptly. "I just know she didn't want to be cut up. She wasn't even an organ donor. It freaked her out."

"Then I'm sorry she didn't put that information in her file, but even if she had, we might have still needed to overrule her wishes."

"So what happens next? I get to go home, right? Down south?"

Silence. Then Dalton says, "Why would you think that?"

"Because she's gone, and she's the reason we were here. I need to take her home for a funeral."

"That isn't how this works, Grant. All that was in the paperwork you both signed before you came up."

This, too, is something new, and a lot more complicated. With Rockton, arriving alone meant we didn't need to worry about next of kin. When you came to Rockton, you disappeared, and if you didn't make it home, you just stayed disappeared.

Dalton continues, "Lynn will be buried here with a proper funeral. Then, when you return, you will be provided with all documentation regarding her death, including cremains, if needed. As for leaving, that can all be figured out later. *After* we finish our investigation."

CHAPTER EIGHTEEN

The interview moves into details after that—how Grant can see Lynn's body, what will be done for the burial and funeral. Dalton switches the recording to double speed, and I can see enough to know there's nothing useful for my purposes.

"Next we need to build a timeline for Lynn," I say. "Question everyone in town, and find out when they last saw her. Also check whether anyone else spotted her with someone during the storm—even if someone only saw two people and can't confirm one was her."

"I notice you're not specifying that you'll do this questioning, which I hope means you're acknowledging that you don't need to."

I hesitate. I want to, obviously. I'm still stinging from Grant's jab about me taking a nap. Off-loading this on others makes me feel like one of those senior detectives I hated working with, the ones who'd sit back and let the younger detectives conduct the routine interviews and then swoop in for the major ones when we neared a solution.

But if I were my usual self, with all my energy and zero restrictions, I still wouldn't insist on personally interviewing all seventy residents. That's inefficient. I'd ask Dalton and Anders to help, and the three of us would canvass and then I'd fully interview anyone who had something useful to say.

The last part is the most important. I need to talk to those who have something to say.

"I'll ask you and Will to canvass," I say. "Tell them about Lynn's death and question them. If anyone has anything of interest, I'll be at the town hall, sitting on my throne, waiting to grant audiences."

"You want a tiara, too?"

"No, just a stool for my sore feet, a roaring fire for warmth, and a sleeping dog for atmosphere."

"Can't promise the last, but she seems pretty tuckered out. You've got a good chance."

"Excellent. Then my royal pup and I shall relocate to our throne room."

When the last person has been questioned, Anders pokes his head in to say that he's meeting Grant at the clinic with Dalton, so Grant can see Lynn and decide what arrangements need to be made. I feel no obligation to be there for that, so I take advantage of the break to rest my eyes for a moment and then . . .

I startle awake to Dalton lifting me from my chair. When I scramble, confused, he sets me back down.

"I tried," he says. "Can I carry you home? Or you gonna insist on walking?"

I rub my bleary eyes and give my head a shake. The baby kicks twice, as if in annoyance at the sudden flurry of activity.

I rub my belly, and my nerves calm at this reminder that all is well. Our baby is kicking, and I feel fine.

I roll my shoulders. Then I remember where I am and what I'd been doing, and I snatch up my notebook like a student caught sleeping during class.

"I have a timeline," I say.

"Can it wait until we're home?"

I shake my head. "I'd rather go over it now, in case you see anything I need to follow up on."

He makes a show of checking his watch. "It's almost ten, Butler."

I peer at the window and see only darkness. "Let's just get through this."

He sighs and dramatically flops into a chair. "Go on."

"The period in question starts after Thierry allegedly left Lynn in the store, before the storm hit. You and Will made a list of everyone who spoke to her before that time, in case any of it is relevant."

"We did, and I doubt any of it is, but we have the list."

"Okay, so Thierry leaves the store at about noon. Then we have three people who went in before the blizzard struck. Carson was picking up things for his mother while Thierry was working with Max. He didn't speak to Lynn beyond asking for the items. He says she may have asked some questions, but he can't remember. It was just 'normal stuff.'"

"The annoying mundane questions grown-ups ask thirteen-year-olds, and the kids forget the conversation two seconds after it ends."

"Yep," I say. "Carson leaves as Yolanda is coming in. That's from Yolanda—Carson didn't remember it."

"Being thirteen and trying very hard to ignore the grown-ups."

"Yolanda is looking for a new shirt. Lynn helps with that. They talk a bit about Kendra—Lynn is still freaked out and eager to help in any way she can. That's the entirety of the conversation. No mention of Thierry, Grant, or any other man."

"Huh," Dalton says. "Weird. I definitely see Yolanda as the boy-talk type. A missed opportunity."

Yeah, I can't imagine anyone engaging Yolanda in that sort of chatter. That doesn't mean she wouldn't be up for it, but the vibes she gives off say she expects serious conversation only, and that is *not* serious.

I continue, "Up next is Mathias."

"Who lied and said he didn't go in the store."

I lift a finger. "Uh-uh. Mathias never mentioned the store. Will asked whether he saw Lynn yesterday, and he said he didn't. A technicality, and yes, I still gave him shit for that, because I don't appreciate having someone else need to tell us they saw him go in the store. But, according to him, Lynn was gone."

"Gone? With the door left unlocked?"

I lean back in my chair. "When it comes to Mathias, 'gone' is open to interpretation. He went in to get bootlaces, didn't see her, and grabbed a pair from the shelf. He made no attempt to find her. She might have been in the storeroom or stepped out for a moment. Or she may have actually left before the storm and didn't lock up."

"Which she could have done by accident—being in a rush to beat the storm—or intentionally—in case anyone needed anything after she left."

"Yes. And I really wish it had been anyone other than Mathias, someone who would have at least made some attempt to find Lynn."

Dalton snorts. "I'm guessing he didn't even leave a note saying he took the bootlaces, for inventory."

"Of course not. But that isn't why he wouldn't have tried finding her. He just counted himself lucky he could get his laces without interacting with humans."

"Some days, I get that." Dalton stretches his legs out. "But it's fucking inconvenient for us when he's the last person in the store. And after that? No one on my list saw her once the storm started. Can I hope Will's interviewees did?"

I shake my head. "Yolanda was the last person to see Lynn at the shop, and the only other person to see her after that was Marlon."

"Who identified her by her scarf. Which we haven't found."

When I glance over, he shrugs and says, "Maybe I've been reading too many of April's mystery novels, but if someone was identified only by a well-known scarf, it'd be a sure bet that wasn't actually them."

"It was the killer's accomplice wearing the scarf? To muddy the timeline?" I tilt my head and consider. "That would only apply if spotting her in town at that time *did* muddy the time-line, which it doesn't."

"Yet."

"True. I'll bear it in mind. Marlon made the ID based on a scarf. Otherwise, no one saw her after Yolanda did, shortly before the storm started." I push to my feet. "I want to have a look at the store."

"It can't wait until morning?"

I look at him. "I don't know. If it's clear enough to fly out in the morning, are you okay with waiting until I've searched the store? I can't let a potential scene sit until I come back next month."

He grumbles under his breath. "Fine. We stop by the store."

"Has anyone been in there?" I say. "Besides me, when we were searching for her?"

"Not that I know of. It's been closed since the storm."

"Let's see whether Lynn left any clues behind."

I'd been in the store earlier, doing a cursory search right after we discovered that Lynn had gone missing. Now I'm looking at the scene with fresh eyes. I start with the accounts book at the counter. The last note is that Yolanda picked up a new shirt. Earlier, I'd noticed that the book was open, but now I pay more attention to how it's been left open—facing toward the store, with a pen on the page. In light of what Mathias said about the store being empty, the placement of the book suggests Lynn hadn't been grabbed or lured out unexpectedly. She'd opened the book, turned it toward the customer side of the counter, and left the pen there. That's what she'd do if she just stepped out for a minute, trusting that any resident who isn't Mathias would note what they took in her absence.

So the question becomes whether she popped out for a moment or did indeed leave ahead of the storm, keeping the store unlocked in case anyone needed something.

There's no washroom in the store. Given the town setup, toilets are kept to a minimum. Inconvenient yes, but also efficient, minimizing the number of plumbing setups required.

Being the only person on staff, Lynn would need to leave to use the bathroom or to grab food or to get something from the main storerooms. In all cases, while she could lock up, we'd see no problem with leaving the store open.

If she went for food, someone would have seen her. The toilet or storeroom then.

We found one of her gloves, and Marlon saw her wearing her scarf. I double-check, but there's no sign of any outerwear left behind. Would she put all her outerwear on to go to the toilet or storeroom? Probably not, given that the temperature had been above freezing. She *could* have, though. So while I suspect she'd been leaving for good, ahead of the storm, I can't rule out the possibility she was only intending a quick stop before she returned.

If so, *did* she return? Just because no one saw her doesn't mean she couldn't have popped out before Mathias arrived and re-turned after he left. If she really had closed early for the storm, that wouldn't explain Marlon seeing her being escorted through the whiteout.

Unless she'd left early . . . but hadn't gone home.

Lynn uses the storm as an excuse to leave work early and visit someone. She spends some time with that person and then heads home in the storm, which is when she was taken and Marlon saw her being "escorted."

Is that the story? Is whoever she visited lying because he fears being blamed for sending her into that storm?

Or did she visit someone who then *pretended* to lead her home during the worst of the storm?

I turn to Dalton. "She was seen at—"

A shout from somewhere in town. Dalton strides to the door and throws it open. In the distance, a voice that is unmistakably Grant's bellows, "Come out you son of a bitch! You did this to her, and I am going to fucking *end* you!"

"Shit," I say.

Dalton glances back, as if ready to say he'll handle this. Then he shakes his head and lopes off. And I follow.

CHAPTER NINETEEN

I call Storm over and beeline for the residences. Grant has gone to confront Thierry and . . .

And that is not where the voices are coming from. I frown and peer through the dark town until I see Dalton. He's up ahead, planted in front of Grant, who's trying to get around him to the butcher shop. Mathias stands on the front porch, arms crossed, one hand holding a large knife.

"If you cannot handle him, I will," Mathias says. "You do not want that."

"Get the fuck inside and *let* me handle it," Dalton snaps.

"Are you going to handle it?" Mathias says. "I question that right now. If you cannot—"

"Stop your fucking posturing bullshit, Mathias. You are *not* helping. Get your ass inside. *Now.*"

"Mathias!" I shout, and I sound as if I'm calling a growling dog to heel, I'm okay with that. He *is* posturing, which he does to shore up his reputation—and keep people at bay—but he usually doesn't interfere with our job.

"Get inside," I snap in French.

Mathias turns a gaze on me, and for two seconds, it's ice cold, sending a chill through me. But then he blinks and sniffs.

"Tell your husband—" he begins, in French.

"I'll tell him nothing," I say. "Show a little damn respect and address him yourself."

The front door opens, and Mathias wheels, knife raised. "I told you to stay inside."

Sebastian only fixes Mathias with a look . . . and then steps past him.

"You!" Grant shouts. "Get the hell out here and face me."

Two figures come running between buildings. Anders and Marlon. They both advance on Grant, but Dalton lifts a hand, telling them to hold off for now.

"What's going on here?" I say as I walk over.

"He's the one Lynn was with," Grant says, jabbing a finger at Sebastian. "He was screwing around with her and he killed her."

For a second, I think Grant saw Sebastian walk into the butcher shop and, from the back, mistook him for Thierry. They're about the same height and build, with dark blond hair. From the front it's clearly Sebastian, and it's light enough to see his face.

"Sebastian?" I say. "You think Sebastian—"

"I was going through Lynn's drawers. I need clothing to cover her *dead body,* after someone left her in a storm *naked.* I found this in her underwear drawer."

He lifts something I can't quite make out. Dalton takes it gingerly with a gloved hand and holds it out to me. I walk closer. It's tiny feathers braided into a heart.

"It's a fishing lure," Grant spits. "Like the ones *he* makes."

"Sebastian is not the only person who knows how to tie a lure," Mathias says.

"Those are his feathers. Lynn bought one of his damn lures.

Or she *says* she bought it. She didn't even fish, but she said the feathers were so pretty."

They are very nice—iridescent black interwoven with white. Pretty . . . and distinctive.

"They're my feathers," Sebastian says, ignoring a warning growl from Mathias. "Lynn did buy a lure from me, with those same feathers. I brought them back from the settlement when I went to see Felicity. Lynn liked them."

"Is this the one she bought?" I lift the lure.

"No," Grant snaps. "It's not."

Sebastian opens his mouth.

"Do not answer her," Mathias says.

"Lynn bought a regular lure," Sebastian says. "That one's mine, which Mathias knows because he saw me making it last month. It's for Felicity." He looks at me. "I did *not* give it to Lynn." He looks at Grant. "Your wife was a nice lady, and I enjoyed talking to her, but that was it. I have a girlfriend. I—"

"You killed her. You screwed around with her and then you murdered her. There is something wrong with you, boy. Lynn couldn't see it, but I can. You're not right."

"I did not kill your wife," Sebastian says. "I was not having an affair with her. I did not see her yesterday. I did not kill her. I'm very sorry for your loss—"

Grant lunges, but Marlon and Anders leap forward to grab him even as Dalton catches him and blocks his path.

"You can't hide behind that old man forever," Grant snaps.

"Grant . . ." I say. "If someone did kill Lynn, we will investigate. You need to—"

"He did it. Search his place. Interview him. He murdered my wife, and if you won't do something about it, I will."

Dalton shakes his head. "Grant? You're under house arrest. Come with me—"

Grant snarls and lunges for Sebastian again, but the others easily hold him off and then haul him away. Once they're gone, I turn to Sebastian.

"*Non,*" Mathias says.

Sebastian turns and murmurs something I don't catch to the older man. Mathias scowls and stomps into the butcher shop, slamming the door behind him.

"Ignore him," Sebastian says. "He's just a little . . . overprotective."

"Just a little," I murmur.

"I know you need to talk to me and probably search the apartment again."

"I do. Last time I was only looking at the sleeping pills."

"I know. Come on up."

Before I can climb the stairs to Sebastian's apartment, Marlon comes loping back and motions that he needs to speak to me.

"I'll go up—" Sebastian says, and then stops. "I'll wait here."

I nod my thanks for his understanding—if he's even remotely a suspect, once again, I can't let him enter his apartment before I search it. I lead Marlon off.

"I wasn't going to come back," Marlon says. "But Eric thought I should. I told him . . ." He rubs his arm, as if cold, and glances behind me. I look back to see Sebastian sitting on the porch, looking the other way, giving us privacy.

"I told him that the figure I saw with Lynn, it could have been the kid."

I nod. "Sebastian's the right size. I know."

"So is Thierry. Hell, so are a bunch of others, men *and* women. I don't think he'd ever hurt Lynn. He's a good kid, and he's crazy about his girlfriend, and I know that doesn't mean he couldn't . . . whatever, but I just can't see it."

"Okay."

"It's just . . ." Marlon trails off and shakes his head decisively. "That's all. I'm just having . . . Shit, Casey. I was the last person to see Lynn alive. I probably saw her with her killer. I could have saved her."

I squeeze his arm. "You had no way of knowing, and her killer was almost certainly armed. If you confronted them, they might still have killed her—and also killed you."

I don't know that, but I need to say something. I can't imagine the guilt he must be feeling. He nods, slowly, mumbling, "Maybe. Okay. I should go."

He glances toward Sebastian again.

"Marlon?" I say. "What is it?"

He hesitates, and then says, "Will asked whether I could say the guy I saw absolutely *wasn't* the kid. I think he hoped I'd say yeah, it wasn't. I said he was the right size, and Eric said you need to know that. So . . ." He smacks his hands down at his sides. "That's it. That's all I had to say."

He turns. I let him get two steps. Then I say, "Marlon . . ."

He turns, slowly, almost reluctantly. "Yeah?"

I walk over. "That's not all, is it?"

He hesitates, and glances in the direction the others went, as if wanting to leave this and catch up with them.

"Marlon . . . ? If there's more, I need to know it."

He exhales. "It's nothing really."

"Tell me, and I'll decide whether it's nothing."

He glances after the others again and then says, "I thought it was Sebastian."

"Thought . . . ?"

"When I saw Lynn being escorted by someone, my first thought was that it was Sebastian. Something in the way he moved." Marlon throws up his hands. "I don't know. It was just an impression. But then Grant thought I said Thierry's name, and I realized I didn't have any proof about who it was, and if something happened to Lynn, I shouldn't be making guesses."

He looks at me. "I didn't tell Grant I saw Thierry escorting Lynn. But I didn't say I just saw 'someone' either. I said I saw Sebastian."

Sebastian takes me up to his apartment. He offers tea or a cold drink, but I say no. I need to interview him quickly. My talk with Marlon had given Sebastian time to come up with a story, if that's what he needed.

Do I think Marlon's right? No, but what I think isn't important. If there are detectives who can tell the guilty from innocent, I will never be one of them, and I've honestly begun to believe they don't exist outside detective stories. The ability to "tell" monsters from ordinary people is a fiction we tell ourselves, because we don't want to accept the truth, which is that nothing gives away the monsters among us.

Grant said he knows something's wrong with Sebastian. So that's proof that you *can* tell, isn't it? No. What Sebastian has isn't a streak of evil. It's sociopathy. Call it mental illness or neurodiversity. What it means for him is that, as hard as he tries, he'll never quite act the way we expect of neurotypical people.

Hell, the longer I live in Rockton or Haven's Rock, with such a small community of people, the less I'm convinced that neurotypical is even a thing and not just a name given to a mental construct humans have declared "normal." To someone like Grant, confident in the presumption *he* is "normal," it's easy to look at Sebastian, or April, or even Dalton and me, and to narrow his eyes and decide something isn't quite right.

In Sebastian's case, yes, Grant is correct that the deviation in the young man's brain does make him dangerous, and so I cannot absolve him of this accusation outright, as much as my gut says the crime doesn't fit the young man I know.

"That *is* the heart I made for Felicity," Sebastian says as we crest the stairs into the apartment. "I'm sure of it, but I'd like to check where I was keeping it, if that's okay."

I nod and follow Sebastian to his room. On his dresser, there's what looks like a jewelry box. When he opens it, I see that it's his lure-making equipment. He pulls out a drawer and removes tissue-wrapped objects. He takes out one, starts to unwrap it, and then stops.

"This one's been opened." He points at the bottom. "I fold them under when I wrap them."

"Those are . . . ?"

"My lures." He takes out another one. "This one's been opened, too." A third. "But not this one." He shows me how he'd tucked it under, forming a perfect pouch for the elaborate and delicate lures.

He opens the three. They're all lures—none a heart-shaped decoration like Grant found.

"It was in here," he says.

"When did you last see it?" I ask.

He shrugs. "When I made it last month. I wrapped it up and put it away."

"And you didn't notice one missing?"

"The other three were already in there. That's the drawer for Felicity's lures. I finished hers first, and then moved on to doing ones for others. Once they were done, I didn't open the drawer again."

He doesn't say that someone stole the heart. He doesn't even point out that the opened ones suggest someone was looking through the lures. Sebastian isn't only smart—he's a convicted felon. And he trusts me to draw my own conclusions.

"You sold a fly to Lynn?" I say.

He nods. "About a month ago. Someone heard I do them and was asking about them, so I promised to bring some to the Roc. I did. A few people wanted to buy them for spring fishing. Selling them is awkward—I don't need credits—but if I give them away . . ." He shrugs.

"If they're free, everyone will want one because they *are* pretty. That's why Lynn bought one?"

He nods. "She said she doesn't fish, but she wanted it." He glances over. "She wasn't flirting or anything. To her, I'm a kid. Yeah, she hit on Gunnar, who isn't much older than me, but she definitely saw me as a kid."

"Who all was there when you were showing them off?"

"Uh . . . I can give you a list of those who were at the table, but others stopped by for a look. Anyone in the Roc that night saw them, and more people know I make them, from conversations and such."

"Did you mention the heart one to anybody?"

"I don't think so. Mathias saw it and . . ." He stops. "Lynn. Not that she saw it, but I asked whether she actually wanted a fly or just something else, maybe for a necklace. I said I'd made a heart for my girlfriend. She said the fly was fine."

"Was that at the Roc?"

He nods. "And before you can ask, others were there, but I don't remember who."

Sebastian lowers his voice. "Is it true what Grant said? I heard that Lynn died of exposure. But you think it was murder?"

"Grant knows it was hypothermia, and he knows we're investigating the possibility it was murder. Anything else is his own conjecture."

He shoves his hands into his pockets, going silent. Then he says, "I don't have an alibi. It's the same as for the night Kendra was attacked. During the storm, I was here in the apartment, working on my flies. Mathias was, too, which is technically an alibi but . . ."

He shrugs. Again, Mathias would tell us whatever it took to exonerate Sebastian.

"He wouldn't let me get away with murder," Sebastian says, as if reading my thoughts. "He's been very clear on that. If I screw up, that's it."

"No exceptions?"

Sebastian exhales and lowers himself onto the edge of his bed. "I should say no exceptions but we both know Mathias's ethical code is a little convoluted."

"Just a little."

"If I killed someone in self-defense, he wouldn't turn me in. But if someone hurt me, I wouldn't kill them in revenge. That's a shitty revenge—hurting them back would be correct. Same if someone hurt Felicity. Now, if someone hurt another person I care about, like you or Mathias? I'd probably just turn them in. No offense."

I need to bite my cheek at that. He says it with sincere apology, as if I might be offended that he'd turn in my attacker rather than wreak vengeance himself.

He continues in that same thoughtful tone, as if laying out the circumstances under which you'd commit murder is very ordinary conversation. "But killing someone because they killed a stranger, even horribly?" He shakes his head. "I'd be putting a target on myself, and I don't do that."

Unlike Mathias. That's what he means. I'm sure Sebastian knows what crimes Mathias has committed. While that's hardly part of normal psychotherapy, nothing about their particular therapeutic relationship counts as normal.

"What about an accident?" I say. "What would Mathias do if you accidentally killed someone?"

"Accidentally let Lynn die of exposure?"

I move to a small chair and sit. "Someone was seen escorting Lynn during the worst of the storm. The size of the person fits you. Let's say you're out and you see her struggling to get to her residence. You help her. As soon as you see the residence, you say goodbye, and she gets turned around in the whiteout and heads into the forest."

"But that wouldn't be my fault. Sure, I'd feel bad that I didn't take her to the front door, but no one would blame me." He considers. "No, I guess Grant would still blame me. But if that happened, I'd quietly tell you what happened, and I know you wouldn't go around telling people that I let her die. Or even that I was the last to see her."

"I wouldn't."

"So I'd tell you. But whoever was seen with Lynn, it wasn't me."

I've given him an out here. Someone saw a person escorting Lynn, and that person could have been him. All he has to do is say yes, that's how it happened. Oh, I'd still investigate, because Lynn *didn't* just get lost and die. But without more information, this could seem like a way to explain why he'd been seen with her. He didn't take it, though.

"Wait," he says. "What time did someone think they saw me?"

"Roughly four. During the worst of the storm."

"Then I might have an actual alibi. I stepped outside around three thirty to see what was happening with the storm. I noticed someone outside at Kenny's place, wrestling with a shutter.

I pulled on my stuff and told Mathias I was going out. One of the external shutters on the carpentry store had come loose and was banging away and Kenny was fixing it before it flew off and damaged something. I helped with that, and then we went in and had a coffee. I got back around six and made dinner."

He looks my way. "Please tell me that helps."

It does, if Kenny can confirm the alibi. Or, at least, it helps prove that Sebastian wasn't that person seen with Lynn. Does it exonerate him completely? No. But it's a good start.

"It helps," I say. "I'm going to need to search your room, though."

"Do whatever you need to do, because between the drugs for Kendra and Felicity's heart being in Lynn's drawer, I'm starting to feel like someone here doesn't like me much."

CHAPTER TWENTY

I don't find anything in Sebastian's room, and that's not surprising. If he is being framed, it'd be wise for the killer to hide a "trophy" in Sebastian's bedroom—a piece of clothing or jewelry—but the storm means it'd be hard to have gotten access to this room today. Either Sebastian or Mathias has been here or in the shop all day. Any evidence would need to be hidden later, which is why it's a good thing I conducted the search now.

I'm also quick to warn Sebastian to keep both the shop and their apartment secured, but according to him, they've been doing that since the drugs were found missing.

Do I think Sebastian is being framed? Yes. Stealing the temazepam had seemed a matter of convenience. Someone knew he had sleeping medication and discovered Mathias doesn't lock the doors. But the heart-shaped lure placed in Lynn's underwear drawer is deliberate.

Not only does Sebastian match the basic description of the person Marlon saw, but the way that person moved suggested it was Sebastian. I know what Marlon meant by that. Sebastian carries himself in a way that seems a study in contradictions. He gives off a very casual air, laid-back and unprepossessing. That's what he wants people to see. It lowers their guard and helps them dismiss him. Sure, he might seem a little off, but certainly not dangerous. Just a kid. That's why Lynn would have set her eye on Gunnar while never looking Sebastian's way. He *seems* younger than he is. Just a kid.

And yet, despite that affected persona of nonchalance, there's a watchfulness to him, an alertness. He has a very relaxed stride, like the kind of guy who'd stroll into a bad neighborhood by accident. But the rest of him—his face and especially his eyes— tells a very different story. He is exceptionally aware at all times. That casual walk and eagle-eyed gaze could be emulated by anyone who has watched Sebastian.

Our killer isn't acting on impulse. The theft of the drugs implies planning. What if part of that planning meant setting up a fall guy? Someone who bears a physical resemblance to them, especially when bundled in winter wear.

Who might frame Sebastian this way? Anyone matching his basic physical size, which includes a half dozen men and women in town. But the one that comes to mind first? The one who keeps sliding into the center of this.

Thierry.

From Sebastian's apartment, I pop by and see Kenny, who confirms what Sebastian said about helping him and having coffee afterward. The times match up. Next I go to where we're holding Grant. In Rockton, we'd had a cell in the police station for anyone we needed to confine. The problem came when we needed to watch—or guard—someone and didn't want to make them stay in a cell so small they couldn't even stretch out on the floor. We do have a cell in Haven's Rock, but we also have a windowless bedroom with a guard area just outside the door. That bedroom is where Grant's being held.

I find both Dalton and Anders just outside the building door, talking.

"I need to speak to Grant." I look at Dalton. "Ten minutes tops. Then I'm off to bed."

He grunts and opens the door.

"I'll grab my stuff for the night shift," Anders says, and takes off at a lope.

Dalton and I go inside. The small exterior room has a cot and a chair. That's where Anders will spend the night, right outside Grant's door. Dalton knocks on that door.

When no one answers, Dalton sighs. "I know you're in there, Grant. I'm just knocking to be polite and let you know I'm bringing Casey in."

"Yeah? I just lost my wife. Polite would be not treating me like a goddamn criminal."

Dalton opens the door. Grant is up on the bed, dressed, arms crossed, a kid who's determined to spend his grounding like that.

"You're here because you threatened a resident," I say. "You were warned to stop. Warned multiple times, in deference to what you've gone through. But if you kept threatening, we needed to put you in here to cool off. It's better than the cell."

"You know who should be in the cell? That kid."

As I move into the room, I take a better look at Grant. Could *he* pass for Sebastian? He's a couple of inches taller, but otherwise, if he had the walk right, he could have done it. Heavy winter wear—plus a blizzard—means I can't rely too much on the description.

"You say you found the lure in Lynn's underwear drawer,"
I say.

"Yeah."

"Hidden?"

He shrugs. "It was wrapped in a pair of her underwear, so
yeah, hidden."

"Would that be a safe place for her to hide something?"

He looks at me like I'm joking. "Uh, it's her *underwear* drawer.
I don't go in there."

"Not even to put away laundry?" Dalton says.

Grant's face screws up. "Why would I be putting away laundry?"

"I put away ours," Dalton says. "Including my wife's underwear."

"Well, I don't. The laundry is her job. Always has been. And
before you think that's some chauvinistic bullshit, I do dishes
and she does laundry."

"When was it last done?" I ask.

He throws up his hands. "How would I know? Again, not
my job. She takes the laundry and brings it back."

We have a centralized facility here, as in Rockton. I can check
when it was last done for Lynn and Grant, which might narrow
down the window of when that lure could have been dropped
off. Still, if it'd been a few days, that increased the risk of Lynn
finding it.

"Back up to yesterday morning," I say.

"I wish I could," he mutters, and again, I'm reminded that he
really is grieving. Or doing a good job of faking it.

"When you left your apartment, did you lock the door?" I
ask.

"Lynn and I left together for work. We never lock it."

"What time was that?"

He peers at me. "Are you suggesting someone planted that lure?"

"I'm running through all possibilities. Now, what time did you leave?"

I make notes of his comings and goings that day. Both Lynn and Grant worked all morning, and neither seems to have returned before the storm. Since then, Grant has come and gone, never locking the door. There would have been plenty of opportunities for Lynn's killer to slip in and leave that lure.

The family building is currently being used for couples, too, since the only family is Dana and the boys. Being seen hanging around when you don't live there would be noticed . . . unless you have a reason for hanging around. Unless people are accustomed to seeing you at that building because you're tutoring the two boys who live there.

And, once again, the pendulum swings back to Thierry.

I go home after that. I stay up for a while talking over the case with Dalton, but I'm in bed shortly after midnight, and thankfully, I'm too exhausted to lie there working it through. The next thing I know, it's morning, and I wake to Dalton packing our bags.

"The weather is clear enough to leave?" I say.

He grunts.

I push up into a sitting position. "I'm not going to argue against leaving, Eric. I hate taking off before this case is solved, but I won't risk our baby's life for that. If the weather is good enough to fly, I just need time to talk to Will. He'll be in charge of the case. He can investigate, but mostly, we'll just need the town to be locked down until we return. Which, I know, may not be for a few weeks. I don't expect Will to solve the case, but I do trust him—and the others—to lock down tight and keep the killer from striking again."

"The weather isn't good enough to go," he says. "That's what I'm grumbling about. The cloud cover's too low. I'm hoping it'll clear, though. Meanwhile, you have time to keep working the case."

When he walks close, I pull him into a kiss. "Thank you."

"Don't thank me. Thank the damn clouds."

"I know, and I also know you want to leave as soon as possible. Which we will. I promise."

I start my day with a breakfast meeting. It's supposed to be a private meeting with Anders, in preparation for handing over the case, but I find him at the clinic, and it's hard to call him away without making April feel excluded. And the more I think of it, the more I realize she should be part of this. Not only is she our medical examiner, but she's discovered a love of mysteries. They appeal to her problem-solving brain. Our mysteries might not be as tidy as the ones she reads—and she may consider that my fault, for not being as good as those fictional detectives—but she does appreciate any chance to give her mental muscles a workout.

So it's a meeting for three. Well, four, when Dalton returns with breakfast. But then he also returns with Yolanda.

"She asked the status of the investigation," he grumbles. "I made the mistake of telling her."

"He said you were discussing it with Will over breakfast," Yolanda says. "I decided to join."

I look up at her from the chair April insisted I sit in. "You're always saying you want to be treated like everyone else and not pull rank . . . and then you pull rank."

"Pfft." She sets a plate of bakery goodies on the counter. "I never said I won't pull rank. I totally will, when it suits me. What's the point of privilege if you can't wield it to get what you want? So fill me in. I'm guessing this bullshit about Lynn's death probably being accidental is just that—bullshit. You know it's murder."

April says, "Someone stripped her, tied her down, and watched her die of hypothermia."

The room goes silent and Yolanda stares, as if this might be my sister's developing-but-odd sense of humor.

Then Yolanda says, "Oh," and sways, and Anders darts forward to steady her. She doesn't object until she realizes it and then brushes him off and lowers herself into another chair he'd dragged into the room earlier.

"That was blunt, wasn't it?" April says.

"A little." Yolanda tries for a twisted smile. "But better than cushioning it for me." She leans forward, inhaling deeply. Her hand trembles, and when she notices it, she curses and shakes it hard. "Fucking tremors."

"They worsen with stress," April says. "But I suppose you know that."

Yolanda gives another hard shake of her hands, as if that will help. Then she looks at me. "Is April right about Lynn?" At my sister's small noise, she says, "Of course you're right, April. You wouldn't say it otherwise. I mean, are we sure that's what happened or is that the theory?"

"We're never absolutely certain," I say. "But it's the theory that fits the evidence, unless anyone else can come up with another one. Lynn was found naked, which can happen during hypothermia."

"Getting naked?"

"Paradoxical undressing. There's a medical explanation. It's like a severe hot flash, and the person—already confused by the hypothermia—takes off their clothing. So that seemed to fit. We found some of her clothes before we found her. But then there were very light abrasions on her wrists and one ankle. We went back and found marks in the snow suggesting she'd been lying on her back with her arms and legs out. Abrasions on a tree and two bolt holes in the ice suggest where she'd been . . ." I hesitate to say "staked out" and go with ". . . tied up."

"And the part about her killer watching her?" Yolanda fists her hands and tucks them away. "I know that might not matter. What counts is that she died . . ." She swallows hard. "Horribly."

"But it *does* matter," Anders says. "It shows what kind of person we're dealing with."

Yolanda honestly looks like she's going to be sick. I can argue that she inserted herself in this, and so we bear no responsibility. If I'd tried to dissuade her, she'd only have dug in her heels. But she didn't live in Rockton. She hasn't seen what we have. And whatever tough facade she adopts, that isn't necessarily who she is underneath. I know that better than anyone. Looking as if nothing would faze you doesn't mean you lack the empathy to understand what Lynn endured.

So I soften my tone as I say, "We found evidence that someone sat on a log facing where she'd been tied. Of course, that doesn't prove they watched her—"

"He did," Yolanda says. "That was the point. If he's going to make someone die a terrifying death, he's going to watch." Her voice drips with disgust. "Otherwise, why bother."

"I would agree," April says. "I realize you don't like to speak in absolutes, Casey, but it was a truly horrifying way to kill someone. Sadistic. The point, I believe, of sadism is to observe the suffering."

We all sit in silence as breakfast stays on the counter, untouched. Then I say, "Speaking of absolutes, though, we can't be sure this was a man, so let's not refer to them as he."

"No sexual assault?" Yolanda says.

"No sign of it."

"Then Kendra . . ." Her gaze shoots to me. "Are we presuming it's the same person who tried to take Kendra?" Her shoulders hunch. "That *that* was supposed to happen to her?"

"The only clear link is the fact that we have one attempted and one successful abduction. I think that's enough to link them in theory, but I'd like more."

"Have we run a tox screen on Lynn?" Yolanda asks.

"It is inconclusive," April answers.

"And I'm not sure she would have been drugged," I say. "At least not in the same way Kendra was. It was a storm. Someone was pretending to help her get home and led her into the forest. While we don't see signs of a struggle, she was dressed in heavy outerwear, as was her attacker."

"Scratches wouldn't show," Anders says. "Even blows would have been cushioned."

Yolanda says, "So she let him—*them*—undress her and tie her up without arguing?"

"She may have been in shock. She also may have just been doing as she was told, presuming it was an assault."

"Get it over with," Anders murmurs.

"Or feign compliancy and hope to lower her attacker's guard," I say.

Yolanda shakes her head. "I can't see that. She knows she's in trouble. She's going to fight."

I say nothing. Oh, I would argue—fiercely—in any other

circumstances. Yolanda might not intend it, but she's skirting dangerously close to victim blaming. Sometimes fighting is the answer, and sometimes it's not, and no one can say which they'd do until they're there. At eighteen, my boyfriend and I faced three guys in an alley. They'd come for him. I fought. He fled. He survived . . . until I recovered enough to confront him.

Would I be so quick to fight back again? Knowing I nearly died that time? That isn't a call I can make until I'm faced with the choice, and even then, whatever I decide would be ten percent informed decision and ninety percent animal panic.

I say, evenly, "I don't consider the lack of defense wounds to be proof Lynn was drugged. If she did comply, she was disabled quickly, before she could react."

Anders nods. "It really can happen that fast. She's going along with what her attacker says, plotting her escape, and then they overpower her. Tie her up as she's still processing what's happening."

"And screaming for help," I say. "We can't overlook that. She was only a hundred and fifty feet from town. Her first reaction—correctly—would be to scream."

"Except there was a storm," Anders says. "No one could hear her."

"He didn't gag her?" Yolanda says. Then her face sharpens with bitterness. "No, of course he didn't. He didn't need to, with the storm raging, and it'd be much more satisfying to watch her screaming."

"We found no sign of a gag."

"I did find signs of laryngeal trauma," April says.

Yolanda looks sick again.

I straighten. "We'll go over the case in detail, along with the suspects and all evidence. That's why we're all here. Eric's hoping the clouds will lift enough for us to leave today. If we do . . ." I fight to keep my voice steady. "We'll likely be gone for a few weeks. Which means I can't finish this investigation."

"We've got it," Anders says.

"I hate leaving. I had a scare the night before last, but it doesn't seem to have been anything serious and—"

"You're leaving," Anders says, meeting my gaze. "I know you're going to say you feel fine now, but what if something goes wrong when you *can't* leave?"

"The baby is still in breech," April says. "I am not certain I care to conduct my first Cesarean section on my sister. I would like you to leave." She pauses. "That sounds harsh. I mean that, for your sake, I would prefer you to leave, but also, if it helps convince you to go, I do not wish to be responsible for anything going wrong with my niece's birth."

"It's a girl?" Yolanda says, perking up.

"We don't know that," I say. "April and Eric have just decided it is."

"But we could find out," Yolanda says. "We have an ultrasound here." She looks at me. "It would be a good idea to take a look at the baby. And a welcome distraction right now. You owe us that much."

I snort. "I certainly do not. If I need an ultrasound, April will provide it . . . without checking for the baby's sex. But, back to the case, I wasn't arguing for us to stay."

I glance at Dalton, who has said nothing, but I haven't missed how tightly he's been holding himself during this part of the conversation. "I promised I wouldn't. I agree that, while I feel guilty leaving when we have a murder, my obstetrician strongly urges me to go to Whitehorse, so I will. April doesn't want to be responsible for any problems with our baby, and neither do I. We fly out at the first opportunity. We have satellite phones now, and I can micromanage that way."

"If the phones work," Anders says. "I have a feeling they might stop, depending on how often you call to check up on me."

I shake my head.

"There's not going to be a lot of investigating," Dalton says. "Casey should have time to pursue her leads before we go. After that, it's a matter of you guys following up on any new leads, but mostly just making sure no one else gets hurt."

"Locking down?" Anders says.

Dalton nods. "We'll talk to Phil and then we'll hold a town meeting." He glances my way. "And as proof of my love, I will lead it while you get these guys up to speed."

I smile. "Thanks. The residents may not appreciate that, but I do."

CHAPTER TWENTY-ONE

Anders and Dalton both leave briefly. Dalton goes to speak to Phil, while Anders asks Kenny to gather folks for a town meeting. Then Anders returns, and I take him, Yolanda, and April through the case, laying out all the evidence and the suspects.

"Sebastian's being framed," Yolanda says.

"I think so, too, but you can't discount him—or anyone—as a suspect."

"If Sebastian did this," April says, "he would not have done such a poor job of it. Therefore, I agree with Yolanda."

I lift my hands. "Yes, but we can't start using 'would have covered his tracks better' as a defense. You have all the evidence. This morning, I want to speak to Grant again. It's time I learned why Lynn was here."

"My grandmother can tell you that," Yolanda says.

"She can confirm it, but I'd rather give Grant a chance to explain . . . while I behave as if I can't get it otherwise. Then I'll want to see how his story compares with the real one."

"Clever," April murmurs. "But, as much as I do not care for Grant, I find Thierry a better suspect."

Yolanda's brows shoot up. "Based on what? The fact he flirted with Lynn? There's no evidence they did more than flirt."

"He fits the physical description as well," April says. "Which also matches Sebastian, and I believe that is significant. The killer is framing someone who could be mistaken for them, in case they were spotted."

"I'd like to roll back to motive," Anders says. "If we think it's the same person who attacked Kendra, then it would seem to be random. Choosing whoever took the drink at the Roc. Choosing whoever was out alone in the storm. But the fact that Lynn was also at that table, getting the same drink, might argue otherwise."

"How?" April says. "If they all had the same drink, there was no way of knowing which would go to Lynn."

"I've considered the possibility they were all dosed." I turn to Yolanda. "I meant to ask you about that. How did you feel that night?"

She takes a sip of coffee before answering. "I'm not sure. I have thought about that. I only drank half of mine, and looking back, I fell straight to sleep, which isn't normal for me. But I wasn't going to mention it because it sounds like paranoia."

"But it was Kendra who was grabbed," April says. "If the target was Lynn, and her killer dosed all the drinks, why take the wrong woman?"

Yolanda shrugs. "A mistake? As someone with some face blindness, I can tell you they're of a similar build. I wouldn't make that mistake face-to-face—even with my condition, I can tell a brown person from a white one, but at night, bundled up . . . ?"

"Except they also live in different residences," Anders says. "Kendra was grabbed going into hers. That argues *against* the killer making a mistake. I think it was random. The fact our second victim was also at the table is a coincidence."

I clear my throat. "All that is to say we need to look at all possibilities."

Dalton comes in the front door. "Well, that's done. How's it going in here?"

"Wrapping up," I say. "I'd like to speak to Grant. Is he still in custody?"

"He is."

I'm alone with Grant. That seems best for this conversation. Dalton joins me long enough for Grant to vent his frustration at being under house arrest. Dalton says he'll be allowed out tomorrow morning. He frames it as a courtesy for the grieving husband, but really it's for Anders and the others. Needing someone to guard Grant at all times would pull them away from protecting the town at large.

And what if Grant really is the one we're protecting them from? Well, if Grant killed Lynn, it was personal, and that's not likely to endanger anyone else.

Once Grant gets that promise of freedom, he's ready for our interview. Of course, after I tell him what he needs to know, we cycle back to complaints.

"So my wife *was* murdered? What happened to promising us safety? That's why we came to this backwoods shithole. To keep her safe."

I struggle not to flinch. I've heard this before. Every time someone died in Rockton—or was in danger—this became the discourse. How could that happen in a place that guaranteed safety?

I could point out it wasn't a guarantee. The entry process is extremely clear on that, so residents can make informed decisions.

But when something goes wrong, it feels like breaking a promise. Like when someone dies in a car accident despite wearing a seat belt. Or drowns in a boating accident despite wearing a PFD. Isn't that why we endure the inconvenience and discomfort of those safety measures?

Those things do make us much safer. Coming to Haven's Rock makes people much safer. But it's a matter of degrees, not absolutes. In a time of crisis and grief, though, no one needs to hear that. It puts the blame back on them for accepting a less-than-perfect solution.

"We are investigating all the safety measures that could have prevented this," I say. "On that note, though, I do need to ask about why you came here. I know that's confidential, and of course I can't force you to answer, but I am asking. In case it proves relevant."

"I thought that's why we went through all that cloak-and-dagger stuff. To be sure no one could follow her here."

"The chance of that happening is infinitesimal. While again, I can't say no one could *ever* track a resident here, the storm makes that particularly unlikely."

"What about a resident coming on false pretenses?" He waves off my protest. "Yeah, yeah, I know there's a system and an investigation, but what if someone offers your investigator a million bucks to falsify documents?"

"There's a fail-safe. Everything is thoroughly verified by a second party. If there is even the slightest concern, the application is denied."

"What about the person who makes the final decision? What if they're bribed?"

I shake my head. "Financially, they're bulletproof. However, that's why I'm asking about Lynn's story. To determine whether it might be worth extreme measures to kill her. Also, given the way she died, I'm wondering whether her story might have compelled someone to enact a form of twisted justice."

"Fuck." Grant slams back against the wall as he shakes his head.

"Grant . . ."

"She thought she was doing the right thing. That was the problem. She had this very . . ." He gestures, as if unable to find words. ". . . *rigid* sense of right and wrong. I told her it was going to get her in trouble someday, but even when it did, she didn't see that she'd done anything wrong."

He rubs one temple. "And she didn't. What she did *was* the right thing, but sometimes, you need to protect yourself, you know? Stick your nose where it doesn't belong and someone's going to bite it off. That's what my mother always said, and Lynn could never understand that."

Before I can comment, his head jerks up. "Look at Dana and her kids. Look at what they've suffered because Dana and her husband couldn't just keep quiet. Now he's dead, and she's permanently injured, and they're stuck here. For what? If you see something you shouldn't see, keep your damn mouth shut. Mind your own fucking business. But when I told Lynn that—look, here's proof of how bad it can get when you stick your neck out—what did she do? Started thinking Dana's story can't be that simple. Sticking her nose into *that*. Surely your husband wouldn't be murdered for doing the right thing. There must be more to it."

He looks at me sharply. "Someone put a fucking bomb in Lynn's car, and she still didn't think she was in real danger. To her, it was just a warning. She said it didn't go off because it wasn't supposed to, not because the fucking guy screwed up. She would not listen to reason, so if you're asking whether she would have told someone what she did? Yeah. Because she was so sure she'd done the right thing."

"Which was . . ."

He throws up his hands. "Sticking her nose where it didn't belong. She worked for this lawyer, a lot of rape cases and whatnot, and Lynn discovered this doctor had been bought off. Big-name guy, did a lot of expert-witness stuff. Was that wrong? Of course it was, but it wasn't her job to rat him out. Let someone else do that. It wasn't her job to get involved. But she swore nothing bad would happen to her. And it did, didn't it?" His voice cracks. "I told her it would, and I was right, and I wish to God I wasn't."

I'd told Anders, April, and Yolanda that I only wanted Lynn's backstory to see whether Grant would tell the truth. I didn't actually think it could be a lead. Was I wrong? I don't think so. I still can't see how that would lead to her murder. Down south, yes, to silence her. Up here? The "damage" was done, at least in the eyes of the person she accused.

Dana's husband was murdered because they bore witness to a murder. That was pure vengeance—the person they accused had already died in jail. But there's no point in chasing a whistleblower. The whistleblower only initiates the investigation, and nothing they retract will change the outcome.

What if Lynn told someone here what she'd done? Even bragged about it? That's not grounds for murder.

I'll need to confirm this story with Émilie, but my time is ticking. I'm reminded of that when I step outside and look up. I don't like the color of that sky, but the cloud cover has lifted. Dalton is going to be eyeing the clock—and the number of hours of daylight. It's already late morning. I'm guessing I have about two more hours before he declares it's time to go.

Before I interviewed Grant, I'd sent a message to Émilie requesting a meeting. She might be elderly, but she's not sitting in her rocker beside the phone. In this case, I'm not sure talking to her is the most efficient use of my waning time. I could do that from Whitehorse more easily, and do it via video. But she's replied to say she's available, so I take the phone into the town hall and make the call.

I tell her what's happened to Lynn. I also tell her that Dalton and I need to go to Whitehorse for the duration of my pregnancy. I approach the former with far more care than April did with Yolanda, but Yolanda is her grandmother's child, and I know better than to leave out details.

It takes a few moments for Émilie to recover from the shock and horror of Lynn's fate, but when she hears why I'm leaving, she's quick to agree. Anders, April, and Yolanda are more than capable of handling the situation, however much I might hate leaving a killer uncaught.

As for Lynn's background . . .

"Grant was telling the truth," she says. "As Lynn said, she worked for a law firm that took a particular interest in sexual assault survivors. Of course, that is mostly civil litigation against offenders. There's no money to be made simply helping survivors."

Sadly true. A survivor or victim of crime can retain a lawyer, but that's mostly for support. Technically, the prosecution is their advocate.

Émilie continues, "In the course of her job, Lynn learned that a psychiatrist expert witness was taking bribes. He was providing testimony that set the accused free. The man was exceptionally well known and well regarded, and seems to have been above reproach for most of his career, but then, with retirement looming, he got greedy."

"And realized he could leverage his reputation to pad out his retirement plan."

"Yes. The problem, of course, was that this man had done a lot of good earlier in his career. His list of supporters was long and vaunted, and they could not believe such allegations. I'm sure you know how that goes."

"They called the accusations a smear campaign," I say. "Someone wants to take this poor doctor down and paid Lynn to do it. Or, even if he did do these things, his reputation should absolve him. Forget that rapists were set free. The doctor screwed up, but he should be forgiven based on his illustrious career. Everyone makes mistakes."

"Exactly. The vitriol against Lynn was breathtaking. Or, it was to me, though you might not have been as shocked. She received rape threats, death threats, and a bomb in her car, as Grant said. I reached out and offered sanctuary, and I believe it was Grant who talked her into it."

"The same Grant who grumbled constantly about being forced to come here because of her? The same Grant who apparently also supported her by having an affair during that whole mess, 'cause it was stressful, you know. For him."

Émilie sighs. "Grant is an ass, and from what you've already told me, he was likely psychologically abusive. This is one of the issues I didn't consider with letting in couples."

"We focused on signs of physical abuse."

"Yes. Back when my husband and I took refuge in Rockton, couples were allowed, obviously. I will be blunt and say that, back then, we did not really consider spousal abuse an issue."

"It was a different time, as they say."

"*Serious* abuse would have been a concern, but otherwise, it was seen like spanking your children. Distasteful but nobody else's business. The problem, I fear, going forward, is that in a case like this, I'm not sure what we would have done. I doubt you would have refused to let Lynn into Haven's Rock because her husband was psychologically abusive. Even if he'd been physically abusive and she insisted he come with her . . ."

Now it's my turn to sigh. "In trying to make Haven's Rock better, we've opened ourselves up to a million more moral and ethical dilemmas, haven't we?"

"We'll figure them out. For now, the unhappy marriage only gives Grant motive for murder. I don't suppose he's hinted at leaving early?"

"He's done more than hint. Since they were here for Lynn and she's gone, he wants to leave. He's been very clear on that, which gives him a definite motive for murder."

"It does indeed."

Émilie and I only talk for a few more minutes, mostly nailing down any potential problems with Dalton and me leaving mid-investigation. While residents sign a zillion forms absolving us of all liability, that's mostly for show.

What if someone is injured by the killer while Dalton and I are away and the victim threatens to go to the authorities? Émilie would certainly try to buy their silence, but if they refused that, it doesn't matter whether those forms protect us from liability—Haven's Rock would be exposed. More importantly, are we in breach of duty by having *both* me and Dalton leave? I'm the one with the health emergency.

Émilie doesn't see an issue. Unlike Dalton, Anders has formal training from his experience in military policing. Leaving our deputy in charge of the investigation works, and with such a small town, we have more than enough staff for security.

After that call, it's time to interview Thierry again. I've been postponing this one in hopes of finding more to use. Hell, I'd settle for proof that he was having an affair with Lynn. I just need leverage. Otherwise, I'm asking the same questions in hopes of spooking him into slipping up.

That's what I do. I ask the same questions, hammering particularly on his whereabouts the day of the storm. He does start to sweat, quite literally perspiring. Is that a sign of guilt? Not necessarily. When the police keep harping on the same points, a suspect begins to worry that we're about to reveal the big gotcha.

Tell me again where you were the night of the murder. Are you sure? Absolutely sure? Well, then explain why you were seen . . .

I push hard, but all he does is sweat, which could mean he's guilty or could just mean he's worried about being framed for a crime he didn't commit.

I've arranged for Anders to come by twenty minutes into the interview. That lets him tell Thierry that he'll be taking over and do a bit of posturing.

Casey's leaving, but I'm in charge now. I'll be keeping an eye on you. She's told me everything. If you're seen talking to a woman or setting foot in the Roc or stepping outside the town boundaries, you're being shipped south for a proper interrogation.

We leave Thierry and head out into the cold, as I pull my scarf up higher against the wind.

"You get anywhere with him?" Anders asks.

"Nope. He's sticking to his story, even under threat."

"Hmm. I will definitely keep my eye on him, but I suspect the guy's only crime was some gentle flirting with a married woman."

I don't answer. I agree, but I don't want to influence his investigation.

"Also," Anders says, "Eric's over at the hangar getting the plane ready. He says you've got about another hour."

"I shouldn't even need that much. I just have one more stop, and then I'm ready to go."

"We'll figure this out," Anders says.

When I don't answer, he says, "You need to leave, Case. If you don't and anything goes wrong with the baby, you'll blame yourself, whether leaving could have helped or not."

I nod.

He squeezes my shoulder. "You go, relax and have a baby, and when you come back with the little one, everything here will be quiet." He glances over at me. "Note that I said everything *here* will be quiet. Your house will be another story. Non-stop crying and fussing . . . and that's before the baby chimes in. You're going to be itching for a crime to solve, to get out of the house."

"Just make it a small crime. Maybe a nice theft. We—" I see Mathias stalking from the butcher shop ahead. "And there's my interview target. Let me talk to him, and I'll catch up with you before we leave."

"Have fun!" Anders calls as I stride to catch up with Mathias.

CHAPTER TWENTY-TWO

"Mathias!" I call. "I need to speak to you."

I'm speaking in French, but he keeps walking. I repeat it in English.

Then, "Mathias! If you fucking make me run after you in my condition, I swear I will see you evicted from this damn town no matter what goddamn blackmail you threaten me with."

He turns slowly, his expression impassive. "You have been with your husband too long. You are starting to sound like him, all profanity and empty threats."

"You think that's an empty threat?" I stride closer. "Try me, Mathias. I understand you're protective of Sebastian—"

"I am not 'protective' of anyone. I am angered that you are the victim of very obvious framing and do not see it."

I plant myself in front of him. "Do you honestly think I'm not very aware that someone seems to be framing Sebastian? If I wasn't, he'd be coming south with us. His medication was used to dose Kendra. His lure was found in Lynn's drawer. And an eyewitness claims to have seen him with Lynn during the

storm. I would be a shitty detective if I didn't suspect he's being framed, and I'd be an inept one if I *presumed* he was being
framed and didn't question him. Now I don't know what's gotten into you, but I need you to stand down."

He crosses his arms. Then he says, "How are you feeling? I
know it has been a difficult pregnancy."

"If you are implying that baby brain is affecting my ability to
investigate, just say so. If you are implying that hormones are
making me blow up at you, go to hell."

"I am simply asking after your health," he says mildly.

"Yeah? Then you're trying to lower my guard. You don't
give a shit."

"*Non,* Casey," he says. "I do give a shit. I also give a shit that
someone seems to have . . ." His gaze flits about. While we're
speaking French, that doesn't mean a passerby couldn't hear and
understand our conversation. There's no one around—I made
sure of that—but when he checks, I wave toward the butcher
shop.

"Go inside," I say. "I have something to discuss with you,
and it seems you have something to discuss with me."

Mathias takes me up to his apartment. "Sebastian is out," he
says before I can ask. "He is with the boys and Gunnar, playing
some sort of board game in the community center." He glances
back. "I presume he is still allowed around children."

I don't even dignify that with a glare. We head inside, and
he waves me to a seat.

"You first," I say. "You said you give a shit that someone
seems to have . . ."

"Do you think Sebastian was targeted at random, Casey?"

I ignore the patronizing tone. He's still in a mood, and if he pokes me any more, I'll switch to English. That'll teach him.

"No," I say. "I have two leading theories on that. The main one is that he was targeted by someone of a roughly similar build, so that if the killer is seen with a victim, while wearing winter garb, Sebastian will fit. Considering that's exactly what happened—someone resembling Sebastian was seen with Lynn during the storm—that's a strong theory. My second possibility is that he was targeted because of the temazepam. If the same person who killed Lynn also dosed Kendra's drink, then it's likely they heard something to suggest Sebastian had strong sleeping medication. Once they stole that, Sebastian became the patsy, who would continue to be framed."

Mathias's grunt allows that this is decent detective work. Then he says, "And the third theory? There is another, perhaps stronger. Something that makes Sebastian the perfect target."

"The fact that he's a convicted killer? Or the fact he's a diagnosed sociopath?" I adjust my posture as the baby decides now's a fine time to start punching me. "I've considered those, but I can't think of any way for someone to get that information. Core staff knows it, but that's a very limited number of people. There's no record of it for someone to stumble over. Sebastian's not going to raise it in conversation. Neither are you. So unless you're telling me you got drunk and told someone . . . or let it slip in pillow talk . . . ?"

He only gives me a hard look.

I throw up my hands. "Then since that's clearly your theory—that someone knows he's a sociopath—how do you envision someone getting that information?"

"Too many people know." He crosses his arms again. "I do not like it."

"That was Sebastian's choice."

"Perhaps someone wrote it down."

"Wrote down that Sebastian is a sociopath? Someone needed to make a note because they were liable to forget it? Also, except for Will, Eric, and me, the staff only know about the sociopathy. Not the murder conviction."

Mathias leans back in his seat. "I am only asking."

"There's one person who might need to write something down about Sebastian. You, Mathias."

Silence.

I lean forward. "Do you have notes on Sebastian's past? His condition?"

"*Non.*" Another hesitation, and I let it drag on until he says, "I have some treatment notes, but nothing that would clearly state his condition or his crime."

"Could they be inferred?"

"I do not think so."

"That's not exactly heartening."

He folds one leg up over his knee. "The papers are very secure, and I see no sign they have been touched."

"But someone did enter your apartment—possibly twice—to steal from Sebastian's room, which he didn't notice. Neither of you realized anyone broke in, right?"

"*Non.*"

"Then I think I'd like to see where you keep those papers."

"I am going to need to relocate them now," Mathias complains as I return the locked box under the floorboard.

"You should anyway," I say. "Have you never read a single mystery novel? Watched a single mystery film?" I shake my head. "I suppose I should be glad you didn't shove them under the mattress."

"I tried, but the box made a terrible lump, and I could not sleep."

I put the floorboard down. "I agree there's no sign it was tampered with. Even if someone found it in that ridiculously obvious spot, the contents are about as secure as you can get." There's a key lock on the outer box and a combination on the inner one.

"*Merci.*"

"However . . ." I give him a look. "Someone determined to get into it could just take the whole box and figure out how to pry it open. We have a safe in the town hall. I would suggest you store it there."

I take some time struggling back to my feet, noting no offer of help from Mathias. "I will consider the possibility that Sebastian was targeted because someone found out about his past, and I'll pass on the tip to Will."

"Do you expect William to solve this case? He is a fine police officer, but he is not a detective."

"I'll be continuing to work on it remotely, through him. Now, as for my question . . ." I wave him back into the living room so I can sit. "I don't know how much you've heard about Lynn's death."

"That she was apparently left in the forest during the storm, where she became lost and perished of hypothermia. Sebastian also heard a rumor that she was not simply lost, but tied up and left there."

I tell him the full story. When I finish, he's quiet. Very quiet. I can't read his reaction. He seems to just sit there and consider what I've said.

I continue, "I'd like to ask a bit about the psychology of that. It's sadistic, obviously."

"*Is* that obvious?" He gives me a sidelong look. "It would depend on whether the killer believed Lynn had done something for which this was a fitting punishment."

From what I understand of Mathias's past, this was his own modus operandi. Horrible deaths that he considered justice for the crimes committed.

I shake my head. "No resident gets in without a full background check, and no one gets in who's running from crimes they committed. I know why Lynn was here and I've confirmed it with Émilie. No one is going to punish her for that. Of course it's possible there's something else in her past that someone might punish her for. Something involving hypothermia? Maybe she got lost with a friend and left that friend to freeze to death?"

"That would not be justification for killing her in such a manner."

I'd say nothing is justification for what was done to Lynn, but I keep my mouth shut and let him continue.

"In order for her to deserve such a fate, she would need to have done something such as abandon her friend, taking all the supplies and not telling rescuers where to find her companion. Which, yes, is a highly manufactured scenario. Another possibility might be if, as a teenager, Lynn had a baby and abandoned it to die. Now, that is certainly not justifiable cause to punish her—she would have been panicked and acting irrationally—but someone could . . ."

He sees my expression, and that my hands have instinctively moved to my belly.

"That was inconsiderate of me," he says. "I apologize. There is little point in guessing at what Lynn might have done to make someone think she deserved to die in such a manner. But yes, she might have done something and her killer might have decided it deserved such a death. The stronger possibility is, as you say, sadism, which is the real reason you are here and not to ask why someone might consider that a justifiable fate."

His gaze rests on me, his piercing look suggesting he knows there was some of that in my question, too.

He continues, "Such a murder suggests extreme sadism. They did not simply abandon her. They did not simply tie her up. They did not even simply strip her down and tie her up. They watched. That was the point. The watching."

"Watching her slowly die, freezing to death, screaming for help that wouldn't come."

"Yes. So who does such a thing? We can talk of psychopaths and sociopaths and the difference ad nauseam, but as you doubtless realize, this is not sociopathy as we see with Sebastian, who might kill to achieve an end."

"But if someone did frame Sebastian because they knew he's a sociopath, they might not realize that."

"They likely would not. Or, even if they did understand the difference, would they expect *you* to know it? Or would you see evidence pointing to a sociopath and close the case?"

"So what are we looking for?"

He sighs and leans back in his chair. "Are you looking for me to play profiler, Casey? It is a game for fools and Hollywood detectives."

"I know profiling isn't the science we wanted to think it was. You can't tell me I'm looking for a white male between the ages of twenty-five and thirty-four."

His lips quirk. "But you probably are, as that is a simple matter of statistics. Yes, I can give you some insight into the mind of someone who might do such a thing. Just do not take it as gospel."

"I won't."

Mathias tells me what he can. He's right that profiling isn't what we see in the movies. There can be value in it, but the way it's portrayed makes it seem like hard science.

We can't only blame Hollywood either. Hollywood seized on an idea that was already popular in law enforcement. What if you could take crimes and extrapolate backward to come up with a profile of the killer? That works best if you're saying that the person who killed Lynn is a sadist and getting clues about their personality from that. It does not work well if you decide that the method of her murder is symbolic and suggests they grew up with maternal attachment issues and felt "left out in the cold" by their mother.

As for things like "white male between twenty-five and thirty-four," as Mathias said, that's just statistics. It's like saying that someone committing a sexual assault is probably male. Probably, yes. Absolutely? No.

The most important thing Mathias tells me is that this is unlikely to be a first offense. You don't start with something this horrific. It's probably not even a valid jump from "tortured small animals as a child" to this.

If this is pure sadism, we're looking for a serial killer, at least in the sense of someone who has killed before.

Here is yet another problem we're discovering in Haven's Rock. Just because there's no record—or even suspicion—of a resident having committed violent crimes does not mean they've never done it.

What's the chance that, in our first batch of residents, we've let in a serial killer with no police record? One who has never even been questioned in connection with violent crimes? It must be exceptionally low. My vengeance theory makes more sense.

Mathias walks out with me. Then he continues on to the coffee shop while I stop to say a quick goodbye to Nicole as she passes with Stephen. Finally, I start making my way toward the hangar, presuming Dalton will be there with Storm and our luggage.

Shit. I wanted to ask Mathias something else.

I turn to see him in the distance. He's bundled up, but I pick him out easily from the others. He's a slight man, not terribly tall, walking with purpose . . .

I slow as I watch him. A slight man below average height. A man I believe has a history of enacting vicious punishments he considers justified.

"Detective Casey?" a voice says, and I turn to see Carson walking toward me.

I force myself to shift mental gears. "Hey, I heard you guys were playing a board game. How'd it go?"

The boy shrugs. "I got bored and let myself lose." He motions down, and I see Raoul tagging along. "I said I was taking the dog for a walk." He looks back at me. "Do you have a sec? Before you leave? There's something . . ." He shrugs again, now in a way that suggests he's uncomfortable. The language of a teenager—every shrug and grunt and eye roll having its own meaning.

"Something you need to speak to me about?"

Another shrug. "Maybe? It's probably nothing, but if you leave, and I don't say anything?" He glances away. "I'd rather not do that again."

When Max went missing, his brother had withheld details, not for long, but enough that his teenage ennui had fallen away to reveal the young man under it, panicked and guilt-stricken.

"Sure, let's pop into the town hall. I should sit for a minute anyway."

CHAPTER TWENTY-THREE

"I was outside during the storm," Carson says, even before we get our boots off. "I snuck out. That's why I didn't say anything earlier." He pauses. "If I had information that was definitely useful, I'd have come forward. But since it didn't seem useful, there was no point getting in trouble."

I lead him to the chairs, and we both sit.

He continues, "I'm still not sure it's useful, but I feel like I need to say something, and if I catch shit, then I catch shit."

"While I can't guarantee your mother won't find out," I say, "I see no reason at this point to tell her."

"But if it leads to an arrest, I'd need to testify."

He speaks calmly, but his face is taut with tension. Yes, of course. He's in Haven's Rock because his parents were eyewitnesses to a murder. His father died because of it.

"Absolutely not," I say. "I will never reveal anything you said to anyone here. If we believe someone committed a crime like murder, they'd be taken home. Any punishment would happen there, and that's where they'd get the chance to defend themselves, but no one up here would be involved—or even *could* be involved, for privacy. Our only concern is the danger people pose to other residents. Once they're gone, they aren't our problem."

"Okay, that makes sense." He toys with the seam on his jeans. "I guess me worrying about making Mom mad seems like a very small thing, considering what happened to Lynn. I wouldn't keep quiet just to avoid getting in trouble. But Mom . . . She has nightmares about Max going missing, and if I admitted I slipped out during a storm . . . She doesn't need that."

And she definitely doesn't need to learn that her son may have been eyewitness to an abduction leading to murder. The echoes to her own past will mean—between that and memories of Max's disappearance—she might never sleep again.

"Whatever information you have, I will do what I can to avoid telling your mother. Teens sneaking out is just . . ." I shrug. "Part of being a teen. But after Max's kidnapping, it's different for her."

"I really *would* have come forward sooner if I thought what I saw was helpful."

I want to hug him for that. In spite of what happened to his parents, he still wanted to do the right thing. That takes unbelievable courage. Of course, the last thing he wants is a hug, so I settle for an encouraging smile.

He continues, "It was during the whiteout. Max was playing on the Switch, and Mom was napping. I got bored, and I was looking at the storm and wondering what it was like to be out there. We've mostly lived in places that don't have snow. Sheriff Eric gave us that talk about blizzards and whiteouts and snow blindness, but it sounded weird. The idea that you couldn't actually see anything. It's just snow. I wanted to see what it was like."

He looks at me. "I was very careful because I knew if I even got a little lost, Mom would have a heart attack. I put on my winter stuff in the hall and slipped out. I just walked around the building, while keeping one hand on it."

"Good," I say. "Because you really can get lost out there."

"Yeah, I saw that. The wind was whipping the snow around, and at one point, I couldn't even *see* the building. If I wasn't touching it, I'd have been screwed. But then, the wind died down for a second, and there was someone there. Like maybe fifteen feet away. Two people walking."

"Did they see you?"

"Nah, they had their backs to me. They were heading the other way. Then the wind came up again, and I couldn't see them. I didn't think much of it. Just people getting home in the storm. But then I heard someone say Lynn had been spotted with a guy, and I started wondering whether that's who I'd seen. Except, even if it was, you already had that information, and I couldn't add anything. I just saw two figures, one a lot bigger than the other, like a man and a woman. He seemed to be holding her arm, but not restraining her or anything. Just helping her along."

"What can you tell me about them?"

He shrugs. "Nothing, really. Just that it was two people that I automatically thought were a man and woman. Wearing the usual stuff we all do. I didn't take a good look."

"Lynn wears a very distinctive scarf. Did you see that?"

He shakes his head. "Whoever it was, she had her back to me."

I hesitate. "So you didn't see her scarf tied around her neck?"

Now he's frowning. "She wears it inside, like most of us. Which I know because I mistook her for Mom once, which was really awkward."

"Were you behind your residence or beside it?"

"Around back."

"And they were heading where exactly?"

"I was coming around clockwise, and they were up ahead of me. I figured they were going to the residence next to ours."

Which they might have been. Two people in the storm, unrelated to Lynn's disappearance, just heading home, as he figured. Otherwise . . .

I need to give this more thought. For now, though, I thank Carson and send him on his way, and then it's time for me to go.

Talking in a plane is never easy. A small plane means there's little chance of speaking without our headsets, but even with those, it's too much effort for a conversation. With Dalton being the pilot, I'm never keen to divert his focus at the best of times, and this isn't the best of times.

While it's an easy takeoff and the cloud cover is well overhead, he's focused on distant dark clouds. Very distant and not very dark, meaning any bad weather is far enough off.

Storm is in the back, having been trained to stay there so she doesn't interfere with the pilot. I glance back at her. She's an experienced flier, but not necessarily a happy one. I offer her a smile, and then I let myself fall into my thoughts. While I'm technically the copilot, this small plane doesn't need that. I was in the process of learning to fly when morning sickness derailed me. I'll still get my license—it'd be good to have another pilot, besides Dalton and Phil. For now, Dalton will let me know if he needs my eyes.

I'm deep in my thoughts when I see his lips moving. I check my headset. It's on. I just can't hear him, which means—coupled with the fact that he isn't looking my way—that he's talking to someone on the radio.

I look out the window. Snow, trees, more snow. It's gorgeous landscape, particularly after the storm, but there's nothing to see except that landscape, no sign of civilization in sight. Mountains. Frozen lakes. Endless green conifers. Anything that looks like a road is just a creek or river.

I peer at the sky. It's dark to the southwest, which is where we're flying, but it's clear here. I glance at Dalton. He's still talking, but I can see his expression now. It's grim, a little angry, his lips forming curt, clipped words. He nods, as if pushing back his annoyance. He says something more and then hits a button to end the transmission.

Then he hits another to open the communication between us.

"Got a problem," he says. "Cloud cover's dropping in Whitehorse. Storm's blowing in. They're suggesting we redirect to Dawson." A pause, at least five seconds long. Then a quick glance my way. "What do you want to do?"

"Divert to Dawson City or push on to Whitehorse?"

He shakes his head, attention back on the cockpit window. "I wouldn't take the risk of pushing on. I mean head to Dawson or turn back?"

I consider that. Dawson City is the second-biggest urban center in the Yukon. Except, at barely over a thousand people, "urban center" is pushing it. Yet it has a regional health facility. Even then, it's not as if I'm in imminent danger of having this baby tonight. We're looking at a day or two at most in Dawson, and then pushing on to Whitehorse to resume the plan.

"Dawson's good," I say.

He nods, and it's a little abrupt.

I lean to see his face. "That's not your choice."

"No, it is. I just . . ."

He trails off and refocuses on flying. I let him do that and wait to see whether more is coming. When it's not, I decide to table the conversation until he's not at the controls of a plane. If he had concerns about landing in Dawson, he'd say so. I'm guessing he's just annoyed about not being able to get to Whitehorse today. He'll feel a lot better once I'm minutes from a hospital.

He switches to the outgoing radio to make plans with the Dawson City airport. We deal with them a lot, and he knows most of the people who work there. I let myself drift into my thoughts as the plane takes a slight turn west.

It's about thirty minutes later when I'm roused from my thoughts by Dalton shifting in his seat. There's a crackle in the air, as if I can sense his annoyance again, and I glance over to see him back on the radio. I frown. We should be getting close to Dawson. Is there a . . . ?

I see the problem. Right outside the windshield.

We've started our descent, and we're flying straight into a snowstorm.

I glance at Dalton but push down the urge to signal him. Do not pester the pilot. He's on the radio, presumably with the Dawson City airport.

I turn my attention back to the windows, and my stomach does a little flip as the snow rushes at us.

"I've got this," Dalton says, his sudden voice making me jump.

I look over. He reaches to squeeze my leg before taking the yoke again. His gaze never leaves the front window.

"It's just a little squall," he says. "I can fly us down. Helps that we have a better plane now."

I force a smile at that, even though he can't see it. The bush plane we had in Rockton was fine but old, and this is an upgrade, with the latest tech. Courtesy of Émilie, of course. It's not her fancy Cessna TTx—that would draw too much attention. But it's a solid and modern aircraft, and a "little squall" isn't going to stop Dalton from being able to land.

"I'm just pissed off at myself," he says. He flips a switch and checks a screen. "We shouldn't have left. You didn't want to. You didn't need to. This was on me."

"No, Eric, it wasn't. April agreed—"

"April agreed for my sake. Because I'm freaking out at the chance of losing you. I just never . . . I never really understood the risks, and I know no pregnancy is risk-free, and maybe I'd still be freaking out if we were living in Vancouver and you didn't have any prior issues but . . . I let my fucking insecurities take over when we should have stayed in town."

"You've got this," I say.

He flips another switch. "The landing? Yeah. I've got that. What I don't have is my damn shit together and the fucking common sense not to make things worse because I'm panicking over getting you someplace safe."

I reach over and touch his leg. "Leaving was the right choice. Will said if something went wrong with the pregnancy and I hadn't left, I'd never forgive myself, even if leaving wouldn't have helped. He's right. I wanted to stay. I needed to leave. We made the right call."

"Now land the damn plane?"

"Please."

The window shows nothing but driving snow, and I'm really trying not to worry about that. If I squint, I can see treetops below. Dalton's back on the radio, and he's switched it so I can listen in. I appreciate that. I keep quiet, and I listen as the air traffic controller helps guide us in.

Landing in a snowstorm introduces the triple threat of poor visibility, high winds, and an icy runway. It helps that this is a northern airport, where runways can be icy for most of the year. It also helps that Dalton is a northern pilot—even when the skies are clear when he takes off, he might be landing in a flurry. That doesn't mean this is easy or that there aren't a few times when I close my eyes and wrap my hands around my belly, as if that will help. But in the end, it's as perfect a touchdown as we could hope for.

The plane idles on the runway. The air traffic controller gives final instructions, telling us to take our time. We're parked, and there's no one else coming in behind us.

Catch our breath, she means. Take a moment and just breathe.

We're doing that when Dalton blurts, "I don't want to do this again, Casey."

I'm silent for a moment. Then I say, carefully, "I'm guessing you don't mean flying in a snowstorm."

"Fuck." He presses his hands to his face and rocks forward. "I'm sorry. This is not the time."

"No." I twist to lay my hand on his arm. "Say what you need to say, Eric. You don't want more kids."

"I . . . I don't know about that. Maybe? Maybe not? I just mean, if we did want more, I don't want to do this again. I'd rather adopt or foster or . . . something else."

"Okay."

"I don't want to play Russian roulette with birth control again. I want to make sure. I want to have a—" He takes a deep breath. "Fuck. This really isn't the time. I'm sorry."

"No, I get it."

He looks over, his gray eyes cloudy. "You get that you married a selfish asshole with serious abandonment issues who melts down over a pregnancy?"

I inch over to hug him as best I can in the cockpit. "No, I get that you don't want me to die, which is a good thing."

He gives a tight laugh. "Better than the alternative?"

"Much better." I hug him again. "Seriously, though. Remember how I said, if anything went wrong and there was a choice between saving me or the baby, I want you to make that decision? That's the way they used to do it. The husband decided. I heard stories of men who chose the baby and . . ."

My chest clenches. "I gave you that choice for two reasons. One, because I don't trust myself not to choose the baby. Two, because I trust you to choose *me*. I cannot imagine those husbands who let their wives die to save their newborn child. If you don't want me doing this again because you're afraid of losing me, then we don't do it again. We'll have one child—which, honestly, might be more than enough—or we'll come up with other solutions. Okay?"

He lifts me out of my seat and pulls me onto his lap and answers with a long hug.

CHAPTER TWENTY-FOUR

We're in Dawson City. Getting there isn't as easy as it might seem. The airport is fifteen kilometers from downtown, and there's no car rental agency. Taxi service is nonexistent off-season. Luckily, we do business here so often that we have a car stored nearby with people willing to make a few bucks driving us to it.

By the time we reach our hotel, the snow has died down enough for us to stash our bags in our hotel room and take Storm for a walk.

As much as we love Haven's Rock, it's wonderful to escape it now and then. Oh, sure, it's nice to see a different landscape and tread new trails and indulge in all the luxuries of urban life. Hot running water! Fresh veggies in winter! More than one restaurant to choose from! But mostly, I enjoy the chance to just be a woman out for a walk with her guy and her dog. We aren't "in charge" here. We can be ordinary and invisible people, and that is glorious.

We walk from one end of the town to the other. That sounds more impressive if I don't admit it's about a mile. Dawson City is a unique town. Some might say "odd," but in the Yukon, that goes without saying. Dawson is known for its role in the Klondike gold rush and all the ways the town holds tight to that heritage, particularly for tourism.

There are only a handful of streets, in a near-perfect grid pattern. Along the main ones, most of the buildings date back to the gold rush. Dirt roads. Wooden sidewalks. False-front buildings that look straight out of a Western.

This being the tourism off-season, a lot of the shops and restaurants are closed, but I can still get a decaf latte—made with real milk—and some bakery treats. We grab necessities for the night—cold drinks, water, snacks—and then head back to the hotel.

After spending the flight mulling over my case, I'm itching to talk to Émilie, but I don't want to make that call around Dalton. He'll be going out in an hour or so to pick up dinner, so I've only texted her to say I need to speak again. At the hotel, I indulge in a long hot bath in an actual bathtub. By the time I'm done, Dalton is ready to talk dinner. We do that and call in an order, and then he takes Storm to go get it, leaving me to phone Émilie.

"I need to ask about another resident's background," I say. "I don't need details on why he's in Haven's Rock. I won't ask for the story of everyone I consider a suspect."

"But you could, Casey," Émilie says, with obvious patience. "I know you and Eric think it's important not to know resident stories for their privacy, but I believe you are overthinking that. You are no longer council employees. This is *your* town."

"I know, but we feel better keeping that wall in place wherever possible. We promised them that no one in town would know their backstory unless absolutely necessary."

"And I have suggested we reword that to exclude management. But this is a discussion for another time. You and Eric have a suspect."

I hesitate. Then I say, "I have one, and I'm being especially careful because . . ." I inhale. "It feels like a long shot. Eric is friendly with this person. We both are. And they don't match the profile of someone who commits a murder like this, if we're looking at a serial killer."

"A what?"

I back up to tell her about my talk with Mathias.

"I understand the logic," she says, "but I think you're going to need to look more closely at this being a case of horrible revenge. The checks we perform are so thorough that I cannot imagine we've let in a serial killer. If my investigator finds *any* history of violence, they stop immediately and that person is removed from consideration."

"What if there's never been any recorded history?"

"How often does that happen, Casey? That a serial killer turns out to have no red flags in their past? Never been investigated, charged, or even disciplined in school for violence?"

"The chances are extremely slim. But I'm having a very hard time seeing this as a vengeance killing. Lynn did work in the justice system, and she was sure to have pissed people off, even without the whistleblowing. Let's say they reopened that expert's cases and some guy's not-guilty verdict is being questioned. Would that make him put a bomb in her car? Maybe. Would it make him somehow manage to track her down to Haven's Rock—despite all our precautions and security measures—sneak into town, find her, lure her out, and horribly murder her? No."

"Agreed. This isn't about vengeance for something she did down south. Now just tell me who you want to know about."

I take a deep breath. "Marlon."

"Marlon?"

At her tone, I wrap the hotel bathrobe as far as it'll stretch around my belly. "I know. He's a very unlikely suspect, which is why I'm being careful about saying anything in front of Eric. I like Marlon. We all do. I cannot imagine him doing something like this."

"But . . ."

"He was our only eyewitness. He says he saw Lynn being escorted by someone he believed to be Sebastian. He based his ID of Lynn on her scarf, which someone else has pointed out—correctly—that she wore inside her jacket. This other eyewitness says there was a greater height differential between the two figures—significant enough that they automatically identified it as a man and a woman, unlike Marlon's description."

I take a deep breath. "However, none of that means Marlon lied. If Lynn were in a hurry, she might have wrapped her scarf on the outside. The larger figure may have been hunched into the wind, making them look closer to Lynn's height when Marlon spotted them. And the second witness didn't see anything to identify the smaller figure as Lynn, which is why they didn't come forward—they thought they may have seen someone else."

"Yet now that the question has been raised, you need to investigate."

"Yes."

"Because you're a detective, Casey. And a damn good one who chases answers even when it's uncomfortable and inconvenient. All right then. I think I might be able to put your fears to rest easily, given Marlon's service record. He served nearly two decades in the military, only leaving it recently, and the majority of that time was spent overseas. I won't specify which branch he worked in or what he did, but it wasn't frontline. He worked in a support capacity. I don't know whether that makes a difference to your profiling—the fact he had a desk job."

"Was he traveling, though?" I ask. "That'd make it easy to hide a pattern of violence. Or a trail of victims."

"No, he was stationed in only a few places, and his records in all of them were spotless. He never married, but he did have a few long-term relationships, with no hints of trouble. I will still run deeper checks on the places he was stationed, looking for unsolved murders, but I would expect, if he were a serial killer, he would have requested more travel, which he did not. He preferred to settle into an area for as long as possible."

"What about the non-serial-killer option? Can we check for overlap between him and Lynn? When he was back home, did they live in the same region? Work in the same field? Is there any chance that he was connected to her job—as someone affected by her work. Could they have been here together by coincidence and he recognized her? Is there *anything* that might have brought them into contact?"

Clicking sounds across the line, as if she's typing. "At this stage in recruitment, we're actively avoiding residents from the same region. Of course, if we had two critical cases from the same area, I'd allow it, particularly if their trouble hadn't been newsworthy. But both Lynn's and Marlon's situations received local media coverage, which means I would have flagged a potential privacy issue. I am double-checking, though. . . . No, they lived nearly on opposite coasts. There's no overlap in employment. I will dig deeper, of course, and have my investigator do the same. But I think it might also help to know Marlon's story. I know you didn't want that."

I check my watch. Dalton will be back any moment. "If it will help, go ahead."

"I think it will, and I think it will also explain why I'm expressing significant doubt at the thought of him killing Lynn, certainly in such a way. Marlon had become involved with a woman. It was, in his words, a casual relationship. They met at work. This woman had recently left another relationship with a man who . . . While there was no clear history of abuse, her partner was known to be violent in general."

"Ah."

"He had a lengthy police record. When he discovered his ex-girlfriend was involved with Marlon, he went after Marlon. There were several encounters, one of which required police involvement, but the reports make it clear that Marlon did no more than defend himself. By this point, Marlon was no longer even seeing the woman. Yet the attacks continued. Then he was kidnapped at gunpoint by two men. He managed to escape. The ex-boyfriend had an alibi, and so he couldn't be charged, though my investigator says even the police have no doubt he ordered the kidnapping, which was likely a hired hit. Luckily, the men the ex-boyfriend hired were less than competent."

"They usually are."

"At that point, though, Marlon didn't want to rely on ineptitude to keep him safe. He reached out for help through another organization, which is where we found him."

"And the fact that he was the victim suggests he's not my killer," I say. "I'd agree with that assessment. I can't imagine someone coming up here to escape persecution that they could have resolved, which they could if they were a violent killer themselves."

"Yes. While Marlon was in the military, and he's certainly

physically capable of defending himself, he did only that. He defended himself when attacked. He escaped when kidnapped. But he did not seek to eliminate the threat, which I presume your killer would have."

A sound at the door, as if Dalton is there with his key card.

"Eric's back," I say. "I'll let you go. Thank you for this."

"I will check into overlap between Marlon and Lynn. Just in case. But I really don't expect to find anything."

Neither do I, but I appreciate her checking. I say so and sign off as Dalton comes in with dinner.

We eat on the bed while watching TV, which is another in-dulgent luxury of being away from home. Sure, we could eat in bed at Haven's Rock. We could even bring the laptop up to the bedroom and play a recorded show. But it's not the same as lounging in a king-size bed watching a giant screen and not worrying—apologies to the hotel staff—about getting pizza sauce on the sheets.

I have no urge to tell Dalton about my suspicions regarding Marlon. I've already sent Marlon back down the suspect ladder far enough that I'll only reconsider him if something comes up. So we eat pizza and watch TV, and then watch more TV, taking full advantage of having access to streaming services.

It's nine when my phone rings. Dalton has gone to take the pizza boxes downstairs to the trash, and when my cell shows a blocked number, I know it's Anders because we'd planned a pre-bedtime call. I also realize he doesn't know we aren't in White-horse.

I answer and start to explain, but he cuts me off with, "I already got the 411 from your husband. He called me on his way to grab pizza. I told him to send me one, but apparently, he didn't think the delivery drivers would travel this far."

"Kids these days. No sense of adventure."

"Yep. I'll just need to schedule a trip after you guys settle in with the little one." That's another huge advantage to Haven's Rock for our staff—they can actually take getaways and vacations.

Anders updates me on the situation in town, which I presume he'd also done with Dalton, though the version I get is slanted more toward the case rather than security measures. As for security, there's a dusk-to-dawn curfew in place as well as a buddy system that ensures someone has seen every resident both at the end of the day and the beginning. While they've had a bit of snow, there hasn't been a storm, but if one hits, it'll be a lockdown with those buddy checks in place.

As for the case . . . There's nothing for him to tell me. Everything has been quiet, and no one has come forward with extra information. On that note, though, I need to ask Anders to do something tomorrow.

"I did have a last-minute report of a couple being seen the day of the storm," I say. "It doesn't match Marlon's, which means they probably saw someone else. Can you and Yolanda canvass, though?" I give him the approximate time and location. "Just see whether two people were out at that time and place. They may not have mentioned it in interviews because they didn't see anything, but I'd like to strike this potential sighting off the list."

"Got it. Oh, and we've released Grant, but he's staying with Kenny. Is there anyone else you want us keeping an eye on?"

I hesitate. Then I say, "Between us? Mathias."

A long pause. Then, "That's not a joke, right? I mean, in general, I think we all need to keep an eye on Mathias, but you mean in conjunction with this case."

"It's a long shot, but he fits the basic figure of the person Marlon saw with Lynn, and he'd have access to easily frame Sebastian."

"If you've considered the possibility, we should keep an eye on him. I'll do it personally and keep mum. Anyone else?"

I hesitate. Do I mention Marlon? I've mostly dismissed him, but Anders just said that if I've considered a possibility, he needs to be aware of it. And yet . . . He's friends with Marlon. Do I risk damaging their relationship by pointing a finger?

No, the real question is whether I trust Anders to be a competent law-enforcement agent who can separate those things. The answer to that goes without question.

"Like I said, I have a potential witness sighting that contradicts Marlon's," I say. "So as much as I hate to even mention this . . ."

"Got it. No worries. Marlon's been helping with security, and that's keeping him front and center. Makes it easy to keep an eye on him."

I exhale. "Thank you. Again, it's a long shot, and I hated to mention it."

"Don't ever hesitate, Case. We've both had to suspect friends . . . and sometimes been right to do it, sadly. Everything's under control here. What time do you plan to fly out tomorrow?"

Dalton returns at that moment, and I put the phone on speaker as we discuss our plans for the next day.

CHAPTER TWENTY-FIVE

I can't stay asleep, and for once, it isn't the baby. During all this turmoil—landing in a snowstorm plus the stress over our change in plans—the pregnancy has been fine, the baby occasionally moving and kicking or punching with no cramping or other danger signs.

What keeps me from staying asleep is the case. I drift off easily enough, and I sleep soundly until nearly four. Then I have a nightmare where I know the culprit is Marlon, but I don't mention it to Anders, and Marlon goes on a killing spree, murdering Anders and April.

I startle awake and swear under my breath. None of that happened. I don't strongly suspect that Marlon killed Lynn, but I still *did* warn Anders. Everything is fine. It's my damn subconscious poking at me, my generalized fear that I've abandoned Haven's Rock to a killer.

But when I try to sleep again, it's not general anxiety that has me tossing and turning. It's Marlon. Have I dismissed him too quickly? Dismissed him because I don't *want* to consider him? His military service doesn't remove him from the profile.

If anything, it places him more firmly in it. Serial killers often aspire to military or paramilitary service, and while they don't necessarily get in, they may find adjacent careers.

The fact that Marlon joined security in Haven's Rock is a red flag, as is the fact that he socializes primarily with local law enforcement. That strengthens the paramilitary-interest aspect, but it also means he has a direct pipeline to any investigative efforts. And his military job gave him the ability to move around, which as I said could help him hide assaults or murders.

What about the situation that brought him here? It would seem, logically, that a violent person would retaliate with violence if they were being threatened. But is that faulty logic? If you were a serial killer being hunted by your girlfriend's violent ex, would you end the threat? Or would you duck and weave to avoid drawing too much interest from the police?

Marlon matches the size of the person Carson saw. By telling us he saw Lynn with Sebastian, Marlon could be redirecting us to the false suspect he'd chosen . . . and also removing himself from the suspect pool. He'd even solidified his "alibi" by hailing Grant and saying he'd seen Lynn.

Am I really considering Marlon as a suspect? Or is it just that middle-of-the-night phenomenon where even ridiculous fears seem reasonable?

I catch sight of my laptop on the desk. Then I slide out of bed, patting Storm when she rouses and whispering for her to go back to sleep.

I ease into the desk chair and turn my screen brightness down to the lowest setting before I flip on the browser.

Émilie gave me enough to look up Marlon's case, and she said it made the local news. If I find it, I find *him*—his real name—which goes against every assurance of privacy we give residents.

I should just ask Émilie to . . .

To do what? Keep digging? She said she would. But she clearly thinks I'm wrong. I need to do this myself, and I know I'll regret it later, but this is a breach of confidence I need to make.

I barely start before stress sweat trickles down my back. I move the chair so if Dalton wakes and I'm deep in my work, he won't see what I'm doing before I have the chance to Alt-Tab away. That launches a wave of guilt so overwhelming that nausea overtakes me, and I crawl back into bed and tell myself I am not doing this.

As I lie there, all I can see is Lynn dead on the ice, her eyes open.

They wouldn't have been open when she died, right? While she'd have screamed at first, eventually hypothermia would have set in. That's why we hadn't seen as much struggling as we might have expected—by the time she realized she was going to die, her mind would have already been wandering. She would—I expect and sincerely hope—have drifted off in a fog, overwhelmed by the need to sleep.

Her killer opened her eyelids. Opened them and looked into her eyes and left her like that.

I push up from bed. I need to find Lynn's killer. I need to make sure they don't do that to anyone else, and I need to make sure they don't get away with what they did to Lynn. If that means violating a resident's right to privacy, then I need to remember what Émilie said.

We are in charge here. We are not beholden to some faceless council and even more faceless investors. Our duty is to resident safety, which trumps privacy.

Back in Rockton, we'd thought nothing of researching a resident online if we needed to. Dalton had been doing that before I arrived. But that was because we couldn't easily ask the council for their backstory, and even if we got it, we couldn't be sure it was real.

I trust that Émilie gave me Marlon's real backstory. But if I don't dig myself then I feel as if I've half-assed this. I'm the detective, the investigator.

What's really holding me back isn't guilt over betraying Marlon's trust. It's guilt over betraying someone else's trust.

I tap Dalton's shoulder. "Eric?"

His eyelids flutter. Then they spring open, and he vaults up, blurting, "The baby?"

I squeeze his arm. "No, sorry. The baby's fine. I'm fine."

He blinks and looks around. His gaze goes to the window, where it's pitch-black outside. "Okay. So what's . . ." He glances over. "The case."

I nod. "I have a suspect that I haven't shared with you, and I believe I need to research them. I got their backstory from Émilie but . . . I need more. I was going to start digging online, and then realized I was going behind your back."

He arches a brow. "Going behind your boss's back or your husband's?"

"My husband's. I'd have no problem sneaking behind my boss's back."

He lets out a low laugh.

"And not even my husband's as much as my partner's," I say. "I didn't want to tell you that I suspect this person, because it's awkward. Then Émilie gave me his story, which she thinks means he couldn't have done it, and I agreed at the time but . . ."

"Then you went to sleep and woke up second-guessing."

I nod.

He pushes up onto his elbows and looks over at me. "Are we talking about Marlon?"

I exhale. "Yes."

Dalton nods. "I started wondering about that myself last night. We're resting a lot of the investigation on what he said because it's an eyewitness report from a reliable source. But if Carson saw something different, then the answer is either that Carson saw someone else or . . ."

"Or Marlon lied."

"What did Émilie tell you?"

I relay the whole story, along with my doubts.

"We need to confirm all that," Dalton says. "No question about it. We've already worried about relying on Émilie too much. This is one situation where that's a problem. She's confident in her recruitment methods, and no one likes being questioned on their work."

He pulls on his sweatpants and stretches as he stands. "I'm not saying she'd hold anything back, but she thinks her methods are foolproof and if Marlon's background suggests he can't be our killer, she's not going to dig as deep as we need her to."

"Agreed."

He picks up his watch and checks it. "Still too early to grab coffee, but let me take Storm for a walk while you start digging. I'll make coffee when I get back."

I'm on my second cup of decaf. Dalton is stretched out in bed, wearing only his boxers again, and it's proof of how engrossed I am in my work that I barely notice. Barely. I'd need to be wearing blinders to not notice at all.

I tried working in bed, but with a basketball for a belly, there's no lap for a laptop. So I'm at the desk, searching while he half dozes, ready for questions but not interrupting.

I'm halfway through that second cup when I find Marlon.

Or I find his case, at least. Émilie might have given me his story, but I soon realize how few details she provided. Correctly, I might add, but that makes searching for his case tricky.

What helps in the end is, well, Marlon himself. Or Martin, as it turns out. That's his real name. I know he served in the military, and I know he's not white, which helps narrow it down. Any article on him is likely to mention the military service—that this idiot of an ex was foolish enough to go after a serviceman. As for "not white," that comes into play because, as it turns out, the ex isn't just some random guy with a propensity for violence. He's a card-carrying member of a white nationalist group. Okay, maybe they don't have cards, but they should—preferably stapled to their foreheads. In any event, the guy who went after Marlon had clear ties to some Aryan group I've never heard of, and one paper speculated that's why he went after Marlon so hard. No shit.

From there, the story is as Émilie described it, though I now get the details filled in. Marlon was working at a software firm when he started a relationship with a coworker. The coworker's ex confronted him in a local bar and there was an altercation. Two more altercations followed, with the reports making it clear that Marlon was being targeted and only defended himself in the fights. The relationship ended, but the persecution did not.

One thing that Émilie skipped in her account? That Marlon's stalker started posting garbage online about Marlon's behavior as an employee, accusing him of sexual harassment and theft and everything else he could come up with. It was laughable really, how obviously the ex was behind it, with his ridiculous scattershot accusations. The not-so-laughable part was that the negative publicity must have made the software firm uneasy. Marlon and his firm "parted ways" with a severance package. All this information comes in articles written after the fact, because the incident that got it in the paper was the attempted kidnapping, with the rest as backstory.

The kidnapping attempt hadn't been something as simple as grabbing Marlon in a parking lot and trying—but failing—to get him into a panel van. No, he'd been Tasered and stuffed into a car trunk, driven into the wilderness and told to dig his own grave. That's when he finally leaned into his military training. He slammed his shovel into the back of one guy's knees, taking him down, and then smacked the other guy in the head hard enough to daze him. But the dazed guy managed to get into the car and take off, leaving Marlon with a wounded—but armed—assailant . . . miles from civilization.

He'd fled the guy with the gun, and he'd been shot at before making it to safety. That's what got the story in the local papers—the kick-ass escape.

As I read those articles, I find it impossible to keep seeing Marlon as a guy who'd stake a woman on the ice and watch her die. I read them rooting for Marlon and being impressed as hell by how he handled it. In the same situation, would I have been able to run after disabling my attackers? Or would I have used that shovel to beat them until they couldn't fight back?

I glance over at Dalton. He only arches his brows.

"I found him," I say. "There's nothing in his story that gives me any cause for concern, but now I'm going to dig into him personally. Okay?"

"Of course. Do whatever you need to do." He sits up. "Can I go grab you breakfast? The bistro must be open by now."

"Please."

He pulls on his clothing as I begin my search. I've just found Marlon's social media when Dalton picks up the leash and heads for the door.

"Not going to ask what I want?" I say.

"You're my wife. I know what you want."

I arch my brows. "Do you?"

"Sure. One of everything."

I grin. "Good man."

He calls Storm over, and I return to the screen. Marlon doesn't have a lot of social media, but like many people of his generation—a little ahead of mine—he has a Facebook account for keeping up with family and former colleagues and old school chums.

When the page pops up, the profile picture is of a guy in fatigues, chilling with his feet up. It's one of those shots that probably looks great at full size, but as a profile pic, it's a blob of camo green. I click it, hoping to get a full picture, but he's uploaded a low-res file, and it's still blurry.

I move to his last update, which was made a few days before he left for Haven's Rock. It's a personalized variation on the one we give all residents to post. The trick to disappearing successfully, as I'd been told, is not to disappear at all. Tie everything up and walk away.

It helps that our residents are already in difficult situations. When they say they're going traveling and will be offline, no one questions that. Marlon's post says he needs a break from "everything that's been happening" and his new job allows him to work remotely, so he's going to travel. While he'll be taking a social media hiatus, expect lots of photos when he gets back.

I flip through a few more entries. He's a sporadic poster, and once the trouble started, the endless advice became more than he cared to deal with.

Hire a lawyer!

Why aren't the police arresting the guy?

Show that asshole who he's messing with.

He'd stopped posting—probably went offline so he didn't need to see that.

I'm going to need to go back farther if I hope to find . . .

I stop. All the updates have been text only, but I reach a photo of a guy at a party. He's hoisting a beer and grinning at the camera. I wouldn't have paused at it except for the caption.

Finally got my hair cut.
Now that's a cause for celebration, right?

I frown at the photo. Is that Marlon? The answer should be obvious. I've spent four months with the guy in Haven's Rock, and this photo is less than a year old. The haircut matches the short hair he has now, as does the meticulously trimmed short beard. In the photo, his skin tone is a tad darker, but this photo was taken in the summer, which means it's probably from the sun. The eyes are brown, like Marlon's. The facial shape and the eye shape are the same. So why am I hesitating?

Because it's not Marlon.

It looks like Marlon . . . but it's not.

The guy in the photo has a different smile. He's also leaner, without Marlon's bulky muscles.

Still, we all have different smiles for different circumstances and audiences. And the photo was taken six months before he came to Haven's Rock. With all the stress of the stalking, he could have been hitting the gym hard and bulked up. Also, it's just one photo. I've seen photos of myself where I do a double take because of the angle or the lighting.

All of that could explain it. But none of that stops my brain from screaming that this is not Marlon.

And maybe it's not supposed to be him. I might be misinterpreting the caption.

I open the images tab and breathe a sigh of relief. My gaze goes straight to Marlon, in a photograph taken on what looks like a hike. The other guy has his arm thrown around Marlon's shoulders.

I click and read the attached post.

A rare visit from my favorite cousin (sorry to all the others . . . you'll be my favorites when you come to visit, ha!) Out for a hike with Jerome, whom I can't tag because the guy's a Luddite without an FB profile.

Okay, so that explains it. The guy in the other photo was Marlon's cousin Jerome. I click the back button to read more posts, but instead it returns me to that page of images. I'm about to get out when I stop as my gaze slides over the gallery of photos.

I see more now of Marlon's "cousin." And none of the person I know as Marlon.

CHAPTER TWENTY-SIX

Dalton walks in with a bag of breakfast sandwiches and finds me standing by the door, as if I've been waiting to pounce.

"That hungry, huh?" he says. Then he sees my expression.

"Marlon isn't Marlon," I say. "He's his cousin."

"I . . . What?"

I back onto the bed and take a moment to corral my thoughts as I pet Storm. Then I try again: "The man from those articles—the one Émilie admitted to Haven's Rock because he was in trouble—is Martin Moyer. Martin Moyer isn't the person we know as Marlon."

"I . . . What?"

I point to my laptop, with the photo of the two men on it. "The man on the left is Martin Moyer."

Dalton looks at the image. "The left? No, Marlon's the guy on the right."

"That's Martin's cousin Jerome."

Dalton rubs his eyes and then pulls over the desk chair and sits.

"I'm not explaining this well," I say.

"You are. I'm just wrapping my head around it. Give me a sec." Another rub. "Okay, so Émilie recruited a guy named Martin Moyer, who is the one in those articles, the former military man who was kidnapped and nearly killed for messing with some neo-Nazi's ex."

"Yes. None of the articles I found had a photo. Understandably—as the victim, the last thing Martin wanted was more attention. However, after I saw the photos of Martin and Jerome, I did more digging and found social media articles on the kidnapping that *did* include Martin's photo, which leave no doubt that the man we know as Marlon is not Martin Moyer."

"The man we know is the guy on the right." He points at the photo. "His cousin."

"Jerome Moyer. I took that from Martin's socials. Jerome doesn't have a social media presence. At all. I did, however, find a couple of deep online references that seem to be him, including another photo, older but definitely our Marlon."

Dalton takes a deep breath, then exhales a long "Fuuuck." After a moment, he turns to me. "So Martin got accepted and let his cousin take his place? Could that work?"

I pick up my notepad from the bed. "I think so. Émilie's investigator is the one who worked with Martin. He does all the interviews and provides all the data. Then Émilie needs to provide the fake passport to get Martin across the border. Did they supply Martin's photo, hoping their superficial resemblance would get Marlon past security? Jerome grows a beard and cuts his hair to match, and that's good enough? Or did they supply Jerome's photo, presuming whoever's making the passport either hasn't seen Martin's photo or—again—would figure it was close enough. We'd need to run that past Émilie."

"Ask her what checks and balances are in place to ensure the person admitted is the person who arrives."

I nod.

He shakes his head. "You know what check *isn't* in place? Making sure we've seen a photo of the person who's supposed to be showing up. There's a resemblance, but there's no way we'd have mistaken Jerome for Martin. We're more paranoid than any border guard."

"We need to start getting photos," I say. "Photos that have been seen all the way up the chain. But fixing that is a problem for another day. For now, it's clear that the wrong guy is in Haven's Rock. The question is why Martin did the switcheroo." I pause. "And my fear is that he didn't."

Dalton frowns. Then he swears. "Martin *did* need to disappear. So why give his spot to his cousin?"

"Also, Martin *has* disappeared," I say. "He posted a goodbye on his socials, just as he'd been instructed. Is it possible that coming up here wasn't what he wanted? That Émilie gave him all the resources he needed to vanish, but he didn't actually want to come *here*? So he let his cousin come up instead, while he hightails it to Mexico? Possible but convoluted."

"There's another reason why Martin would disappear and Jerome would show up here instead."

"If Martin didn't give his cousin that slot. If Jerome took it."

"And Martin isn't around to tell anyone." Dalton exhales. "Fuck."

"I'm calling Émilie," I say. "You need to get on the phone to Anders. We have to get Marlon in custody. Now."

I don't bother texting Émilie to warn her I'm calling. She picks up, sounding groggy. I realize it's barely seven. I know the polite thing would be to apologize for waking her, or at least ask *whether* I've woken her, but that's wasted time, and this is urgent.

I tell her what I've discovered. Like Dalton, she needs to ask me to repeat myself a few times while she processes. But she's soon up and tapping on her laptop.

"Is there any chance I could be mistaken?" I say. "Some way you can tell me that this kind of mix-up is impossible and we've misidentified Marlon?"

"I wish I could, Casey, but I'm looking at all the photos now, and if you say this man on the right is the man in Haven's Rock, then there has indeed been a switch. The biggest sticking point would be the passport, as you mentioned. I'm just pulling up Marlon's file, and the photo submitted is . . ." She curses.

"Jerome, not Martin."

"Yes. I can very clearly see the difference. Jerome cut his hair and grew a beard, but he is not Martin."

"There's just a superficial resemblance."

She exhales. "Yes, and I fear it's worse than that. It's a lack of checks and balances, as you said. Most of our interviews are conducted by encrypted video, unlike when you were admitted and Eric met you in person. Video is never ideal for lighting and image quality. We also minimize points of contact. In Marlon's case, only the interviewer saw him, via video. The person they spoke to would have been Martin. Then the passport photo goes to the same person. Presumably they would confirm it's the person they saw in the video interview, but that is not a clear checkpoint."

"They aren't asked to study the photo and confirm that it matches. It's just presumed that they'd notice if it didn't."

"Yes. Also, in this case, the person who conducted the interview and received the photo is white."

She doesn't need to explain what that means. There's a known predisposition for people of one race to misidentify people of another. While Émilie is white herself, she has biracial grand-children. She might not have made that mistake, but she never saw pictures of Martin. She only received the passport photo of Jerome for her files.

"Plugging these holes comes later," I say. "For now, Eric is outside calling Will and getting Marlon quietly put into cus-tody. The cell, not the apartment."

"Good."

"Eric and I will, if we can, continue on to Whitehorse later."

"Absolutely. Will can handle this. I will send a plane to pick up Jerome as soon as possible. Whether or not he killed Lynn, this is a clear violation of the agreement, and we can remove him. I will deal with any exposure threat he might present."

"Good. You do that, and I'll interview him from White-horse. I can have Will search his apartment and look for evi-dence that he's responsible for Lynn's death. So far, I don't really have anything except the very strong feeling he lied about see-ing someone escorting Lynn."

"Someone who happened to physically resemble the person being framed. Right down to Marlon actually saying he thought it *was* Sebastian, in case you failed to make the connection."

I stretch out on the bed and rub my stomach. "I know. But that's not evidence. Neither is the lack of an alibi—most people don't have them with the blizzard. I'll have Will search after Marlon's safely in custody. He can build a timeline for Marlon from talking to others. My concern right now is why Jerome is in Haven's Rock instead of Martin . . . and what happened to Martin."

She curses softly. "Of course. Martin would have needed to

disappear. We monitor residents' social media to be sure no one asks too many questions. We'd have noticed if he resurfaced."

"There's no sign of that. Also, I need to know more about Jerome Moyer. I've started searching, but he's a ghost online, which is . . . troubling."

"It is. All right. We've established that Marlon is Jerome. I'm going to stifle the urge to investigate how that happened. My focus is on getting Jerome out of Haven's Rock. I'll dispatch a plane to retrieve him. Are you all right with me setting my investigator on Jerome's trail?"

"Yes. Whatever happened, it wasn't the fault of their investigation. You do that, and I'll do my own digging until we can leave for Whitehorse."

I'm off the phone before Dalton returns, so I put on my outerwear. If we'll be here for a while, I need a walk before I settle into more online searching.

I don't see Dalton and Storm until I round the corner. Then I spot them near the rear of town, where it rises into forest.

Dalton has his back to me, and the phone to his ear. Before I make it to him, he turns to head back and lowers the phone at the same time.

He spots me, lifts a hand and picks up speed. I do the same, giving my legs a welcome stretch.

"How's Will taking it?" I say.

"I can't get through to him."

"What?" I peer up at the sky. It's overcast, but nothing that suggests a storm.

"It's not the weather. The phones are connecting. Well, one

is at least. I've tried both numbers. One rings but no one answers, and the other goes straight to voicemail. I've left messages on both."

My heart thuds, and all I can say is "Okay." But it's not okay. It's *very* not okay.

Dalton continues, "One phone should be with Will. That's the one that's going straight to voicemail. The other is with either April or Yolanda—last I heard, they were bickering over who got custody of it while we were gone. That's the one that keeps ringing."

"If *that* one was going straight to voicemail, I'd say whoever has it forgot to recharge it. But Will's wouldn't."

Dalton nods.

My racing heart jams into my throat, and I struggle to speak. "I told Will to keep an eye on Marlon."

"Good," Dalton grunts. "Maybe there really is a storm out there. Or the satellite network is . . ." He waves a hand. "On the fritz. I don't know. We'll keep trying until we get through. In the meantime, Will knows to watch Marlon."

"No, I meant . . ." I take deep breaths of the icy air. "Maybe, yes. He knows to watch Marlon so it's not as if he'll be caught off guard, but if I told him to watch Marlon, what if . . ."

Silence. Then, quietly, Dalton says, "What if Marlon figured that out."

CHAPTER TWENTY-SEVEN

We're at the hotel packing as fast as we can. Dalton has con-tacted the airport to make sure we can take off in the next hour. We can, since our destination isn't on a route that coincides with other flight paths.

We aren't heading to Whitehorse anymore. We're going back to Haven's Rock.

There's no choice here. It might turn out that the phone problem is a temporary glitch. If so, then we can turn around. But it doesn't seem like a glitch. It seems like someone is mak-ing sure we can't contact Haven's Rock. Someone who knows where those phones will be and can take them.

The whole time we're packing and driving to the airport, I'm calling those numbers. Endlessly calling. At the same time, I dig for more on Jerome Moyer. It's an online slog. The name isn't uncommon enough for me to easily sift through the chaff, and the fact that "our" Jerome Moyer is an online ghost means most references I find aren't him. It doesn't help that I'm look-ing for a Jerome Moyer who might be a killer and there's an unrelated Jerome Moyer who *is* a convicted killer.

At the airport, I wait with Storm as Dalton runs through his preflight checks. Émilie has already sent me a quick-and-dirty history for Jerome Moyer, proving why she has a professional investigator instead of just relying on a former police detective with a laptop.

Jerome Moyer. Forty-two years old. His father was Black, that being the Moyer side, but his dad had died in the military when Jerome was young, and he'd been raised by his white mother and her new husband, a big-game guide in Montana.

Jerome moved out before his eighteenth birthday, and his mother and stepfather never bothered reporting him gone, as if they'd all decided he was close enough to legal age. From there, he seemed to have held down a string of jobs that I'd expect to be above the reach of a guy who hadn't finished high school, including a stint as a paramedic . . . despite having no paramedic training.

The "Marlon" I know is even-tempered and easy to get along with. Charming, but not so charming that it puts people like me on edge. He's self-effacing, happy to help out. On the surface, he's a far cry from a manipulative sociopath, but even in his Haven's Rock persona, I see a form of manipulation, a far more clever one.

Marlon has been who we need him to be. Friendly and helpful without causing any waves. Looking at him more critically, he reminds me of Anders . . . or the version of Anders most people see. The popular guy everyone wants to have a beer with, wants to be paired up with on a job. The guy who always has a smile and a warm greeting and a sympathetic ear, if you need it.

Is the Marlon I know Jerome's usual persona? Or did he come to Haven's Rock, zero in on the most popular guy—another man of color, no less—and craft his facade to match? I think it's a combination, given that string of seemingly impossible jobs he held down, often for years at a time. He got away with it because he seems like the last guy who'd lie to get ahead.

Along with that data comes a list of cities where he's lived. He likes cities—easier to disappear in. And when he relocates, he doesn't just hop in the car and drive a hundred miles. He crosses the country. Putting distance between where he was and where he wants to be next.

I use those cities as the starting point for my search. This is where I *do* have the skills to search, though again, I could do better with access to databases and contacts. Still, since Jerome seems to have stayed in the US, I'd have been limited there, too.

My search for unsolved murders is nothing short of depressing. These are major cities. Of course there are unsolved murders, and narrowing it down to "female victim" and "sadism" doesn't help.

I'm aware of time ticking by. If I'm close to any kind of breakthrough, Dalton will wait, but otherwise, we cannot afford for me to surf the internet while something may have happened in Haven's Rock. Nor can we risk missing our takeoff window.

I need to be more specific. Search on hypothermia. How about exposure? How about—

The link doesn't come where I expect it. I've searched on Jerome in connection to murders in all the places he lived and found nothing, but then I get a hit on his name and a death by . . . dehydration.

It's a strange story, one I need to read twice to parse it out. The connection comes because Jerome attended high school with the girl who died. They'd been in the same class, and in one article, he'd been referenced as having helped organize the search when she disappeared.

The strange part is the girl's death. It happened over the

summer break. She'd gone missing, and the whole town had searched for her. She'd been found five days later . . . in the high school, which had been closed for the season.

It seemed she'd broken in through a window to retrieve a necklace she'd accidentally left in her former locker. After she had the necklace, she went into the accessible bathroom, and the door locked behind her. The janitor had been on vacation, and no one was in the school to hear her shouting and banging on the door. This was back at a time when few kids—especially in small-town Montana—had a cell phone.

A horrific and tragic accident. One that I would have taken a helluva lot closer look at. A girl described as a "model student" breaks into the school for a necklace rather than wait until the janitor returns and ask to get it? After breaking in, she decides she really needs to use the bathroom before making her escape? She chooses the accessible bathroom . . . which also happens to have the water turned off for the summer, leaving her with nothing to drink and survive? And how the hell did the door lock behind her? The article says something about it being an automatic door that failed, but add that to the other oddities, and I'd be very suspicious. The local sheriff was not. The school raised money and installed emergency alarms in all the bathrooms. Problem solved. Future tragedies averted.

That sets me on a new search. Girls or women dying in bizarre and horrible accidents, particularly involving things like exposure to the elements or dehydration. Something where they were trapped and died slowly.

The next one comes quickly, because in this case, the family didn't accept the manufactured explanation. Twenty years ago. College student in a city where Jerome lived. Her death was ruled a suicide after she apparently tied a cinder block to her leg and stepped off a dock into a small lake near the school. Her family argued that she wouldn't have done that, but when it looks like suicide—especially with someone that age—the police will often ignore the family's protests. Her parents no longer lived with her, so she could hide her college-induced depression from them.

In this case, though, it wasn't just the parents—no one who knew the victim had seen any sign that might indicate suicide. All this wouldn't get my attention except for one tidbit that didn't make it into most respectable publications. The investigators believed the victim had underestimated the depth of the lake, because the cinder block hadn't pulled her under to a relatively quick death. She'd been held under just enough to cover her mouth and nose, leaving the top of her head above the surface.

I imagine what that would be like. How she'd have been able to get snatches of air as she struggled, swallowing water when she tried to scream. How long would it take to die like that? How horrible would it be?

And what if your killer was right there, on the dock, watching? And with your eyes above water, you could see him watching.

"Casey?"

I look up to see Dalton standing there.

"Ready to go?" he says.

I nod and I go to snap the laptop shut, but then keep it open. "Can I keep working while we have a signal?"

"Of course."

We're in the air, ten minutes outside Dawson City, when I finally lose the last flicker of cell signal and shut my laptop.

Then I glance over at Dalton. His attention is on the sky, but it's clear today.

"You okay to talk?" I ask through the microphone.

"I am." It's hard to make out tone through the connection, but his voice sounds tight, as if he's dreading hearing what I have to say. "You found something."

"Possibilities. Deaths in areas where Jerome lived. Girls and then women, all around the age he'd have been at the time. He went to school with the first victim, but otherwise, there are no connections to him."

"No connections to *him*. But connections to Lynn. How she died."

"Yes. I started looking at unsolved murders, but then I thought more about Lynn. What if Will hadn't noticed the abrasions? Would we have chalked it up to death by misadventure? A tragic accident?"

He grunts, letting me continue.

"Removing Lynn's clothing was risky," I say. "After Kendra had been dosed, it would automatically have us thinking sexual assault. But maybe that was part of the game. We'd jump to that conclusion but be confused by the lack of any signs of assault. Then someone would mention paradoxical undressing or April would find it in her textbooks or, if all else failed, Marlon could mention he'd once heard something weird about victims of hypothermia undressing."

"Which he would be able to do because he knows everyone involved in the investigation. Classic sign of a serial killer, isn't it? Interest in law enforcement? Even inveigling their way into the investigation?"

I nod, remember he can't see that, and say, "Yes. The people he befriended the most were Will, you, and me, along with our inner circle. His supposed military background made him perfect for our militia. That fits. Not everything does. Serial killers are usually white, but there have been serial killers of all races. He was raised by a stepfather who made a career out of hunting. Jerome dropped out of high school and left his family behind, suggesting issues there. He's older than the average serial killer, but he seems to have the ability to pace himself. He started as a teen and only takes one victim every five years or so."

"You found more?"

"A few possibilities. His MO seems to be what we saw with Lynn. Not hypothermia per se, but deaths that were ruled accidents or suicides, the circumstances of which were . . ." I swallow. "Horrible. The girl from his high school died of dehydration after getting locked in a windowless and waterless bathroom during the summer break. A college student who drowned of apparent suicide, weighed down by a cinder block that didn't submerge her enough to die quickly. Just before I lost service, I found a case from five years ago, a woman who died while hiking, after falling into a crevice and breaking her leg." I pause and then add, "Her cell phone was on a ledge just out of her reach. She could see it, tried to get to it, but couldn't. That's what caught my attention. That cell phone."

Dalton doesn't curse. He doesn't say anything. He's silent. We both are. Silent with the horror of these deaths.

"I'll keep trying to call our sat phones," I say. "Émilie is, too. She thinks it might be a service failure."

"I hope so."

"If so, then we'll get there, quietly take Marlon into custody, and get him out of Haven's Rock. Then we can push on to Whitehorse."

Dalton glances over. "How are you feeling?"

"Sick that this guy got into Haven's Rock. But you'll notice that I didn't say *we* brought him in. I didn't even say Émilie let him in. He took advantage of a loophole no one saw. We've had them, and we're going to keep having them until we plug every one." I take a deep breath. "In this case, the outcome was . . . as bad as it can get. But no one in the process made an unforgivable mistake. We just need more checks and balances."

"Agreed. However, I was actually asking how you're feeling physically—you and the baby."

I manage a weak smile when he glances over. "We're fine. Just regular punches and kicks and movement. I even think they may have gotten turned the right way—I was sure I felt kicks up top this morning."

"Good."

"At least one thing is."

We share a brief, worried smile, and reach out for a quick hand squeeze before Dalton focuses on getting us home.

CHAPTER TWENTY-EIGHT

I was telling the truth about how I feel. There really hasn't been more than normal movement since our scare. And I definitely felt kicking near the top, which suggests the baby is moving into the correct position. Yet no sooner do we spot Haven's Rock below than a cramp nearly doubles me over. Luckily, Dalton is too busy landing the plane to notice. I hold my breath as I stare at my watch, waiting for the next one.

The "next" one doesn't come, thankfully. We're landing when I feel another cramp, but it's much lighter, and it feels more like regular intestinal distress. That is not unexpected, given the way my stomach is twisting with worry over why no one is answering those phones.

I want to land and see Anders standing there, having heard the plane and come to the hangar to meet us. He'll be there, arms crossed, giving us shit for coming back, teasing that we couldn't stay away.

What? The sat phones aren't working? Huh. I never even noticed. Been too busy . . . running this investigation, which I can totally handle.

Marlon? I just passed him. He was heading for the café. Coffee break time. I've been keeping an eye on him.

Anders is not at the hangar. No one is, and my heart seizes at that, and I climb from the plane even as Dalton growls for me to wait and let him help me down.

Then I see Anders, coming at a lope, and I exhale.

"Hey," I say. "Satellite must be down. We can't get through."

Anders gets close enough for me to see his grim expression and my gut twists, another cramp hitting. "Will?"

"My phone's missing," he says. "So is Marlon. I just—" He breaks off with an angry shake of his head. "I just realized about the phone. I went to bed late and gave mine to April. Yolanda has the other one, and April was pissed, worrying about you since you couldn't make it to Whitehorse yesterday. She came barreling in this morning and woke me up, thinking I'd taken the phone back. It was missing from her . . ."

He trails off, gaze slipping to mine and then away. I know what his next words would be, because if April was worried I might need late-night medical attention, she would have left the phone beside her bed.

Marlon went into April's room, while she slept, and took the phone. While she'd been lying there, with her eye mask on, alone and vulnerable.

"April's fine," he says quickly. "She doesn't even seem fazed. But, of course, that's April. I told her to grab the other phone from Yolanda. Then I went to check on Marlon. His apartment is empty, and I'm worried that's not a coincidence—one of your suspects is gone along with the sat phone."

"Taken it to try getting a ride out of here," Dalton says as he joins us.

"How long's he been missing?" I say as we start toward town, moving as fast as my waddling body can move.

"I'm not even sure he *is* missing. He's just not in his apartment, and I was starting to search when I saw the plane. He was
supposed to take a patrol shift starting at eight, but I asked him
to switch to Grant's job, which doesn't start until ten."

I check my watch. It feels as if it should be early afternoon,
and it's only 9:55. That's what happens when your day begins
before dawn.

"For all I know," Anders continues, "he could have been
grabbing breakfast before his shift starts, and someone else stole
the phone. I was about to search for Marlon myself while getting Yolanda or Kendra to check on our other suspects, see if
anyone is missing."

"It's Marlon," I say grimly. "That's why we came back. We
were trying to call to tell you Marlon isn't Marlon. That is to
say, he's not the guy we admitted as Marlon."

Anders stops short before resuming his walk with, "What?"

I give him the quickest possible rundown as we near town.
When I tell him what I found, about the murders I think could
be Jerome's work, his face goes ashen.

"Holy shit," he whispers.

"Yep," Dalton says.

"I . . . Part of me says I should be furious because he played
me. Played me like a goddamn violin." He swallows and rubs his
mouth. "But all I can think about is those girls, those women,
and I want to ask if there's any chance you're wrong but there's
not. He was exactly what we needed. Especially what *we* need—
you, me, Eric."

I nod. "A resident with military experience to fill the gap left
by me being pregnant. And a gap in general. We're all working
our asses off to build and protect this town. To have a resident
with the skills, the personality, and the willingness to help out?
Gold."

"Casey?" Dalton says, lowering his voice as we enter town. "I'd like you to take Storm and get that sat phone from Yolanda."

"Got it," I say. "I'll tell her what's happening, and I'll get in touch with Émilie while paying April a visit to check on her. You guys are looking for Marlon, I presume."

"We are. Will? Can you round up Kenny, Phil, Kendra, Jacob . . . Find Gunnar, too. Put him in his perch. Get the others up to speed."

"You want to lock down?" Anders asks. "Everyone inside?"

Dalton shakes his head. "If Marlon's still in town, the last thing we want is him being tipped off by too much activity. Kenny, Kendra, and Jacob should be on patrol. Gunnar in his perch. Phil is working with Isabel on a plan for a lockdown, if that's needed."

"Eric?" I say as he starts veering left.

He glances back.

"If he's not around, come see me before you leave town? Take Storm and backup?"

"I will."

I head straight for Yolanda's apartment. Anders hadn't gotten a chance to check in on her. She's not doing any regular job right now, having been semi-recruited to help Anders on the case and town security. He says she was on patrol yesterday afternoon, ending early evening when her Parkinson's tremors started up. He hasn't seen her since her patrol shift began—he'd spoken later to Kendra, who said Yolanda passed on a message that she'd be back on duty by late morning.

Yolanda has an apartment in the general residences. We've tried getting her to take a larger one in the family building, but she's never as stubborn as when she's determined to be treated like everyone else. Except, you know, when she doesn't want to be treated like everyone else.

Her apartment is on the first floor. That's one perk of having been here during construction. She might not want upgraded quarters, but she does have the most conveniently located apartment—main level, near the doors and close to the washrooms and common areas, but not right beside them, where noise could be an issue.

Her door is locked. I knock. No answer. I knock again.

"Looking for Yolanda?" a voice says.

I glance over. It's one of our newest residents, Ingrid, a young woman with an easy smile.

"I am," I say.

"I saw her getting coffee with Marlon this morning." She waggles her brows, still smiling. "Maybe he's finally getting his shot, huh?"

My gut goes cold.

"Detective Butler?" she says. "Are you okay?" Her gaze drops to my stomach. "Wait. You're supposed to be gone, aren't you? Having the baby?"

"Something came up," I say, smoothing out my expression. "I need to speak to Yolanda *and* Marlon. Town business. So if they were together, that's perfect. You said they were grabbing coffee? When was this?"

She checks her watch. "It's been a while. Maybe just after eight? They were in the café line ahead of me. I guess they'd be back to work by now."

I thank her and start to hurry off as another cramp hits. Definitely stress, and for very good reason now. I tamp down the pain and pick up my pace as I beeline for the café.

★ ★ ★

On the way to the café, I spot Anders and wave him over. I quickly tell him what Ingrid said, and his expression drops the way my stomach did.

"Yolanda," he whispers. "Oh no."

"It might be nothing," I say. "If Jerome did bolt, he could have been making a show of being seen. The coffee line is the best place to do it, and if Yolanda's there, even better. Everyone including her will confirm he was in that line, chatting and acting normal."

Except that we can't get hold of Yolanda. She has the other sat phone, and it's ringing through to voicemail.

Maybe because she left it in her apartment. She's obviously been up and around for hours, despite not working until later. She goes out, forgets she has custody of that phone, and it's ringing away in her apartment.

I test that with the sat phone we brought back with it. I don't hear anything.

We reach the café. Inside, our bakers Brian and Devon are hard at work. We pull them both aside into the back room and ask about Yolanda and Marlon.

Devon grins, not unlike the way Ingrid did. "Yep, they were here, and they were *together*. Chatting away and everything. I think that fire might finally be sparking."

Anders shakes his head. "She's not interested in Marlon."

Devon's brows rise. "And you know that how? Because you've been keeping tabs?"

Is it my imagination, or does Anders flush a little? He definitely glances away as he shrugs. "We talk. She knows he's interested, and she's not, and I've been subtly trying to tell him that without him jumping to the wrong conclusion."

"That *you're* interested in Yolanda," Devon says. "Which would be totally the wrong conclusion, right?"

Brian elbows his husband. "Stop matchmaking. Will's right. Yolanda's not interested in Marlon. She must have really wanted that coffee today. Otherwise, she'd have cut out of line again, like she usually does when Marlon shows up."

I frown. "What's this?"

Brian takes a batch of muffins from the oven. "It's only been a couple of times, but it's pretty obvious. Marlon comes strolling along when Yolanda's at the back of the line, and she suddenly forgot something and has to leave."

"Ouch," Devon says. "Poor guy."

Brian shakes his head. "If she's not interested and he isn't taking the hint, that's on him. But today they actually joined the line together. They were deep in conversation. It seemed serious—not the usual early-morning-crowd small talk."

"Any idea what they were talking about?" I ask.

The two men look at each other. Then Devon says, "Brian was in the back when they got to the counter. I heard something about a noise in the night? Marlon seemed concerned? I didn't really catch it. They were keeping their voices down."

"Did they grab a seat?" I motion at the dining area.

"Nah. They got their coffee to go. Oh, I did hear something else. Yolanda said she might start her patrol early. On account of what Marlon heard, I think? He said he didn't start work until later, so if it was okay, he'd join her, since no one should be out there alone."

"See?" Brian says. "That's why they were together and talking. Business."

We take our leave. Once we're out the back door, on the empty patio, I murmur, "That makes sense. She would talk to him about business."

Anders doesn't answer. That gives me pause, but then another damned stomach cramp hits, and I wait it out before continuing, "Business being town security. He says he heard something and . . ."

And then it hits hard enough for my breath to catch, and I realize why Anders is so quiet, why he's staring out at the forest, breathing hard, a stricken look on his face. I'd been completely focused on why Yolanda and Marlon were together, and the "security" answer came as a relief, when it should have had the absolute opposite effect.

Marlon says he heard something last night, out in the forest.

Yolanda says she'll start her patrol early and take a look.

He offers to come with her, and she won't argue because he's right—no one should be out there alone with a killer on the loose.

Except the killer is the guy saying he "heard something." And he just found a way to get Yolanda—the woman who's been blocking his interest for months—into the forest with him.

"Eric," I say, my voice coming out strangled. "We need to get Eric."

I go hunt for Dalton while Anders uses the two-way radios to call whoever's on patrol. Yolanda said she was going to start early, but she'd be overlapping with others, rather than taking over. There's a decent chance whoever else is patrolling saw them.

I find Dalton talking to Phil and Isabel at their place, and I make them pull on their boots and follow as I talk. We soon hear Anders ahead, and we pick up speed and find him talking to Kendra and Jacob, who just got back from patrol.

"We never saw them," Kendra says as we approach, as if knowing this will be our first question. "We were just saying that we need to lock down. I was going to go talk to Phil but . . ."

"Yes," Phil says. "We're in lockdown. Kendra? Jacob? I'll get your help with that—"

"We need Jacob," Dalton says. "He's a better tracker than me. You get Kendra and Casey."

I shake my head. "Storm works best with me. And if we need to split up, there should be four of us, so we can stay in twos."

Dalton hesitates.

"He won't have gone far," I say. "He's not getting Yolanda miles from town, whether he's luring her or carrying her."

"All right then. Let's take one of those radios and head out."

CHAPTER TWENTY-NINE

It doesn't take me long to realize I was mistaken. These are not "stomach cramps." They're labor pains. It feels like another round of prodromal labor, which means it's nothing to worry about. My body is just fussing. Or, better yet, getting the baby in position for birth in a few weeks.

I don't tell anyone. I really am fine. It's just sudden bursts of pain that make me want to double over. No big deal.

Okay, yes, it's a big deal, but compared to Yolanda being in the forest with a sadistic serial killer? I can handle the pain. The baby isn't coming yet.

We only need to circle the town once before finding Jerome and Yolanda's trail. Even without Storm, I could have tracked them—there are two sets of prints leaving the main trail, only partly obscured by thick brush.

Halfheartedly obscured? Yes. Jerome could have found a better place to leave a trail, like the flattened mess of prints leading to the lake, from our investigation.

I look at these prints, and I see a sneer. At us? Because we left, taking Storm and Dalton and leaving the town—presumably—

without a tracker. Jerome had little interaction with Jacob. He wouldn't have realized Jacob would find this trail faster than Storm or Dalton.

Or is the sneer for Anders? Hopeless without his boss? While the forest is not Anders's forte, he *would* have found this trail, because he'd have searched until he did.

I set Storm on it, and the others let her take charge while they scan for trouble and clues. It's a clear day, which is a relief. Sunny but cold. The only thing slowing us down is the forest itself, thick with fresh snow. That makes it slow going, but it also means I can keep up easily.

Okay, "easily" might be an exaggeration. I'm keeping up, following in the path Storm cuts, but it's still a slog and the cramps don't help. At least the others are behind me, meaning I'm free to pull faces when the contractions hit.

With a trail Storm could follow half-asleep—plus three pairs of eyes on alert—I don't need to do much more than guide Storm and encourage her. When she stops to snuffle the snow, I move up alongside her and bend over as best I can.

The snow here isn't as deep. It's an open area with scant tree cover, and the snow has blown away, leaving it only a few inches deep. I still can't tell what Storm's snuffling until I spot a small hole in the snow a foot to my right and then another beyond it. Telling Storm to stay where she is, I peer into the hole.

"Blood," Dalton says.

I glance up to find he's walked past us and is looking at another spot.

"Blood drops in the snow," Jacob says. "They've sunk in, but we can see them."

"It's from that," Anders says.

He's pointing at one of the few trees. Dalton's already bearing down on it. I waddle over as he takes a piece of fabric from the branches. It's dark with blood.

"Part of a shirt," he says, holding it up for me.

It's the torn bottom section of a standard-issue jersey. It's been ripped, and it's drenched with drying blood.

"Is that Yolanda's?" Jacob says quietly.

I shake my head. "The shirt is too big for either Yolanda or Lynn. It's a lure."

Jacob frowns over at me.

"Jerome said he heard something in the forest," Anders says. "That's how he got Yolanda to go in with him. This would have been the lure. He says it sounded like it came from this direction. Wait, is that blood in the snow? Holy shit, what's that in the tree?"

"How the hell did he get it in the tree?" Dalton says. "These are the only tracks."

I squint across the clearing. Then I track the blood droplets.

"Threw it." I point to the tree line off to our left. "He'd have stood over there and thrown it. Drops fall and it gets tangled in the tree."

"He was our snowball pitcher for a reason," Anders mutters. "He has one hell of an arm."

"So he comes in over there." Dalton points. "Where Yolanda won't later see his trail. He throws it to create a tableau guaranteed to get her attention."

"Is anyone going to ask where the blood came from?" Jacob says. "That's a lot of it."

"It's not blood." I gesture for him to get closer to the rag and sniff it.

"Ketchup?" he says. "And something else?"

"Some mixture that looks a lot like blood, at least on a piece of fabric and some drops in the snow."

"Uh, guys?" Anders says. "There's something over there, too."

I can't see what he's pointing at. The perils of being a short woman with tall guys. I start heading that way when a contraction hits, and I manage to hide it by glancing sharply left, as if I heard something. Then I shake my head before anyone can comment.

The footprints proceed toward whatever Anders saw, though they meander a bit, and I can imagine Yolanda in tracking mode, scanning the clearing, walking around trying to find anything else.

Then she does. There's a red patch in the snow, as if something else had been there but is now gone. I don't spend more than a second looking at that, though. What seizes my attention are the marks in the snow. The smaller boot prints from Yolanda, and then the spot where she crouched for a better look . . . and the drag marks behind it, the wild thrashing as she struggled against Jerome hauling her backward into the thick woods.

I hurry after those marks. We all do—Anders and Jacob going on ahead with Storm, while Dalton stays with me, making sure I'm not left behind.

Jerome set this all up in advance. Then he brings Yolanda and leads her along until she's engrossed in what has happened here, worrying that someone else is missing, wanting to process the scene as best she can before alerting Anders, trusting that Marlon has her back because she might not be interested in him romantically, but she trusts him as a person, as a colleague.

She bends to examine something in the snow. He needs that distraction. She's smart, and she's probably armed with her own gun, but her guard is down and she's crouched, and it's easy to grab her and drag her off and get her gun away before she can pull it on him.

I see the signs of that final struggle in the snow, where he must have gone for the gun and she tried to get to it, but he's so much bigger and stronger and her brain is still trying to process what is happening.

With that, I realized he was even more careful in his choice of location than I thought. He'd needed the clearing to stage the tableau. But once he had Yolanda, he either needed to move her by force or carry her. The other option would be to kill her where he grabbed her, but we already know he likes to take his time. He's not going to lay a trail that could bring Anders running before Yolanda is dead.

No, after he had her, he needed to move her and hide their trail. Just beyond that clearing, we hit rock, which the wind has swept nearly clear of snow. He was able to avoid the pockets of snow and get Yolanda out of there without leaving a trail.

Or, without leaving a trail that he expects Anders can follow. Jacob and Dalton pick up the signs of passage here and there. But it's Storm who shines, easily able to follow Jerome's scent across the rock.

And after all that, the trail heads to the place we would have expected him to take her. The lake. He circled around it, though, coming across the rock to the opposite side. Being careful, because without a snowstorm for cover, he needs to be farther from town.

Is he taking a risk bringing Yolanda to the lake? Of course he is. Anders might skip finding a trail and head straight here, knowing that's where Lynn died.

Jerome is taking risks because he likes that. Added danger. Added excitement.

We're already onto him. He hasn't just happened to kidnap Yolanda at the same time I started getting suspicious. He'd probably breathed a sigh of relief when Dalton and I left mid-investigation. Then Anders took him off patrol.

Oh, Anders had been careful about it. With Grant grieving, someone needed to do his job, and the patrols were under control, with no sign of trouble. Would Marlon take over Grant's job, please? Of course. But he'd also gotten suspicious.

There was probably more. Maybe he overheard something. Maybe he just got vibes from Anders that said he was a suspect. So, since it looked as if he wouldn't get away with killing Lynn, why not take another victim before he escaped? And he didn't need to worry about Storm being summoned to track him, because he had both satellite phones.

Anders will know who took Yolanda, and when she's found dead, he'll know who did it. So Jerome doesn't need to throw Anders off the trail completely. He just needed to slow him down.

When we reach the lake, the footprints resume, sporadic but clear. He's pushing her ahead of him. A scuffle. Then blood spatter, as he must have cut or stabbed her to keep her moving. My chest clenches when I see those.

Don't fight, Yolanda. That might be the hardest thing you've ever done, but we're on the way. We'll get to you in time.

I pray we'll get to you in time.

Is it already too late? I'm trying so hard not to calculate. If they left Haven's Rock around eight thirty, and we didn't arrive until nearly ten . . .

It's tight. If Jerome moved quickly, it's too damn tight, and he *will* be moving quickly. Especially if he heard our plane.

Why the hell did I take so long to realize Yolanda was gone? That could make all the difference here. When Anders said Yolanda had the second phone—the one going to voicemail—I should have been more worried than I was.

Storm barks, shattering my thoughts, and I look to see she's trying to get my attention. Her tail is moving with excitement and she's looking over the lake to a spot on the ice.

Shortcut! I found a shortcut!

"She smells Jerome and Yolanda on the wind," I say. "Over there."

The footprints continue straight, hugging the shore. Jerome and Yolanda headed along it, but they're over to the right now.

"Split up?" Jacob says. "Eric and I keep tracking while you, Storm, and Will head that way?"

Dalton shakes his head. "If Storm smells them, this is the shortcut. We're downwind of where she's scenting. We mark this spot, in case we have to come back."

"It's awfully open," Anders says, shading his eyes against the sun.

I see what he means. If we take the shortcut, it'll put us out on the ice, where our approach can be spotted.

"And he'll be armed," Anders says. "Yolanda always carries her gun, and he'll have taken it from her by now."

"The safe path is along the shore," I say. "There's cover. But we could be running out of time. He's bound to have heard the plane."

"I'll find us a path," Dalton says. "Everyone fall in line behind me and keep quiet."

Dalton picks a path that doesn't satisfy either part of me—the part that worries we'll be too late or the part that worries Jerome will spot us and kill Yolanda faster. But there's no way to eliminate both those concerns, and the route he takes is the best we can manage, not quite cutting across the open ice, but not quite hidden in the thick trees either.

We move fast. It's all we can do. When I can't move fast enough, Dalton tells Anders and Jacob to go on ahead.

"You can go, too," I say. "I have Storm."

He doesn't even answer that. I made a mistake coming out here. Yes, Storm works best with me, but this has been such an easy trail to follow that she didn't need my guidance. I'm slowing them down. I'm holding Dalton back. And the contractions haven't stopped. If anything, they're getting stronger.

Could it be actual labor?

I push aside the panic. Even if it is, I know from my research that labor lasts for hours. Many hours. Early contractions are just a signal to start thinking about packing a bag for the hospital.

We'll get Yolanda and return to Haven's Rock. I won't tell Dalton, of course—he can't afford to be distracted right now, when we're so close. But I do need to issue one warning.

"Don't rely on me," I whisper. "I'm doing okay, but I'm struggling. If there's a confrontation, I'll keep myself safely out of it, but I can't help."

Dalton lets out a low chuckle. "You're eight months pregnant, Butler. I wasn't planning on relying on you for backup. No offense."

"Hey, my trigger finger works just fine."

"But you can't charge and wrestle him to the ground?" He sighs. "There goes that plan."

"If you wrestle him to the ground, I can sit on him. I'm big enough for that now."

"You're fifteen pounds heavier, Butler. That's not much help." His arm goes around my shoulders, and he gives me a squeeze. "When we get close, I'm going to find you a place to hunker, and you will hunker. With your dog and your gun at the ready, but you will hunker."

I nod. "I will."

I'm breathing easier now, the conversation easing my worry and lightening the tension. We're so close. We will get to Yolanda. We—

Storm goes still, nose lifted. Then she whines, and her entire body shakes with excitement. She's looking to our left, inland instead of across the lake. Jacob and Anders are still moving forward in the old direction—heading away from wherever Storm seems to be scenting her target.

Dalton seems ready to bird-call to them, but then he stops. Jerome knows that birdcall. Dalton shifts his weight, glaring at his brother and deputy, as if he can mentally force them to turn around.

"Go on," I whisper. "I'll stay right here with Storm."

He glances at me. I move closer to a bush and maneuver Storm in front of me as a blockade.

"Look, I'm hunkering," I whisper.

He grunts. Then he takes off at a silent lope. I watch as he catches up with Jacob and Anders. There's a quick conference. Jacob peers around and points at something. Dalton nods and ducks his head, half crouching as he runs past a line of low bushes back to me.

"Jacob spotted tracks," he says. "On the hillside."

I hesitate. That's in the general direction where Storm was indicating, which is away from where she'd originally indicated. But it's also heading inland from the lake. Does that make sense?

Yes, it probably does. There's no reason to think Jerome would kill Yolanda the same way he killed Lynn. As far as I could tell, he's never repeated an MO. The apparent destination of the lake could be a decoy.

"You should go," I whisper.

Dalton starts to shake his head.

"Go," I say. I lift my gun and point to Storm. "I'm fine. Storm and I are downwind, and I have a clear sight line across the ice. Jerome isn't going to sneak up on us. They need you out there."

"You'll stay here?"

"Hunkered in place," I say.

He pauses for another two seconds. Then he gives an abrupt nod and takes off.

Dalton's soft footfalls have long since faded to silence. I check my watch, and only five minutes have passed, but it feels like an hour. Storm isn't helping. After Dalton left, she started to fuss. Then the fussing turned to low whines. When that didn't work, she tried to leave her stay position. She'd step forward, and I'd stop her and she'd fidget, like a child forced to sit too long. Except she *can* hold a stay indefinitely without more than a grunt of complaint.

She keeps looking to her left. I think she's glancing in the direction Dalton went, a clear message to me that we should be following. But then I notice her gaze is fixed farther left.

She seems to be looking at the bush we're crouched behind, and I check that, as if Jerome could somehow be on the other side. Of course, he's not, but when I move to peer around it, Storm rocks forward, as if I've finally understood her message.

I creep until I can see past the other side of the bush. She takes two steps in that direction.

"Wait," I say.

She looks back and huffs, frustration pouring off her.

They've gone in the wrong direction. Yes, Jacob saw tracks, but Jerome and Yolanda must have circled back this way.

And, if they have, the guys will be on it. I just need to be patient.

A call comes. It's not Dalton's usual birdcall, but I know it's him letting me know he's okay. Except the call comes from even farther off than I expected him to head.

Jerome has a two-hour head start on us. Just because he may have circled back my way doesn't mean he didn't leave a winding trail first.

Storm lets out a low whine. She thinks I'm not understanding what she's telling me. Her target is over there, and I'm just crouching here, doing nothing.

Her whine sharpens, and she nudges me. I take a closer look at her eyes and her body language.

Not frustration. Anxiety. She isn't annoyed that I'm ignoring her. She's worried, because something is wrong.

A little voice whispers that I'm overreacting. Willfully assigning emotions to my dog that suit my purpose, because I'm concerned that the men are heading in the wrong direction and I'm so conscious of that ticking clock and—

I clench my fists against a fresh contraction.

The voice whispers that maybe this is what Storm is stressed about. Me. Because I may very well be in active labor and Dalton is gone.

But while she presses against me and licks my face during the contraction, once I'm breathing normally, she's focused to our left again, whining.

I have a gun. A gun and a very big dog, and Dalton isn't *that* far away.

Move toward whatever Storm senses. If it's Jerome, stop and assess. If he's sitting on a log watching Yolanda die, then it only takes one shot to end it. Otherwise, I can get Dalton.

I will only go as far as I need to. I'm not being reckless. I know my limitations right now, where I could get into a showdown with Jerome only to be doubled over by a contraction.

I creep forward with Storm at my side. When I veer to a section with larger trees, she doesn't like moving from our trajectory, but she accepts it. That lets me straighten and continue forward a little faster. I get past that line of trees to see windswept rock to the right. It's a big open area, and I can easily scan it and see nothing more than scrubby bushes. Patches of snow are all unbroken by footprints.

I look down at Storm. She's focused on one cluster of those bushes. It's not big enough to hide Jerome and Yolanda, though. It's barely big enough to hide one—

There's a foot protruding from the bushes. A slender, bare brown foot.

CHAPTER THIRTY

My heart stops. A contraction hits, and I grit my teeth through it. Then I squint at that foot.

It's not moving. There's a bare foot just visible through a cluster of bushes, and it isn't moving.

I look each way across the open landscape. I can see one large bush to my left and a small cluster to my right. Is either big enough to conceal Jerome? That cluster is too low to the ground—if he's there, he'd be on his stomach, unable to leap up quickly. The single bush to my left is a possibility, though.

But if this were a trap, would he set it up so I can just barely make out Yolanda's foot?

I don't know. I just know that I can't stay here and hope Dalton gets back before Yolanda . . .

Before she what? Freezes to death?

I look at that bare foot, completely still, and my chest clenches and my eyes fill and I want to scream.

If Jerome left her there, it's already too late. He chose a spot on these rocks, where he could pick his way across without leaving a trail, and he dumped her naked body in a cluster of bushes, where we won't find her until we return with Storm to sniff out whatever remains after—

Another contraction, and I embrace this one. It snaps the doom spiral and forces me to focus on nothing but breathing for a few moments. Then I peer at that single bush, adjust my gun, and move out into the open. I walk with Storm at my side, and all my attention is on that bush. After a few steps, I can see through the snow-laden branches. There's nothing on the other side.

I break into a waddling run, and I practically fall beside the cluster of bushes. I dive in, shoving aside barren branches, snow tumbling down onto . . .

Onto Yolanda. She's barefooted, her jeans and parka gone, panties and button-down shirt still on. And she isn't moving. She's curled up fetal-position on her side, her arms wrapped around her bare legs, and she isn't moving.

When I move around her, I can see cuts on her feet and smears of blood on the rocks. She'd been partially undressed when she escaped Jerome, and she ran here, out on the rocks where he couldn't track her prints, and then she curled up under the biggest cluster of bushes she could find and . . .

I push the rest aside. I'm not just sitting there, crying over her still form. I'm checking for a pulse, for breathing, for anything, and I'm not finding it. She's cold. She's so cold, and there's no pulse, no heartbeat, no sign of life.

There! Her throat fluttered. I put my face right up to hers and feel the faint stream of warm breath on my cold face. Tears prickle my eyes. She's alive.

After Lynn died, I read April's reference entries on hypothermia to refresh my memory. In stage one, the victim is conscious and shivering uncontrollably. Stage two, they stop shivering and become mentally impaired. Stage three? Loss of consciousness, during which it may be difficult to detect vital signs as their body slows down.

Warm her up. That's the treatment for all of the early stages. Here, I remember reading something about cardiac danger, but I can't recall exactly what the book said. Probably to warm her gently and not move her.

I'm stripping off my coat when I remember Anders is out there, along with Dalton and Jacob, all of whom will know how to handle hypothermia.

And all of whom need to know I found Yolanda.

I open my mouth to shout. Then I pause. What if Jerome is nearby, searching for Yolanda?

Too bad. I have my gun, and if he comes first, I'll handle that. I'm not letting Yolanda die for fear I'll accidentally summon her would-be killer.

"Eric!" I shout at the top of my lungs. "I have Yolanda!"

I stretch my coat over her legs. I need Storm to help warm her with body heat. The problem is the damn bush. We can't get to Yolanda properly and I don't dare pull her out.

I shout again as I rip at the bush, snapping branches so Storm can get in there and lie against her bare legs. Then I hear footfalls, and I swing my gun up to see Dalton running full out in my direction, Anders and Jacob behind him.

"She's here!" I say. "She's unconscious but alive."

Dalton goes to lift her, but I quickly tell him my fear. By then, Anders has caught up, and he says it's fine—warming her up is the main thing, and we need to gently get her away from the bush to do that.

All three men work to move her as carefully as they can. Then coats and scarves and sweaters come off, everything they can spare and more. I stay back. When Dalton tries to return my parka, I shake my head and try to hide my chattering teeth, but Anders says, "Take it. We have enough."

I put on my coat and watch. Two more contractions hit in the time it takes Dalton and Jacob to grab armfuls of dried bush branches and set them ablaze while Anders tends to Yolanda. Not wanting to interfere, I refrain from asking for details, but he tells me she seems stable. She's cold, but there are only two toes he's worried are frostbitten.

"There was no sign of Jerome," I say, when Dalton finally crouches beside me. "I think Yolanda got away and hid in the bushes."

He nods.

"The smoke is probably going to tip him off," I say. "Nothing we can do about that, except keep watch."

He grunts. "He's not taking on all of us. Not when we already have Yolanda. Yeah, we need to watch the tree line, but he's still got both the other sat phones."

"Meaning, if he's smart, he'll cut his losses and call for help."

"Which he's not getting," Dalton says. "Émilie should have her pilot here soon. They'll have a phone, and I already let Émilie know to monitor any emergency pickups."

I nod. It's an unsatisfying resolution, and I really don't want to think of us spending the next few months worrying about a sadistic serial killer in the woods.

How many times has something happened in the forest here or in Rockton and someone—resident or staff—brings up the old stories of serial killers hiding in the wilderness? It does happen. There are cases of it in Alaska. But mostly, it's an urban legend. Unless you're running a hidden town in the forest and you *import* the serial killers, who then run off into the forest.

"Jacob and I should stay on his trail," Dalton says. "We had it, up there. Only one set of tracks, which we were worried about, but now it makes sense. Jerome was searching for Yolanda. Looks like he headed farther inland."

"As long as you have a trail, you should keep on it. Otherwise, once the snow flies again, it disappears."

"And it will snow." He squints at the sky. "Probably tomorrow."

"You'd take Storm, right?" I say.

He nods. "You and Will can get Yolanda back to town. It's a straight shot over the ice." He points. "Stick close to shore, and the ice will be thick enough."

He really means that Anders will take Yolanda *and me* to town. I don't argue. I'm in no shape to keep going, and each new contraction screams that I need to get back to Haven's Rock.

"How're you doing?" he asks.

I make a face. "Tired. I *should* get back to town, and I can help Will by keeping watch and clearing the way. You guys can . . . Wait, Jacob doesn't have a gun."

"He can take mine," Anders calls over, obviously listening in.

I shake my head. "I'll give him mine. Your big-ass forty-five isn't for beginners."

"Hey, I know guns," Jacob says.

"Rifles and shotguns, not handguns," I say. "You'll take mine. I'm tired enough that I'm not sure I'd shoot straight anyway."

Dalton peers at me, gaze piercing. "We don't need to head straight out. Why don't we walk you two back to town—"

"I'm fine, and conditions are perfect right now. Once Yolanda's warmed up a little, we'll head out. Like you said, it's a straight shot to town."

★ ★ ★

Yolanda is still unconscious, but Anders deems her warmed up enough to travel, especially since her continued lack of consciousness means we really need to get her shelter and proper medical attention. I manage to disguise my contractions long enough to see Dalton and Jacob off. I could be impressed with my acting ability, but really, it's just that everyone's so distracted that it's easy for me to turn away and hide my grimaces.

I'm in labor. There's no more kidding myself. When I'd had Dr. Kapoor on the line earlier this week, I'd asked about future contractions. She said that if they weren't "progressing"—getting longer in duration and shorter in frequency—it would just be the baby repositioning. But they've gone from once every fifteen minutes to once every eight, and from fifteen seconds long to forty. Yes, I'm timing, as surreptitiously as I can.

My biggest concern is that Dalton might miss the birth of his child. It'd be an impossible choice for Dalton—to protect our town, he must catch a killer, but he also wants to see his baby born and he doesn't want, in later years, for our child to feel as if he chose his job over their birth. So I'm removing that choice, and I can only pray he'll understand.

I'm almost certainly worrying about nothing anyway. Active labor—where you need to get to a hospital—doesn't start until contractions are less than five minutes apart and last more than forty-five seconds.

I still have time.

Plenty of time, right?

I'm overreacting because I'm tramping across a frozen lake, escorting an unconscious woman in medical distress—a *friend* who nearly died. My body is just freaking out because this is the point where I should be packing a hospital bag while Dalton paces and asks me how I feel and I snap at him that I'm in labor, damn it, how do you think I feel?

Haven's Rock is only a kilometer away. Once I'm there, I'll have my sister and all her medical equipment and a top-notch obstetrician on speed dial—I have the sat phone we took with us to Dawson.

April will tend to Yolanda while periodically checking my dilation and telling me there's plenty of time, and then Dalton will come home with Jerome, hear where I am, and run to the clinic just in time to see his child enter the world.

On the bright side, while Dalton was fully prepared to be my birthing coach, is it wrong of me to admit this might be easier if he really does sail in at the last possible moment, once mother and baby seem certain to survive the delivery?

I'm leading Anders across the ice as I fantasize about this perfect birth, where all this will be a story for our baby book.

Well, when I went into labor, I was actually hunting a serial killer and I'll admit, I started to panic about having you out there on the ice, but everything went fine.

When it comes to "where were you when you went into labor" stories, I'll win every time.

Then ice cracks underfoot and I'm catapulted from my thoughts as I leap backward . . . and nearly fall on my ass.

"Case?" Anders says behind me.

I bend—as well as I can—to peer at the ice. There's a deep crack, but it's well below the surface, no need for concern.

I tell Anders but also suggest we veer a little farther out. We're close to the shore here, in a sunny section that's going to melt before the rest. And while I may be carrying a baby, Anders is carrying a full-grown woman. Best not to test the ice.

Once I've picked a new direction, we continue on. Ahead, I can just make out the smoke rising over—

Another crack.

"I don't like that," Anders mutters.

"It's fine," I say, "but yes, we're close enough to head to shore."

"That'd make me a whole lot happier."

We do that, and I take the lead, slowly, testing the ice as we walk. Soon we're on shore, and we've barely gone five paces when Anders says, "Whoa."

I spin and stumble when a contraction hits, but all his attention is on Yolanda.

"She's stirring," he says as I grit through the contraction. "I'm going to set her down for a second. I don't want her startling— not with the cardiac concerns."

"Good idea."

Anders is bending when Yolanda wakes with an "Oh!" She spasms, limbs flying out, fist narrowly missing Anders's jaw. Then she goes still. "Will?"

"I gotcha," he says with a smile.

She stares at him. Then she bursts into tears, the sound ripping through the silence, jagged sobs that are painful to listen to.

"Hey, hey, hey," he murmurs as he lowers her to the ground.

"No!" She claws at him, scrambling to get back up. "Don't leave me. Please. I-I can walk. I'm fine."

"Yolanda," I say, moving up to her. She startles again, and I squeeze her arm as Anders rearranges her in his arms.

"No one's leaving you anywhere," I say. "Will only wants to take a look at you before we keep going."

She shakes her head vehemently. "I just want to get home. Please. I can walk if that helps."

Anders adjusts her. "No need, and it's not safe. We need to check your heart before you walk. I won't set you down."

She nods. Then she looks over at me, her eyes welling. "I was wrong."

"About . . . ?"

"Lynn. I wondered why she didn't fight. Why she undressed. You explained, but I still didn't understand. I thought I wouldn't have done that. I'd have fought, but then he had me, and he's so much bigger than I am, and he'd taken my gun. I still tried to fight and . . ." She touches her jaw, where there's a gash already bruising. A pistol whip. "After that, I did as he said and looked for my chance."

I smile. "Which you got."

Her eyes fill again, but this time, her face suffuses with anger. "And what did I do with it? I got cold. So cold, and all I wanted to do was curl up and sleep."

"That's the hypothermia. It impairs your thinking." I squeeze her hand. "But you found a safe spot first, and we found you, and you're fine."

"Let's get you to April," Anders says.

Yolanda nods, and his arms tighten around her as he continues walking.

CHAPTER THIRTY-ONE

The contractions are worse. So much worse, and I fall behind to hide them now that we're off the ice and I don't need to lead. As I start to lag, I tell Anders to go on ahead.

"Like hell," he says.

"The town is right there." I point.

He shakes his head and slows his pace.

"Will," I say, with a bit of a snap. "Yolanda needs medical attention. I'm going as fast as I can, and I'd really like to slow down." I pause. "I think I'm having contractions."

He turns sharply enough to make Yolanda hold tighter. "What?"

"Early contractions," I say firmly. "But I'd like to go a little slower. Can you get Yolanda to town and send someone back for me? I'll keep moving. I just need to slow down."

"I'm fine," Yolanda croaks. "We'll go as slow as you need, Casey."

I bite back my frustration. The contractions are coming stronger and lasting longer, and I want to just stop walking and rest. Give me five minutes, and I'll be fine. But I can't do that because Yolanda needs to get to April now.

Anders has me go in front so he can match my pace. Which means I need to keep moving even when a contraction has my legs wobbling—

"Who's there?" Anders says.

I stop fast. Someone's to our left, sitting or crouching by the lake.

"Just me," a voice says. "Move along."

"Grant?" I say.

A grumbling sigh, and Grant stands. Then he squints over at us.

"Is that Yolanda?" Grant says. "Where are her boots?"

Not the first question I'd ask seeing Anders carrying Yolanda, but yes, I guess bare feet in winter is odd. I back up to tuck her feet into the scarf we'd wrapped around them.

"She's hurt," I say. "Will needs to take her to town, and I can't keep up. Would you escort me, please?"

Anders starts to protest. Then he stops and looks at me and murmurs, "Right. Not a suspect."

Yep, since we know who killed Lynn, Grant is off the suspect list. Leaving me with him for the short walk to town is fine.

"Go," I say. "Please."

"Grant?" Anders says.

He's still staring at Yolanda. "Is she okay?"

"I'm fine," Yolanda croaks again. "Casey is having contractions."

"Shit." Grant stares at me like I've sprouted a second head. "The baby's coming?"

"Eventually," I say. "Right now, I'm having early contractions and can't keep up. Would you please escort me to town?"

He nods and turns to Anders. "You go on." He pauses, peering at Yolanda. "Wait. If she's not wearing anything on her feet, does that mean the same guy—"

"Will really needs to move," I say. Then to Anders, "I've got this."

"Twenty minutes," Anders says. "I'm taking Yolanda to April, and if I don't see you within twenty minutes, I'm heading back."

I wave a hand. "I'll be there. Just let me rest for a few seconds."

"A *few*."

I shake my head, and Anders leaves with Yolanda. Then I turn to Grant.

"Yes, she was attacked. Eric and his brother are tracking the suspect now."

His gaze sharpens. "Who is it?"

"I'm not authorized to say, but you'll be the first to know."

"So it wasn't me?" he says as his jaw sets. "You blamed me—"

"You were a suspect." I give a grunt as I find a boulder and rest against it. "The victim's current or former partner is always a suspect. You know why? Because half the time women are murdered, that's who did it. If you want an apology, you aren't getting one. We had to consider you, but obviously, we were also considering other suspects, since you aren't the one we came back to arrest."

"What are you doing?"

I think he means why am I not with Dalton, then I see he's frowning at me. I have one knee up against the boulder and I'm leaning into the stretch as a contraction builds.

"It helps, okay?" I say. "At this point, please don't question the pregnant lady. She's in a hell of a lot of pain and needs two minutes to rest before she gets her ass to the clinic."

I stretch, and my body whispers that it would like to stay here. Just lean into this rock. Lean a little more, squat down—

I quickly straighten. Okay, I really need to get to the clinic. "Let's—" I begin.

"I loved her," he says. "I know it didn't look like it, but we were going through a rough patch. If I didn't love her, I wouldn't have come here. I wouldn't have admitted I screwed around and expected her to get her revenge and been okay with that. I wanted to fix things, whatever it took."

I nod and summon all the sympathy I can muster with this pain arcing through me. "I know. I'm sorry. I really am." I look toward town. "We should get moving."

"You don't need me to carry you, right?"

I could almost laugh at his expression. "No, I'm fine. Walking it out feels good."

I start down the path, only to hear him behind me, still standing in place.

"It happened out here, didn't it?" he says.

I want to just keep walking, but I can't do that to him. So I glance back and nod. Then I continue on.

"Where exactly?" he says.

When I don't answer—because I'm breathing through a contraction—he says, "I have a right to know." A two-second pause, and his voice drops. "I didn't mean it like that. I want to know. Maybe it would help."

I nod, focused on breathing in and out. I can see the town buildings through the trees.

"Is it near here?" he says. "Can you show me? Quickly?"

I slow. With the contraction ebbing, I want to snap that I'm having a baby—literally, right now—and this really isn't the time. I don't say that, not because it wouldn't be fair to Grant, but because the hairs on my neck are rising.

I turn slowly.

Grant's peering out at the lake. "Over there, right? Not far. I heard it wasn't far. Can you just show me? Quickly?"

Can I take him farther from town? Out toward the lake? Past the trees? Where no one can see us?

Anders and I thought it was safe leaving me with Grant because he wasn't the killer. Are we sure of that? Absolutely sure?

Jerome must have murdered Lynn. Anything else would be too great a coincidence, especially given what just happened to Yolanda.

But what if Jerome wasn't acting alone?

My hand slides down toward the talisman of my gun, just a touch to remind me I have it.

Except I don't have it.

I gave my gun to Jacob.

"Casey?" Grant says, frowning.

He never calls me by my name. It's always "Detective Butler," often with a twist of derision.

Grant rubs his face. "You need to get to town. I shouldn't have asked. I'm sorry. I'm just . . . I'm not . . ." He swallows. "I'm sorry."

I search his face. It's haggard, eyes dark with exhaustion. Grant didn't help Jerome murder his wife. He's tired and grieving, and he wants to see the spot where his wife died. That's common. Not necessarily a good idea, but when people are groping for closure, they grasp at everything.

See where their loved one died. See the body. Visit the killer in prison. Sit in court through gruesome testimony.

All the things they hope will help.

"If you want to see the spot tomorrow, someone will take you," I say. "Give it more thought first. But we'll do what you want."

He dips his chin, gaze downcast. "Thank you."

We resume walking. I'd like to ask him to get in front of me, but I can't do that without coming up with a logical explanation for an illogical request, and my brain isn't capable of handling that right now. So I listen to his footfalls. They're hard to pick up—we're heading through the trees now, with very light snow cover.

My stressed brain is trying to figure out a solution when he provides one by talking, and I can hear he's at least five paces behind. Lagging, not wanting to take me to town, wanting to go back to the lake.

"Was it Thierry?" he says.

I give a quick "No," mostly because we can't have him going after Thierry while we deal with Jerome.

"The kid? Sebastian?"

"No," I say. "It wasn't any of the initial suspects, and I need you to stop asking, Grant. You'll know as soon as Eric brings him back to town."

"A guy then. That's what I figured. It had to be a guy to overpower her. She was stronger than she looked. She took Pilates and did some weight training and . . ." His voice drops. "She stopped doing the weights because I was always making jokes about how light they were. I don't think she took it as teasing."

No woman takes that as teasing. But I only keep walking, focused on his voice, which has dropped a little farther back as he dawdles.

"I think that's why she did the Pilates," he says. "And some yoga. Because she knew I wouldn't come along, so she could do it in peace. Without me teasing her or getting cranky because other guys were checking her out."

I can see a storage building just ahead, through the trees.

He continues, "I was an asshole. I don't know why she put up with me."

"She loved you."

A pause. "She did, didn't she?" Another pause. "Can I ask for something else, Casey?"

"Hmm?"

"Five minutes. When you bring the guy back, just give me five minutes alone with him."

I exhale and slow. Words are on my lips. *You don't really want that. I can't do that.* With a shake of my head, though, I decide to say nothing. Leave this fight to others. I have a baby who really wants to meet the world. Now.

Grant makes a low choking sound, a stifled sob. I slow some more but don't turn. I'll let him cry in peace, which is half consideration and half that I really don't have time to comfort him. Again, someone else will need to do that.

A soft thud behind me, and I wheel, as if he'd used the distraction of a sob to catch me off guard and lunge. But he's on his knees, hands to his face, making ugly, half-stifled crying sounds.

Or that's what I see at first, exhaling in the relief of *not* being attacked. Then the image reprocesses. He's on his knees, yes, but his hands are at his neck. Those sounds are half-strangled gasps as his eyes round . . . and blood seeps through his fingers.

CHAPTER THIRTY-TWO

I run to Grant, and I'm halfway there when hands grab me from behind. An arm slaps over my mouth, a forearm in a thick parka sleeve. Then something presses against the side of my belly.

"That's a gun, Casey," a voice says. "Go on, look down and check."

His grip eases just enough for me to look and see Yolanda's gun digging into the side of my protruding stomach.

"You fight, you try to scream, you do anything except what I tell you to do, and I'll fire this gun. You know that's not an idle threat. You saw what I did to Lynn, and you are a good enough cop to understand how much I'd enjoy pulling this trigger and watching you as your baby dies inside you."

Rage explodes, so intense I can't breathe. But I don't move. I do not move one muscle because I know the truth of his words. He let Lynn die without a gag because he enjoyed her terror and agony while she desperately screamed for help. He'd happily watch me with a gunshot wound to my stomach, desperately trying to save my baby, knowing I can't. And the best part of all? It'd be my fault. He warned me, and I didn't listen.

I remember what Yolanda said when she woke. How she'd realized I was right about why Lynn didn't fight harder. Because there is a point at which you absolutely do not fight back. And this is mine.

When the rage clears enough for me to see, my gaze lands on Grant, slumped forward, dead. His hands have fallen from his throat, and there's a gash in his jugular. Jerome came up behind him through the thick trees, while Grant was talking—while he was talking about wanting time alone with his wife's killer—and Jerome reached around the smaller man and sliced his throat open.

"Nicely done, isn't it?" he says behind me. "My stepdad would be proud. He always told me those hunting lessons would come in handy."

It *is* Jerome behind me. I know that even if I can't see him. Even if his voice doesn't sound like I've ever heard it. Because that was Marlon, and this is Jerome.

The gun digs into my side. "Start walking. Back toward the lake."

For a second, my knees lock. Head *away* from town? Hell, no. Then I feel that gun, and I remember something.

Twenty minutes.

Anders said he'd give me twenty minutes. Then he'd come looking for me. He'll come, and he'll find Grant.

I nod and start walking, moving slowly. When I speak, I keep my voice low, to be clear I'm not trying to summon help. "I'm having contractions."

"Yep, I figured that. I saw the way your face was scrunching up when you were listening to him prattle. Not an attractive look, Casey."

"I just wanted you to know, in case I make any sudden moves."

He gives a low laugh. "You mean that you want me to know so you *can* make a sudden move and get away from my gun."

"No," I say firmly. "I won't do that."

"But you can try, if you like. I don't mind. You try something, and I shoot you in the stomach and kill your baby. That would be fitting, I think. You're such a go-getter, Casey. Poor Eric could barely get you to slow down. Let me kidnap and murder you? Never. You'll fight to your dying breath, because that's the kind of woman you are."

I say nothing. I don't need to. He's having too much fun on his own.

"I have another plan for you," he says. "A more elaborate scenario. I'd rather stick with that, but if you try anything, I will happily make the adjustment. Shoot you in the belly and then kill you the way I want, after you experience your baby dying inside you." He pauses. "Babies do feel pain, right? At this stage, certainly."

I grit my teeth and force myself to walk as another contraction surges.

"Let's not talk about your baby dying in horrible agony," he says cheerfully. "You must have questions."

I want to say no. I can tell he's eager to give answers. That's the type of killer he is—so damn proud of his work. On the one hand, he's smug about never having been caught. Hell, as far as I can tell, his victims' deaths haven't been investigated. That has to be very satisfying . . . but also very *un*satisfying because no one knows how clever he's been.

But here's his chance. Someone he can tell. Better yet, someone who hunted him and lost. Predator turned prey. An audience who won't live to reveal his secrets.

I want to refuse to be that audience. Deny him and watch him choke on it.

But I can't take that risk.

I told Yolanda that Lynn went along with her killer likely hoping she'd see an opportunity to escape—or someone would hear her screams. Yolanda went along with him and *did* get a chance to escape. Now I must do the same. Play the good victim. The cowed victim. Wait for Anders.

"It was Yolanda all along, wasn't it?" I say. "You never wanted Kendra or Lynn. Yolanda was the target." Too late, I realize that I'm bringing up the one who got away, and I quickly add, "And now she's dying. Will is taking her back to the clinic, but she's not going to make it. She was out there too long."

He laughs softly, the sound thrumming with satisfaction. "Clever, clever Yolanda. Escaped and thought she was safe. I knew she wouldn't get far. Then I heard your bunch found her, and I thought maybe she'd survived."

"She won't," I lie. Then I add more horror, to feed his hunger for it. "Even if April works a miracle, she'll lose her hands to frostbite."

"Then you know what? I hope April does save her. Can you imagine Yolanda without hands? She'd grab the nearest scalpel and finish the job. Well, no, I guess she couldn't grab anything, could she?"

His laugh grates through me, and it takes all my willpower to keep walking.

"Turn here," he says. "We're heading onto the lake."

Good. It'll be easier for Anders to spot me out there. I make the turn toward the snow-covered ice.

"To answer your question, Detective, you're half right. Yolanda was my preferred victim, but obviously I was fine playing Russian roulette with those drinks, letting the victim self-select, so to speak. If I'd been set on Yolanda, I'd have gotten Yolanda."

"Instead you got Kendra."

"Which was a disappointment. Of the three, she was my last choice. Yolanda thinks she's tough, but you can *smell* money on her, however much she tries to hide it. Tough in a boardroom but not out here. Kendra is different. Even drugged, she'd have been a handful. So when I had the excuse, I let her go."

"And Lynn?"

"Happenstance," he says. "That storm hit, and she was in her shop. I waited for the storm to whip up, and then I let myself in the back door, where no one could see me. Then I did a bit of theater, acted as if I'd seen someone through the windows, thought she'd be gone for the storm and a thief was taking advantage. Can't help playing cop, ha-ha. She notices the two beer bottles in my hand. Yeah, I was going to hunker down with Will, but the way this storm is blasting in, I'm never getting to his place. Don't suppose you'd like to share a beer, wait out the storm? Of course she does. Even lets me open them and slip something in hers. Oh, sure, she was the one telling women to be careful, but that doesn't apply to good ol' Marlon. So we drink our beer and talk, and shit, the storm's getting worse. I'd better walk you home."

He pauses to tell me to turn right. That's not the direction I want to go. Straight ahead or to the left, it's open ice, where Anders would easily spot us. Rocks and trees cut into the lake to the right, forming a secluded peninsula. But I can't hesitate. Hesitation will make him think, and I don't want him to realize help is coming.

He resumes his story without prompting. "So I help Lynn through the storm. She's a little woozy, but just laughs it off, blaming the beer. We get close to her residence building and, shit, I'd better not let Grant see me bringing you back. Wouldn't want him to get the wrong idea, ha ha. You okay if we go around the back? Then I can watch you go inside, make sure you're safe. Sure, that's fine. Only by then, the snow is coming in so hard we can't see our hands in front of our faces. That makes it almost too easy. We're out in the forest, surrounded by trees, before she even realizes we're off target. Whoops, shit, better double back . . . only she's too woozy to realize that I take her in a circle and then keep heading out to the lake, where everything's set up. I don't think she even understood something was wrong until I pulled the knife and told her to undress. Even then, she thought it was some weird sex thing and told me, very politely, that she wasn't interested."

He barks a laugh. "I should have been insulted. She's been chasing half the guys in town, and she turned me down. Poor Lynn. Always just a little too eager to please. When she realized I was serious, that clothing came off fast, and I was invited to do whatever I wanted. Just get it over with and let her go. I did what I wanted. Don't think it was what she expected."

He chuckles. "You should have heard her scream, tied up on that ice. Oh, she struggled in the beginning, but between the drugs and the hypothermia, her mind went fast, and all she could think to do was scream for help. Scream for you and Eric. Scream for that useless waste of a husband. Scream and scream and scream. It was fucking *delightful*."

I bite my lip hard to keep from lashing out. Then a contraction starts, and this time it's so strong that I have to stop walking, heaving breath.

"Keep going," he says, gun barrel digging into my side.

"Just . . . just a minute. They don't—they don't last long."

The contraction has my knees wobbling. I just want to sit down. No, I want to squat, with the overwhelming urge to find a toilet, as ridiculous as that seems.

Except it's not ridiculous at all. I want to bear down, in any way I can. The next phase of labor. When my child is ready to be born.

Tears prickle my eyes.

Not yet, baby. Please. Not yet.

Jerome pokes me before the contraction has even finished. He's making sure I don't use them to slow us down. Which, yes, would have occurred to me after the agony of this one passes.

I resume walking. It's a shuffling stride, and that's not me dragging my heels. Even after the contraction passes, my legs feel like rubber, from relief now, my body getting a break before the next contraction hits. Only it's not the same as before, when the contraction passed and I felt mostly fine. My stomach twists, and I'm not sure if it's nerves or nausea.

I want to stop walking. I *need* to stop walking.

If I take one more step in these soaked sweatpants . . .

I mentally slow down. My sweatpants and panties are wet, my thighs chafing. I hadn't even noticed that until now. It feels as if I wet myself.

My water broke, and I never realized it.

All things considered, that's hardly a shock.

"I . . . I need to sit down soon," I say.

"You will. Just up ahead." His free hand reaches over my shoulder to point. I follow his finger and realize he's leading me around that peninsula. To a secluded spot where Anders won't be able to see me.

My knees lock involuntarily.

"Uh-uh." Jerome digs the gun in. "None of that."

"I . . . I don't think I can go any further."

"You will. Or I pull this trigger, and if you're hoping that means Will's going to hear it and come in time to save you . . ."

He leans down to my ear. "*Tsk-tsk.* Such a bad mother already. Willing to sacrifice her baby to save herself."

I bristle, and that makes him laugh.

"Oh, don't be so offended, Casey," he says. "I know you'd never do that. Which is what makes this so much easier. And I also know that we have a limited amount of time together before Will rides to the rescue. It'll take him a while. First, he's going to find Grant, and that'll slow him down. Then he needs to track us, and the fact that we retraced our steps partway is going to screw up what little tracking ability he has. He'll get here. Eventually. But you know who I'm really hoping shows up?" He leans to my ear again. "Your husband."

I must flinch, because he laughs before continuing, "Yep, my ideal scenario has Will Anders blundering around before shouting for Eric, who'll track us easily. Then he'll show up and . . . No, let's save that part. For now, yes, I know you don't want to go where I'm leading you. But I also know you will, because you don't have a choice."

He moves the gun barrel, and I resume walking. I'm moving slow, hissing in pain that's only fifty percent feigned.

He digs the barrel into my stomach. "None of that shit, Casey."

"I'm really having trouble. My water broke."

"Oh, did it? And I suppose when I question that, you'll want me to check, which gives you a chance to do something. Not sure what you'll do, since you don't have your gun, and you're a little unwieldy right now, but even if your water did break, I don't actually give a shit. Walk."

I continue the way he's prodding me. We soon disappear into the curve between that peninsula and the shore.

"Over here," he says. "Remember this spot?"

It takes a moment. Then I do. We'd come ice fishing here just last month—Dalton, Anders, Marlon, and me. The remains of our party are still here, in the cut logs we'd sat on.

I slow. "That ice won't be safe."

"I know. That's the point."

My knees lock. Ahead, I can see the spot where we fished. Anders and Marlon had gone out ahead to make the hole, and instead of making a bunch of ten-inch holes, they cut a single big one, nearly three feet square. I'd laughed at that. A couple of big guys proving their strength with an epic ice-fishing hole . . . when small ones would have been fine and much safer.

That hole has iced over, but I can see the divot of it, and that ice won't be more than a few inches thick.

"Walk *around* the hole," Jerome says with a dramatic sigh. "Sit your ass down on that stump, and if you think of trying anything, let me remind you that I'm an excellent shot and that stomach of yours makes a very prominent target."

He is a very good shot. He'd gone hunting with us a few times, and we never questioned his skill with a gun because he was supposedly ex-military. Now I know the skill comes from hunting with his stepfather instead.

"Hands up," he says. "Walk to that stump, face me, and lower your ass onto it."

I do as he says. As soon as I start to squat to sit, my body screeches in joy. I'm finally getting into the right position. I clamp my legs shut, as if that's going to help.

"You were always my first choice," he says. "If I could have picked anyone, it'd have been Detective Casey Butler. There's a certain thrill to taking down prey that thinks it's smarter than you. But with that bun in your oven, Eric wasn't letting me get near you, and if he wasn't around, there was Will, your sister . . . everyone keeping such a close eye on Casey."

"Yolanda made a decent substitute, though," I say. "Especially since she turned you down."

His cheek tics, and I try not to smile. I might not have wanted to piss him off earlier, but I'm away from that gun barrel now. I can see his finger isn't on the trigger. That hunting experience also ingrained trigger control.

He covers the reaction with a smirk. "Sure, that's the answer. The killer who targets women who turn him down. Such a cliché."

Another contraction. I struggle to think past it. I can't pause. I must keep him talking.

"Did Emma Kim turn you down, too?"

He blinks at the name of the girl he locked into a high-school bathroom.

"Nice work, Detective, but no. I was just a curious boy, and Emma was a convenient target for that curiosity. Not *that* kind of teenage curiosity, though. Mine is a little more complicated."

He's lying. He's trying to lift himself above the "common killer." Act like he didn't make a move on Emma. Like she didn't reject him. That would be passé, the teenage boy held hostage by his hormones. He was more complicated.

He continues, "As for Yolanda, that was feigned interest. She isn't my type. I knew I'd be rebuffed, and so I could play the potential suitor, interested but not aggressive enough to be a suspect in her murder. If I liked her and hoped for a relationship, why would I kill her? It was cover."

He's full of shit. Or maybe full of self-delusion. From the articles I read, Emma Kim had been a lot like Yolanda—smart, opinionated, and far more focused on her future than romance.

She'd rejected Jerome. I'm sure of that. Then he'd realized he'd dodged a bullet there—if she'd told friends he'd pursued her, he'd have been a suspect. So I doubt his other victims had any connection to him. Until Yolanda, because in a town this small, everyone has some connection to you, so he might as well let his bruised ego pick a victim.

Would I have suspected him if Yolanda died? Yes. My attention would always turn to a rebuffed suitor, however gentle his pursuit.

He's looking at me. Waiting for a response.

"What did you do to Martin?"

Something flickers over his face. Actual regret? It vanishes as he finds his sneer.

"Martin was a fool," he says. "All that time in the army, and he was still too much of a coward to deal with that Nazi. He couldn't even bring himself to kill the guys who kidnapped him." He shakes his head. "Weak."

"He told you he was coming to Haven's Rock, didn't he? He wanted someone to know, and he trusted you."

The smallest flinch.

I push on. "But you were in trouble yourself. You messed up and the police were closing in, so you snagged his ticket."

It's a guess, but a flicker on his face shows I'm right.

I have a moment here, where he's distracted, but it's not enough. I can't fight him in my condition, and a momentary distraction won't keep him from shooting me as I lumber away across the ice.

I resist the urge to shift my weight on this log. I'm uncomfortable, something deep in my brain screaming at me to move, to get into position, to be ready, but if I fidget, even a little, he'll mistake it for nerves. I will myself to stay calm and still.

"Sweating a little there, Casey," he says.

"Because I'm having a damn baby," I snap. He's right, though. I'm trying to cover up the signs of my discomfort and growing panic, but I can't hide the physiological tells—my face reddening and sweat dripping under the hem of my wool hat.

"Well, then, let's get on with it." He turns to that wide divot in the ice. "Lie down there."

CHAPTER THIRTY-THREE

I bite my tongue against saying the ice is too thin for me to lie down safely. As he said, that's the point.

"You're clever enough," he says. "You can figure out how to lie so you don't fall through. Spread your weight. Even distribution, that's the key. Except . . . Well, I guess you can't fix that huge center of gravity, can you? But you'll do your best. You'll want to be on your back, obviously."

He moves toward the hole. "Once you're out there, I'm going to shoot holes in the ice. That will bring Will—and hopefully your husband—running. By the time they get here, I'll have taken cover to watch the show. I don't need to go far, though. They'll be too focused on your predicament. If you get up, you'll crash through the ice. If they step close enough to grab you, you'll both go through the ice. And if you really are having that baby?" He grins. "That adds a whole new layer of fun, doesn't it? Because there's no way in hell you're going to be able to do that and stay still. One false move and . . . Crash."

I snort.

He startles. Then his eyes narrow. "What's that for?"

"Nothing."

His jaw works. He has just outlined a horrifying scenario that should have me begging for mercy. And my reaction? A derisive snort.

Finally, my body's exceptionally bad timing works in my favor, because it lets me hide what I'm really feeling. I can act calm, as if my sweaty red face and quick breathing are entirely due to the fact that I'm in active labor.

He peers at me, and I think I've overplayed. Then he laughs. "Oh, you really are a confident bitch, aren't you? You think you'll get out of this. That I'll make a mistake, and between you and your hubby and Will Anders, you'll figure out a way to get off that ice."

He waves. "Fine. You just keep thinking that. Now get undressed."

"You're going to need to take off my boots."

He laughs again, louder now. "Oh, am I? I need to get down on the ice and pull off your boots, using both my hands, which means setting the gun aside."

"I don't care how you do it. But I can't reach my boots." I demonstrate, stretching over, and my body shouts for joy. I'm moving. I'm getting into some kind of position that will help birth this baby and—

I straighten. "I haven't been able to take them off myself for the past month. You know that. You've seen Eric do it for me."

His mouth tightens. "Fine," he snaps. "Start with your coat."

I take off my coat. He orders my hat and gloves to follow, and my body sighs in relief as cold air rushes over my sweating body.

"Shirt," he says.

I glare at him, but I don't argue. I hike the oversized sweatshirt over my belly and then I stand as I wrestle with it, cursing when it gets stuck going over my head. I have it off one arm and my head before he hisses in frustration and bends down to pull it off my other arm.

I wrench the shirt as hard as I can, and the surprise of that pulls him off-balance. He still has the gun in his right hand, but it's lowered, and when he loses his balance, I start to run. There's a massive spruce right there. I just need to get behind it—

A contraction hits, so hard I gasp. My right boot slides. It shoots over the edge of that divot and through the ice. The contraction doubles me over before I can right myself, and my right leg plunges into the freezing water as I fall to my left knee.

Jerome grabs me by the hair and drags me away from the hole. I'm gasping, the pain of the contraction and the icy water making me want to scream. I bite it back—

No.

I let the scream out. I scream as long and hard as I can, doubling over and grabbing my stomach.

Something hits me in the cheek. There's a crack, and I see stars as I fall. Then I'm on the ice, lying on my back, staring up at Jerome. He pulls back the gun as if to strike me again. Then he grabs my right leg. Pain crashes through me and I can't even tell if it's my leg or the contractions. I howl. He yanks off my one wet boot and sock and then the dry ones.

"There," he snarls. "Problem solved. Now take off the rest."

I can barely process his words. My head is ringing from the blow. My leg feels as if it's on fire. I'm shivering convulsively. And all that is swept away by a sensation I can't quite identify.

Instinct. The overwhelming need to bear down. Something almost like relief flutters through me. It's almost over. The baby is coming, and all I need to do is bear down and the pain will end.

Jerome grabs my legs. He heaves them into the air, holding the fabric of my sweatpants and pulling, his face twisted.

I scream again, doubling over as if in pain, but I no longer feel pain. Just need. I need to have this baby, and I am not going to be able to do it like this.

That instinct takes charge, laser focused on what is standing between me and giving birth. I continue to double over, scream-ing and feigning agony. Jerome lifts the gun, but he seems to know a threat won't help. I'm writhing on the ice, as if blinded and mad with the pain of labor.

He jams the gun into his waistband, grabs my pant legs again, heaves and—

I kick with my left leg, the foot slamming into his jaw. He staggers back, and I push up, ignoring the pain and shock of the ice against my bare feet. I take one step, the foot that went into the water numb. Then I hit him with both hands. He stumbles. I hit him again, falling onto him for the extra weight. When I feel him topple, I drop sideways fast, letting my entire body fall as he goes over backward.

He grunts in annoyance. That's it. Not fear. Not concern. Just annoyance. I've knocked him over. Big deal. I couldn't even manage to stay upright afterward.

Then he hits the ice—the thin ice that I'd already broken through. It crashes beneath him, and his eyes widen as he goes under.

His head and torso fall through the fishing hole, but his feet are still on the side, and as he splashes down, he manages to twist and grab the edge. He's caught himself there, with his calves still on solid ice, and one hand holding fast, head out of the water. The hole might have been huge for ice fishing, but it's only three feet across, and Jerome is over six feet tall.

He'd told me I could stretch over the hole, and that's what

he's doing as he pulls his other hand out of the water. He's trying to get a grip, but he can't, because his hand—like my foot—is numb.

I crawl over. My body has gone quiet now, as if it knows I'm doing my best to have this baby.

I keep crawling until I reach the hand gripping the ice. Then I kneel. At first Jerome doesn't see me. He's too focused on getting a grip with those numb fingers. When he does, he blinks. Then he sees what's in my hands and his eyes widen with horror, and I drink it in . . . before I bash the rock down onto his hand.

He screams, and the ice under his hand breaks. His torso drops under the surface. I crawl down to his feet, and with a calm that I'm sure will haunt me later, I take hold of his boots and push. He manages to flail, but it's a weak effort, his arms barely breaking the surface. Then his feet are over the edge, and he drops fully into the water.

A contraction hits, the strongest yet, and I fall back as the world dips to black.

When the world returns, I'm lying on the ice. I manage to crawl to my coat and drag it to shore. Blood pounds in my ears. Pain fogs my vision. I can't seem to find the energy or the will to stand. I barely make it to land and tuck in behind a sheltering rock. Then I drop the coat on the ground and fall backward onto it and scream.

I let myself scream, and it feels so damned good. Then I'm panting and shaking and the urge to bear down takes over. I struggle out of my soaked sweatpants and underwear.

Am I going to do this?

Really do it?

Alone? Beside a frozen lake?

Do I have any choice? My body says no.

Time moves slowly, me locked in this bubble of pain and instinct. Groggily, I look around. There's a partially buried boulder behind me. I inch backward with the coat until I'm half propped on it. That feels better. Use gravity. It's the only birth partner I'm getting.

I try to find a position there, secure but half squatting. I brace myself to push—

"Casey!"

It's Anders.

"Here!" I manage to shout. "Fishing hole!"

Follow the trail of discarded clothing. That's what I want to say, but it's far too many words.

"Over here!" Anders shouts.

Is Anders telling me to come to him? Can't really manage that right now.

I grit my teeth and focus on pushing, which is the only important thing right now. When someone runs around the bend, it's not Anders. It's the person he must have been shouting to.

Dalton races over, red-faced and wild-eyed. Then he sees me and stops so short, it'd be comical if I weren't really focused on giving birth.

"Baby's coming," I manage. "Now."

He just stares, unable even to muster a curse, apparently. Then Anders shoves past him and says, "Holy shit!"

"Having a baby," I grunt.

"I see that."

He runs over, and Dalton snaps from his shock and runs toward me.

"Position?" I get out.

"You're in a good one," Anders says. "Squatting. Taking advantage of gravity."

"Meant the baby."

He gives a short laugh. "Right. Eric? Can you get behind her? Give her something more comfortable to lean against? Give her your hands, too."

Dalton nods. "To squeeze."

"Or break," Anders says as he crouches in front of me. "Depends on how much she blames you for her current predicament. Case? You're going to need to excuse me sticking my head between your legs."

"Absolutely my last concern right now."

Dalton moves me forward gently as he gets in behind me and helps support me by holding my hands. Anders peers up from the ground.

"In position?" I grunt.

"Either the baby is in perfect position or your kid has a very hairy ass."

I let out a whooping laugh of relief.

"I see a little head," Anders says. "Covered in black hair. Though it might not feel so little right now."

"It does not," I say.

"Remember this is the toughest part, and it's already well underway. Also, from the looks of that hole in the ice, you just drowned a serial killer while giving birth. This part's a piece of cake."

No, it's not a piece of cake. But it's easier than I expected, and I presume that's the endorphin rush from escaping Jerome, coupled with the relief of having both Dalton and Anders here. I'm not alone, and the baby is in position, and I can do this. I can really do this.

There's a lot of screaming. Anders helps me time the pushes and reminds me to use my abs to push out and away. Dalton just holds me and tells me how much he loves me and that it'll all be over soon. That last part is what I really want to hear at this moment. It will be over soon. I can feel that. The baby is right there, and I just need to push harder and—

"We have a head!" Anders says. "Just a little more and . . . She's out!"

"Clear her airways," I croak. "You need to—"

"Got it. April made us all go through the basics last month, remember? Cut the cord. Clear her—"

The baby's howl swallows his last words, and then Dalton's helping me to the ground, atop my coat, as Anders holds out a tiny screaming baby with a shock of black hair.

"A girl," I say. "It's a girl."

"And I will not say I told you so," Dalton says.

My eyes fill as I turn to him, and his arms go around me and he hugs us both, as tight as he can.

CHAPTER THIRTY-FOUR

This is not how I expected our baby to be born. At least it'll make a good story, although we'll keep out the serial-killer part until she's older. Much older.

Dalton and Anders wrap me and the baby, and then Dalton insists on carrying us back to town.

"I was carrying them both upstairs when she was pregnant," he says when Anders hesitates. "Only difference now is that the baby is on the outside. Oh, and they're a little lighter, without all that . . ." He waves a hand back at the placenta and fluids on the snow. "Goop."

"You have such a way with words," I say.

"I have an excellent way with words," he says. "And I may have learned a few new ones today, while you were giving birth."

He adjusts me in his arms as he walks, and I check on the baby, sound asleep again and swaddled in Dalton's sweater.

"Speaking of words," Anders calls from behind us. "Do we have a name, now that you've met her?"

"Eric Junior," Dalton calls back.

Anders laughs. "I think that should be *Casey* Junior."

"What?" Dalton glances over his shoulder. "That's a little sexist, isn't it?"

"We'll discuss names," I say. "No rush." I lean back into Dalton's arms as they tighten around me. "No rush at all."

It's such a peaceful walk back that I almost fall asleep, between the slumbering baby in my arms and the rhythm of Dalton's gait. He says something about Jacob and Storm being back in town and hearing my screams, but I barely register his words. Then we reach the clinic, and all hell breaks loose.

Okay, that's an exaggeration. But after that peaceful wilderness walk, it feels as if I'm plunged into the maelstrom. That maelstrom being my big sister.

Baby? Why is there a baby? Why didn't someone come for me? No one said she was having the baby? Give her to me. No, give them both to me. Did Casey pass the placenta? Is she bleeding? Why is the baby sleeping? Has she woken yet? Have you checked her breathing? Is she breathing?

The fact that April can think, for one second, that we'd hike back without checking that the baby was breathing is a testament to her worry. Also, a bit insulting to all of us, but I'll let that pass.

Then she finds out about me being held captive by Jerome, and I realize it's probably a good time to mention that my foot went through the ice—which I hadn't told Dalton or Anders, being a little busy, you know, giving birth.

Cue a freak-out from everyone, as April and Anders both check my leg. It's fine. It really was a quick plunge, with my boot on, that boot having been removed shortly after by Jerome. The bigger issue would have been me walking around without boots and sweatpants, but labor seems to have kept my body warm enough for that.

It's then—in testament to my own muddled mind—that I finally remember Yolanda, who went a lot longer half dressed. She's in the next room, sleeping, and April says that's what she needs. Sleep, lots of sleep. She'll need plenty of recuperation time—her heart went through a trauma—but the only real worry April has is those couple of toes that seem frostbitten.

As for the baby and me, we're fine. The pregnancy may have been rough, but the birth process went as designed. Still incredibly painful and not something I want to do again anytime soon. Really, like Nicole said, it is a wonder anyone has more than one child. Of course, it might be slightly easier in a hospital, with medical professionals and painkillers, instead of on a frozen lake fighting off a serial killer.

During the examination and discussion, my adrenaline kicks in again, and I'm wide awake, especially when April examines the baby and starts making little noises of dissatisfaction.

After the examination, we get "She's a bit small," and "We need to keep an eye on that umbilical cord" and "Did you cut that with a sterilized knife?" and "Her hair will probably fall out."

Yep, April is April, but she ultimately declares we have produced a perfectly adequate offspring. Okay, she says "she seems in excellent health" but of course qualifies that with pointing out that she's not a pediatrician.

All that poking and prodding rouses the baby, and I feed her. Well, I try to feed her. It looks so much easier in movies, where babies latch right on as if they've been eating that way for months instead of through an umbilical cord. I won't say it goes well. I won't even say she gets more than a few drops. But it's a work in progress. We'll get it.

After that, Dalton takes me where I want to be, more than anyplace else in the world. Home.

It's evening now, and I can barely believe this is the same day we woke in Dawson City. I've napped. The baby has napped. I've tried to feed her again. I got most of the milk on myself, but again, I'm not going to stress about this. Oh, who am I kidding— I'm totally going to stress about it once the endorphins of giving birth wear out and I start to panic that my child is starving.

She won't starve. However it goes, we'll get her fed. She seemed satisfied enough with the dribbles she got, and she's back to sleep. I'm not the only one who had an eventful and exhausting day.

I'm curled up in my chair as Dalton rests stretched out on the couch, with the baby nestled against his bare chest. Storm has been rescued from her brief stay with Nicole and Stephen, and she's dozing in the corner, one eye cracked open to watch this strange little creature and make sure it doesn't cause any trouble.

"You two look adorable," I say to Dalton. "She has your snore."

He lifts a middle finger. "She sounded a whole lot more like her mother when she first came out. Roaring at the world."

"You'd roar too if you came out butt naked in subzero temperatures."

"She has your hair."

"Which, as April pointed out, is probably temporary."

"She has my eyes."

"Closed?"

He shakes his head. "Also, you're supposed to point out that the gray-blue is probably temporary, too."

"I'm not my sister."

"Speaking of which, what do you think she'll say when she finds out we're using April as a middle name?"

I pull the blanket over me. "She'll be delighted, of course, and will definitely not point out how it doesn't go with the baby's first name at all."

"We haven't chosen a first name."

"Doesn't matter. It absolutely does not suit, and what were we thinking?"

He smiles and strokes the baby's head. "Thoughts on a name?"

"Leaning toward Riley, but I'm not sure."

"Could go with Rory."

I arch my brows. "Please tell me that isn't a bad pun because she came into the world roaring."

"Of course it is. Rory April Butler Dalton. Or Dalton Butler." His lips purse. "Or should that be Dalton Duncan? We haven't discussed that part."

I shake my head. "Dalton Duncan really is a tongue twister, and April and I don't use Duncan up here. Butler would be better but . . ." I shrug. "It'd get complicated for legal purposes." Butler is my "Rockton" surname, which I continue to use. "I think just Dalton is fine. Rory April Dalton. Initials 'RAD' because you are totally rad, right, baby?"

"I . . . don't even know what that means."

"Slang from my distant youth. It means cool, so it's good."

"You like Rory then?"

I slide from the chair and walk over to sit beside them, my head leaning on Dalton's arm around the baby—around Rory.

"It's perfect."

CHAPTER THIRTY-FIVE

It's been a week since Rory was born, and Dalton and I are out on our first post-baby hike with Storm. We've already abandoned our child. She's with April, who wanted to get in some auntie time.

I'll admit that made me nervous. Our parents left me with April exactly once, when I was seven, and I ended up playing in the backyard until I fell asleep—at ten P.M.—because she'd gotten caught up in a book and "Casey likes being outside." Growing up, I'd seen that as a sign of how much my sister disliked me. Forced to babysit, she'd left me outside. Now I know she really did get caught up in her book, and since I did like playing outside, it seemed reasonable, especially considering she'd have only been twelve at the time.

April and I didn't grow up around babies, so I was nervous until Kenny volunteered to help. He has a passel of nieces and nephews, and with a few instructions, I could confidently leave Rory in their care. It helps that she'll just sleep. That's mostly all she does, and yes, I was worried until Nicole assured me that it's normal for these first few weeks. They sleep a lot, and once that ends, you'll start wishing for those early days again.

Feeding is going okay. Still not perfect, but it's getting better every time. Dalton also takes his turn with pumped milk and bottles, which is what he wants.

At this point, with a sleeping baby and tons of help, it feels easy. I know that's an illusion, but while it's lasting, I should take advantage and do things like going on walks with my husband and my dog.

Today's hike actually serves another purpose. We're searching for a place to bury Grant and Lynn, once the ground is thawed enough. That makes it a quiet walk. We'd done this many times in Rockton, but we'd hoped to avoid it here. While we have had one death—a construction accident—that body could be sent home for family. This is different. Lynn and Grant are both gone, and they will both stay gone, buried in a place neither of them wanted to be.

"I know he really liked fishing," Dalton says as we walk. "But this should be more about her, and I don't really know what she liked."

"None of us did, and not because she wouldn't have happily told us, if we'd taken an interest." I exhale a long breath. "It was complicated. With both of them." I squint out over the sun-dappled snow. "She did enjoy the hikes. Oh, I remember her saying there's a spot where she could see the lake in the distance, and she liked it when they paused there. That would work for both."

"We'll do that then." He reaches for my hand. "What happened to them was terrible. Especially Lynn. We didn't screw up, though. Jerome exploited a flaw in our system, and Rockton had the same one. The only difference is that, in Rockton, he wouldn't have needed to exploit it. Not if he had enough money to buy his way in."

I nod, knowing he's saying this as much for himself as for me. Whatever complaints we had about Rockton, we'll both admit it was a whole lot easier when we could blame someone else for letting in a dangerous resident . . . and then pat ourselves on the back for catching them.

"On a much happier subject," I say, "that is an awesome new sled Kenny built for Rory. I know she's too young to appreciate walks in the woods, but do you think, if she's bundled up enough, we can take her with us that way? Or should we stick with the baby pouch?"

"The sled would work. We have plenty of skins to line it with, and it's not as if we're going to just drag her along behind and forget she's . . ." He trails off, looking to the left and frowning.

"Eric?" I say when he keeps looking.

He pauses and tilts his head to look into the forest. "Slight detour," he says. "I'm not sure what I'm seeing. It might be more of Lynn's clothing. Or Yolanda's."

"Or my sweatpants, which you guys abandoned back at the lake."

"You really wanted your pregnancy pants back?"

I pluck at the sweats I'm wearing. "Until this belly goes down, the looser the waistband, the better."

We've veered off the trail into the forest. It's been a quiet week, weatherwise. Warmer than usual, with bright sun that makes it feel downright balmy. In open areas, the snow glistens as it melts. Here, deeper in the trees, it's still solid but getting crusty, and each footfall pauses before breaking through with a crunch.

Dalton takes the lead. Storm follows behind me. She's been quiet, still getting used to our new addition, and a little out of sorts. I'm making sure she gets plenty of attention and playtime. When she makes a noise behind me, I turn and see her sniffing the air. She gives an uncertain whine and looks at me.

"Eric?" I say. "Storm's picking up something."

"Yeah, I can see why," he says from two steps ahead of us. "There's a campsite. Must be one of the damn miners."

He means the mining company, who are absolutely not supposed to be on this side of our boundary line.

Dalton strides toward the small clearing. Ahead are the remains of a campfire and a makeshift shelter. One of the miners or guards looking for a little winter camping experience? Whatever the reason, having them this close to Haven's Rock makes me very nervous.

"We'll need to take this up with Rogers," I say. "It's a clear violation—"

Dalton stops short.

"Eric?"

"This isn't the miners," he says.

I start forward, and his hands shoot out as if to stop me. Then he settles for taking out his gun. I do the same, and we move into the campsite. He's busy scanning the perimeter, as I draw closer to the site, where clothing has been hung above the fire to dry.

I stare at that clothing. It's Haven's Rock issue. A pair of jeans, socks, and boxers. There's a shirt, too, one that isn't standard issue—a burgundy pullover, the sight of it making something inside me spasm. I'd seen that shirt, complimented the wearer on how nice the color looked on him.

"Jerome," I whisper. "That's . . . that's his shirt."

Dalton nods grimly.

I keep looking, my brain racing to process what I'm seeing.

"A fire, where he dried his clothing after he . . . No, that's not possible. This is just his clothing. Someone must have taken it."

That doesn't make sense. No one is removing wet clothing from a corpse. Then I see the duffel on the ground. Dalton glances over to track my gaze to it.

"That's his," he says. "It was missing from his room, along with a bunch of his belongings. He stole some supplies, too. Protein bars, an extra canteen, a whole carton of matches. Will and I figured he packed a bag and left it in the woods for later, knowing he wouldn't be going back to town."

"He did that before he took Yolanda. Preparing. Someone else found his bag. One of the miners maybe."

Found Jerome's duffel and settled in for a campfire? Used his clothing and then hung it to dry? Got bored, wandered off and left it all behind?

My gaze moves from one item to the next. To the canteen hanging from a tree. To the empty wrappers. To the boot prints all around the clearing.

"I didn't watch," I whisper. "After he went under the water, I knew I should watch in case he came out, but I blacked out. I thought it was only for a moment . . ."

"You were in labor," Dalton says, "and you'd seen him fall in ice-cold water. Even if he got out, he wasn't going to be in any shape to bother with you."

"He climbed out," I whisper. "While I was unconscious. His duffel must have been nearby. Dry clothing. Matches."

"We need to get back. Now." Dalton turns to me. "He might be long gone. That fire is cold. But I'll put together a party and come out to track him."

I nod, still feeling dazed. Was it possible that Jerome had climbed from the ice and stumbled into the woods and I never noticed? I should say no, but I think back to that moment, and I know it's entirely possible.

Even after I came to, I'd been deep in labor. I couldn't hear, could barely see, intent on finding a spot to have my baby.

"I should have said something," I say as Dalton scans the clearing and grabs an item of clothing for Storm. "I should have told you I wasn't watching to make sure he went under and stayed there."

"We never asked. Never checked either. Will and I should have gone back later to look for a body. Or signs he climbed out."

"But there was a baby and Yolanda and Grant to think about, and we were just all relieved it was over."

"Yep, so we're going to skip the blame game and be thankful we found his camp in time. I have a feeling that even if he's still around, he'll stay far from Haven's Rock. But we won't take any chances. We'll track him and bring him in."

"And I'll stay out of that unless you need me to help with Storm," I say as we leave the clearing.

"I can be her handler, but we'll bring you in if there's a problem."

Dalton falls in behind me as Storm takes the lead. We both keep our guns out and our senses sharp as we walk. Earlier, I'd found the crunch of the snow reassuring and peaceful. Now each step sounds like a gunshot.

"If he's around, he'd have already heard us," Dalton murmurs.

"Is he armed?" I whisper. "I presume Yolanda's gun went in the water with him."

"Would it still work?"

"It depends on how long it was under. He only had it shoved in his waistband. I doubt he was making sure he kept it as he hauled himself out, but we still need to be aware he could be armed."

"Gotta admit," Dalton mutters, "I liked the idea of him drowning in a frozen lake. Fitting . . . and saved us from dealing with a new threat."

"Hopefully, he just calls for help. I'll notify Émilie as soon as we get back so she can prepare—"

Storm stops. She lifts her head, sniffs the air, and then her muzzle swings right and she whines.

I move up beside her as I aim my gun in the direction she's looking.

She whines again. It's a different whine than when she scented the campsite. This one's low and anxious, and when I go to pat her head, she ducks it.

Once Dalton gets close enough, I whisper, "I'll take lead."

He hesitates.

"Jerome likes sneaking up from behind," I say.

A grunt. That reminder will keep Dalton in the rear. I signal for Storm to move forward with care. She does that, as well as a dog her size can. She creeps to the edge of another clearing and then stops and ducks her head again, a whine rippling through her.

The sun doesn't penetrate this tiny clearing, surrounded by massive pines, and I have to squint to see. There's something in the middle of it and—

"Oh!" I say, just as Dalton says, "*Fuck.*"

My hands fly to my mouth. "Is that . . . ?"

Dalton only grunts and moves past us. I take another step, my gaze fixed on the scene in front of me.

It's a body, spread-eagled on the snow, limbs tied to trees. There's . . . not much left of the corpse. Scavengers have been feasting. One arm is no longer attached to the torso. One leg is gone completely.

The body is naked and lying on its back. It's a man with a gag in his mouth. His eyes are missing, and something has pecked at his face, but enough remains for a positive identification.

"Jerome," I whisper. "It's Jerome."

We're back in town. We left Jerome's body there. We need a witness to confirm how he died.

Once in town, Dalton goes to find Anders while I walk to one particular door.

I find Mathias in his shop, working on a trio of grouses.

"Fresh meat?" I say. "I didn't think anyone was out hunting."

"These are from traps."

"Ah, right. Your traps."

Last fall Mathias had decided he wanted to take up trapping. We figure it was mostly an excuse to tramp around the woods alone.

"It is good weather for it. The sun comes out, and all the animals peek out from their hidey-holes. Especially the predators."

"Caught any predators lately?"

"A mink, in fact. I am curing the hide for a new baby. You may have heard we have one."

I move up to the counter. "We found Marlon."

"Who?" He looks up. "Ah, him." His lip curls, and he goes back to his work with the grouse.

I lean against the counter and take a feather, turning it in my fingers. "We thought he drowned under the ice. Seems he escaped and had provisions. But then . . . well, he must have poked his head from his hidey-hole."

Mathias only nods and separates a wing from the body.

"He was stripped naked," I say. "Tied to trees and left to die."

"Ah."

"And you have nothing to say about it?"

Mathias tilts his head. "Only that it seems . . . What is the word in English?" He looks me in the eye. "Fitting."

CHAPTER THIRTY-SIX

I'm at home with Rory and Storm. Dalton is working—with everything that happened, we decided he needed to get back on duty. In a couple of weeks, we'll start shift-sharing. I suspect I'll feel guilty about going back to work so soon, but it's the right thing for me, and Dalton having time alone with his daughter is right for both of them. It's not like working in the city, with an hour-long commute. We can easily pop home for lunches, coffee breaks, or just to check in.

I'm half dozing on the sofa while Rory sleeps when a knock comes at the door, one I've heard often enough to recognize it—firm and a little bit imperious.

"Come in, Yolanda!" I call.

She does, and the sound of outerwear being shed follows.

When she enters the living room, she goes straight to the bassinet. "Sleeping? Are you sure that's a kid and not one of those creepy lifelike dolls? I haven't even seen her with her eyes open."

"Don't worry. Once they're open and she's screaming, we'll bring her to you."

She jabs a finger my way as she plunks onto a chair. "You jest, but I'll have you know I'm actually very good with kids."

I smile. "I do know. I've seen you with the boys."

"I like kids," she says. "Never wanted my own, but I am the *best* auntie." She leans toward the bassinet. "You're going to be very lucky to have me around, kiddo. Just wait."

Yolanda thumps back to the chair. "And, in case you were wondering, I *am* sticking around. Gran thought this might finally bring me home, but I'm not giving that bastard any power over me, even in death. I got away. I'm still alive. Seems like I'm going to lose one of those toes, but I figure that's for the best, really. It's a piss-poor serial-killer-escape story if I don't have something to show for it."

She looks over. "Will has even promised me a T-shirt. 'I escaped a serial killer, and all I lost was this lousy pinkie toe.' I will be sorely disappointed if he's joking. I want that shirt."

I smile. "I'll make sure you get it."

"Oh, he's getting you one too."

"'I escaped a serial killer, and all I got was this lousy baby'?"

"*Awesome* baby. Wouldn't want to give the kid a complex too soon. Plenty of time for that later."

"True."

She pulls her legs up under her. "I know you thought I've been hanging around hoping to say I told you so. Well, that and not wanting Gran to know about my Parkinson's, which is true. Also true that I wanted to be sure you and Eric weren't fleecing my gran. I realized you weren't a while ago. But I was never trying for a gotcha, Casey."

She looks me in the eye. "I want you to succeed. I want all of you to succeed. I'm not sure you can pull it off, but if you guys can't, then no one can."

She leans back, gaze going to the ceiling. "Growing up

rich, Gran and Pops taught us we had a responsibility to the world, especially because of where our money comes from. Big Pharma has a problem, and some families might love to throw money around and play philanthropists, as if opening a wing at a museum makes up for getting millions of people hooked on opioids, but it really doesn't."

"Shocking."

"Right? Gran and Pops were never into those, but they still profited from lifesaving medicine, so they taught us to give back. I thought I was, with my company. Environmentally conscious, hiring mostly women, doing plenty of pro bono work, but . . ." She shrugs. "Corporations like to pretend they'd lose money if they did that shit, but my coffers filled faster than I could empty them."

She rises and walks to the window. "This feels right, for now. It's more active. Take a break from being the bitch in charge and be the bitch who criticizes those in charge."

"You do an excellent job at that."

"Keeping you on your toes." She looks over at me. "I'm not your enemy, Casey."

"I know."

"Good."

She looks out again, leaning on the thick windowsill now. "Gran told me what happened to Jerome. She thought I should know."

I say nothing. We'd asked Émilie about that, and she'd said yes, Yolanda should know and she'd tell her herself. Except for Anders—who bore witness—everyone else only knows we found Jerome's body, and if they think we mean we found it under the ice, that's fine.

"I keep thinking about it," she says. "Not how he died, but that moment when he realized what was happening."

"Eric and I didn't do that to him."

She snorts a laugh. "Uh, yeah, obviously. You guys wouldn't do that to *anyone*. I have a good idea who did, but that's between me and myself, though I suspect, if you aren't charging around looking for the person responsible, you already know, too. That's fine. Jerome deserved what he got. What I think about is that moment when he understood his fate. He survived falling in freezing water. He must have been so fucking pleased with himself. And then . . ." Her lips curve in a slow smile, and she doesn't finish the line.

"He suffered," she says. "More than he would have dying in freezing water. He had time to think about Lynn, to experience what he did to her. So I'm glad he suffered. For Lynn and all the others. What he did to them. What he tried to do to you."

"And you," I say softly. "For what he did to you."

She goes quiet. I rise from the sofa, go to the window, and stand beside her.

After a moment, she says, "Yes, for what he did to me, too," and we stand there together, looking out at the falling snow.

ABOUT THE AUTHOR

Kathryn Hollinrake

Kelley Armstrong is the author of more than fifty novels in mystery, fantasy, and horror. She believes experience is the best teacher, though she's been told this shouldn't apply to writing her murder scenes. To craft her books, she has studied aikido, archery, and fencing. She sucks at all of them. She has also crawled through very shallow cave systems and climbed half a mountain before chickening out. She is, however, an expert coffee drinker and a true connoisseur of chocolate-chip cookies.